Fire of Love

Gently sliding his arms under and around Amethyst, Damien pulled her close against him, his heart pounding and throbbing in his ears as his mouth sank deeper and deeper into hers. Then, gently, he explored the slopes of her body as his mouth probed hers, searching, demanding an answering need that he prayed would not be denied him.

Suddenly, Amethyst was fighting his embrace, her body twisting and turning in a dreadful rage. "No . . . no, Damien, please understand." Amethyst was frightened past guile and stammered uncertainly, "I couldn't ever . . . William and I . . . we're going to be married."

"Never!" Damien protested. "William Sheridan will not have you!"

Then, Damien clarified his objection—by resorting to more than words. . . .

THE BEST IN HISTORICAL ROMANCE

LOVE'S FIERY JEWEL (1128, $3.75)
by Elaine Barbieri
Lovely Amethyst was on the verge of womanhood, and no one knew it better than the devilishly handsome Captain Damien Staith. She ached with passion for him, but vowed never to give her heart.

CAPTIVE ECSTASY (738, $2.75)
by Elaine Barbieri
From the moment Amanda saw the savage Indian imprisoned in the fort she felt compassion for him. But she never dreamed that someday she'd become his captive—or that a captive is what she'd want to be!

AMBER FIRE (848, $3.50)
by Elaine Barbieri
Ever since she met the dark and sensual Stephen, Melanie's senses throbbed with a longing that seared her veins. Stephen was the one man who could fulfill such desire—and the one man she vowed never to see again!

WILD DESIRES (1103, $3.50)
by Kathleen Drymon
The tempestuous saga of three generations of Blackthorn women, set in the back streets of London, glamorous New Orleans and the sultry tropics of the Caribbean—where each finds passion in a stranger's arms!

TENDER PASSIONS (1032, $3.50)
by Kathleen Drymon
While countless men professed their adoration for Katherine, she tossed her head in rejection. But when she's pirated away from her safe world by a man whose object is lust, she finds herself willingly committed to one man's desire!

Available wherever paperbacks are sold, or order direct from the Publisher. Send cover price plus 50¢ per copy for mailing and handling to Zebra Books, 475 Park Avenue South, New York, N.Y. 10016. DO NOT SEND CASH.

LOVE'S FIERY JEWEL

BY ELAINE BARBIERI

ZEBRA BOOKS
KENSINGTON PUBLISHING CORP.

ZEBRA BOOKS

are published by

KENSINGTON PUBLISHING CORP.
475 Park Avenue South
New York, N.Y. 10016

Copyright © 1982 by Elaine Barbieri

All rights reserved. No part of this book may be reproduced in any form or by any means without the prior written consent of the Publisher, excepting brief quotes used in reviews.

Printed in the United States of America

LOVE'S FIERY JEWEL

Chapter 1

1775

A cold, pitiless wind slapped icy swells against the weathered hulls of the ships docked in Charleston Harbor, rocking the huge, tethered maidens of the sea with awesome ease. Overhead, dark, angry clouds whirling across a bleak February sky effectively obliterated the last meager rays of afternoon sun. Shouts of harried sailors loading cargo, their breaths frostily visible on the frigid winter air, grew louder as they cast occasional apprehensive glances upward at its threatening visage and accelerated their pace in an attempt to win their race with the impending storm. Their gruff, anxious voices contributed to the steady din of street peddlers hawking their wares, the snorts and whinnies of skittish horses, and the shrill laughter and calls of determined harlots bidding their faithless beaus goodbye while keeping a surreptitious business eye in search of quick and willing replacements.

Moving slowly amongst the milling throng, their progress hindered by the confusion of liveried carriages carrying some of the more affluent passengers, the crush of rough freight wagons delivering cargo and provisions, and pushcarts heavily laden with all manner of barter for the imminent voyage, a small group clutched their hand baggage and made their resolute way toward the tall-masted *Sally*. Heads bent against the bite of the wind, they cast occasional worried glances at the fast moving clouds, apprehension obvious in their wind-reddened faces. One drop . . . then two . . . and the bustling scene appeared to freeze for a fraction of a moment before bursting into frantic activity as the heavens suddenly opened to release a freezing deluge on the tableau below.

Dashing for cover, departing lovers moved their last-minute caresses into the shelter of doorways, small business transactions were brought to premature halts as vendor and customer alike scampered for temporary shelter, and lingering goodbyes within the elegant carriages were hastened to allow for rapid retreats from the fury of the storm. Within minutes the driving rain had swamped the street, forming huge, dirty puddles on the slippery ground, creating yet another series of obstacles for the hapless pedestrians.

Caught in the ensuing melee, the small group's sudden rush toward the *Sally* was blocked countless times before they were able to begin a headlong dash toward the distant gangplank and eventual shelter. Separated temporarily from the group as it finally succeeded in working free of the crowd was a frail young woman tugging a small, shuddering girl behind her, their cloaks flapping wildly in the piercing wind. Within a few minutes' time the driving rain penetrated their inadequate protection to plaster their sodden apparel against their bodies like icy shrouds, and almost blinded as the full force of the storm blew into her face, the woman struggled to keep her fellow travelers within sight. Clutching her daughter's cold, chapped hand even tighter, she raised her voice over the fury of the storm.

"Hurry, Amethyst. They're over there! Run, darling, run!"

Following the direction of her mother's glance with her own, Amethyst saw the other members of the troupe moving quickly up the gangplank of a ship docked a considerable distance away and unprepared for her mother's sudden surge forward, she fell painfully to her knees on the sodden ground. Biting her lips against the sting, the child righted herself within seconds to take her mother's hand and run unfalteringly toward the ship behind her.

When at last Amethyst's water-blurred vision allowed her a glimpse of the ship merely a few yards away, her mother's hand was unexpectedly jerked from hers. Horrified into immobility, she saw her mother pitch head over heels along the water-soaked ground, jerking and tumbling like an absurd mechanical toy, to fall finally in a small, sodden heap at the base of the gangplank.

Not realizing the shrill, prolonged scream echoing in her ears was her own, Amethyst had just reached her mother's inert form when rough hands pushed her aside, and a huge seaman assumed the place at her side. Enraged by the stranger's presumption, Amethyst shoved hard at the man's broad shoulder, and when her supreme effort had no effect on his massive frame, she began pounding on his back as she screamed shrilly, "Get away from my mother! I'll take care of her . . . get away, I said!"

Turning suddenly, the man leveled a menacing glance in her direction.

"Behave yourself, little girl, before I take a hand to you! I'm trying to help your mother, little fool!"

Turning back to her mother, he took just a moment longer for a quick assessment of the woman's condition before scooping up her unconscious form like a weightless rag doll. Turning, he started quickly up the gangplank, hesitating only a second to throw a brief glance over his shoulder at Amethyst's forlorn, motionless figure and growl impatiently, "Are you going to stand there in the rain all day? Pick up the bag and follow me, you little idiot! MOVE!"

Hidden in the darkest corner of the small cabin, still clothed in her dripping garments, Amethyst watched as the stranger administered to her mother's semiconscious form. Without a moment's hesitation he stripped away the woman's drenched cloak and wet shoes, and reaching up beneath her skirts, pulled off her torn and bloodied stockings.

Glancing to her mother's bruised and swollen face resting against the pillow, Amethyst knew a moment of almost paralyzing fear, and swaying with momentary weakness, finally managed to steady herself by sheer strength of will just as a familiar figure bustled through the doorway.

"Captain Straith, is Marian alright? Oh, I'll never forgive myself for abandoning her in the crush like that. I should've waited for her . . . I know how frail she is . . ."

"There's no time for hindsight now, Miss Hallam." Bluntly interrupting the young woman's gushing regrets, Captain Straith continued in an urgent tone. "She seems to be badly shaken and bruised, but no bones appear to be broken. Her heartbeat is strong and her breathing regular. I've sent one of my men for the doctor, but she must get out of these wet clothes quickly before she develops a chill."

Obviously embarrassed by her brief lapse of control, Nancy Hallam answered quietly, "We'll take care of that, Captain. Thank you." Turning, she shouted over her shoulder, "Margaret . . . Margaret! Come in here and help me! Quickly!"

Rising to his full height, Captain Straith relinquished care of the injured woman and was almost out the doorway when a small movement in the corner of the room caught his eye and he spied the child. Shuddering convulsively as she stood in her sodden garments, her hair plastered darkly against her small elfen face, she stepped further back into the shadows of the corner as his glance turned in her direction.

Experiencing an unreasonable surge of annoyance, he

growled with obvious impatience, "Have you no sense, girl? Why haven't you removed those wet clothes? Are you waiting for them to dry on your body? You will become ill, and your mother will be relying on your help . . ."

Stopping abruptly, he was at her side in two brief strides as the child swayed weakly. Grasping her arms to steady her, he realized she was painfully thin and freezing cold, her body quaking so hard that she was unable to speak.

"Don't waste your strength trying to talk." His voice was gruff. "Just help me get these clothes off you now."

In a quick, efficient movement, he stripped away her cloak and proceeded to work at the buttons at the back of her dress. Suddenly pulling away from his hands, Amethyst turned wide, violet eyes to stare at him with horrified maidenly modesty.

Glancing back toward the bunk, Captain Straith saw the two women working diligently to remove their semiconscious patient's wet clothing and realizing no help would be forthcoming from their direction, he mumbled disgustedly, "In a few years, little girl, that outraged expression will have some merit, but right now you are a Child. You can't be more than eight or nine years old and from what I've seen so far, you're not a very bright child, either!"

Jerking her back toward him again, he resumed unbuttoning her dress, muttering under his breath as he did, "Only a fool would stay in wet clothes as long as you did!"

Finally pulling off her dress, he followed with the wet petticoat, wincing slightly at the sight of the small, badly lacerated knees peeking through the holes in her shabby stockings. Reaching around her slender shoulders, he pulled the blanket from the unoccupied bunk and wrapped it tightly around her.

"Now, take off those wet underdrawers!" His sharp command was accompanied by a direct, steely stare into violet eyes which succeeded in finally wearing down the brief display of rebellion on Amethyst's small, pinched face. Wriggling and squirming inside the voluminous covering, she finally raised the bottom of the blanket to produce a small pair of underdrawers hanging wetly around her ankles. In a swift movement, the tall captain had scooped her up and depositing her heavily on the unused bunk, proceeded to pull off her wet shoes and stockings.

Finally realizing the girl was still struggling to speak through quivering lips, he stopped long enough to say with extreme exasperation, "What is it you're trying to say?"

Directing a surprisingly heated glance into his eyes, the child stammered through blue, defiant lips, "Then y . . . you must b . . . be a f . . . fool too, Captain, b . . . because your clothes are as w . . . wet as m . . . mine and y . . . you haven't y . . . yet had the s . . . sense to ch . . . change!"

His only answer the slight narrowing of silver gray eyes and the raising of one dark, arched brow, Captain Straith, in a very slow, deliberate movement, took a corner of the blanket and began vigorously rubbing her hair dry, shaking her small frame in Amethyst's estimation unnecessarily roughly as he did.

After a few seconds, he mumbled tightly, "You're a cheeky little brat, aren't you? Didn't your mother ever tell you children should be seen and not heard?"

When silence was his only reply, he said imperiously, "Well?"

"Yes, she did," was the hesitant, small-voiced response, ". . . but she didn't t . . . tell me I sh . . . should l . . . let anyone c . . . call me stupid!"

For the briefest second the broad, tanned hands drying

her hair slowed, and a small unseen smile hovered around the corners of the captain's mouth.

"Lassiter!" His sudden shout startled Amethyst almost into jumping off the bunk, but the captain held her firmly as a small, gray-haired man came rushing into the room.

"What is it, Captain?"

Still effectively holding her captive in his strong grip, he growled in a tone Amethyst was beginning to believe was his norm, "Bring this young . . . lady a cup of hot broth. She needs something to warm her insides and dull her sharp tongue."

Darting a quick glance upward at his face, Amethyst saw the Captain stare at her expectantly, his brow raised as if challenging another retort. Suddenly deciding discretion to be the better part of valor, she lowered her head submissively and allowed him to continue rubbing her hair.

Within the hour, the broth and warm blanket having accomplished their task, Amethyst lay sleeping, cuddled into a small, innocent ball as Captain Straith returned to check his passengers' conditions. Noting she still gave an occasional involuntary shudder in her sleep, he took the blanket from the other empty bunk and covered her lightly, tucking the corners around her to seal in the warmth.

Turning quickly, he caught Nancy Hallam's scrutiny and feeling suddenly and inexplicably uncomfortable, he said coldly, "Feisty little brat, isn't she?"

A small smile breaking over her delicate features, Nancy whispered in return, "Oh, she's a sweet child, to be sure, Captain, but she considers herself her mother's protector instead of the other way around. Marian's health is somewhat delicate, you know."

"She's doing better since the doctor has seen her, is she not?" Shooting a quick glance to the frail, sleeping woman, he turned back quickly to Nancy Hallam's response.

"Yes, I'm sure she'll return to her normal state of health soon. The doctor confirmed everything you had already said, but she's in for some strict care when Amethyst is again back on her feet. The girl adores her. Her father was second lead in our company for some time, you know, and while Marian is not as talented as her husband, she is still a skilled enough actress to be one of our walking ladies."

At the captain's puzzled expression, she interjected quickly, "She plays a series of small parts in our repertory... When Morris was killed in a coach accident last year she remained with the company. So now I'm afraid she and Amethyst find themselves outcasts from the colonies like the rest of us."

"Oh, I wouldn't put it that strongly, Miss Hallam." A conciliatory note entered Captain Straith's voice despite himself as he recalled Nancy Hallam's triumph of just a few short months before, when she was touted the toast of Annapolis, and the American Company was hailed as the most talented theatrical troupe to touch American shores. Dramatically, the highlight of their years of struggle to be recognized was followed by the Continental Congress's law forbidding entertainments during the crisis with the Mother Country.

"The law against theatrical entertainments and frivolities has no personal overtones, you know. You and the rest of the troupe are free to stay in the country if you will find some other means of employment..." Captain Straith's deep voice trailed to a halt at Nancy Hallam's unhappy face.

"And there you find the crux of the matter, Captain, and for that reason you find what remains of the American Company sailing with you for Jamaica." A new note of optimism entering the light lyrical voice that had earned her fame, she continued, "But Mr. and Mrs. Douglass assure me that their troupe was well received in Jamaica before they came to the colonies. I wasn't with them then. My cousin, Louis Hallam, and John Henry have returned to London where their talents are recognized rather than face an uncertain future, but the rest of us have elected to stay closer to the colonial shores in the event that foolish law is repealed. Mr. and Mrs. Douglass, Mr. and Mrs. Morris, Miss Tuke, the Storer sisters, Marian Greer, little Amethyst and I will form the nucleus of a new troupe which will delight Jamaica! You'll see, Captain, we'll . . ."

Her brilliant expression suddenly dimming, Nancy glanced toward the bunk and the sleeping woman, and mumbled softly, "A very inauspicious beginning, is it not? We have begun our adventure by almost reducing our small number by two. Perhaps this does not portend well for the future . . ."

"I think you have the heart and strength of mind to overcome all odds, Miss Hallam, and I have no doubt you will." Bowing his tall, lean frame in a gallant gesture, Captain Straith raised her slender hand to his lips, bringing a flush of pleasure to the worried young woman's face.

"Captain, you are indeed a gentleman. It is our pleasure to sail with you."

With a small smile the captain turned and left the cabin. After a few moments staring thoughtfully in the direction in which he had disappeared, Nancy Hallam gave a small sigh, and turned back to her patient.

Watching surreptitiously from the bunk, two wide lavender eyes followed the captain's broad frame out the doorway. Still smarting from his insulting comments of a few hours before, Amethyst pulled a revealing, unseen grimace and stuck out her tongue at his retreating back.

"He thinks he's so smart! Stupid, am I? Well, he can

keep his advice to himself from now on. I'll take care of Mama and he can go to the devil!" Feeling fully justified for her silent cursing, Amethyst struggled to her feet, still clutching the blanket around her. "I'll show him," she mumbled as she picked up the dry clothing Nancy Hallam had laid out for her and began to dress. "I'll show him!"

Moving slowly along the narrow corridor, Captain Damien Straith approached the cabin door, not really certain what it was that drew him there again for the second time in two days. The *Sally*'s sailing had not been delayed by the small accident on the dock and now the second day out, all was well. They were making excellent time. Still he felt a strange sense of disquiet. Certainly he was sorry for the unfortunate group of actors forced to abandon the colonies at the very pinnacle of their success, but he had seen less fortunate people than this group before. It was the terribly frail young woman and her daughter that surprisingly seemed to weigh on his mind. Unless he missed his guess, Marian Greer's time was limited . . . he had seen women in her dire condition before. There was a look to her eyes . . . she would probably not live to reach thirty.

Stopping momentarily, he ran a broad hand through his tawny, sun-streaked hair, his brows drawing together in consternation. He was not accustomed to the nagging concern he had been unable to dismiss from his mind, and he was impatient with the hold the unfortunate pair appeared to have effortlessly secured over him. His mind usually followed a different line of thought when he was unoccupied by shipboard matters. At 26 he was one of the youngest and most respected captains in the colonies, having won that position with his quick mind and strong, willing back. And since the Continental Congress had authorized privateering the year before, he had increased the fortunes of his men and himself with several ventures that had only added to his stature. Now with war with the Mother Country appearing imminent, his services would be of even more value. In his personal life, his wide reputation and more-than-pleasing appearance availed him of endless romantic liaisons which he was able to achieve with a minimum of effort and serious involvement. His world was too wide to content himself with one place or one woman for very long.

"So," he asked himself for the hundredth time, "why the nagging involvement with this unfortunate woman and her child?" He would have no control over their destiny in the long run. The woman would surely recuperate from this accident, but the child would undoubtedly be orphaned before she entered puberty.

Unable to answer his own silent questions, he frowned deeply, not conscious of the formidable sight he presented. Extremely tall, a few inches over six feet, his shoulders were broad and heavily muscled from the active shipboard life that also kept his waist and hips flat and lean. Obvious in his trim fawn britches were the powerful muscular thighs that bespoke years of heavy manual labor that had preceded his position as Captain. Light gray eyes under dark brows within a deeply tanned face imparted to his gaze a penetrating, unnerving quality that was not easily dismissed, and his strong, even profile, full lips and firm chin completed the aura of masculinity and power he effortlessly exuded.

Shaking his head in bewilderment at his own confused thoughts, he resumed his approach to the cabin and within a few seconds was knocking on the door. Whatever it was that drew him to these two unfortunate victims of uncertain times and hapless circumstances, he would not know peace of mind until he had satisfied himself as to their present well-being.

The opening door interrupted his thoughts as a small,

belligerent voice inquired, "Oh, it's you. What do you want?"

An embarrassed gasp was heard from the bed as Marian Greer's shocked voice called out, "Amethyst!"

Looking down severely into the small, unfriendly face, Damien shot the girl a withering glance, mumbling under his breath for her ears alone, "Still the discourteous little brat, aren't you?" Stepping past her as if she no longer existed, he turned the full warmth of his smile on the embarrassed sick woman.

"Mrs. Greer. It is good to see you looking so well today."

Obviously pained at her daughter's discourtesy, the woman's pale face flushed hotly. "Captain Straith, you have my apologies. I don't know what has come over Amethyst!" Then addressing the girl who still stood in the open doorway, "Amethyst! You will apologize to the Captain for your unforgivable behavior this minute! Besides having been immensely helpful after my accident, he is captain of this ship and deserving of our respect and courtesy!"

Suddenly becoming frightened as her mother's agitation seemed to rob her of breath and color, Amethyst turned toward him, making sure to keep her back to the disturbed woman. Apologizing in a sincere tone that contrasted vividly with the expression on her small face, she said sweetly, "I'm sorry for my *unforgivable* behavior, Captain Straith."

Using her mother's words, she managed to convey ever so subtly without increasing the woman's anxiety that the idea for her apology was entirely her mother's, and conceding to himself he had to admire the little brat's deviousness, Damien managed to subdue his annoyance.

"*Sincere* apologies," he answered with a double entendre of his own, "are always accepted, child."

Satisfied that he had incensed the little twit even

further by his condescending use of the word "child" when she so obviously considered herself adult, he walked toward the bunk with extreme satisfaction and a wide smile.

"I trust you are feeling as well as you appear, Mrs. Greer. We were all considerably worried by your nasty fall."

The woman's pale blue eyes reflected her appreciation of his concern. "Oh, yes, Captain, I'm much better today by far. But the doctor warned I was to stay in bed until my headaches passed, and Amethyst is determined I will not move a muscle in defiance of his orders." Looking to the corner where Amethyst had retired to sulk, she shot the child a forgiving and obviously loving glance before addressing her again.

"Amethyst, dear, would you see if you could bring me some broth from the galley? I feel a slight chill."

Without a word, the child was on her feet and out the door, and once it had closed behind her, Marian Greer turned apologetically back to Captain Straith.

"Please sit down, Captain." Indicating a chair beside the bunk, she continued, "I wanted a few words in private with you, Captain, to apologize for Amethyst's behavior. She is a very strong-willed child . . . her father's daughter in every way. Morris, my husband, and she were very close and during my most recent illness he seemed to instill in her a strong sense of responsibility for my welfare. Since his death she has assumed complete responsibility for my care, as much as I try to convince her I am quite well."

Nodding his head in polite assent, Damien inwardly realized the girl was far too observant even at her young age to be taken in by her mother's valiant protestations of good health.

"Sometimes I fear," the woman continued in a worried tone, "that she is far too strong-willed for her own good. Surely a woman must be a more pliant creature... not possessed of such fierce determination... I fear for her future, should I..."

Suddenly lifting her eyes, she continued with a new brightness of expression, "Morris was such a handsome man, Captain, and possessed of tremendous talent. He was so proud of Amethyst. He called her his little jewel... She has worked so hard since his death to compensate for my occasional inability to fulfill my obligations to the troupe when I have been ill. She is a surprisingly accomplished seamstress for such a slip of a girl, and is endlessly helpful." A cloud seeming to settle over her expression, she continued, "She has grown quite thin with her constant running and fetching for this purpose and that... but I will soon be well and then she will grow as plump and lazy as a child should be..."

Suddenly intensely serious, Marian Greer's pale eyes filled with tears. "I hope you will not hold her childish rebellion against her, Captain. She is so very young, you know..."

Overcome with pity for the poor woman's plight, Damien took her small, cold hand into his. "You need not worry, Mrs. Greer. I certainly would not..."

A sudden sound at the doorway drew both their eyes to Amethyst who had returned, a small tin of broth balanced carefully in her hands. Walking slowly into the room, she placed it carefully on the shelf beside her mother's bunk, darting a quick, obviously heated glance to the large, tanned hand that held her mother's. Oddly discomforted by the open disapproval reflected on her small face, Damien allowed the woman's hand to slip from his grasp before continuing to speak.

During the course of the polite conversation that ensued, Amethyst moved in a series of seemingly endless tasks between Damien and her mother, waging a casual, deliberate war of interference with their conversation, and the small pinch of annoyance Damien felt at the outset of her campaign slowly grew despite his resolve. Finally barely able to control his anger, he abruptly rose to his feet. Realizing he would soon be at the point of agitating the sick woman even further by taking her darling daughter over his knee to give her the wailing of her life, he put his best effort into a smile and said tightly, "Now that I'm satisfied you are recuperating well, Mrs. Greer, I will return to my work." Was it his imagination or did a flash of relief momentarily move across the woman's face? Whatever her reaction, the child could not suppress a small victorious smile which had the effect of infuriating him even further, and shooting her a thunderous look which appeared to have no effect at all on her apparent satisfaction, he turned and left.

Once outside, Damien stared hotly at the door he had just closed behind him in a supreme effort to swallow his anger.

"Damned interfering little chit!" he mumbled between clenched teeth. "Maneuvered that situation to her own benefit, did she?" The small victorious smile flashed across his mind again, serving only to incite his anger even further.

"One day you will push me too far, little Amethyst Greer," he muttered to the small violet-eyed image in his mind's eye, "and when that time comes, neither Hell nor high water will save you from me!"

Turning abruptly, he started down the hall, the true source of his irritation the fact that he had been outwitted and outmaneuvered by a nine-year-old child.

Crystal clear, turquoise waters gently lapped against the *Sally*'s hull while a brilliant morning sun bathed her in its golden haze. An increasing warmth permeated the gently moving air currents, enveloping the tall, graceful ship in an aura of lethargy that was only one of the many deceptions of the wildly beautiful tropical island of Jamaica.

Leaning indolently against the rail of the ship, sun glinting warmly on his thick, tawny hair, Damien Straith watched the systematic unloading of the *Sally* with a keen eye that belied his casual posture. They had reached Kingston in record time with the cargo of foodstuffs so essential to the tropical island. Shaking his head, he gave a low, disgusted snort. Sugar . . . the island existed mainly for the production of the money crop that would bring wealth to the landowners, a quick fortune to the often sadistic overseers, and endless revenue to the Mother Country. In the meantime the island was being exploited with shocking ruthlessness, the land exhausted with no thought to the future. In the present scheme of things, when the land was no longer productive, it was merely abandoned . . . there was always another section where they could move on. As stupid and short-sighted as this was, there were no complaints from the proprietors in England. As long as they could count rising profits, they would not question the handling of their estates. No land was wasted on the planting of anything as mundane as food, and except for the small plots of ground utilized by slaves for their own use, food was imported from the American colonies and Great Britain. It was cheaper that way. Overseers hired to manage absentee owners' lands were often cruel, merciless men. Bent on the accumulation of a quick fortune for a glorious return to England, they often worked the slaves until they dropped and within the few short years that Damien had been sailing to the islands, the insatiable demand for slaves had raised their population on the island to over 90,000, ten times that of the whites. An island of incomparable natural beauty, Jamaica was unusually barbaric and uncivilized. Unlike the other British islands where settlement was encouraged, there was little polite society, with the small number of landowners that actually lived and worked their own plantations the only inhabitants even concerned about improving their circumstances. It was a greedy, uncultured, often violent world in which the accumulation of wealth was the primary concern, and any and all manner of vice was tolerated and enjoyed in a disordered, mostly ignorant society.

With a peculiar sense of weariness, Damien watched as his eager passengers made their way down the gangplank, barely able to conceal their excitement with the alluring beauty of the island. David and Margaret Douglass were no strangers to the island . . . they knew what they were getting into . . . but the others . . . How many would be lambs led to the slaughter? Unwillingly his gaze lingered on the slight woman trailing behind the small group, tightly clutching her daughter's hand. That gentle, fragile woman would be child's play for the human sharks that inhabited the port. And the girl . . . ? Walking slowly beside her mother, Amethyst's dark head moved from side to side in an effort to digest the unfamiliar surroundings. Despite himself, the small sense of disquiet inside Damien grew. He knew what it was to be orphaned at an early age in a hostile environment. Would she survive . . . ?

At that moment, as if sensing his perusal, Amethyst turned her head toward the ship, her brilliant violet eyes raised to his as she moved almost directly below him on the adjacent dock. Catching his glance, she held his steely gray eyes with her own in a deliberately mocking expression that went far beyond her years. She had not forgiven him his high-handed behavior on the day of their meeting, and if he was any judge of character, she never would. A small smile hovered around his lips despite himself . . . the girl had spirit . . . only to be replaced moments later by a hard, angry line as, unknown to her mother, Amethyst pulled a deliberate grimace for his benefit. Concluding by sticking out her small, pink tongue in his direction, she effectively removed any doubts as to the manner of her final farewell. Smiling shortly at his obvious anger, she raised her nose in the air and looked away haughtily, sending the blood rushing to Damien's face at the little twit's deliberate provocation.

"Little bitch!" he mumbled, his fists clenching and unclenching as he subdued an almost overpowering urge to chase after her and wring her dainty little neck. "You wouldn't try that if you knew you were within my reach . . ." Muttering through clenched teeth, he watched as the anxious group slowly moved around the corner and out of sight. "I'd like to see how cocky you are a year from now. . . ."

But unhappily, the thought gave him little satisfaction. Merely a strange, inexplicable sense of loss . . .

Chapter 2

1779

"Tillie, you are being absolutely stupid and ridiculous about this!"

The exasperated cry from the lips of the slight thirteen-year-old was unthinkingly uttered and regretted only moments later when black eyes opened wide in anger, and the motherly mulatto drew herself proudly to her full, impressive height. A big woman, standing close to six feet, she was broad of shoulder and full breasted, more than ample in weight. Her proud but angry face was fine featured, displaying her mixed blood boldly, and the dark curly hair pulled tightly to the back of her head in a severe knot was only beginning to streak with gray. Dressed in the simple but colorful native cotton dress of the islands, she was a handsome woman.

"Tillie tell you now, missey, not to forget this be Tillie Swann you speak to, free woman of color, educated at the free school. Tillie no fool . . . wiser than you! You mama sick and when him sick you listen to Tillie . . . him in charge of you!"

"No one is in charge of *me* but *me*, Tillie!"

Ignoring a reluctant surge of pride in the child's vociferously defended independence, Tillie continued in a reprimanding tone, her aging but still beautiful face stern and unrelenting.

"You still be child, Amethyst Greer, and like or not, you mama ask me to see to you care when him unwell! You listen now to what Tillie say. You stay away from that man! Him obeah-man. Tillie know!"

"Oh, Tillie..." Dismissing the woman's warning with an impatient wave of her hand, Amethyst succeeded only in incensing her further.

"You don't be facety with me, missey! Tillie tell you him obeah-man! How else him ship get past gunboats like shadow? They look fe him here, him there... they look fe him there, him here! Everybody know him on island, but nobody know where! Nigromancy! Obeah!"

Despite her irritation, Amethyst felt a flash of amusement. Usually taking particular pains to be correct in her grammar, Tillie was beginning to slip into the island dialect, a sure sign of her mounting anger. But she had no patience with Tillie's superstitions. Witchcraft ... magic ... those were the answers the islanders put to every situation they could not understand. As far as she was concerned, it was all nonsense, and Tillie's superstitions were not going to stop her... nothing was going to stop her.

"I'm going tonight, Tillie!"

"You will not! And if you speak any louder, you mama going to get out of bed and come right out here and say so!"

Glancing quickly toward the door behind which her mother slept, Amethyst frowned and continued in a lower tone, "I don't need anyone to tell me what I have to do, Tillie. I have to get Mama some good food, not these achees and mangos we've been living on... or she will... she won't get better very quickly!"

The welling of tears in soft, violet eyes and the child's faltering words dismissed all anger from Tillie's voice, but her manner remained adamant.

"You will not go!"

"I will!"

"Amethyst?" A weak voice from the next room brought the first sign of contrition to the small, flushed face as Amethyst responded in a light voice, "Yes, Mama?"

"Could you come here a moment, dear?"

Not waiting to answer, the child raced across the room to her mother's summons, leaving Tillie shaking her head in despair.

"That child gowan be the death of me...," she mumbled, a worried frown creasing her brow despite the unsquelchable pride in the child that always prevailed within her.

Tillie Swann, daughter of a white plantation owner and negro mother, automatically free by the laws of Jamaica, had begun work for the professional troupe of actors three and a half years before, after their first performance in Kingston. Well received by the culture-starved residents of the island, the troupe was finally financially able to hire a woman to tend to their basic needs while they pursued their art. Cook, housekeeper, and laundrywoman for the troupe, and in her spare time—and out of the goodness of her heart—nurse to the almost continually ailing Marian Greer, Tillie was immediately impressed by the nine-year-old's intelligence and maturity. Her respect for Amethyst's fiery independence and unfaltering dedication to her mother's welfare had fostered a growing affection that had turned into a deep love for the beautiful young girl she now was.

"Him my soul child," Tillie whispered to the silent room, a deep pride bringing a light flush to her smooth cocoa skin.

Slight and graceful as a reed, Amethyst was a delight to the eye. A strong, almost motherly glow swelled in Tillie's heart at the long, glossy, unruly black curls that streamed down the girl's slender back; the wide lavender eyes that sparkled with undaunted spirit; the smooth, white skin; the short, straight nose and full generous mouth that vacillated between childish whispered confidences to her surrogate mother, and unthinking, blatant insults such as she had uttered just a few moments before. With the slim, almost boyish figure of immaturity, Amethyst was unconsciously beautiful, and growing more so each day, and Tillie alternated between overwhelming pride and fear for the hapless child.

These were bad times in Jamaica. England's censure on trade with the colonies during their rebellion against the Mother Country was proving to be more detrimental to Jamaica's stability than to the rebels'. Dependent on imported foodstuffs that were no longer allowed in from the American continent, the price of food had tripled during the last years, and starvation in the slaves' quarters on plantations was rampant. A hurricane having destroyed the emergency crops that were planted, food was desperately sought by all legal and illegal means. A few American smugglers, grasping the opportunity for quick, hefty profits, chanced the British gunboats to smuggle food to the anxious islanders. Outlaws with a price on their heads, they were heroes to the islanders, and were welcomed and protected with a sense of reverence.

"But Tillie not such a fool," she muttered under her breath as she bent to her laundry basket. "No way him come past gunboats like shadow if him be ordinary man! That captain . . . him be obeah-man! Him make himself invisible and steal past ships. . . ."

A hesitant step interrupted her thoughts and Tillie looked up to see Amethyst return from her mother's room, her bright eyes downcast as she walked slowly toward the unsmiling mulatto.

"Mama thought she heard us arguing, Tillie . . ." Amethyst's expression was contrite as she slowly raised her eyes. "She was upset . . . but I told her not to worry because I was just behaving poorly, and would apologize to you. I'm sorry, Tillie," she whispered, suddenly moving forward to throw her thin arms around the older woman. "You are my only true friend. We shan't argue anymore, shall we?" she said hopefully, awaiting a break in the stern countenance staring down at her.

With a relieved sigh, Amethyst saw a smile break through the stern facade, but Tillie's voice was strong with unwavering authority. "No, we won't argue anymore if you listen to me, missey."

Smiling with relief, Amethyst countered with a quick but evasive, "Thank you, Tillie. . . ."

Keeping close to the shadows of the buildings, her light footsteps echoing eerily in the deserted street, Amethyst moved quickly down the poorly lit lane. Why had it taken so long for Tillie to fall asleep tonight? Was she suspicious? No, she couldn't be or she would never have made it out the door! Oh, Tillie would be furious when she found out she had sneaked away during the night, but Amethyst couldn't leave anything more to chance. Mama wasn't getting any better. Dr. Martens said she needed to be "built up." She was weak. There was only one place where she could get fresh milk and eggs . . . the Sheridan Plantation. They had a few goats and a few chickens that had managed to survive. If she could only get some flour or rice, she could hide some of it and trade some for fresh milk and eggs. She had heard two men talking at the performance the previous night. The *Sally* had arrived the night before with a cargo of food and was secretly docked somewhere on the island. Captain Straith . . . a small grimace of distaste crossed her youthful features at the mere thought of his name. Four years had not lessened her instinctive, well-remembered dislike of the man, but he was her only hope. He had liked her mother . . . he had been holding her hand that day on the ship, hadn't he? She would explain how sick Mama was. She'd beg if she had to, although the mere thought revolted her, but she'd wring some supplies out of his cold heart. She had to . . .

With a determination born of desperation, Amethyst increased her speed. Her light footsteps skimming over the ground, she was mindless of the danger of her solitary mission when with heart-stopping abruptness a large figure lurched out of a doorway as she passed, catching her leg and knocking her to the ground. Aided by the strength of pure, unmitigated fear, Amethyst pushed and pounded at the clutching hands, wriggling and squirming until she had worked herself free. Struggling to her feet, she ran as fast as her slender legs would carry her. Her heart pounding in fear, Amethyst ran blindly down the winding street until her heaving lungs could take no more. Gasping painfully, she finally slowed her pace and threw a frightened glance over her shoulder. No one followed! With an immense sense of relief she realized the man had probably been drunk . . . there were many drunks in the dock area. It was a dangerous place to be, which had been the main reason for Tillie's objection to her plan. But dressed as she was in boy's clothing, her long hair stuffed into a hat that she wore pulled well down over her ears, she could go on without further problem . . . she hoped.

"Just a few blocks more," Amethyst mumbled under her breath as she cast apprehensive glances into the shadows. Despite her resolve, the superstitions of the island began to play on her mind. In each wavering shadow she half expected to see the Old Hige, the hag who shed her skin each night to wander in the dark in the shape of a ball of fire and suck the blood of sleepers. Or the Rolling Calf with its fiery eyes, dragging its chain behind it . . .

Shaking her head clear of rioting thoughts, Amethyst stopped to get her bearings. The bawdy house should be near. It was usually easy to find by the noise emanating from the many well-lit rooms, but it was so late that all was quiet. Oh, she hoped she hadn't missed him, but if she could judge from the snickers of the two men, Captain Straith would be at his favorite streggah's rooms until the early morning hours. Amethyst's education on that score had been quite broad. She had learned a long time ago how these women made their living, selling themselves. As for her, she would rather die than let that vile man touch her.

Finally judging she had indeed arrived at her destination, Amethyst glanced up and down the street. It was quite empty, and realizing she could do no more than wait, Amethyst moved into the shelter of a doorway and sat down. Pulling her knees up to her chest, she locked her arms around them in a small, tight ball. She would wait until morning if she had to. If only she hadn't missed him . . .

Shooting an absentminded glance into the ornate vanity mirror in the gaudy bordello room, Captain Straith quickly brushed his heavy sun-streaked hair into place. He had stayed longer than he intended. It was nearly daylight and he had a lot of work ahead of him before he sailed. By now the cargo would be unloaded and the reloading underway. A small smile curved his full, sensuous mouth. A run to Jamaica always proved well worth the risk. The residents of the island were near panic for food, and his cargo of flour, rice, Indian corn, meat, and the dried herring which was the staple of the slaves' diet, was anxiously awaited. He was especially pleased that on this voyage he had been able to negotiate in advance for a full return cargo of gunpowder and military supplies that were not generally available to Yankee buyers and were so badly needed by the colonial army. It made no difference to General Washington whatsoever that his needed supplies were smuggled past British gunboats. In fact, it appeared to increase his appreciation of them.

The first gray shafts of dawn were beginning to squeeze through the drawn blinds in the small opulently furnished room and Damien glanced regretfully toward the wide disheveled bed that dominated the center. And damned if Ruby hadn't made it worth the risk to come see her last night. The sensuous octoroon was well versed in her trade, and Damien suspected that the bags of rice and flour he had brought her were more welcome than diamonds. Stopping just a moment longer to run his eyes over the dusky-skinned beauty sleeping so soundly, Damien gave a small laugh. She had fair worn him out last night in appreciation, and, he suspected, in hopes that her performance would insure a visit on his next voyage to the islands—which indeed it had.

"You have well earned your rest, Ruby," Damien snickered lightly to the sleeping streggah, and throwing her a farewell kiss, he quietly opened the door and moved down the dark stairway. "Hell," he mused as he stopped midway to stretch his tired, aching body, "it's going to be a long day." Suddenly remembering the touch of those full, demanding lips against his skin, he sighed contentedly. "But it was worth it . . ."

With another small, self-satisfied laugh, Damien continued down the steps, casually and effectively dismissing the sleeping woman from his mind. He had more important things to think of now and Ruby would not enter his thoughts again until he returned to Jamaica. The important thing now was to get out of the area as quickly as possible without being recognized and return to his ship. With a strong sense of purpose Damien continued down the staircase, his mind already running ahead to the tasks of the day that was just dawning. Loading of fresh water and cargo would have to be completed so they could sail on the evening tide. They could not risk another night on the island. There was always the chance that someone would find the reward on his head just too tempting to turn down, even though the individual who dared would suffer the wrath of the entire island if he were found out. After all, he was a hero, wasn't he? And in addition to that, he had strong obeah! Chuckling lightly to himself, Damien reached the foot of the steps and turned into the alleyway. He was well aware that the islanders were in awe of his powers of witchcraft, and their superstitious beliefs served his purpose well . . . were in fact his best insurance against being turned over to the . . .

"Captain Straith!" A small whispered voice cut into Damien's wandering thoughts and brought him up sharply for the briefest second before he continued briskly down the street. Light footsteps sounded behind him and the voice hissed again, "Captain Straith!" but Damien strode purposefully forward, effectively ignoring the urgent summons.

The running footsteps behind him came closer, and Damien braced himself the second before a small hand grasped his arm, simultaneously jerking him around.

"Captain Straith! Please, I want to talk to you a moment."

Glancing down sharply at the boy standing beside him, every nerve in his body alert to impending danger, Damien responded with feigned annoyance, "You have the wrong man, boy. My name is not Straith. Now get along and leave me alone. I have places to go." Shaking off the small hand that clutched his arm, he continued down the street, shooting quick, surreptitious glances out of the corner of his eye for a possible trap, for which this boy was possibly the lure.

The running footsteps continued behind him, as did the small, determined summons which grew annoyingly louder. "Captain Straith . . . please wait . . . Captain Straith, I must talk to you . . ."

"Damn the blasted boy!" Damien cursed softly under his breath. "If he keeps this up, the entire island will know I'm here!" Shooting one more glance around and satisfied that the street was indeed deserted, Damien turned the corner, simultaneously stepping into an alleyway and drawing back into the shadows as he did. Expectedly, within a few seconds the boy turned the corner. In a swift movement, Damien's strong, powerful arms snaked out, covering the insistent mouth with one hand as the other wrapped around the boy's waist, jerking him full back against his body in the darkness of the alleyway.

"Now, what is it that you want?" he hissed menacingly into the boy's ear as the slight figure squirmed and wriggled in his grasp in an effort to break his hold. "Are you the lure for some sort of trap?" he growled. "Well, if you are, it would seem that the tables are reversed, wouldn't it?"

The boy continued struggling and kicking, his thin arms flailing about ineffectively, his feet kicking wildly in an effort to land a few savage kicks in his vulnerable shins. Despite his great strength, the boy's unyielding resistance was seeing results. Damien's grip around the boy's narrow waist began to slip and the boy suddenly turned and began pounding and scratching fiercely at his chest and face, while directing sharp, well aimed kicks at his legs.

Momentarily stunned at the fierceness of the child's attack, Damien dropped his defenses, only to receive an unexpected, well aimed kick to his knee that sent sharp shooting pains the full length of his leg and left him gasping.

"Damn the little bastard!" he swore under his breath, simultaneously raising his hand to deliver a hard, resounding slap to the angry face of his small opponent. The blow connected squarely and the boy staggered backwards, his small fists dropping lifelessly to his sides in prelude to complete collapse. Realizing he had almost knocked the boy senseless with his light blow, Damien grabbed him quickly around the waist, jerking him forward against him before the wobbling legs buckled completely. For a few seconds the boy's weight hung lifelessly against him, his head laying lightly against his chest as he struggled to regain control of his senses, and Damien froze with momentary shock. Were those budding breasts pressing so intimately against his chest? Suddenly jerking the boy away from him, he held the slight figure at arms' length. Still supporting him with one arm, he raised his hand to jerk the hat from the boy's head. To his amazement black, silky curls tumbled down around the slender slumped shoulders, and realizing he—or she—was found out, the child raised slightly dazed but furious eyes to his. The moment of contact with the enraged glance sent an inexplicable jolt through Damien's body. Unable to explain the peculiar sensation, still holding the girl at arm's length, Damien took a few quick steps to the right and thrust her face out of the shadows and into the brightening light of morning.

The dazed expression had left the small, pointed face, and raging lavender eyes glared into his. Immediate recognition surged through him for all the girl had grown since Damien last saw her. Amethyst . . . the child named for the color of her eyes . . . how could he ever forget the little brat?

Jerking her roughly back into the shadows of the alleyway, he growled into her furious face, "I see you haven't changed a bit since we last met, Amethyst Greer. Still the same thoughtless little idiot you were four years ago. What were you trying to do, bring the whole street down on me?"

"No, I was not, Captain Straith." Amethyst could not stop herself from sneering in return, but suddenly realizing she would have to change her tactics if she was to ask a favor of the odious man, she struggled to overcome her fury. With a supreme and obvious effort she managed a small smile and a more pleasant voice.

"I was desperate to see you, Captain, because," taking a deep breath and managing an even wider smile she continued, smiling up into his dubious expression, "because you are my last resort. I am desperately in need of a favor."

To Damien's descerning eye, the picture before him was too inconceivable to be believed. The damned little witch who only moments before was ready to scratch his eyes out was suddenly purring... trying to charm him... with the mark of his blow still burning hotly on her cheek. That she still felt its sting there was no doubt, but she obviously was ignoring the pain. Common sense told him she longed to scratch his eyes out in retaliation. She was up to something.

"A favor? What is it?" When she hesitated a moment, he ordered sharply, "Hurry up! I've no time to waste with you. What is it that brings you scurrying after me in the dark? Do you realize that I might have killed you?"

"Since I did not think you were in the habit of murdering children, Captain," Amethyst cooed acidly, "I did not realize I would be in danger trying to speak with you."

Raising his brow slightly at her words, Damien muttered under his breath, "You wish to be considered a child only when it suits your purpose. Now what do you want?"

Closely watching the play of emotions over her small face, Damien was suddenly struck by the brilliant beauty beginning to blossom there. Obviously finding it hard to put her thoughts into words, she stammered uncharacteristically and averted her face. Suspicion knawed relentlessly and Damien demanded impatiently, "Well?"

"It's my mother, Captain." The words were mumbled, her face still averted. "She's ill. She needs nourishing food if she is to regain her strength, but . . . you must realize that it's almost impossible to get what she needs." Slowly the small face raised to his, but her eyes were still lowered, unwilling to return his questioning gaze. He waited in silence for her to continue, and slowly, effectively, the heavy black lashes lifted from clear, ivory cheeks, allowing the full power of wide, tear-filled lavender eyes to glow into his. Momentarily startled with the impact, Damien swallowed hard, shocked that the glance of a child such as she could have such a dizzying effect on him.

Angry with himself, he demanded harshly, "What do you want from me?"

Obviously disconcerted by his harshness, Amethyst stammered, "I . . . I would like some food . . . maybe a few bags of flour or rice . . . anything I can trade for milk . . . eggs . . ." Her small voice trailed off as she stared into the captain's stony face.

"And I suppose you expect me to lead you to the ship, show you our docking place . . . so you may go directly to the authorities and turn me in for the reward?"

"No, Captain! I wouldn't . . . I mean, I had no intention . . . please believe me . . ."

"You must think me a fool, Amethyst!" His face was livid with anger. The girl had disliked him from the first and probably considered this a good chance to line her pockets and get back at him for his imagined slights at the same time. Obviously it was a poorly contrived attempt to trick him. He continued harshly, "Now go home, little bitch, and try to think up a better story the next time you attempt to betray someone. Your plan this time is too childishly transparent to work on me!" With a rough shove, he pushed her toward the alleyway entrance. "Go home, little girl." As her expression slowly turned to rage, he whispered menacingly, "And if you try to scream the authorities down on me, I swear I'll snap your little neck!"

Not doubting his words for a moment, Amethyst took an involuntary step backwards, her small hands doubling up into tight fists as burning fury suffused her. "You are too stupid to know when a person is telling the truth! Fool! Buffuto! You and your streggah make a good pair! And I warn you now, Captain Straith," she hissed in suppressed violence, "if Mama should die, I will tell Tillie to turn her obeah against you! She is a puckoo woman . . . her obeah is strong . . . she will set a duppy on you and you will need no one to turn you in. You will be caught and you will die . . . and . . . and . . . I will be GLAD!"

Suddenly sobbing wildly, Amethyst turned and ran down the street. Taking a few, hesitant steps forward, Damien watched the small retreating figure, a heavy scowl covering his face. The child was either an extremely good actress or truly desperate. Suddenly remembering Marian Straith's small, pale face and Amethyst's obvious devotion to her, it seemed no longer unlikely that Amethyst had attempted such a dangerous mission merely in the hope of obtaining a few bags of rice. A dozen conflicting thoughts seemed to rush through Damien's mind as Amethyst's slim figure disappeared around the corner of the lane, and suddenly unaware of his own intentions, Damien started walking briskly in the direction in which the sobbing girl had disappeared.

Slowly Amethyst approached the small frame house that housed her mother, Tillie, and herself. A series of identical four-room houses lined the street, one indistinguishable from the other, but the barren facade of her own home seemed to glare at her, accusing her of inglorious defeat at the hands of the ignominious captain.

Standing stiffly, Amethyst took deep, heavy breaths, forcing herself into control, and carelessly wiping her face dry with the sleeve of her shirt, she walked toward the door. She would have to face Tillie sooner or later. She would rather have faced her with her arms loaded with rice and flour, but since that would not be the case, she walked slowly up to the door and turned the knob. One step into the room and Tillie's face glared angrily into hers. Her sober expression suddenly crumbling into tears, Amethyst ran forward to throw her arms around the worried mulatto, sobbing heavily against her neck, "I tried, Tillie . . . I tried, but he wouldn't help me . . . he wouldn't help me . . ."

All trace of anger fled in the face of the child's anguish, and wrapping her arms around her comfortingly, Tillie cooed softly in the child's ear. "That's alright, child. Lord knows you tried."

So involved was Tillie in the child's grief that she did not hear the slight noise at the door the second before it suddenly burst open. Snapping back against the wall with a loud thud, it revealed a huge, angry man standing in the doorway.

Gasping audibly, Tillie cried in a hoarse voice, "It be him . . . him be the obeah-man!" To the frightened woman's horror, Amethyst pulled free of her protective embrace to shout angrily, "What are you doing here? Get out of my house!"

Damien frowned, slowly closing the door behind him. Tillie's petrified gaze fastened on the specter's penetrating eyes. Commencing a low moaning chant, she began rocking gently from side to side in a graceful hypnotic motion. Before Damien could respond to the child's vehement command a weak voice called warily from the next room.

"Amethyst . . . Amethyst, dear. Is something wrong?"

Appearing to suddenly snap into movement, Damien started for the room from which the voice had called, and seeing his intent, Amethyst charged him violently, kicking and punching him wildly as he continued to advance. Abruptly flicking the furious child off like a fly to send her bouncing against the far wall, he opened the door and walked toward the bed. Startled, the woman gasped and after a brief moment, said weakly, "It is Captain Straith, is it not?"

His stern expression suddenly changing into a warm smile, Damien advanced. His hand outstretched in greeting, he gently took the hand lifted to his in return and raised it to his lips. "Mrs. Greer! It's good to see you again. I realize it is a bit early to call, but I happened to run into Amethyst this morning, and she told me you were unwell. Since I was so close to your home, I decided to stop in to see you . . ."

Flushing with true pleasure, Marian Greer moved her glance to the doorway where Amethyst stood watching the captain warily. "Amethyst, dear, wasn't it nice of the Captain to stop in? Would you please bring us some tea, dear?"

Within the half hour the captain had left. Departing the house with a friendly goodbye to Mrs. Greer, he deliberately neglected to speak to Amethyst and the wide-eyed Tillie.

A few hours later a heavy, insistent pounding at the front door drew both Tillie and Amethyst. Upon opening it they found four sacks, clearly labeled flour and rice, and two more that smelled suspiciously like smoked fish. Quickly stepping out into the street, they found it empty, despite that fact that it was an hour when there were normally many people abroad on the lanes.

Gasping audibly, Tillie turned anxious eyes on Amethyst, whispering in a shaken voice, "It be him . . . it be the obeah-man . . ."

Shooting her an exasperated look, Amethyst said, "Oh, do be quiet, Tillie, and help me drag these sacks inside."

Struggling with the weight of the heavy sacks, Amethyst mumbled vehemently under her breath, her small face flushed with emotion, "I don't care . . . I don't care . . . I hate him! I hate him anyway!"

Chapter 3

1780

Walking rapidly along the dusty road, Amethyst stopped from time to time to shake her foot vigorously in an effort to rid her worn sandals of stones that occasionally wedged inside and jabbed her small feet annoyingly. Vast, flat sugar fields stretched out on either side of her, a familiar but ever changing landscape which she viewed with interest only because the fields were being prepared for planting, the beginning of the fifteen-month cycle of creole cane. Black, naked backs glistened with perspiration as huge work gangs of slaves labored their way across the field in a system of cultivation that had gone unchanged since its inception. Working in pairs, the strongest slaves were "holing" the ground, the muscles in their powerful arms bulging with the strain of breaking two-foot holes in the soil with antiquated hoes, as their partners assisted in making the trenches. Walking behind, supporting huge baskets of ash and dung on their heads, the female slaves were spreading fertilizer in the trenches, while the work gangs following implanted cuttings in the prepared beds. Black drivers were keeping the gangs moving, while white overseers guaranteed the ultimate was demanded and derived from the exhausted gangs. It was not quite mid-morning, but Amethyst knew the slaves had been awakened by the sound of the conch at dawn, and would continue at the unrelenting pace until they were unable to work any longer. With a small sigh, she gave a silent word of thanks that she had not been born into slavery, and as happened each time she saw those backs bent in endless labor, she valued even more her own freedom, however meager its circumstances.

Shaking off her dour thoughts, Amethyst hastened her pace. She was accustomed to the long walk, having made it every other day for well over a year, but she was always happy to see the pitched, shingled roof of the great house of Sheridan Plantation come into view. Although it was similar to so many of the plantation great houses, huge and square with great louvred windows and spacious balconies adorned with graceful wrought ironwork, it had a native Jamaican charm of its own. Her destination, however, was not the great house, but rather the small, detached outhouse and attached buttery in the rear, in which all the cooking was done. Since her fateful meeting with Captain Straith, almost two years before, sacks of rice and flour and other food staples arrived at her door with regularity, apparently each time the *Sally* successfully eluded the gunboats to smuggle food ashore. With an ample supply of foodstuffs available to her, she had been able to strike a bargain with William Sheridan, master of the plantation, to have the greatest part of the food supply picked up by his wagon and taken to the plantation for his use, saving a small but ample amount for her own household. In return, she collected fresh milk and eggs on alternating days until the next shipment arrived and their bargain was renewed. It had worked out well, despite the need for the hour-long walk each way to collect the proceeds.

Her mother's health had improved with the change in diet, and while still not healthy, she was at least able to maintain her position with the troupe. Although not quite up to the slapstick entertainment provided between acts and at the conclusion of the performance, they had worked out an agreement with Mr. Douglass that her mama would fulfill the acting commitments and Amethyst in costume and heavy makeup would take care of the more active entertainment that actually required more physical dexterity than skill. Since between the two of them they were merely fulfilling the commitment of one member of the troupe, they were paid accordingly. But it was of no matter to Amethyst as long as her mother was reasonably well and they could live in a minimum of comfort. In truth, she fully realized their lot was far more fortunate than most on the island. All but destroyed by a series of hurricanes, the food crop had been meager. Many of the slaves were in desperate straits, but with Mr. Sheridan a resident owner and concerned about the welfare of his "black gold," the Sheridan Plantation slaves were not so badly affected. Absentee owners living comfortable lives in England unaware of the true reasons for their slaves' deaths, and actually uncaring until it affected their profits, usually accommodated their overseers' requests for more slaves without question. As a result, many of the large plantations were poorly run and mortgaged to the hilt, with futures that were exceedingly dim.

Surprisingly, the theater had not been affected by the hard times. A sizeable audience continued to appear twice weekly, apparently in an effort to put aside for a few hours the worries that filled the greatest part of the island residents' days.

If there was one fly in the ointment, it was Marcus Peters. A small shiver of distaste passed over Amethyst's delicate frame at the mere thought of the lecherous overseer of Sheridan Plantation. From the first, Amethyst had been aware of his interest . . . could feel the weight of his obvious fascination with her slight young body. In the last year his interest had become decidedly more active. He had taken to accosting her unexpectedly, his large dirty hands mauling her at the smallest opportunity, until she had been forced to flee their last two confrontations. So far she had been lucky, but her stomach knotted in fear of the outcome should he continue to press his advances. She dared not tell Tillie. There was no one else to send in her place, and she feared that should she complain to the lofty master of Sheridan Plantation, he would laugh in her face. Well, she would have to take it a day at a time, and hope the man would finally desist in his unwelcomed attentions. Raising her chin a notch higher with resolution, Amethyst turned on to the well worn path to the kitchen.

At fourteen years of age, Amethyst was a much different figure than the one that trod the same paths a year before. Still not much taller than a few inches past five feet, her boyish proportions were a thing of the past. A full, rounded breast now filled the narrow chest and the still minuscule waist was accented by slight, gently curving hips. Long, well shaped legs, hidden in the fullness of her dark skirt, contributed to the graceful swaying walk which caused her brilliant black curls to bob enticingly. But the splendid metamorphosis did not stop in the maturing of her lovely, young body. Still not at the full height of its beauty, Amethyst's face had nonetheless lost its childish prettiness and had begun to show the exciting promise of a more mature beauty. The fragile, clear complexion remained, contrasted even more heavily by the widening of incredible lavender eyes, magnificently fringed in a breathtaking sweep of long black lashes. Her nose was much the same, short and straight with classic appeal, but the new delicate contours of her cheek gave added emphasis to the full red lips that moved so expressively over perfect white teeth, drawing the eye to their fullness . . . tender, potent, almost overwhelmingly inviting. Innocently unaware of the formidable power she wielded with one sweeping glance of violet eyes, or the unconscious pursing of full red lips, she swept open the kitchen door. Surprised to find a stranger chatting so amiably with Delsea, she took a small step backward, feeling the intruder.

Both heads turned in her direction and the slender young man appeared momentarily startled. Tall and fair complexioned, his hair a rich mahogany color that matched the color of his eyes, he was extremely pleasant looking and seemed to find Amethyst similarly appealing. His eyes moved warmly over her, missing nothing and stopping to dwell for the briefest second on her soft, vulnerable mouth.

Smiling widely, Delsea welcomed her reassuringly. "Come in, Miz Amethyst. Him standing here be Massa Sheridan, Jr., fraish frem him schoolin'!"

His eyes suddenly widening, William, Jr. exclaimed surprisedly in a voice that held an appealing richness of tone, "You couldn't possibly be Amethyst Greer!"

Uncertain how to take his blatant astonishment, Amethyst nodded politely, "Yes, I am. I'm happy to meet you, Mr. Sheridan." Her face drew into a small frown of confusion at the obvious shock her soft confirmation had produced. Why he should be aware of her existence, much less appear shocked at the sight of her, was a mystery!

Awkwardly extending his hand in greeting, William Jr. shook hers lightly and stammered in response to her questioning expression, "You must excuse my reaction, Miss Greer, but I didn't expect the shrewd businesswoman who had contracted with my father for an exchange of supplies furnished to her by a well known smuggler to look . . . to be . . ." His youthful face flushing more deeply to his obvious dismay, the young man dropped her hand and said with considerable embarrassment, "Suffice it to say, I was taken by surprise." In an apparent attempt to conclude what was turning out to be a very awkward moment for both of them, he turned to Delsea.

"I must be going now, Delsea, and I'm pleased to have met you, Miss Greer . . ."

Turning toward the doorway, he made a quick exit, leaving Amethyst and Delsea staring at his fast disappearing back.

Completely unaffected by the awkwardness of the moment, Delsea said warmly, her old black eyes following him affectionately down the path, "Him growed t' be a good man. Him be true boonoonoonoos. An dem Creole men, dey sure pleasin' fe deh eyes . . ."

Amethyst smiled as the old woman raised her brows expressively and shook her gray head. Obviously Delsea thought highly of Mr. Sheridan, Jr. She had heard few white men given the great compliment of being referred to as "boonoonoonoos" by their slaves. With regard to the second part of her statement, Amethyst had not always concurred with the rather prejudiced general consensus of opinion that creoles, whites born on the island, were essentially better looking and better natured than other whites, but if this young man was to be considered a prime example of his race, Amethyst suddenly found she might happily agree.

Without further ado, Delsea turned to the larder and began to fill Amethyst's empty container with milk, and after she had carefully placed four large eggs in her small basket, offered her the ritual cool drink before bidding her another farewell.

So caught up was she in her speculation of young Mr. Sheridan's abrupt departure while she made her way along the winding trail to the main road, Amethyst failed to hear a step behind her until rough arms caught her in a crushing embrace. Even before she saw his face, Amethyst recognized the fetid breath of Marcus Peters and struggled wildly, her strong physical protests hampered by the weight of her fragile burden.

"Let me go, you fool!" she shouted, suddenly furious

that he should attack her when he knew she was least able to resist.

"Ya weren't expectin' to leave before sayin' goodbye to Marcus, were ya, honey?" he leered, his breath coming in short, heavy pants as he savored the feeling of her ripe, young body wriggling against his.

Amethyst's stomach rebelled wildly, and she fought to control the urge to gag. The man was utterly disgusting, wretched. And in addition to that, he was unclean, with unkempt, graying hair, and the foulest of body odors.

"Leave me alone, you filthy swine! Shower your attentions on some other woman who will welcome them . . . if there is any such desperate creature on the island!"

His face flushing hotly at her insult, he answered by tightening his embrace, almost stealing her breath. "A simple workin' man ain't good enough for ya, is he, princess! Your tastes run more to smugglers and thieves."

Gasping from the pain of his captive embrace, Amethyst groaned, "You are a vile man . . . boogoo-yagga!"

The whispered native insult appeared to suddenly inflame his anger and releasing Amethyst with a suddenness that sent her staggering backward, Marcus raised his fist to strike.

"You'd better not try that, Marcus!" A low warning came from a short distance away, and both heads snapped to the side to see William Sheridan, Jr. swing down from his horse and walk to stand between them.

"This little bitch!" Marcus Peters raged. "She comes swingin' her ass in front of me, deliberately tauntin' me, tryin' . . ."

"That's not true!" Amethyst's words were a shocked gasp.

". . . tryin' to get my attention, and when she does, she

plays hard to get . . . She's been askin' for . . ."

"That's enough, Marcus!" His face flushed in anger, William appeared barely in control of his temper. "Get out of here, now! You have work to do and it's obvious Miss Greer does not welcome your attentions!"

"She was tryin' . . ."

His face flooding with deeper color, William took a menacing step forward and hissed, "Go . . . *now!*"

Startled by the suppressed violence flaring in William's eyes, Marcus swallowed thickly and without another word, turned on his heel and stomped away.

Trembling visibly and shocked into silence, the metal container and basket still in her shaking hands, Amethyst stared at the retreating figure. Suddenly glancing down, she saw eggs oozing through the bottom of the basket, and quickly placing the metal container on the ground, she uncovered the basket.

"He's broken them . . . they're all broken . . ."

Her soft, forlorn cry suddenly turned into a deep, gulping sob, in delayed reaction to the fright of Peters's unwarranted attack. Dazedly she repeated again, lifting her gaze to William's concerned face, "He lied . . . he lied . . . that terrible man . . . I didn't try . . ."

Within seconds she was enclosed in a comforting embrace, her tear-streaked cheek resting against a sympathetic chest as William whispered soothingly, "You don't have to say anything, Amethyst. He is a vile man . . ." Smoothing the damp tendrils back from her face as she lifted her eyes to his, he whispered consolingly, ". . . and you are only a child."

"I am not a child." A flash of spirit sparked her tear-filled eyes, causing a small smile to move momentarily over William's lips.

"How old are you, Amethyst?"

"I can understand that you must think I am a child by the way I have been carrying on, b . . . but I was frightened . . ." Swallowing tightly, she pulled free of his arms to wipe away her tears with the back of her arm in a decidedly childish gesture, before raising her chin resolutely and continuing. "But I'll be alright now, except . . ." Glancing down again, her eyes came to rest on the basket of broken eggs.

Sliding an arm around her shoulders, William squeezed her arm lightly. "Since it was the fault of our overseer that the eggs were broken, we'll replace them. Come on." Urging her toward the kitchen, he walked with his arm around her, noticing that for all her bravura, the girl still trembled.

"You didn't answer my question, Amethyst. How old are you?"

"I'm fourteen years old. How old are you?"

Suddenly laughing, charmed by her audacious response, William smiled a rich, warm smile into her eyes. "I'm just twenty-one . . . quite a few years older than you."

"But that still doesn't make me a child," Amethyst said stubbornly, her violet eyes daring him to contradict her positive statement.

"I suppose not." William's eyes had gone suddenly serious just the second before they entered the kitchen to Delsea's wild exclamations.

Within a few minutes, whole eggs had been exchanged for broken ones and Amethyst and William walked side by side to the main road. At the end of the path, Amethyst turned soberly to William.

"Thank you, Mr. Sheridan. I must hurry home now. I shall be late and mother will be worried."

"Since I've been calling you Amethyst for the last half hour with no objections on your part, Amethyst, please do me the favor of calling me William. We are friends, aren't we?"

A small smile lit her face and William was once again

struck by the girl's selfless beauty.

"Yes, I believe we are friends . . . William. Goodbye now."

Suddenly unwilling to let her go so abruptly, William took Amethyst's arm in a brief, detaining gesture. At her questioning glance, he dropped it to reach for his horse's bridle and swinging up quickly into the saddle, extended his arm toward her.

"Come on, I'll ride you home."

"Oh, no! It'll take you out of your way, William."

"And our overseer has put you behind schedule. Tit for tat, Amethyst."

His sudden contagious grin sparked her own spirit of adventure and handing him her cargo to hold with his other hand, Amethyst took the arm extended to her and was pulled firmly up onto the saddle behind him.

"Hold on to my waist," and as she slid her arms around him, William shot a small smile over his shoulder, "That's right, now hold tight. Here we go!"

With a small jolt they moved from the uneven path onto the road.

His shirt smelled lightly of soap and sunshine as she pressed herself lightly against him. Unable to suppress a small giggle, Amethyst laughed lightly.

"Oh, William, this is fun!"

Chapter 4

1781

Walking along Harbor Road side by side, the two women, alike in so many ways, were still in vibrant contrast with one another. Both small, slight of build and conservatively dressed, one was excruciatingly thin, with an air of fragility that manifested itself most obviously in her precise, calculated movements. Her skin, though fairly unlined, bore a pallor that belied the tropical sun and was indicative of many bedridden days. The straight brown hair, caught into a neat bun at the back of her neck, was liberally streaked with gray and lacked luster. Dull blue eyes shadowed by dark circles mirrored accurately her state of health. Her general appearance was that of a fading bloom for which time was very short.

Contrasting vividly, a younger woman walked beside her. On closer inspection it became apparent that she was more girl than woman as evidenced by the youthful beauty of her face, and her naturally graceful but uninhibited walk. About her was a vitality that flashed in the gleam of the dark hair bobbing against her back, the glow of a golden, lightly tanned complexion that defied convention, and the sparkle of brilliant violet eyes and a flashing, dimpled smile that turned heads all along the street. Beside the fading bloom she walked, an exquisite flower in only the first magnificent stage of full glory.

Shooting a short glance to the small woman walking beside her, Amethyst felt the warmth of her mother's smile and sighed. It wasn't often that Mama felt well enough to venture out for a walk, and her obvious joy in her however temporary feeling of good health was exhilarating in itself. The past six months had seen Amethyst taking over more of her mother's acting commitments while she was incapacitated, and she knew her mother was extremely proud of her accomplishments. It was with great determination that she refused to acknowledge the inevitable, which was written more clearly on her mother's face each day.

With a positive effort, she directed her thoughts once again to William Sheridan, but try as she might, she still could not figure out what had set off his tirade a week ago.

The creole cane was a few months from harvest. She had arrived at the plantation that day by wagon, along with the new supplies which she had found on her doorstep a few days previous in the same mysterious manner as usual. Inexplicably, her arrival with the provisions had seemed to spark William's irritation, and her greeting was acknowledged with only the briefest of nods. Despite the fact that he had made a point of riding her home from the plantation at least twice a week during the past year, allowing an easy and pleasant companionship to grow between them, he was suddenly acting decidedly remote. When she left the kitchen with her exchange of supplies, he allowed her to walk alone down the trail to the road for a few yards before accompanying her with obvious reluctance.

"So, you've had a visit from your smuggler friend again, I see. He certainly goes out of his way to take care of you, doesn't he?"

Momentarily stunned at William's peevish tone and veiled innuendo, Amethyst stared speechlessly at his lightly flushed face for a few moments before answering haughtily, "Captain Straith isn't concerned about me . . . it's Mama. I've told you that before, William. He took a liking to Mama when we sailed here on the *Sally*. He doesn't really like me, and I certainly dislike him."

Flicking a contemptuous glance over her in an insulting manner, William's voice was a low sneer. "Of course . . ."

Aghast at his behavior, Amethyst eyed him unbelievingly. He was the same William for whom she had developed a great fondness . . . the same thick, mahogany colored hair and boyishly handsome face, tall, the same slender stature . . . he had not changed much in their year of acquaintance, but the flashing, heartwarming grin that so typified his personality was not present. Instead, his lips were pressed into a straight line, and a small muscle ticked in his cheek with suppressed anger.

"William! What is the matter with you today?"

"It just seems to me that the infamous Captain Straith goes to a great deal of trouble just because he took a 'liking' to your Mama . . ."

Suddenly feeling the blood rising in her own cheeks, Amethyst responded heatedly, "Are you insinuating, William Sheridan, that there is some type of . . . of . . . illicit relationship between Captain Straith and my mama?" Without waiting for his response, she continued furiously, "Well, you are wrong! Neither Mama nor I have even seen him in over a year, and he doesn't go to 'so much trouble' to see to us. It's not so difficult to send a few of his men."

"Well, I don't like it, that's all!"

"You don't like it!" Exploding with anger, Amethyst shouted, "And what concern is it of yours? My business agreement is with your father, and he seems to be well satisfied with the arrangement!"

"I don't like your associating with a man of that type."

"Oh, you would rather Mama and I go hungry, like the majority of the people on this island. Well, I don't find that thought too appealing, and neither does Mama. We don't choose to turn away help, even if it comes from a smuggler! So you can keep your opinions to yourself, William Sheridan, and go wash your mind in the creek!"

Amethyst's blazing temper seemed only to inflame William's anger, and glaring heatedly in return, he shouted, "You are left far too much on your own for a respectable young lady. You need . . ."

"Now you're telling me that I'm not respectable?"

". . . you need someone to take care of you . . . to watch out for your welfare."

"I don't need anyone *now,* William Sheridan, and I never will! Mama and I have done quite well for ourselves since Papa died. We support ourselves and run our own lives, *and we do not need or want you to tell us how to behave!"*

With that last shouted, unmistakable declaration, Amethyst had turned on her heel and stepped off the path onto the road. Without turning back once to see William staring moodily after her, she had stomped proudly down the road to town.

Frowning slightly, still puzzled with his behavior of the week before, Amethyst caught her mother's silent scrutiny and flashed her a short smile. Mama had met William several times and liked him immensely. It wouldn't do to upset her with his confusing behavior. In an effort to relieve her mother's mind by appearing intensely interested in shopping, Amethyst directed her glance toward some of the market stalls across the street. As she did, a mahogany colored head standing above the crowd caught her attention, and when the crowd of shoppers shifted for a moment, she saw William. His eyes were trained on the face of a slender blonde girl hanging tightly on his arm, her face turned up to his as she cooed appealingly.

"So," Amethyst mumbled to herself angrily, "that's

the reason he's suddenly so critical of me . . ."

Slipping her arm through her mother's, she urged quietly, "Let's look at the wares across the street, Mama," and before Marian Greer realized what had happened, she felt herself being propelled across the street. Within moments she was facing William Sheridan and his female companion. Startled, Marian Greer said lightly, "William, how pleasant to see you!"

Before William could respond to her mother's greeting, Amethyst smiled brilliantly up into his face, fluttering her silky black lashes in flagrant imitation of his companion's soleful expression. Directing the full power of her violet gaze into his eyes, she cooed sweetly, "Yes, William, it's sooooooo good to see you, but I'm afraid we have no time to chat right now and must run along." Flashing him another dazzling smile, she mumbled under her breath for his ears alone, "Yes, *she* does appear to be very . . . *respectable.*"

Satisfied to see the beginning of a bright flush suffuse his face as she turned away, she urged her mother forward, chatting amiably as she did, "It really is such a lovely day, isn't it, Mama? I'm so glad we decided to come out for a walk . . ."

Amethyst turned the bend in the road and immediately caught sight of William's tall, spare frame as he stood waiting at the turnoff to Sheridan Plantation. Nero was tethered to a tree close by, his black coat gleaming in the early morning sun. She had started out a few hours earlier this morning with the hope that she would be able to pick up her supplies and go before William even expected her to arrive. Somehow she felt William would make an effort to meet her today, and she was in no mood for another of his outbursts. She realized her behavior the day before when she had mocked Cecily Hargrove so blatantly was not that expected of a "proper" young lady, and her mother had upbraided her severely. She did not wish to give William the opportunity of saying she had proven him right. She could not really say she regretted her actions, either. Oh, what great satisfaction it had been to show Cecily Hargrove up for the simpering, thoughtless idiot she really was! And if that was the kind of girl William wished her to emulate, he was more of a quashi than she had thought him to be.

Head held high, she approached him, swinging her milk container and basket casually. As she drew closer, Amethyst noted that William did not appear angry as she had expected, but seemed extremely sober, more serious than she had ever seen him. Somehow this serious William unnerved her far more than the raging William of a week before.

Suddenly very serious herself, Amethyst stepped onto the trail to the plantation, and said softly, "Good morning, William. You're out quite early today, aren't you?"

Without a flicker of a smile, William answered quietly in return, "Somehow I had the feeling it would be safer to get here early today, Amethyst, if I wanted to see you."

"And is it so important to see me today, William?" Amethyst was once again puzzled by his behavior and tried valiantly to draw him out, but William would not be budged. Nodding his head slightly, he refused to say more than, "Yes, it is," before moving forward onto the trail to the kitchen, indicating he had nothing more to say at present.

Except for an exchange of pleasantries with Delsea, they maintained complete silence until they returned to the road. Mounting up on Nero, William held out his arm in a familiar gesture, saying as he did, "Come on, Amethyst, I'll ride you home. There are some things we must discuss that have been put off far too long already."

Abruptly wary of this new William, Amethyst shook

her head. "No, William, it's a nice day . . . I think I'd like to walk."

His eyes suddenly catching and holding hers, William did not allow her to continue. "Please, Amethyst, don't be difficult. It's important to me that some things be straightened out."

The soft quality of desperation in his voice persuaded her far more effectively than a command, and reaching up, Amethyst accepted his hand and was pulled up behind him.

As before, there was an uneasy silence between them that went unbroken for the duration of the ride until Amethyst noticed that William was directing Nero off the road.

"Where are you going, William? I have to go home."

"I just want to talk to you for a few minutes, Amethyst, and I can't do it while we're bumping along the road and you're staring at my back."

Within a few minutes, Nero was tethered at a small tree and William had seated her on a log in a lovely little glade beside a small brook. Once seated alongside her, he seemed reluctant to begin, and feeling extremely uneasy, Amethyst nervously looked away from his troubled mahogany eyes.

The spot William had chosen to talk was lushly beautiful. Small trees common to the area were in full blossom, their dark, glossy leaves contrasting brilliantly with the profusion of mauve-blue flowers that preceded the fruit. Nearby a fat green lizard scampered up the trunk of a large palm, his throat fan flaring colorfully for the benefit of a drab little female close by, and Amethyst could not suppress a small smile at his vain display.

"It's lovely here, William. This area must have been glorious before so much of the land was cleared for cane. I've never seen these trees in such profuse bloom before."

"Yes, it is lovely, Amethyst, but all beauty pales to insignificance beside yours."

Startled by his compliment, Amethyst turned her gaze to his and saw that he was in complete earnest. Amethyst's heart began a slow pounding as their glances met and a light giddiness stole over her. Unable and undesirous of looking away, she continued to hold his gaze as William raised a tentative hand to touch her cheek lightly.

"You know what these trees are called, don't you Amethyst?" he said softly, referring to the brilliant blooms. "They're called the 'tree of life.' A very appropriate place to bring you to discuss . . ." Appearing suddenly unable to say more, he swallowed tightly and in one swift movement had pulled her into a crushing embrace, straining her tight to his chest as he whispered unevenly against her hair. "Oh, Amethyst, darling, don't you realize why I was so unreasonable last week when you arrived with the supplies? I was jealous . . . insanely jealous of that damned smuggler. I still am."

"But William," she whispered softly, the heady sensation of his heart thudding so wildly against her breast sending little shivers along her spine, "I told you there is no need . . ."

"And I believe you, Amethyst, I really do . . . but darling," he released her slightly so he might look down into her eyes once again, "I don't want anyone else taking care of you. *I* want to take care of you! *I* want to be the one you come to for help, not some smuggler. Oh, God, Amethyst," his voice was a soft, anguished cry, "don't you realize I love you?"

Without waiting for her response, William's mouth covered hers, a small groan escaping him as he pulled her more tightly against him, straining her closer still as his lips devoured hers. Completely overwhelmed by the new violent feelings flooding her senses, Amethyst's arms slowly circled his neck, her fingers tangling in the thick hair at his neck to move with an inborn sensuousness that set him to trembling.

Finally loosening his embrace to hold her at arms' length, he said softly, his breathing uneven as he stared longingly at her soft, bruised lips, "But damn it, Amethyst, you're still a child ... and so damned innocent! You don't even realize how close I am to ... God! You're barely fifteen!"

Abruptly releasing her, he stood up and turned away, running his hand through his hair in an anxious gesture. "That's why I stayed away from you for a week and tried to find an interest in Cecily Hargrove. I thought if I could manage to put you out of my mind for a while ... but the moment I saw you again, Cecily no longer existed."

Without her realization, Amethyst moved to stand beside him, and placing her hand on his arm, she said softly, "William, why are you so upset?" Turning him gently toward her she smiled into his tortured expression, inadvertently increasing his passion by the sheer power of her sublime beauty. "I'm fifteen years old now, but next year I'll be sixteen ... Certainly sixteen is considered quite mature. Can't you wait a year for me, William?"

For a small, wordless moment William's eyes roamed her face, a small smile appearing on his lips only seconds before he pulled her against him in an abrupt movement, holding her tightly as he whispered against her hair in a choked voice. "God help me, Amethyst, that's the problem. . . . I don't think I can . . ."

In the next moment he was kissing her wildly, his lips sending a madness racing through her body that she seemed powerless to control. She had never been kissed before, much less allowed a man to arouse her so violently, and inundated by a sweep of unfamiliar emotion, Amethyst found herself drowning in pure, unadulterated desire. William's kisses went on and on, raising her passion, destroying her resistance, until she found herself lying prone on the ground with William's young, lean body lying atop hers. His hands were on her breasts, exciting even deeper emotions than before and gasping with ecstasy, Amethyst strained him closer as his lips trailed across her shoulder. Frustrated by the clothing that lay between them, he began to fumble at the buttons on her skirt. Suddenly he was unable to wait and reaching down, he awkwardly pushed it aside. The second his hand touched the skin of her thigh, Amethyst was wrenched from her passion-induced lethargy and she gasped hoarsely, "William, what are you doing?"

Raising his eyes to hers, William pleaded softly, "Amethyst, darling, don't stop me now . . . darling, I love you . . . I must have you . . . darling . . ." His hand was on her stomach, moving sensuously downward when Amethyst felt the first jolt of fear.

"William, stop! Stop, please!" When her panicky entreaty had no effect on his passion, Amethyst pushed at his hand wildly, only to feel his arm stiffen and refuse to be moved aside. Mumbling incoherently, his lips pressing hungry kisses against her face and neck, William's hand moved unalteringly to the soft warmth of her crotch where he began an intimate caress. Suddenly Amethyst was fighting frantically, pounding and scratching at his hands and back, twisting and turning beneath him as she cried out softly over and over again, "No, William . . . no! I don't want it this way . . . stop!" And then as anger overran her emotions, "Stop! William, how dare you treat me like this? You are a beast . . . stop, I say!"

But he was deaf to her pleas and immune to her blows. Suddenly overwhelmed by fear and succumbing to a strange weakness slowly stealing over her, Amethyst began sobbing softly as she sought frantically to free herself from his arms.

Where all else had failed, Amethyst's heartbroken sobs appeared to suddenly penetrate his raging passion and raising his head, William stared in a startled manner at her tear-streaked face.

"Don't cry, darling, I'm sorry. I didn't mean to frighten you . . . Amethyst . . ." Smoothing his hand across her cheek, he gently wiped away the tears, contrition shining brightly in his eyes as he whispered softly, "You don't have to be afraid anymore, darling." Kissing her mouth lightly, he rolled off her, straightening her skirt as he did, and rising to his feet, he gently pulled her up to stand beside him.

Her body was rigid and trembling and when he reached toward her, he saw her tense for flight. Taking her hands gently in his, he looked deeply into her eyes, remorse clearly defined in his unhappy expression.

"I'm sorry I frightened you, Amethyst. Darling, you're right, I was behaving like a beast. Can you forgive me . . . please, darling . . . can you try to forget what just happened? Just remember I love you, Amethyst. I wouldn't do anything to make you unhappy or frightened."

Still unable to speak, but touched by William's obvious sincerity, Amethyst nodded slowly, her breath catching on a small sob as she made a positive effort to regain control.

His own eyes bright, William slowly enfolded her in a gentle embrace, stroking her hair soothingly until her trembling subsided. When he was finally satisfied that the hysteria of the moment had been conquered, he slackened his embrace enough that he might look into her face. Content that he no longer saw fear in her eyes, his own tense expression relaxed into a tentative smile.

"I haven't destroyed your trust in me, have I, Amethyst?" His voice held an urgent, hopeful appeal that tugged at Amethyst's heartstrings, and managing a small smile of her own, she whispered shakily, "No, William."

"Then you have my word now, darling," William's voice was firm with conviction. "We'll wait . . . I won't rush you into anything. And you're right, Amethyst. Sixteen is a mature age . . . even mature enough to marry."

Amethyst remained silent, her eyes traveling the smooth unlined planes of his handsome face until he chafed at her silence and urged quietly, "What do you say, Amethyst?"

Her violet eyes still a bit wary, a tentative smile touched her lips as she whispered huskily in response, "I suppose that's so . . . we'll see, William . . ."

Chapter 5

1782

Long, slender fingers curling tenaciously in the thick hair at the base of his neck drew his mouth down possessively to meet parted lips inviting the invasion of his tongue. Somewhere in the back of his mind a warning bell sounded shrilly as the tactics of the woman in his arms became more and more transparent to Damien's mind's eye. He had been through this same scene many times before and was wary of the shrewd maneuvers of calculating females who sought to insinuate themselves firmly into his memory and his life with their willing bodies. This knowledge was not a matter of conceit, merely a matter of experience gained from repetition, the few close calls he had managed to escape in the past. But he was determined to avoid the allure of inviting arms which promised much while demanding far more in return. A life at sea was not conducive to long, binding relationships and he did not intend to be tied down.

Slowly freeing himself from the soft, clinging embrace, Damien pulled his head back to look down into Merrell's sultry glance, unable to deny the persistent tugging in his groin her expression evoked. Concealing the self-derisive smile rising to his lips, he whispered firmly, "I must be leaving, Merrell. The tide will be high within an hour and I have many last-minute details to accomplish."

"Damien, darling," Merrell cooed, her caressing, dark-eyed glance moving provocatively across his mouth, "you don't really want to leave me, do you?"

"I have to admit," Damien countered evasively, "you make it damn hard for a man to think of business, but," his hand moving purposefully to the handle of the coach door, he continued, "we can continue where we left off when I return to port in a few months. In the meantime, try to behave yourself while I'm gone ... if that's possible."

"Can you give me a good reason why I should behave myself, darling?" Merrell's voice was petulant as her expression took on a faintly victorious glow. "Will you be behaving yourself for me?"

Damien's direct response was delivered in a soft, even tone. "Merrell, dear, you wouldn't want me to lie to you, would you?"

Her eyes snapping wide in surprise, Merrell Bristol stared silently into his face for a few brief seconds, her lips tightening ever so slightly in concealed anger. The spoiled daughter of a wealthy Philadelphia merchant, she was not accustomed to being thwarted once she had set her mind on any goal, and she had definitely set her mind on becoming Mrs. Damien Straith. However, far too wise to press a situation where she was obviously beginning to lose ground, she replied slowly, "Of course not, darling. And neither will I lie to you. But when you return, we'll make up for lost time, won't we ..."

Leaning forward to press her ample bosom against his chest, Merrell slid her arms around his neck, offering her mouth again as she moved sensuously against him in a tantalizing promise that could not be ignored.

"Damn if she isn't an efficient little seductress," Damien thought silently, regretfully tearing his mouth from hers as he firmly disentangled himself from her clinging arms. Flashing her a brief smile, he slipped out of the carriage door without a reply.

Striding briskly toward the *Sally*, he turned to extend a brief salute in the direction of the elegant black carriage and the lovely woman staring unsmilingly out the window at his retreating figure. Turning back to mount the gangplank, the smile swiftly dropped from his face as his thoughts moved quickly to the imminent voyage. Within a few brief seconds, all thoughts of Merrell Bristol were completely dismissed from his mind.

A steaming tropical sun beat mercilessly on his head as Damien stared sullenly at the placid, gleaming waters of the Caribbean Sea. The voyage was not going well. Directing another glance upward, he snorted disgustedly at the sight of limp sails against the masts, lifeless ghosts of the full billowing beauties that should be carrying them smoothly toward Kingston. With a small shake of his head, Damien's lips curled in an ironic smile. Smuggling was still extremely profitable in Jamaica. The necessities of life continued to be in short supply on the island and the cessation of the war the previous year had not discouraged the islanders from welcoming smuggled merchandise. He was well on his way to becoming wealthy while still maintaining the devotion of the islanders for his steady provisions of needed supplies, smuggled or not. But he had decided he would enter port legally this time. Rather than risk a problem with his American registry, he would use the set of false ship's papers he maintained for just such an occasion. The *Sally* would not be challenged. He owed himself and his men some leisure time in a port where they were practically an institution even if it was a whispered fame. And that was the irony of the situation. Having made the decision to enter Jamaica legally for the first time in many years, the *Sally* had become becalmed. She had been floating in the same area for three long days, seeing less movement than she had seen in dry-dock the last time around!

"Hell!" he thought, impatiently shifting his broad frame for a brief glance across the motionless horizon. He had had his fill of still, hot air that sat on a man's shoulders with soul-wearying weight. He was anxious to be on to Kingston.

His brow knitting into a small frown, a persistent thought returned to his mind, effectively mounting his agitation even as he attempted to ignore its nagging presence. It was only by chance that he had learned that Marian Greer had died a few months ago. The damned brat with the purple eyes was an orphan . . . she was alone . . . Refusing to acknowledge the sudden tightening in his stomach that recurring thought evoked and the influence that bit of information had had on his sudden desire for leisure time in Jamaica, he rationalized silently, "Well, at least she is assured of an ample supply of food." He had seen to it on his last trip to Kingston that the usual portion of supplies was delivered to her door, and if she continued to be as shrewd as she had been in the past, he was relatively certain that food would not now be a problem for her. He had also learned through a few inquiries that Amethyst had been gradually assuming more and more of her mother's acting duties while the sickly woman recuperated from repeated illnesses, and had been well received by the audiences in Kingston. A scoffing expression covered his handsome face for a few brief seconds. In his own silent estimation, Amethyst's reception as an actress only served to prove the stupendous ignorance of the famous Jamaican Creoles. But why he was actually spending any time at all in contemplation of the surly little beggar's plight was a complete mystery to him. Unexpectedly the vision of a small, angry face turned up to his, heated purple eyes blazing furiously into his own stormy expression returned to his mind and a peculiar sense of urgency increased inside him. Damn that lazy wind! Damn the obstinate sea! The *Sally* lay as dormant as a leaf on a stagnant pond and he was helpless against the situation.

Damn the... But what was that? Suddenly alert, Damien pulled himself erect. Glancing upward, he saw a slight puffing of the shrouds that only moments before hung so still. Damned if there wasn't a breeze coming up!

A slow grin gradually widening across his face, he watched as the sails began to fill firm and sure, and feeling the ship's instantaneous response beneath his feet, Damien experienced a jolt of exaltation.

Turning, he shouted over his shoulder to the slender first mate who stood a few yards behind him, staring up at the billowing sails with a relieved expression, "Barnes, get the men to step lively! It looks like we'll see Kingston within a few days!"

Turning slowly, Amethyst surveyed the small bedroom, her eyes running over the familiar furniture with a dispassionate glance. A room of her own at last... for which she had paid an exorbitant price. Mama and she had shared the small room and the lumpy double bed for almost seven years. Amethyst had only relinquished the room to her mother in the last year of her life when the woman's failing health had demanded more privacy. But the room was hers now... it had been for almost three months, and Mama was buried in the small cemetery on the hillside. It wasn't a fair exchange. Not fair at all.

Angry with the tears that filled her wide lavender eyes, Amethyst tossed her ebony tresses impatiently, moving to straighten the bedclothes as she did. It would do no good to be maudlin. She was on her own now and would have to make the best of the situation. But she wasn't really alone. Tillie, bless her loving heart, stayed on in the little room off the kitchen, even though she had not been paid in countless months for all the time and work she had lavished on Mama and herself. Maintaining that a roof over her head and food to eat was enough for her, and that her small income from the other members of the troupe provided for any essentials she might need, the tireless mulatto had been an endless comfort in the terrible days just before and after Mama had slipped away.

And there was William. A small frown creased Amethyst's smooth brow. William's devotion to her was matched only by his father's abhorrence of a possible match between them. Had the elder Sheridan not been such a highly principled man, she was certain he would have dissolved their bargained food exchange the moment Marcus Peters had snidely informed him of his son's attentions to the "waterfront actress." Since her mother's death, things had proceeded from bad to worse between father and son, quickly escalating to the volatile stage with William's declared intention to marry her.

Her frown deepening, Amethyst shook her head. William's declaration had been a bit premature as far as she was concerned. She had no intention of marrying so quickly, despite her circumstances. She was only sixteen years old, and since she was fortunate enough to have been accepted to fill her mother's spot in the repertory company, she was not pressed to make any hasty moves. She needed more time to be certain that the feelings between William and herself were the same and of as enduring a quality as those that had existed between her mother and father. The beauty of her parents' love was extremely vivid in her memory, sustaining Amethyst in her darkest moments of loneliness. In her heart Amethyst knew she would accept no less in her own life. Marriage was a step she would contemplate very carefully before committing herself. But William was so impatient . . . and stubborn. Ignoring his father's vehement disapproval, it was only her own hesitation that held them back from immediate marriage. In all sincerity, Amethyst could not say she doubted William's love. Considerate, attentive, loving, even if a trifle jealous and possessive since she had been fully accepted as a permanent member of the troupe, she did not doubt the feeling that shone from those mahogany eyes when they rested on her so warmly. Nor did she doubt the depth of emotion between them when William took her into his arms. She also realized that each day it grew more difficult for William to release her from his embrace, and felt a deep guilt at the obvious suffering her hesitation caused him.

But she was truly offended by his father's blind prejudice against her profession. Once again feeling the heat of anger, she gave a short, unladylike snort. Perhaps her entrance on stage was occasionally met with bursts of enthusiastic calls and comments that were not entirely gentlemanly, but at least she and Mama had been self-supporting and independent. And even if Mama and she performed only bit parts, Papa had been a true artist. She had no reason to be ashamed and would refuse to accept begrudging approval even if it were offered . . . which it wasn't. But William had countered that argument by pointing out she was punishing him for his father's ignorant prejudice. Maybe she was . . . she didn't know . . . she was just so unsure. . . .

Of one thing, however, Amethyst was not unsure. She did not wish to add to the troubles already besetting Sheridan Plantation as well as the other plantations on the island. The prices of imported goods in Jamaica, whether arriving legally or illegally, were considerably higher than before the war. The cost of living continued to climb while sugar prices fell rapidly. Even the increase in coffee production was not sufficient to overcome the generally bad economic situation. Hit by another severe storm in the past year that had damaged crops and killed thousands of slaves, many of the Jamaican owners faced ruin. With the depression worsening and no relief in sight, William Sheridan, Sr. needed his son more than ever. Despite her anger at his prejudice against her, she did not wish to be a bone of contention between them. She appreciated the ties of blood far too strongly, especially now that Mama was gone, to dismiss the estrangement of father and son lightly.

As if she did not have enough problems besetting her, Amethyst had learned only last night that overtures were being made to inquire if the American Company would be welcomed back in its homeland now that the revolution had been brought to a successful conclusion. Were William to find out that the troupe was even contemplating leaving the island, matters would become unbearably complicated. Well, she was certain he would not . . .

The sound of a male voice in low conversation with Tillie in the next room interrupted her thoughts. Glancing to the small clock on the nightstand, Amethyst felt a small stab of apprehension. William wasn't expected for another hour or so. Something must have happened to bring him here so early in the afternoon. Throwing the bedclothes across the bed in a haphazard manner so she might go out to ascertain the reason for William's unorthodox arrival, Amethyst moved rapidly to the doorway. Opening the door with a quick movement, she began worriedly, "William, what are you doing here so early? I didn't expect . . ."

Her words dying on her lips, Amethyst stared dumbly into unforgettably piercing gray eyes that caught and held her speechless.

Arriving that morning, the *Sally* and her anxious crew had sailed boldly into Kingston harbor. Immediately exhibiting the false ship's papers to the port officials awaiting them on dock, Damien ignored the raised brows and questioning expressions the forged credentials evoked. The papers were in perfect order and there would not be time to verify them before the *Sally* sailed again. For once grateful for the inefficiency of maritime bureaucracy, Damien was completely at ease in his charade, realizing that even though he and his men were well known in Kingston, no one dared betray him. His friends were loyal, and his enemies were in fear of his strong obeah. Hah! That really was a joke! Suppressing a smile as he strode swiftly toward his cabin to change his clothes, Damien marveled again at the manner in which the whispered fantasies of his magic powers had become accepted as fact by the islanders. A fantasy that had served him well, he snickered to himself as he closed the cabin door behind him and reached for a clean shirt. And it would continue to facilitate his relations with the highly superstitious inhabitants of the island. Even the brat's mulatto servant was in awe of him. Damien chuckled, remembering the woman's terrified expression when Amethyst defied and then attacked him on his last visit to her home. His brows suddenly drawing together in a small frown, he sobered quickly at the memory. Everyone was in awe of him with the exception of the violet-eyed brat, and she had hated him with a passion that stirred her to fury. For some reason, the same sense of urgency that had filled him since the inception of his voyage to Kingston again nudged him annoyingly, and he hastily buttoned the fresh white lawn shirt he had donned over his well fitted fawn britches. Turning, he walked quickly out the doorway and down the passageway, still refusing to admit to himself he would not be free of this peculiar sense of disquiet until he was certain as to the fate of the little chit possessing the purple eyes that haunted him.

A short time later he stood outside the small house where Amethyst and her servant still resided. His heart throbbing a thunderous stacatto beat inside his chest, Damien stood for long moments before the unimpressive frame building. Angered at his own emotional reaction to the anticipated meeting, his scowl darkened as he approached the door. He raised his hand to knock, but suddenly refusing to submit to a request for entrance to the household he had steadfastly supported for the past three years, Damien jerked open the door, startling the tall mulatto woman who gasped audibly at his appearance. Her eyes wide with a mixture of apprehension and awe, Tillie immediately clasped her hands in front of her chest, commencing the slow, hypnotic, swaying motion she had assumed on his last visit.

His irritation increasing irrationally, Damien fixed his penetrating gaze on her face, demanding harshly, "Where is your mistress? I want to speak with her."

"In her room, Captain." The mulatto's voice was low and wary.

"Well, tell her I'm here, woman! I don't wish to wait all day!" In reality, Damien did not believe he could wait another minute, so strong was the strange anticipation building inside him. God! What was the hold that child had on him?

As if sensing his presence, a familiar voice demanded as the bedroom door opened unexpectedly, "William, what are you doing here so early? I didn't expect . . ."

Startled lavender eyes suddenly met and held his, the moment of confrontation freezing Damien into immobility at the sight that met his gaze. Her eyes were the same . . . great purple orbs rimmed with sweeping black lashes, but, Lord, the remainder of the vision that met his scrutiny left him speechless! Allowing himself the liberty of slowly assessing the changes three years had wrought on the girl/woman standing before him, his gaze moved openly over the marvelous face staring up into his. Still dominated by those unforgettable eyes, the promise of beauty he had recognized on her childish visage was fulfilled to perfection in the high cheekbones and graceful contours of her cheek; the clear, creamy complexion that glowed with natural vibrant color; the short straight nose; the full, appealing lips gradually tightening into a hard, straight line which was softened only by the irrepressible dimple winking in her cheek. She was still small in stature, her shoulders narrow, their graceful curve covered by the glorious black mane that streamed to her mid-back in a fall of gleaming, unruly curls; but the small, budding breasts that had shocked him into realization in that dark alley three years before had bloomed into a fullness that filled her chest with breathless appeal.

Her narrow ribcage was flat and straight beneath, narrowing even further to a minute waistline. Her plain gray skirt flared out softly, obstructing the continuation of Damien's assessment, but remembering the long, straight legs revealed in the boy's britches at their last meeting, Damien could only surmise the beauty hidden from his view. Returning his gaze slowly back to her face, Damien noted absentmindedly that the slender arms hanging at her sides were growing tense and the small, delicate hands had balled into tight fists. Still oblivious of the heat of increasing anger in her expression, Damien was aware only of the sheer magnificence of the Amethyst standing before him and the overwhelming desire growing inside him to take that magnificence in his arms and hold it tight against him, safe and secure, under his protection. The warm glow inside him spreading with a rapidity that shook him to the core, he was about to reach for her when he was stopped abruptly by the fury in her voice as she spoke.

"What are you doing here?"

Conquering his driving desire to snatch her into his arms, Damien's eyes narrowed as he responded with spontaneous anger at the challenge in her tone, "For all you've changed on the outside, you're still the same obnoxious brat, aren't you, Amethyst?"

Purposely ignoring his insult, Amethyst continued with a barely controlled sneer, "You're a little late, aren't you, Captain Straith? Mama is no longer here to praise your thoughtfulness and flatter your ego with her gratitude."

"Flatter my ego . . ."

"And it is unfortunate, isn't it, Captain, that any other plans you may have had in mind have been ruined by my mother's untimely death."

Annoyed and bewildered at the idiotic girl's reception, Damien said impatiently, "What other plans? What the hell are you talking about, Amethyst Greer? Your mother was a lovely, intelligent lady whom I respected. I heard of her death only last month in Philadelphia and came here to express . . ."

Damien Straith's voice faded from her hearing as a familiar rage expanded inside Amethyst. She never had and never would forgive him his insulting attitude toward her, nor had she forgotten the sting of his hand against her cheek when she had approached him for help dressed as a boy. Her mother's undying gratitude and praise of the odious man for the barrels of food left anonymously on their doorstep over the past three years had only contributed to her dislike. Burned into her memory was the picture of her mother's and Straith's clasped hands the day she had unexpectedly entered the cabin during the voyage to Jamaica. Recollection still left a bitter taste in her mouth. Mama had been a lovely woman, overprotected from the world by an adoring husband. She had remained to the day of her death extremely gullible when it came to human deviousness, and it had been her own lot even as a child to follow Papa's wishes and protect her mother from harsh realities and her own trusting naivete. Amethyst was aware of Damien Straith's reputation. He was a notorious womanizer. She was also aware that a man of his character rarely did anything without an extremely strong motive, and it had been obvious to Amethyst from the beginning that the "generous, gentlemanly" Captain fully expected his generosity to be rewarded when Marian Straith returned to good health. Eating at her even more deeply was the fact that Damien Straith was the only man aside from her father that Marian Greer had ever spoken of in such glowing terms. Certainly, the overbearing boor standing before her was not to be compared with her loving father!

No longer attempting to conceal her sneer, Amethyst interrupted ungraciously, "If you regarded my mother so highly, why did you never stop to see her? She was extremely grateful for your 'generosity,' you know."

"And I can see her daughter did not share her sentiments," Damien mumbled, his face beginning to flush a dark red at the girl's stinging attack.

"No, her daughter did not and does not share her sentiments," Amethyst whispered fiercely. "Her daughter is not gullible enough to believe a man like you would continue to flatter and provide for a lovely widow if he didn't expect . . ."

"Blast you, girl!" Damien was barely able to resist the urge to put his hands around that lovely little neck and choke off the stream of nonsense streaming forth from between those two lovely lips. Those soft, inviting lips were not meant for the vicious nonsense spewing forth. More angry still with his preoccupation with the mouth that belittled him so vehemently, Damien continued harshly, "You are a fool, Amethyst Greer! You were a stubborn, headstrong child, and have grown into a young woman who is headstrong to the point of stupidity! How you ever managed to contrive such nonsense in your confused brain, I will never understand."

"Nonsense! My confused brain!" Amethyst gasped

incredulously. "You merely cannot abide a woman who sees through your scheming!"

Taking a few quick steps forward, Damien grasped her slender shoulders and shook her hard, growling between his teeth as he glared down angrily, "I merely admired your mother, I tell you . . . was concerned for her welfare . . ."

"If you were so concerned, why did you never stop to see her? The trusting person that Mama was, she often hoped you would stop to call again."

"My voyages to Kingston were not exactly made under ideal circumstances, Amethyst. In the event you have forgotten, a state of war existed at the time and I had to get in and out of Jamaica as quickly as possible."

"But you always had time for your streggahs . . ."

Amethyst's eyes glittered victoriously as Damien found himself at a loss for a response to the truth of that statement. Furious at being bested once again by the hot-tempered little chit, Damien released her shoulders with a suddenness that knocked her a few steps backwards before she regained her balance.

"I do not feel the need to explain my comings or goings to a nasty little termagant who nurses imagined grievances and is too stupid to listen to the truth!"

Her eyes flaring wide with anger, Amethyst pulled herself up haughtily. "The truth? Alright, Captain Straith, tell me, what is the truth? Why *are* you here?"

"Yes, why *am* I here? I've been asking myself that same question since you first opened your mouth, Amethyst, but perhaps you're right. My streggahs always paid me well for the food I brought them. Maybe I do deserve some sort of reward for everything I did for you and your mother."

Stepping forward, Damien pulled the small, haughty figure into his arms, crushing her against his broad chest as he lowered his head to cover the lips that taunted him so viciously. But strangely, Damien himself suffered the greatest surprise in the encounter. Totally unprepared for the swell of emotion that overwhelmed him at the first taste of her parted lips, his broad frame shuddered with undeniable passion at the pure, sweet sensation of coming home . . . the vague recognition of a blurred dream . . . His mouth plunged deeper, his binding hold on the small woman in his arms effortlessly subduing her struggles to be free. Time ceased to exist as Damien gloried in the absolute pleasure surging through his veins. Lolling in a sea of unearthly sensation, he efficiently ignored Amethyst's ineffective protests as he pulled her closer still. He did not want, he could not bear to let her go. Gradually the wild struggling ceased and Damien drew his mouth from her throbbing lips, whispering softly as he did, "Amethyst, darling, I want . . ."

Stopped abruptly by the venomous glare in the brilliant eyes raised to his, Damien attempted to pull Amethyst back into his arms when she whispered insidiously, "So, now that the Greer you had originally planned to seduce is not available, you have decided to take the Greer remaining in her place! Sorry to disappoint you, Captain, but I am not my mother! I am not susceptible to hypocritical endearments, no matter how passionately rendered!"

His face suddenly flaming, Damien pushed Amethyst from his embrace. "A true and utter bitch, aren't you, Amethyst? Too bad all your beauty is on the outside and none of it within. You're right, you know. You're nothing like your mother. She was a lady—warm, sincere, genteel—not a cold, hardhearted conniving little witch . . ."

"I am a cold, conniving witch because I will not stretch myself out on your bed like one of your willing streggahs? Hah! That's where you're wrong, Captain. There is simply nothing about you that could possibly stir that sort of emotion inside me. Were I one of your streggahs, you would have to pay dearly for that kind of service..."

"I *have* paid you dearly, Amethyst..." Damien Straith's voice was low, his hypnotic stare holding her gaze as he continued softly, "I have paid for three years..."

Her eyes snapping wide, Amethyst gasped audibly. "You don't really expect... you couldn't possibly believe I would pay you in that way!"

A small sneer twisted the strong planes of Damien's features for a few seconds before he gave a short, harsh laugh. "Don't worry, Amethyst. I wouldn't take you now if you begged on bended knee. The man who sleeps with you will probably wake up frost-bitten the next morning. There would be no pleasure in holding a cold fish in my arms." Sweeping her with one last contemptuous glance, he said dismissingly, "You are perfectly safe with me!"

Trembling with fury, Amethyst spoke in a low, barely controlled voice. "In that case, Captain, I believe your business in my home is done! Please leave... *now!*"

His huge hands clenching into tight fists, Captain Damien Straith threw her one last scornful glance before turning on his heel and moving wordlessly toward the door.

"And by the way, Captain," Amethyst called at his retreating back, "your charity is no longer needed here. Save your precious food for the women who are willing to pay you for it in the currency you demand! As for me, I would rather starve!"

His hand on the doorknob, Captain Damien Straith turned slowly, his voice filled with derision. "And as for me, Amethyst, I would rather remain celibate!"

Still seething at his last, well delivered insult, Amethyst watched as Damien moved through the doorway, slamming the door behind him in unmistakable finality. Her face flushed with anger, she turned to meet Tillie's horrified expression. Unwilling to submit to another speech on her lack of gratitude, Amethyst said in a low warning voice, "Tillie, kindly leave me be. I am not in the mood for one of your lectures right now."

Ignoring her as if she had not spoken, Tillie shook her head emphatically from side to side, her voice deep with warning, "You be a fool, Amethyst Greer! You Mama turn over in him grave if him see the way you speak to Captain Straith today! Stupid girl! Do you remember how you Mama was before that man take him under him wing? Him dying, girl, quickly gowan away . . . But that man, him take pity on you and keep you food closet full. That man, him give you three more years with you Mama, and you halla like kas-kas woman! Quashi! Fool!"

"Didn't you hear what he said, Tillie? He admitted he expected payment for his 'pity.'"

"Quashi! Now you have big trouble. That man have strong obeah, Amethyst Greer. Him gowan bring him duppy down on you! Him magic strong . . ."

Turning her back with a scoffing expression while the earnest woman still spoke, Amethyst walked purposefully into her room and closed the door behind her, but not before she heard Tillie mumble under her breath, "Facety miss! Quashi!"

Stepping to the bed, Amethyst absentmindedly began to straighten the bedclothes she had abandoned a short time before. Tillie was the fool, not she! She no longer needed to depend on Damien Straith's charity. She was in good health and could easily exist on the mangos and achees that abounded on the island, with an occasional supplement of fish or eggs bought with her small salary. She would not starve without that conceited oaf's providence.

A picture of Damien Straith returned to her mind's eye

and Amethyst considered it unconsciously. In the three years since she had last seen him, the Captain's broad, muscular frame seemed only to have lengthened and broadened to a more powerful, impressive size. That was undoubtedly part of the reason for the awe he inspired in the superstitious natives. But more likely still, the natives were probably impressed by the light gold hair that shone like the sun, the broad, sharply chiseled planes of his lightly tanned face from which his peculiar light eyes appeared to glow translucently. Had she been a more weakly minded person, she would have felt fear herself at the fury besetting that formidable specter only moments before. Suddenly remembering the bruising pressure of his mouth against hers, gradually softening into a deeply stirring caress, she snorted angrily. A marvelous actor was Captain Straith! Should he decide to give up the sea, the American Company would do well to offer him a prominent spot in their troupe! But she was an actress, too, and could not be fooled, despite her body's own traitorous reaction to those firm lips pressed against hers, those strong, powerful arms holding her passionately close, his softly whispered endearment, "Amethyst, darling . . ."

Abruptly angry with herself, Amethyst dragged her thoughts forcefully from her mental meanderings. "You *are* a fool, a quashi, Amethyst Greer!" she mumbled under her breath as she slapped the lumpy bed vigorously. "But you need not worry. You have seen the last of Captain Damien Straith!"

Moving down the street with long, angry strides, Damien turned the corner, heading instinctively in the direction of the docks. His massive chest heaving in anger, he muttered under his breath, "Damn that girl! Damn that Amethyst Greer! She did it again!" Since the day of their first meeting when she was still a child, she had managed to turn the tables on him, twist his words and his actions until they lost all resemblance to his original intentions. Why was it she was determined to think ill of him? Think ill of him ... that was a masterful understatement. The girl despised him! His pace automatically slowing as unanswered questions continued to swirl in his mind, he examined his actions honestly. He had done nothing to incite the anger with which she greeted him today. In truth, he had been too stunned to do more than mutter her name! God, she had become a beauty! It was no wonder they had accepted her so willingly into the troupe of actors in her mother's place. She wouldn't have to be able to act ... not the way she looked! She probably had to be escorted from the theater with a bodyguard to protect her from the wild young bucks that frequented the waterfront area. His scowl darkening at the thought, Damien felt a peculiar tightening in his stomach as his irritation flared anew. And the damned brat probably gloried in every minute of it!

Suddenly conscious of his boorish conduct of a few minutes before, Damien thought defensively, "Well, she got exactly what she deserved." Everything she said was untrue. That pale, sickly woman, Marian Greer, had stirred nothing more than pity inside him. Hell, she was too unobtrusive, too retiring in her manner to interest him in the way Amethyst had intimated. He had gone to that household today merely to set his mind at ease that the child ... the little brat ... had survived her mother's death well. Humph! He needn't have worried. That little shrew was too contrary to allow the world to defeat her, and she had her strongest weapon in her biting tongue!

And it was a mystery to him why he was allowing that little scene of a few minutes before to bother him at all. He had accomplished his purpose in finding out that the girl was indeed doing well. Then why this sense of discontent that disturbed him so completely? Could it be because the scent of her still lingered in his nostrils . . . because his hands still tingled from the touch of her skin . . . because the memory of the pressure of that small, delicate body against his was still vivid in his mind, the unbelievable sweetness of her mouth leaving him with a lingering desire for more? Stunned, he finally faced the facts squarely as the *Sally* came into view. He had been thoroughly devastated by the touch of her, and she had been utterly repelled! What's more, the conniving little snip had used him and used him well while she needed his help, and now that he had served his purpose, had driven him off like a stray dog! Suffused with a deep, blinding anger, Damien mounted the *Sally*'s gangplank, the thunderous fury pervading him reflected in his raging expression. Amethyst's malevolent sneering voice rang in his ears.

"You are no longer needed here! I will not accept your charity! Please leave . . . *now!*"

Rapidly descending the steps to his cabin, Damien roughly pushed open the door, entered and slammed it hard behind him, muttering a low, ominous oath under his breath, "You will live to regret those words, Amethyst Greer. Oh, yes . . . you will live to regret them . . ."

Silently slipping out of the house, Tillie moved down the darkening street as surreptitiously as her impressive size would allow. Carrying her small, unlit lantern, she would walk to the far end of town and turn into the forest. From there she would reverse herself through the wooded trail and retrace her steps until she proceeded steadily in the opposite direction from which she had appeared to be heading. She wanted no one to guess where she was going. She had no desire to allow her prestige as a free woman of color to suffer as a result of her actions tonight. Having finally reached the edge of town, she ducked into the woods and continued on her preplanned course.

Tillie was all too aware that as a special class of Jamaican, her status depended on steadfast adherence to all customs white in origin. Having been educated by her white father, she, as well as the other mulattos on the island, laid claim to the manner, dress and religion of the white parent, but Mabella Swann had forged a lasting influence on her proud daughter's life. Rearing her to concede outwardly to social pressures, she had allowed her daughter to adopt the white man's ways and religion in public, while secretly indoctrinating her into the religion of the Puckoo people. Dangerously, over the years, Tillie had clung to the Puckoo beliefs and in times of stress turned to their medicine man for aid. Also aware that many of the plantation slaves despised the mulattos for their distinction of class, she was fully cognizant of the chance she took each time she joined the slave gatherings for Puckoo rituals.

Through a chain of whispered messages, Tillie had received word that the Puckoo people would meet that night at the Conway plantation, and although she had not attended a meeting of the cult in many months, she moved steadily toward the meeting place with a deep sense of purpose.

The darkness of evening had shrouded the worn trail as Tillie arrived at the plantation, her clear, unmarked brow covered with perspiration, her full breasts heaving from the exertion of the strenuous pace she had maintained for the past hour. Following the sound of solemn, steady drumming, she arrived breathless at a clearing where a huge fire burned, casting spirals of brilliant light toward the sky while flickering shadows played against the black faces surrounding it. A low, steady humming had already begun as the scantily clothed bodies concentrated there began a slow, hypnotic gyration in time with the gradually increasing tempo of the drums. Lengthening orange and yellow flames stretched up in long, increasingly greedy tongues to lick the darkness overhead as Tillie followed a call more ancient than time and slowly assumed a place in the moving circle. Her body responding automatically to the persistent drumming that seemed to dull her brain, she moved steadily to the savage, hypnotic rhythm. The momentum of the dancers grew gradually wilder, bodies pumping and twisting with unrelenting fury, seeking to hold and conquer the beat that heated their blood. Inhaling and exhaling in gasping, choking coughs, they instinctively followed the ritual of the dance, their short, harsh barks growing increasingly louder until the primitive chorus echoed in the surrounding darkness. Accelerating violently, the drums began to throb in thunderous fury, louder, louder, faster, faster, urging the dancers to greater passion as they writhed and jerked to its sensual rhythm, the short barks of breathing gradually attaining a barbarous crescendo that shook the small clearing with its intensity. And still the drums beat on, throbbing, urging, pushing the entranced dancers to the threshold of a sustained, ecstatic frenzy which plummeted them sharply in increasing numbers to the ground and insensibility, where they mumbled in exhausted voices as their minds wandered aimlessly through the gray, semi-conscious vale where only they existed.

And still Tillie danced on, her tall, graceful figure responding to the tempo of the drums, her full breasts moving rhythmically under her blouse, her ample hips rotating, her powerful legs whirling to stamp a steady rhythm against the ground as her Negro blood pumped in her ears, filling her brain with the power of the beating sound that seemed to sustain her, driving her with endless vehemence beyond the endurance of the other dancers. Finally, she alone danced in violent supplication to Pucku, the possession god of her Negro people. Heaving, gasping, her movement became more spasmatic as her arms flailed about hysterically, carrying her to a whirling, climactic peak that ended in a thin, piercing scream as she swooned to the ground in semi-conscious obeisance. Her body still quaking with the fury of possession, Tillie mumbled indistinctly, her deep voice muttering soft, unintelligible passages that ran endlessly from her lips.

Picking his way carefully among the bodies strewn in reckless confusion around the clearing, a short, wizened old man came to stand above her, his ears tuning in the sound of her voice to the exclusion of all others. Tillie Swann had been truly possessed by Pucku and was speaking in the tongues of his god. Tonight he would listen to her alone. Crouching down beside the prostrate woman, he listened silently until she spoke no more, refusing to leave until the woman's eyes once again looked clearly into his.

Slowly the gray veil lifted from Tillie's gaze. Still disoriented, she felt the ground beneath her body, damp and moist against her perspired skin. Her head was aching, the pulse in her throat still throbbing violently. Finally able to focus her gaze, Tillie was startled to see two bright black eyes staring unblinkingly into hers. Cowering from the piercing brightness of his stare, Tillie awaited the witch doctor's words.

"Tillie Swann be chosen of Pucku t'night. Him speak through you t' him people here. You white blood be weak, you black blood strong. What you want from dis old man t'night?"

Looking purposefully into the old man's face, Tillie said firmly, "My soul-child, him make the white obeah-man turn against him. My soul-child hard-ears, not listen to Tillie. Obeah-man leave house rygin against my soul-child. You speak to Pucku. Break obeah-man's magic."

"Who dis obeah-man be, Tillie Swann?"

"Him be the Captain Damien Straith."

His eyes flaring revealingly, the old man slowly stood and turned to walk away. Quickly scrambling to her feet, Tillie swayed momentarily before turning to run after him. Reaching his side, Tillie took his arm to stay him.

"What you say, old man? You help Tillie Swann? Amassa, old man," she pleaded again.

His face once again inscrutable, the old man muttered almost inaudibly, "Cap'n Straith have strong obeah . . ."

"You help Tillie Swann, old man?" Tillie repeated, her dark eyes glued to the man's face in wordless appeal.

For long silent moments the old man stared into her face, his mesmerizing glance seeming to slip beyond her eyes into her very mind. Suddenly shaking off her restraining hand, he turned to walk toward a small hut at the edge of the clearing, and slipped inside. Reappearing a few minutes later, he carried a small cloth bag. Reaching inside, he handed her a dried, shriveled fowl's foot, mumbling softly, "Foot of fowl dat scratch earth of de dead, him bring strength of spirits t' protect you soul-child. Keep it near you child, 'n obeah-man's duppy stay away."

Having finished speaking, the old man turned on his heel and walked away, leaving Tillie staring gratefully behind him.

"Tenky, old man. Tillie Swann say tenky."

Making no response, the old man walked into his hut and out of her sight.

Swiftly turning, Tillie noticed most of the dancers were on their feet and milling around the clearing. Anxious to return home, she tucked the charm into her pocket and snatching up her lantern, walked quickly to the edge of the forest. She was still unsure of her reception here. Many of the men and women nursed grudges against her as a free woman of color, and the old man was gone, unable to stand between her and any possible antagonists. Relieved when she had reached the edge of the clearing to step at last onto the forest path, she had gone only a few feet when a hand firmly clasped her shoulder, freezing her into immobility.

The unyielding grip turned her slowly to face a powerful shadow towering a head and shoulders above her, the massive masculine frame almost indiscernible in the light of the small lantern. But there was only one man who dwarfed Tillie Swann to that extent. Gradually raising her lantern, Tillie's glance caught and held the steely stare of sharp black eyes. Slowly, her gaze moved over the broad, flat features, the full lips compressed into an angry line, the dark brown skin still smooth despite the gray scattered amongst the short-cropped hair on his well shaped head.

"Why you not look fe Raymond, Tillie Swann? You gowan run fe home n' run frem Raymond?"

In a hard voice contrasting vividly with the familiar weakness besetting her, Tillie responded harshly, "This be important business, Raymond. Tillie have no time to look fe any old slave . . ."

"Raymond not 'any ole slave,' Tillie." The hand on Tillie's shoulder tightened spontaneously and a slight trembling began inside her.

"Besides," Tillie continued with a vague negative gesture as if he had not spoken, diverting her eyes from his intense stare, "Tillie gettin' too old to play games . . ."

The large calloused hand gripping her shoulder moved to smooth back the wisps at her hairline which had worked loose from the tight bun at the base of her neck. Raising her chin with his hand, Raymond forced her to resume contact with his eyes.

"Tillie not too old fe Raymond. Tillie Swann be beautiful woman . . . woman fe me . . . fe me . . ."

"Tillie not you woman, Raymond!" Jerking her face from his caress, Tillie responded heatedly, "Tillie be free woman! Belong to no one! And you be slave, Raymond!" Her glance filled with contempt she continued, "Slave man, him got no woman!"

"Raymond, him have you, Tillie Swann." Raymond's whispered statement bore the power of conviction as he slowly perused her countenance, sending the blood flooding into her face.

"No!" Taking a step backward, Tillie shook her head emphatically. "No! I gowan find a fine mulatto man fe me. No more games with black Guerney Bird!"

His eyes flaring with anger at her insult, Raymond's voice was a low hiss. "Raymond creole black, Tillie. Him born on island, jes' like you!"

"That be right, Raymond," Tillie hissed in return, "but before my father lose him plantation and die, my father *own* you and you mama!"

"Yaw, you faddah own Raymond, Tillie, but him own *you* mama, too!"

"But him not own Tillie!" Tillie countered hotly. "Tillie be free woman, too good for old slave that belong another man now."

All trace of anger suddenly leaving his face, Raymond stared intently into Tillie's flashing eyes for a few long moments. Slowly reaching for her hand, he tugged gently as he spoke in a firm voice. "You come wid Raymond now, Tillie. No more hallah. I'se put up new place to lay. Fraish 'n clean, jes' like Tillie want. Tillie come lay wid Raymond . . . Raymond be mightly lonesome fe Tillie."

The simple sincerity in the black eyes looking down into hers eating steadily into her resistance, Tillie mumbled with a valiant attempt to retain her reserve,

"Lonesome! Hmph! How many women you take since Tillie see you last, Raymond?"

His dark eyes holding hers intently, Raymond responded softly, "Raymond take no woman. Tillie him woman."

Swallowing tightly against the emotion choking her throat, Tillie nodded slightly, allowing Raymond to take the lantern from her hand and pull her against his side as he turned to move slowly along the dark path. Within a few minutes they had reached a small clearing where, standing back, Raymond pointed to a barely visible structure dominating the area. "Dis place be fe Raymond n' fe Tillie . . . fe when Tillie come t' Raymond."

Urging her forward once again, Raymond led her silently into a small wooden hut about twenty feet square, and put the lantern on the ground. His head almost touching the thatched roof as he stood inside, Raymond searched Tillie's face for her first sign of acceptance, watching her expression intently as her eyes traveled the rough dwelling. Her glance trailing the earth floor, Tillie's eyes moved to the simple, handmade table and two stools that dominated one corner and slid slowly to the large platform in the center of the room on which lay a fresh mat and blanket. "Fraish 'n clean, jes' like Tillie want . . ."

Her great, dark eyes filling with tears, Tillie turned in a quick sure movement to put her arms around the neck of the huge man standing beside her. Experiencing a familiar thrill as his long powerful arms closed around her, Tillie reveled at the touch of his broad chest against her cheek as she whispered softly in a voice rich with emotion, "Yaw, Raymond, this be the place we come together. My father gone. Him not hallah anymore. No one see us. We be alone here." Raising her hand, Tillie slowly caressed the firm cheek of the man she had loved since childhood, drawing his mouth down to hers as she whispered softly, "Raymond not belong Massa Conway . . . Raymond belong Tillie Swann . . ."

The sound of the conch broke the morning stillness of Conway Plantation, sending its shrill call to endless labor. Startled from his sleep, Raymond reached out instinctively to the mat beside him to find it empty, already cool to the touch. Raising his hand, he covered his eyes for a few long seconds as a familiar sense of loss pervaded his senses. Slowly pulling his great, naked frame to a standing position, he paused one moment longer to stare down at the mat beside his feet, the memory of the night past flashing before his mind. A small smile curving his lips for the first time, he mumbled huskily under his breath, "Tillie Swann be free woman n' Raymond be slave, but Tillie be woman fe Raymond. No fine mulatto man fe Tillie Swann. Jes' Raymond . . . Raymond n' Tillie Swann."

The creeping light of dawn rapidly moved across the gray sky, faintly illuminating the familiar street as Tillie made her way with unerring purpose toward the small frame house that was her home. Entering quickly, she moved to her room off the kitchen. Immediately stripping off her clothes, she filled the small basin on the washstand and commenced bathing fastidiously. She could leave no trace of the previous night's activities on her clear, light brown skin. Darting a glance to the clothing lying on the floor near her feet, she appraised the dirt stains and small pieces of vegetation adhering to their surface, the result of her frantic bout with Pucku possession, and realized she would have to wash them quickly before Amethyst awoke. Amethyst was aware of her attendance at the cult rituals but was extremely apprehensive because of the danger involved. Tillie did not wish to add another worry to the list already besetting her high spirited soul-child. What was more, should Amethyst become aware she had approached the medicine man on her account, Tillie would be in for a battle.

Reaching into the pocket of her skirt, Tillie extracted the shriveled fowl's foot and stared at it thoughtfully. Her mission had been successful. She had obtained a powerful charm. Captain Straith's obeah could not harm Amethyst while she kept it near . . . but convincing Amethyst to keep it with her was another problem she had yet to face.

Taking the large cloth from the side of the washstand, Tillie began to dry herself, her mind moving to the picture of Raymond's tall powerful figure as she slowly moved the cloth across her faultless cocoa-colored skin. As strongly as she denied it, Raymond was her man. Having grown up on the same plantation, the feeling between them had started young, despite their divergent lives. Progressing from friendship to adolescent attraction, the strong feeling between them had matured into a firm though unacknowledged bond of love. They both realized their relationship could not pass beyond its present boundaries, and except for occasional bouts of defiance against the cruel twist of fate that had trapped her into subservience to the powerful emotion that existed between them, Tillie had come to accept her lot. Extremely beautiful in her youth, her splendidly sculptured face, creamy brown skin, large, velvety black eyes and tall, graceful stature had earned her many proposals of marriage from within the large mulatto community in Kingston. Having long since left her youth behind, Tillie was still beautiful, and still unmarried. It was unfair! Her dark eyes filling with unexpected tears, Tillie pulled on her clothes in sudden anger. Raymond was more man than all the dandified mulatto men on the island put together, but there was no chance for a life between a Negro slave and a free mulatto on the island. Unexpectedly recalling the fury on her father's face when she had declared her adolescent attraction to the handsome black buck Raymond had become, a spontaneous shudder shook her sturdy frame. Ashamed of the weakness that still prevailed at the vivid memory, Tillie mumbled under her breath, "Tillie Swann be grown woman now and lead her own life. No matter what anyone say, Raymond the man fe me..."

The sound of stirring in the next room breaking into her thoughts, Tillie quickly rolled her soiled clothes into a ball and pushed them under the bed. Smoothing back the stray wisps of hair at her hairline, she hastily checked her appearance in the small washstand mirror. Satisfied she was presentable in her fresh skirt and blouse, she picked up the shriveled charm and slipped it into her pocket. Finally drawing her tall frame to its full, impressive height, Tillie took a deep breath, opened her bedroom door, and walked casually into the kitchen.

Inspecting her appearance critically in the long mirror behind stage, Amethyst adjusted the neckline of the plain dark gown that would serve as the costume of a maid in the absence of something more suitable. She nodded unconsciously in approval and adjusted the small white apron. There would be little or no criticism of the fact that the costumes worn by the actors were contemporary, although the action of *Othello* being performed that night was laid in Venice and Cyprus of a bygone period. These inconsistencies of dress did not bother the Kingston audiences who were aware of the company's limited wardrobe. Neither were they bothered by the inadequate scenery consisting of a large cloth painted appropriately, serving as a backdrop, and two large shutters that when pushed together formed one continuous wall at the back of the stage. The performance was in progress and Amethyst was presently concealed, awaiting her cue, behind one of a series of wing pieces painted in an almost unidentifiable design to match the backdrop.

The theater was almost filled to capacity. David Douglass's performance of *Othello* was well known for its excellence, and had drawn a full house. This being the first of many walk-ons Amethyst was to do that night, she had not had an opportunity to view the audience and was slowly scanning the faces of the 300-odd spectators when an elbow jabbed her sharply in the ribs, turning her to the enthusiastic expression of Sally Warren, another of the "walking ladies" in the troupe.

"Did you look at the box to the right of the stage, Amethyst? Lord, but there's a handsome gent sitting there." Giggling annoyingly, Sally continued with a small wink, "Do you think he might have a preference for actresses? I wouldn't mind keeping that young buck company tonight!"

Sally Warren was nineteen, three years older than Amethyst, but in looking at the bright young face painted garishly under a full head of curly blonde hair, and the ripe young figure displayed to best advantage in the tight purple dress she wore, Amethyst felt ages older. Sally was a sweet girl, but her main problem was that she seemed to have a similar enthusiasm for a great many of the male faces looking back at them from the audience. And, all the worse, seemed determined to make her rounds until she had satisfied her curiosity with each and every one of them that was of a mind to cooperate!

Shaking her head, Amethyst looked into the pale blue eyes staring longingly past her face into the box at the side of the stage. "Do you mean to say," Amethyst began pointedly, ". . . that this fellow is even better looking than the one you singled out last week . . . and the one the week before . . . and the week before . . . ?"

Pulling her eyes back to Amethyst, Sally grumbled with a short show of irritation, "Oh, come now, Amethyst, just because you have a steady beau that comes to almost every performance . . . and a beautiful man he is, too . . ." Sally's voice began to lighten as her thoughts drifted in contemplation of William Sheridan's vibrant good looks, ". . . well, you don't have to be so hard on a poor girl who's still searching for her true love."

With a short laugh, Amethyst said lightly, "Sally, dear, my only fear is that you will wear yourself out with this intense search you are conducting."

"Oh, Amethyst," Sally giggled again, finally accepting with her usual good humor the subtle digs Amethyst directed at her promiscuity, "be a good girl now and take a look at this fellow. You'll see what I mean."

Nodding absentmindedly, Amethyst's eyes scanned the audience systematically, moving first over the pit seats directly in front of the stage, then to the better seats in the boxes that formed a horseshoe curving from one side of the stage to the other, and on to the gallery above the boxes, her eyes jerking back to the box to the right of the stage in abrupt recognition of the face that had just turned back in her direction. Her heart pounding wildly in her chest, she stared at the unmistakable features of Damien Straith!

"You see him now, don't you, Amethyst? Devastating, isn't he, with those odd light eyes that send little shivers right up your spine? And do you see the breadth of his shoulder and chest? A real man he is. I bet he . . ."

Sally's enthusiasm bubbled on while her voice drifted from Amethyst's ear. Quickly running her eyes back along the line of boxes, her glance finally came to rest on William's familiar, handsome countenance. He was seated in his usual box and had probably just entered the theater, for she had not seen him on her first perusal of the audience. Unconsciously uttering a small sigh of relief at the moral support of his presence, Amethyst turned her attention back to her babbling friend.

". . . can tell me who he is. I'm sure he's not been here before. I could not have forgotten that face . . ."

"I can tell you who he is, Sally." Amethyst's voice was deceptively casual. "He's Captain Damien Straith of the ship *Sally*. Now isn't that a coincidence?"

Her eyes flaring wide with surprise, Sally giggled again, tossing her blonde curls with a new confidence. "Well, what do you know? That fine looking gentleman might just have a weakness for girls by the name of Sally!"

"If you're smart, you'll stay away from him," Amethyst warned with sudden seriousness. "He's a bad one, a real womanizer. He . . ."

Suddenly interrupting Amethyst's negative statement with a horrified gasp, Sally stuttered unexpectedly, "Amethyst . . . quick! That's your cue!"

Startled as she turned toward the stage to see Othello awaiting the maid's entrance, Amethyst burst onto the stage in a sudden rush, stopping abruptly midway across to commence the measured pace her role demanded. The quick chorus of laughter her unorthodox entrance drew from the crowd brought a spontaneous frown to David Douglass's face, tightening even further the lump that suddenly choked her throat. Managing to continue casually across the stage as she had done many times, Amethyst was about to lift a small tray from the table when Othello turned to speak to Desdemona. Unexpectedly catching her foot on the hem of her dress, Amethyst stumbled momentarily, and watched in horrified embarrassment as the tray and its noisy contents tumbled to the floor in a crash that effectively drowned out Othello's adamant declaration. The laughter grew louder as her apprehensive glance slid slowly to Othello's reddening face, and burst into loud guffaws as she stooped to scramble awkwardly for the metal goblet that had rolled between his feet. Standing abruptly, she was face to face with David Douglass's livid expression, the fury in his haughty eyes the final straw that pushed her over the edge. With a quick turn, Amethyst bent to scoop up the contents of the tray in one fell swoop and beat a hasty retreat from his freezing glance. Suddenly regaining her composure, she came to a jerking halt at the wings and turning, directed a curtsey to the glaring Othello, managing in the effort to send the contents of the tray again crashing to the floor. The roar of laughter that shook the theater as Amethyst scrambled wildly to retrieve the fallen articles, followed her out the wings as she made her ignominious exit.

Finally settling down, the audience had once again turned its attention back to Othello when a small thread of laughter started across the room. Unaware of the reason for the growing hilarity, the small, slender hand reaching out surreptitiously from the wings continued to search blindly for the last goblet that had escaped retrieval when it had rolled onto the forestage. Finally pushed beyond restraint by the growing laughter and the furtive hand, Othello marched boldly across stage, speaking his lines through clenched teeth as he gave the elusive goblet a sharp kick, sending it bouncing noisily into the wings. The searching hand froze momentarily, disappearing suddenly in a movement so rapid that the entire house was brought to sustained, convulsive laughter which finally ended in a round of enthusiastic applause. Turning to offer a low, prolonged bow, Othello then resumed his performance with remarkable aplomb.

Standing wide-eyed in the wings, Amethyst was astounded by the events that had just progressed on stage. She had been performing for years without fault! What had come over her? Hardly able to believe her own wildly amateurish performance, she covered her eyes in dismay, tears choking her throat. She had disgraced herself! She had disgraced her father's good name! The first set of disastrous circumstances had been bad enough. What had possessed her to attempt to retrieve that missing goblet from backstage? Possessed her... Suddenly leaning forward, Amethyst shot a furtive glance into the box to the opposite side of the stage, and met head on the translucent, sardonic gaze of Damien Straith. Quickly jerking back her head, Amethyst missed completely the small, amused smile that flashed momentarily across his dry expression.

It was all his fault! Her mind flashed back to Tillie's warnings of that same afternoon when the worried woman had attempted to persuade her to carry that ghastly chicken's foot on her person as protection from Damien Straith's obeah, but Amethyst quickly subdued the niggling worry that Tillie might possibly be right. Obeah! It was all superstitious nonsense! She had heard her mother say that time and time again, charging that it was a person's own fear that allowed the "obeah" to gain control of his person. Tillie must have unconsciously instilled a fear in her that had set off the chain of unfortunate circumstances once she had realized Damien Straith was in the audience. Well, she would not allow it to happen again! She would have several opportunities to redeem herself tonight, and she would show Damien Straith that he could not intimidate Amethyst Greer!

Moving quickly to the small dressing room that accommodated the lesser female members of the troupe, Amethyst snatched her new sapphire blue gown from the rack. Quickly jerking off the somber black dress, Amethyst pulled the new gown over her head. Hastily taking a brush to her gleaming black tresses, she swept them into a graceful pompadour that softly framed her face, accenting the fragile curve of her cheek and the wide amethyst eyes that reflected the color of her dress, glowing a truer sapphire than the garment itself. Slipping a matching ostrich feather into the back of her elegant coiffeur, she turned to appraise herself critically. The dress had been made specifically for her after her acceptance as a full-fledged member of the troupe, and she was to wear it that night. Possessed of a clear, sweet singing voice that had charmed audiences into keeping their seats between acts since the age of ten, Amethyst had finally been given that spot on the program as her own. Always having performed in outrageous costumes due to her youth, she had been almost unrecognizable as the beautiful young woman she had become, and realizing the potential of Amethyst's unusual beauty, David Douglass had authorized the purchase of the startling gown she was now wearing for the first time. Stepping back to assess herself more fully, Amethyst gave a small astonished gasp. The splendid garment cupped the smooth curve of her shoulders enticingly, the neckline plunging deeply to expose the fullness of her smooth white breasts to an alarming degree. The bodice dipped to a tight deep point at her waist, emphasizing its narrowness from which the skirt flared out to float lightly to small feet encased in matching blue slippers. Dispersed sparingly over the entire surface of the garment, brilliants were concentrated mainly at the daring neckline to outline the graceful swell that indeed appeared as if it would escape the bounds of the glorious gown at the slightest provocation. Astounded by the image that peered back at her from the mirror, Amethyst stared in amazement, her incredulous expression slowly changing to a small, confident smile.

"Amethyst Greer, you will knock them back in their seats tonight . . . yes, you will!" she mumbled under her breath before turning to move quickly from the cramped room. She would wait in the wings until the conclusion of the first act in approximately ten minutes, and she would not miss the cue for her appearance this time . . . not this time or ever again!

Moving uncomfortably in his seat, Damien stared absentmindedly at the stage, his mind far from the Othello who was emoting so eloquently to his enraptured audience. But Amethyst would be appearing again soon, and the fun would begin again. Managing to subdue the laughter rising to his lips, Damien recalled with an almost indecent pleasure the embarrassment reflected on that small, lovely countenance. He was not quite certain why he had been drawn here tonight when just a day before he was certain he never wanted to look on the little chit's face again, but he had enjoyed her mortification immensely. It was almost worth waiting through the damned boring performance progressing on stage, just to see her expression when she came out again.

"Hell!" he thought, barely able to suppress a broad smile, "I could not have conjured up a more enjoyable evening if I had tried!"

The sudden volley of applause breaking into his thoughts drew his attention back to the stage as the green baize curtain moved to cover the frozen tableau for the end of the first act. How much longer would he have to wait . . . he was becoming impatient.

The audience was just beginning to mill restlessly when the piano struck up a loud, attention-getting chord before progressing a few seconds later into the first bars of the hauntingly familiar melody of "Greensleeves." The sound of short, shocked gasps jerked his attention to the opposite side of the stage where a startling vision in blue appeared, her sweet, true soprano ringing out melodically across the hushed theater. Amethyst walked smoothly across the stage with mesmerizing grace, not a trace of the clumsy creature of a few minutes earlier remaining as the clear, bell-like tone of her voice wove a soft, hypnotic spell that brought all movement in the audience to a complete standstill. The candles in the chandelier overhead glimmered in the glow of her ebony tresses, the sparkle of her radiant eyes and the natural glow of her faultless vibrant coloring causing an inexplicable knot to form in Damien's throat. The footlights' glow danced in the brilliants on her dress, their greatest blaze emphasizing the tempting white swells rising above her decolletage. Her slender, graceful arms moved faultlessly at her sides as she approached center stage, her hands finally clasping together in gentle supplication as the melody continued on.

Staring transfixed at the vision standing just a few feet from him on the forestage, Damien's heart began an accelerated beating, his eyes refusing to move from the beauty of Amethyst's face, although the words she sang were no longer audible to his ear. His eyes slowly moving over her, the gradual joy of realization began to sweep over him at last. This was Amethyst . . . the way he had, in the dark, unconscious passages of his mind always dreamed her to be. She was a woman grown at last . . . no longer a child . . . ready for the raw, violent emotion she had stirred in him since the day of their first meeting. He had been helplessly drawn to her when she was a child, her memory refusing to leave his mind despite the momentous events of the past seven years, creating an indelible tie that drew him helplessly to the woman he had dreamed she would someday become.

This then was his preoccupation with the surly waif that defied him relentlessly and continued to defy him . . . the reason for his inexplicable fury when she had run him off . . . the cause of the undeniable wave of growing warmth that had begun inside him the moment she had stepped through the doorway of her room yesterday. This was *his* Amethyst . . . the way he had dreamed her to be . . . the reward of seven long years of frustrated dissatisfaction with the women that had filled his time until now. His eyes caressing the soft line of her cheek, trailed down the slender column of her throat, his hands longing to touch the delicate white skin that shone with virtual incandescence as his eyes swept her with a soul-shaking longing that set his large, calloused hands to shaking. "Amethyst . . . my Amethyst," he thought fiercely. "You belong to me, even if you have not yet come to complete understanding of the course our predestined lives have taken. But I will make you understand, darling. I will teach you. You will give me your purity of spirit, and I will give you all my lo . . ."

But Amethyst's gaze had stopped moving over the audience and had become fixed on a fellow seated in a box at the opposite side of the stage. The obvious warmth of her gaze settling on him, she directed the verse of the song to him as she sang,

> Black is the color of my true love's hair
> His looks are something wondrous fair
> The purest eyes and the strongest hands
> I love the grass on which he stands
> I love my love and well he knows
> I love the grass on where he goes
> If he on earth no more could stay
> My life would quickly pass away.

Amethyst's singing continued on, her voice rising into a gripping chorus that stole the hearts of the audience. Her glance did not falter, remaining locked with that of the unknown dark-haired young man who was the recipient of many envious glances. A slow anger began to build inside Damien, growing into a fury that sent the blood rushing to his head. "No! She belongs to me," his mind raged. "She is mine!"

She had been his since that day on the dock when her

piquant little face had first stared up into his. He would suffer no interruption in the mutual fate that was meant to be theirs. He would put an immediate end to her infatuation with the fellow in the box, and she would turn to him. She would . . . she must turn to him . . .

Staring intently at Amethyst, Damien willed her to turn, to return *his* glance, but the chorus continued on, her eyes refusing to move from the fellow in the box, refuting the power of his mental command. Overcome with a deep, blinding rage, Damien closed his eyes for a few, brief seconds, his hands knotting into heavy, powerful fists which he brought down in furious frustration onto the ledge of box. At the moment of their encounter with the surface of the railing, a startling cracking sound snapped open Damien's eyes in time to view the rapid, hurtling descent of one of the battens stretching a series of ceiling cloths from one end of the stage to the other. Jumping to his feet as fear closed his throat, Damien saw Amethyst glance upward and spring to the furthest edge of the stage, just as the heavy wooden pole struck and splintered the stage in the exact spot where she had been standing. Shook to the very center of his being by the narrowness of her escape, Damien leaned forward to grasp the railing of the box and hurl himself over its edge onto the forestage. In a few quick strides he was at Amethyst's side to take her trembling form into his arms, the frightened reaction of the audience escaping his ears as he mumbled against her hair, "Amethyst, darling, thank God you are safe."

Suddenly rigid in his embrace, Amethyst jerked herself away, her pale face turned up to his accusingly. "You! How dare you thank God for my escape from an evil you planned with the forces of darkness? I could feel your eyes on me . . . willing me to look back at you, but I would not succumb. And you took your revenge . . ."

"Amethyst, what are you saying?" Startled, Damien

stared down into the purple orbs reflecting her rage, inwardly flinching at the hatred burning there. "Don't you know . . . don't you realize that I'd never hurt you, even if it was in my power to do the thing you accuse me of? Good God, Amethyst, is that what you believe of me, that I am . . ."

"Take your hands off me!" Jerking herself from his arms, Amethyst turned and ran out the wings into the arms of the fellow to whom she had directed her song and who had just arrived backstage.

Shaking his head as a familiar fury swelled inside him, Damien covered the distance between himself and the embracing couple in a few long strides. Ripping them apart, he pushed Amethyst to the side and faced the startled stranger, his face a mask of vicious wrath.

"I do not know who you are, and neither do I care," Damien began in a low, measured tone, the intensity of his expression and the barely restrained fury in the tensing of his tall powerful physique an overwhelming specter to behold. "But I will tell you this once and once alone. You will neither go near Amethyst nor touch her again. She is mine . . . she belongs to me. She is my woman, do you understand that, boy? And you will either heed my words now and forget Amethyst ever existed, or as sure as I stand before you this night, I will see you dead!"

At first startled into speechlessness, the young man's astonishment turned gradually into outrage as he demanded vehemently, "Are you insane, man? Who are you anyway? Whatever makes you think you have the right . . ."

Rudely interrupting his questions, Damien responded in an ominous tone, "I am Captain Damien Straith. I have the right of previous claim. Amethyst belongs to me. She has been mine since she arrived in Jamaica as a child, and as a woman still belongs to me."

The young man's eyes widened at the declaration of his name, his glance shooting to Amethyst's face for confirmation as her eyes grew wide in horror.

"No! No, William! Don't believe him! It's all untrue! There was never a discussion of these things between us. He is mad!" Her eyes imploring, Amethyst whispered, "Please believe me, William!"

"William ... William Sheridan, the plantation owner's son. So now I understand," Damien muttered darkly. The coldness in his voice sending a hush over the small group that had gathered around them, Damien continued softly, "I warn you now, William Sheridan. Heed my words. Whatever plans you had for Amethyst are finished."

Without speaking a word, William turned his back on Damien, his glance efficiently dismissing Damien's menacing statement as he turned silently to Amethyst. William's hand had just touched her cheek in a soft caress when a heavy hand closing on his shoulder jerked him around to meet the power of Damien's closed fist as it crashed against his face, knocking him senseless to the floor.

"William!" Amethyst's wild dive toward William's fallen form was halted by the same powerful hand as it jerked her to Damien's side and held her fast.

"Leave him be! I warned him ..."

"You warned him!" Amethyst's voice was a malevolent hiss. "What right have you to ..."

"I have this right!"

Jerking her against his chest, Damien enclosed Amethyst in a crushing embrace, his mouth closing over hers, the power of his kiss forcing open her mouth until he tasted once again the intoxicating sweetness within. Deeper and deeper he pressed, subduing her struggles effortlessly as he slowly overwhelmed her opposition with the strength of his possession. When finally he drew away, his voice was deep, his glance steady as his eyes held hers with the sheer power of his will.

"You are mine, Amethyst Greer. And you will be mine as long as I wish you to remain mine!"

There was neither confirmation nor denial on Amethyst's face as she stared at him in a bemused fashion. Noting the concern in her expression as her eyes suddenly darted to William's prostrate figure, he continued more softly, "It's best for him if you leave him there, Amethyst. You will only do him harm with your attention."

Amethyst's eyes moved to Damien's face in obvious fear, and Damien felt a strange sense of unrest.

"Come with me now," he urged more gently. Shooting a quick glance back to the stage where the debris caused by the fallen batten and short cloths still lay untouched, he said softly, "The performance will not resume tonight. You are extremely shaken. I'll take you home."

Shooting one last, longing glance in William's direction, Amethyst hesitated only briefly before Damien's strong arm closing around her shoulders drew her close to his side to urge her toward the exit door.

The night was fresh and clear, the infinite beauty of the star-filled sky and balmy scented air escaping completely unnoticed by the two that rode silently in the open carriage. Amethyst's face was averted, her eyes staring sightlessly away from Damien's troubled expression. He was aware he had not handled the situation well. Amethyst was angry . . . angrier now than she had been before. Perhaps his actions had been unwise this evening, but the unexpected threat to her life, as well as the jolting experience of seeing her in someone else's arms had been more than he could tolerate. He longed desperately to hold her but knew with a cold certainty that they had much to settle between them before their relationship could progress past the reservoir of icy silence Amethyst maintained. His arm sliding across the back of the seat, he moved a bit closer, touching her chin with his other hand, gently turning her face back in his direction. She was startlingly close, breathtakingly so, her eyes wide, staring up into his, her flawless complexion illuminated by the bright, starlit night, her soft appealing lips only inches from his.

"Amethyst, dear," his voice was husky as he spoke, "I realize you must be stunned by my actions tonight. You probably did not expect . . ."

"But I did expect!" Amethyst's voice was low, her eyes steadfastly maintaining contact with his, the only sign of her mounting anger the spark that burned in their purple depths. "I told you yesterday that I did not believe you had helped my mother and me without an ulterior motive. But I had not realized that you would attempt to come between me and the man I love in order to cancel all debts between us."

"You do not love that young fool!" Damien stated emphatically, his face stiffening in anger.

"And how would you know if I loved him or not?" Amethyst demanded, inching away from him in anger to draw herself up haughtily against the side of the carriage. "Do you profess to read minds as well as perform black magic?"

"Come now, Amethyst, I had thought you far too intelligent a woman to believe all the poppycock that is whispered about my powers of obeah! If I hold a power over you, it has nothing to do with magic."

"You hold no power over me whatsoever, Captain Straith!"

"Oh, is that so, Amethyst?"

In a swift, unexpected movement, Damien pulled her close, his strong, arrogant mouth closing over her slightly parted lips, efficiently shutting off all protest with the strength of his kiss. But once begun, the lesson quickly grew out of hand. A deep, pulsating heat surging through him at the first taste of her lips, Damien pulled her closer, closer still until Amethyst's soft, tantalizing body was crushed roughly against his in an endless kiss that stirred him to the very soul. He could not hold her close enough. His one hand sliding around her narrow waist to press her intimately against him, his other hand slid up her back to close over the white, bared shoulder. Delighting in the coolness of her skin, thrilling as his caress moved up the back of her neck, he slid his hand into her hair to hold her head fast and tight under his kiss. Gradually Amethyst's protests lessened until she no longer struggled against him, her lips softening under the relentless pressure of his mouth, her body growing relaxed and compliant under his touch. And still his kiss went on, searching, devouring greedily the unbelievable beauty unfolding beneath his lips. Finally his mouth left hers, his lips trailing heated, hungry kisses up her cheek, across the fragile, almost transparent lids closed with passion, along her temple and hairline to her small tempting ear, before returning with renewed eagerness to consume once again the welcoming mouth awaiting his kiss. His heart pounding in his chest, all rational thought lost from his mind, Damien finally drew himself away to search the lovely face so close to his. Her expression bemused, almost frightened, Amethyst stared up into his face.

Damien's voice was a ragged whisper. "So, I hold no power over you, Amethyst." Pressing another warm, lingering kiss against her vulnerable mouth, he felt the trembling of her petite frame, and a flush of exaltation slid over him.

"You have answered my question without words, darling," he whispered, circling her lips with kisses, sliding his mouth down the slender column of her throat before pressing heatedly, with escalating fervor, against the soft white swells exposed in her decolletage. Following the daring neckline to the full depth of its plunge, he covered the smooth breasts with warm, moist kisses, his mouth moving and nudging against their softness until they were almost free of their narrow confines. He could feel her heart pounding against his cheek, and barely able to restrain the wild heat pulsating through his veins, he raised his face to gaze into Amethyst's impassioned expression.

"And this, darling," he continued softly, "is the reason I know you do not love that young man in the theater."

His last sentence seeming to shock her from her mindless lethargy, Amethyst suddenly attempted to jerk herself free of his embrace, the heat flushing her lovely face apparent even in the semi-darkness. Her voice trembling as she sought to regain her composure, Amethyst said in as haughty a tone as she could manage, "Do not be deceived by a short, thoughtless lapse, Captain Straith . . ."

"My name is Damien, Amethyst. I want you to call me Damien . . ." His voice a husky whisper, he ignored her shaken statement to continue a barrage of kisses against her cheek and mouth. But she continued to speak.

". . . I have had a terrible fright tonight and am merely reacting hysterically. I'm afraid I'm not responsible . . ."

"You are reacting with the same hysteria as I, Amethyst," Damien interrupted softly, "and that is the hysteria of realizing we . . ."

"I realize nothing, Captain," Amethyst began, stopping abruptly as she became aware that they were in front of her house. How long had they been there in full view of curious eyes? How many people had witnessed her wanton display from their windows? Swallowing hard, she continued determinedly, "I only know that I am exhausted and must go inside now."

His brows drawing together in a small frown, Damien said softly, "Why do you deny the feeling between . . ."

"Please, Captain," Amethyst exclaimed softly, her wide eyes filling with unexpected tears, "I want to go inside now."

The tone of her voice hinted at the true hysteria beginning to overwhelm her senses, and Damien considered her thoughtfully for a few long moments before gradually lessening his hold. Anxious to be out of his arms, Amethyst made a quick move to escape, only to find Damien's grip tightening warningly.

"You don't have to run away from me, darling," he said softly. "I'll take you to your door now if that's what you truly want."

Averting her eyes from his, Amethyst repeated softly, "Yes . . . yes . . . I do want to go inside now."

"'I want to go inside, *Damien*,'" Damien prompted, tilting up her chin so that she looked into his eyes once again. "Come on . . . say my name, Amethyst. It's really not that hard, is it?"

Swallowing hard once again, Amethyst said breathlessly, "Alright . . . Damien . . ."

A small muscle twitching in his cheek at her whispered response, Damien stared unfathomably into her incredible beauty for a few long moments before stepping from the carriage. Turning, he offered her his hand and helped her to the street. Sliding his arm around her possessively, he pulled her close to his side as they walked the few short steps to her door.

Looking up, Amethyst felt the heartstopping impact of his clear gray eyes shake her body. She was speechless against his mesmerizing stare and watched helplessly as he lowered his mouth once again to plunder hers with a rising passion that left her shaken.

Finally raising his head, Damien's voice was ragged,

his hand trembling as he raised it to caress her velvet cheek. "Goodnight, darling. Go inside now and sleep well. We have much to discuss tomorrow."

Her voice a hoarse whisper, Amethyst said softly, "Goodnight."

"'Goodnight, *Damien*,'" was the prompting response.

Shooting him a quick, unreadable glance, Amethyst whispered softly, "Goodnight . . . Damien."

Turning abruptly, Amethyst entered the house, the remnants of the strange trembling she had experienced in Damien's arms still remaining in the small, intermittent tremors that shook her small frame. What was the weakness that seemed to overwhelm her each time Damien forced his attentions on her? Remembering the pressure of his full, hungry lips against hers, the purely male scent of his body as he crushed her intimately close, his voice soft and husky as he murmured, "Amethyst, darling . . .", Amethyst was once again assailed with the same malady. What was wrong with her? She despised Damien Straith for the opportunist he had proved to be. Then why did she seem to forget everything she truly felt about him the moment he took her into his arms?

The sound of movement at the entrance to the living room snapped Amethyst's head around to Tillie's accusing glance.

"What kind of show you put on in that carriage, Miss Amethyst Greer? You mama work hard to keep you names good and clean. Be you tryin' t' wipe out all him work in one night?"

"Please, Tillie," Amethyst's voice was sharp, "I'm not in the mood for a lecture. It's been a terrible evening. You don't know . . ."

"I know everythin' that happened tonight," Tillie corrected in a low, knowing voice. "That man . . . him set him duppy on you. Him make you run across that stage and act like a fool 'til people in the audience split him sides laughin'. Then when you come out to charm the people with you sweet song, him bring the ceiling down on you!"

"Tillie, you exaggerate!" Amethyst scoffed in an effort to deny the same fear that had been crowding her mind. "The batten fell, that's all. It was extremely frightening, but I'm alright now. It was just an accident..."

"It be no accident, Amethyst Greer!" Taking the grisly charm from her pocket, Tillie held it out again in Amethyst's direction. "You take this now and him lose him power over you!"

"I don't want it, Tillie!" Her face flushing in anger, Amethyst shook her head firmly. To accept the charm would be to acknowledge Damien's control over her emotions. The very thought of it raising her color to higher level, she said adamantly, "I can handle Captain Straith by myself!"

"Like you do in the carriage, missey?"

Her face maintaining her hot color, Amethyst drew herself up haughtily. "I was not myself tonight. I had suffered a terrible fright... I was shaken..."

"That man, him got him eye on you, Amethyst, but him not gowan marry you. Him not marry anyone, and if you not be careful, Mr. Sheridan not gowan want you either!"

"You needn't worry about that, Tillie. William loves me."

"But that man gowan take you and use you. Mr. Sheridan not gowan want second-hand woman for him wife!"

"Tillie!" Tears springing to her eyes, Amethyst responded softly, "You know I wouldn't let that happen."

"Tillie see you in that carriage, Amethyst." Tillie's short glance contradicted her protest. "Him already have power over you, but him let you go this time. Next time him not gowan pull away."

Her face suddenly draining of all color, Amethyst took a small, inadvertent step backwards as Tillie put into words the fear that had been permeating her senses. Unable to respond, Amethyst turned abruptly toward her room. Grasping the door knob with a shaking hand, she tossed over her shoulder in the firmest voice she could manage, "I'm going to sleep now. I'll feel better tomorrow and you shall see just how little 'power' Captain Straith has over me. Goodnight, Tillie."

Unable to face even her own thoughts, Amethyst spent the dark hours of the night tossing and turning in her bed as a myriad of emotions swept over her. For the first few hours she waited hopefully for William, but she waited in vain. Why had William not come to see how she had fared? Was he angry because she had left with Damien? But she had had no choice . . . she had not wanted the ghastly scene to continue. Would William really desert her as Tillie had intimated? No, he loved her. He had proved his love for her in countless ways over the past year, and they would be married now had she not been so hesitant. Perhaps she had been wrong in refusing to marry William. If she were married now, Damien Straith would not be a problem. No . . . that was not reason enough to marry. There must be true love on both sides in order to marry, and no hesitation. But she did love William, didn't she? Drawing the image of his face to her mind, Amethyst felt the same sense of warmth steal over her that always accompanied his presence . . . his touch . . . and she relaxed for a few short moments, basking in her temporary escape, until uncertainty again overcame her senses. Well, she would get up at dawn tomorrow and would go to Sheridan Plantation to see William. Perhaps he was hurt far more seriously than she thought. A stab of true fear jabbed her insides viciously at the thought.

Please, God, no! In an attempt to escape her fear, she closed her eyes tightly and turned her face to her pillow. She must empty her mind of thought now and go to sleep. It would do her no good to worry all night long. She had a long walk ahead of her at dawn . . .

Finally falling asleep, Amethyst seemed to awaken only a few minutes later to find the bright light of morning slipping through her window. Shooting a quick glance to the clock on her dresser, she gasped audibly. 7:30! She had wanted to be away at dawn so that no one would be aware of the direction in which she headed. Furious that she had not awakened on time, she jumped out of bed and pulling off her night rail, grabbed her underclothes and began to dress. She would go to Sheridan Plantation anyway, and damn the knowing glances that would follow her! So engrossed was she in her hurried dressing that she failed to hear the rattle of the wagon that pulled up in front of her house, or the soft knock on the door that preceded the conversation that jerked her head away from her reflection in the mirror and caused her to drop her brush as she ran to her bedroom door and pulled it open.

"William!" Without waiting for his response, Amethyst flew across the room to throw her arms around his neck with relief. Hugging the familiar warmth of him tightly against her, she murmured over and over against his ear as he bent to scoop her in a tight embrace, "William, William, I was so worried! Why didn't you come to see me last night? I waited and waited until I became certain something dreadful had happened to you." Running her hand into the thick mahogany hair at the base of his neck, she inadvertently touched a huge swelling at the same moment William winced with pain. Drawing away, she looked worriedly into William's face for the first time, noting his unusual pallor and bloodshot eyes. As he returned her glance, he swayed for a brief second, and reaching out, gripped the chair beside him for support.

"What is it, William? What's wrong?" Suddenly frightened beyond belief, she reached up her hand to touch his cheek in a tentative caress. Turning his head, William kissed her palm and held it against his cheek for a few brief moments before releasing it.

"I struck my head when I fell to the floor last night, Amethyst. I was unconscious for a few hours afterwards and someone drove me home to the plantation. When I finally awoke it was too late to come to see you, darling, and to be very honest, I was in no shape to mount my horse, much less make the trip to town. But nothing and no one was going to keep me away from you this morning." His pale face knit with concern, he continued softly, "Are you alright, darling? Did he . . . did Straith hurt you in any way? If he did, I'll . . ."

"No, William, I'm fine." Her eyes scanning his face, Amethyst noted worriedly that he seemed to grow more pale by the minute, "but please sit down. You don't look well."

Refusing to be seated, William pulled her once again into his arms. Completely oblivious of Tillie's watchful eye, he brought his mouth down to cover Amethyst's lips with his for a deep, searching kiss. Giving him her lips willingly, Amethyst's arms wrapped around his neck, her hands careful to avoid the sensitive area at the back of his head as she pressed herself against him, willing the same surging response she had felt to Damien Straith's kisses.

The sound of Tillie's horrified gasp caused her to open her eyes a brief second before she was ripped from William's arms and pushed to the side.

"I told you to stay away from Amethyst, Sheridan!" Enraged, Damien Straith faced an equally enraged William Sheridan who responded heatedly, his face whiter by the second as he swayed visibly, "And who are you to give me orders, Straith? This is not your ship, and Amethyst is not your possession!"

Rushing between them, Amethyst steadied William and turned heatedly toward Damien. "William is not well, and you have no right in my house! Get out, now!"

His eyes widening in sudden anger, Damien was about to respond to Amethyst's demand when William's knees buckled suddenly and he pitched toward the floor. Unable to support his weight, Amethyst emitted a frightened gasp as he slid from her grasp the second before strong arms grabbed the unconscious man and lowered him gradually to the floor.

"William!" Immediately on her knees beside him, Amethyst placed her hand on his chest, relieved to feel his heart beating beneath her touch. Swallowing the tears that choked her throat, she completely ignored Damien as she struggled to speak. "Tillie, quickly, get some water and a cloth. He's unconscious . . ."

Countermanding her directions, Damien said sharply, "Don't waste time getting water, Tillie. That fellow in the wagon outside belongs to Sheridan, doesn't he?" At Tillie's affirmative response, he continued briskly, "Get him in here. This man should be in bed. I've seen wounds like this before. He must have struck his head when he fell yesterday and has obviously sustained a severe blow to his skull. The only cure for this type of injury is complete bed rest for at least a week. Otherwise, the result could be disastrous."

Immediately turning on her heel, Tillie ran to the door to call the Negro waiting on the wagon outside the door. Turning her tearful expression toward Damien, Amethyst hissed, "You! You did this to him! And now you stand there talking so glibly as if you have some actual concern for his welfare! Hypocrite! Monster!"

Turning, Amethyst lowered her face to press her moist cheek against William's as she whispered comfortingly into his unhearing ear.

A strong hand closing on her arm jerked her suddenly to her feet and whirled her around to face Damien's strained expression. "You will stay away from him, Amethyst. His man is coming." He nodded toward the worried Negro running through the doorway, "and once he is home, his family will care for him."

"You . . . you did this to him," Amethyst sputtered angrily.

"The blame for this man's injury lies on his own shoulders, Amethyst," Damien responded cooly. "I warned him, but he did not choose to heed my warning. In any case, his injury was not due to my blow. It was due to his fall."

"And you caused him to fall!"

"I am not responsible for his weak jaw, Amethyst."

Seething with anger as the man before her completely absolved himself from blame, Amethyst turned her back on him haughtily. Attempting to aid the Negro who struggled to lift William's unconscious body, Amethyst was roughly pushed aside, as was the astonished black who watched as Damien bent and lifted the unconscious man with apparent ease and carried him through the doorway to put him on the back of the wagon.

"Get something soft for this man's head so he will do himself no further damage on the ride home," Damien ordered imperiously as he rearranged the boxes in the wagon beside William so they enclosed him within a small space. "Now he will not slide around on the trip back," he mumbled under his breath as he took the pillow from Tillie and slid it gently beneath the unconscious man's head.

Quickly grabbing Amethyst's arm as she attempted to get into the wagon beside William, Damien demanded harshly, "What are you doing?"

"I'm going to accompany William home to make sure

he's alright." Raising her eyes to his, Amethyst demanded with the same imperious tone, "Now take your hands off me!"

"You are going nowhere," Damien ground out from beneath clenched teeth, tightening his grip before turning to direct his attention to the frightened slave who stood in apparent confusion looking from one to the other. "You . . . what is your name?"

"Quaco, Massa."

"Quaco, take your master home and fetch a doctor immediately. But be sure to drive carefully and avoid bumping him as much as possible. Do you understand me, man? Your master is to have complete rest and quiet, and as little jolting as possible."

"I'se understand, Massa. I'se take Massa William home straight 'way, 'n I'se drive slow 'n careful."

His face cracking into a small smile for the first time that morning, Damien clapped the worried Negro on the shoulder. "Good man. Now get on with you."

"Let my arm loose, Captain Straith! I'm going with them," Amethyst muttered angrily as she jerked her arm back and forth in an attempt to be free of his hold. When her struggles availed her nothing, she muttered again, "I warn you, let me loose!"

Completely ignoring her struggles, Damien watched as the Negro mounted the wagon and clucking softly, started the horse down the street with obvious caution. Finally turning back toward her, he said sternly as he pulled her toward the house, "Sheridan will be alright if he is careful. You will not encourage his feelings toward you any longer. You will only do him further harm."

Rounding on him as he closed the door behind them, Amethyst gasped unbelievingly, "I will do him *further* harm? You are the one who has harmed him, not I!"

"And you were the cause for my actions," Damien stated simply as he looked down into her flushed face.

Huge lavender eyes sparkling with anger looked up into his, and he marveled absentmindedly that with her changing moods, Amethyst seemed to grow more lovely still. Raising his hand, he gently touched the smooth cheek that was still wet with frustrated tears, feeling a resurgence of his own anger as Amethyst jerked her face from his caress. His brow darkening, he said softly, "You were kissing him when I entered, were you not, Amethyst? I think I should remind you what it's really like to be kissed by a man . . ."

Taking her abruptly into his arms, Damien's mouth swooped down on hers, igniting the same thrilling heat in her blood that had defeated her countless times, but this time Amethyst refused to succumb to the mind-dulling, pulsating languor that began creeping over her. Instead, taking his bottom lip between her teeth, Amethyst bit down viciously, smiling victoriously as Damien jerked himself away with a dark oath and raised his hand to his bleeding lip.

"Hellion!" he muttered as he faced her thunderously. "Those tricks will avail you nothing!"

"I'm going with William!"

"They have already left, you little fool."

"Then I will follow when you leave! You cannot watch me all day long, can you, Captain Straith? You have business to attend, goods to sell and a return cargo to contract. Will you spend your time being my jailer? For I assure you, at the first opportunity I will leave for Sheridan Plantation to see William."

"You're right, Amethyst." Once again in control of his emotions, Damien eyed her coolly, "I have no time to waste, and since you were foolish enough to warn me of your plans, I suppose I have no other recourse but . . ." Bending forward suddenly, Damien grasped Amethyst around the knees and tossed her on his shoulder. Holding her kicking ankles with his one hand as she dangled over his shoulder like a squirming sack of grain, her fists beating wildly at his broad back, he finished adamantly, ". . . but to take you with me!"

"Let me go!" Amethyst screamed, her flailing fists beginning to make themselves felt as she pummelled his back unceasingly.

Raising his free hand, Damien slapped her small, rounded backside sharply, smiling at the startled gasp that followed. "Be quiet now, and try not to make a spectacle of yourself," he commanded softly.

Before Tillie's horrified eyes, he opened the door and turned onto the street, still toting his mortified burden over his shoulder as he started in the direction of the docks.

Glancing from side to side as she hung over his shoulder, her long, gleaming hair hanging down past her head, bobbing with his vigorous stride, Amethyst watched the startled expressions of those she passed, her ears burning at the ribald comments of the few.

"Captain . . . please . . . Captain . . . put me down," she implored, close to tears with humiliation.

His pace slowing, thereby affording the curious a better view of his embarrassed burden, he said firmly, "You have sealed your own fate, Amethyst. Since I cannot trust you to obey me, I must take you with me while I attend to my business."

"Captain, please . . . put me down. People are staring. You are making me a laughingstock."

"My name is Damien, Amethyst."

There was a brief hesitation before the soft voice said quietly, "Please . . . Damien, please put me down."

"And will you run from me the moment I do?" Damien inquired softly, his smile growing as he sensed victory within his grasp.

"No . . . I will not."

"And will you accompany me to my ship without protest?"

Again a brief hesitation as Amethyst looked at the curious and somewhat jeering glances directed her way. "Why must I accompany you to your ship?"

"You yourself have said I must be your jailer or you will go to Sheridan Plantation."

"No . . . no, I won't go to the plantation . . ."

"I don't believe you, Amethyst." Damien was frowning once again at the realization that she would do or say anything to go to William Sheridan's side.

"Then . . . put me down. I'll go with you to your ship. I promise."

"It will do you no good to lie, Amethyst."

"I promise! I promise I'll go with you if you'll let me down. Please . . ."

This time the hesitation was on Damien's side, his stride slowing even further while he considered her plea.

"Do I have your word, Amethyst?"

"Yes . . . yes, Captain, I promise . . ."

"'I promise, *Damien*,'" Damien urged, feeling an undeniable sense of satisfaction as he sensed the momentary tensing of her body.

"I promise . . . Damien," was the whispered response, and not realizing he was holding his breath, Damien released it silently as he swung Amethyst to her feet.

Hurriedly smoothing her hair, Amethyst glanced around at the inquisitive glances scrutinizing her openly, adjusting her rumpled clothing before raising a heated glance into the clear gray eyes regarding her cautiously.

"You are a beast!" she hissed softly, "but I will keep my word." Turning wordlessly, she assumed a place at his side as he continued toward the docks at a slower pace. Fuming inwardly as a strong arm stole around her shoulders a few seconds later to pull her against his side so they gave the appearance of strolling lovers, she refused to look up into the victorious smile beaming down on her. Holding her head a bit higher, she continued steadfastly forward, refusing to glance either right or left as she stared ahead unblinkingly. Within minutes the tall masts of the *Sally* came into view, and Amethyst's heart began a slow pounding as they gradually approached the lowered gangplank. Memory suddenly transported her back seven years to the time she had first seen the *Sally* through a veil of freezing rain. Her mother had been running at her side and had stumbled, tripping head over heels . . . A big man had pushed her away from her mother's inert form and called her a fool, his light gray eyes upbraiding her. Her mother had been so still and bleeding . . . she had been terrified that her mother was dead, and he had called her stupid! She hated him then, and looking up into those same translucent gray eyes, she hated him now.

Frowning slightly, Damien allowed his eyes to travel Amethyst's face for a few minutes before whispering calmly, "That was a long time ago, Amethyst."

Not questioning the fact that Damien read her thoughts accurately, Amethyst replied in a lowered voice, "But nothing has changed. You are the same and I am the same, only a few years older. But I still ha . . ."

"That's enough, Amethyst!" Damien's voice was sharp as he grabbed her hand and pulled her forcefully forward and up the gangplank, unwilling to listen to her vehement declaration. Jeremy Barnes's startled expression as Damien jerked Amethyst on deck behind him would have been laughable had he been in a better mood. Instead, frowning darkly, Damien said in a low voice, "We have a guest for a few hours, Barnes. This young 'lady' will wait for me downstairs until we conclude our business."

Pulling her down the stairs behind him, Damien

dragged her relentlessly down the small corridor toward his cabin, and opening the door, roughly pushed her inside. Following her inside, he slammed the door behind him.

While she stared toward him in obvious hatred, Damien returned her stare, his hands moving to his shirt front. Slowly unbuttoning his shirt, he finally removed it and threw it on the wide bunk in the corner of the room, exposing the breadth of his naked chest as it heaved in obvious agitation. His hands moving to the waist of his britches, he began unbuttoning the buttons unhesitantly until Amethyst gasped in a hoarse voice, "What are you doing?"

A faint smirk appearing at the corner of his mouth, he replied arrogantly, "I'm changing into my work clothes, Amethyst, dear. If you wish to pretend maidenly modesty, you may turn your back, because I intend stripping down to the skin!"

Her face flaming, Amethyst turned her back abruptly to his low snicker. Within a few minutes, Damien's low amused tone broke the silence of the cabin. "It's safe to turn around now, Amethyst."

Turning back to face him where he stood in rougher garments that did nothing to lessen his virile appeal, Amethyst's voice was filled with contempt. "You are a beast, Captain Straith!"

Stepping forward in a quick, unexpected movement, Damien crushed her against him in a tight embrace, prompting relentlessly against her lips moments before his mouth closed over hers, "'You are a beast, *Damien*.'"

Within minutes he was gone, leaving her shaken and filled with the same puzzling sense of wondering expectancy. The sound of a key turning in the lock brought Amethyst sharply to her senses as she flew to the door to turn the knob testingly. He had locked her in! Pounding at the door in a fit of fury, Amethyst screamed wildly, "How dare you lock me in! Unlock this door this instant, do you hear me? I demand you unlock this door, Captain Straith!"

Waiting hesitantly for his response, Amethyst heard a low amused voice from the other side prompt softly, "'I demand that you unlock this door, *Damien*.'"

She was still standing in open-mouthed amazement at his audacity when she heard the unmistakable sound of his footsteps turning and heading back down the passageway and then ascending the stairs.

Frustrated beyond belief, Amethyst turned away from the door, her eyes sweeping the cabin furiously. Neat and spotlessly clean, it was of moderate size and furnished sparsely with a broad, wooden framed bunk on the inside wall on which the bedding was meticulously arranged to provide a smooth, nautical appearance. A large desk and chair dominated the far corner, over which a lantern some two feet in height hung from a beam. A black stove was bolted to the floor at the center of the room. A small table, two chairs, and a large wooden sea chest completed the furnishings. Enraged at being confined like a prisoner, Amethyst stomped across the room to the precisely arranged desk and raised her hand to sweep the articles on its surface to the floor when she stopped abruptly. Her brief experience with Damien Straith had taught her one thing. Whatever her vengeful action, he would top her with one better, and she was in no position to put his anger to the test. She had to think . . . stop reacting, and think. It was imperative that she see William, for she knew instinctively should she not appear at the plantation, nothing would stop William from attempting to come to her. And if his condition was as bad as it appeared, he might do himself irreparable damage in the attempt.

"Oh, William . . . William . . ." Covering her eyes with her hand, Amethyst mumbled forlornly, "What shall I do?"

Time moved slowly within the cabin, but within the hour Amethyst had a plan. She would reverse her strategy and pretend to go along with Straith's plans and at the first opportunity would escape to Sheridan Plantation and ask for sanctuary until Straith left the island. It might prove an uncomfortable plan knowing the older Sheridan's dislike of her, but it would work ... if only she could convince Straith ...

The time was shortly past noon, judging from the position of the sun outside the portholes when Amethyst heard a heavy step outside the door. Quickly smoothing her hair and dress, she stood expectantly as the key turned in the lock, anxious to put her plan into effect, only to see as the door opened, the man whom Damien had greeted on deck as Barnes, bearing a tray of food.

His pleasant face creased in a small, apologetic smile, he said softly, "I've brought your lunch, ma'am."

Striving to hide her resounding disappointment, Amethyst said softly, "Where is Captain Straith? He's still aboard, isn't he? I mean, he wouldn't leave me here ..."

"Oh, he's still aboard, ma'am. It's just ... well, the captain doesn't usually bring trays."

"Neither does he usually hold women prisoner on his ship ... or does he?" Amethyst inquired, a new fear born in her mind.

"Oh, no, ma'am," the young man hastened to assure her, "The Captain doesn't usually have a need to hold women prisoners ... I mean ..." Stammering as his face flushed unexpectedly, he continued, "I mean ..."

Her expression wry, Amethyst said wearily, "That's alright, you needn't explain. Thank you very much for the food, sailor."

Turning away, Amethyst allowed the man his escape, her teeth clenched angrily at the sound of the key turning again in the lock. Her eyes filling with tears, Amethyst sat down to her lunch of sliced cold meat, cheese, and dark bread. She had to get out of here. When would he come back . . . ?

Walking slowly down the narrow passageway toward his cabin, Damien hesitated briefly in front of the door, the key in his hand. There was no sound from within but that meant little. The beautiful little virago inside must have formulated some sort of plan by now. Hell, he thought with utter disgust, what kind of a war was he conducting anyway? It had been a long, hard day, during which he had hardly been able to concentrate on the work at hand, so intense was his preoccupation with the girl/woman who awaited him in his cabin. What was wrong with him, anyway? Well, she had had long enough to cool off and he would attempt to reason with her. If she still wanted no part of him . . . he raised his shoulders with a resigned shrug, so be it. It had never been difficult to find a woman with which to pass time.

Inserting his key into the lock, Damien opened the door. To his disgust, his heart began a slow pounding in anticipation of his greeting. But there was none. The room was completely silent. Flicking his eyes around the room suspiciously, his gaze came to rest on the bunk and the slender figure reclining there. With a small smile, he moved to stand beside the bunk, watching as Amethyst's breast rose and fell in a slow, easy rhythm indicative of true sleep, his eyes slowly drinking in undisturbed her complete and devastating beauty. Unexpectedly, there was a thickness in his throat and he swallowed hard against the overwhelming tenderness welling up inside him that refuted his attitude of a few minutes previous. No, he would not let her go . . . Slowly reaching down, he touched the long dark hair streaming across the pillow, his hand tightening in the lengths as his eyes roamed the black fringe of lashes lying against her smooth cheeks, the small straight nose, and came to rest on her mouth, the lips parted in sleep to allow a peep of white straight teeth beneath. Her throat was creamy white and smooth, tempting him, the softness exposed in the demure square neckline of her dress only hinting at the beauty lying beneath. He had felt that softness beneath his lips last night . . . He ached to hold her, to touch her.

Within a few seconds he had slipped out of his shoes and lowering himself to the bunk beside her, was startled to find her instinctively fitting herself against his side. Fearful of waking her and disturbing the beautiful moment, Damien pressed light kisses against her hair, breathing deeply of her fragrance as his mouth moved against her temple, the dark fringes covering her glorious eyes, the small pointed chin, and finally, unable to resist a moment longer, covering her lips with his to drink deeply of the wealth within. Gently sliding his arms under and around her, he pulled her close against him, his heart pounding and throbbing in his ears as his mouth sank deeper and deeper into hers. He was uncertain of the exact moment of her awakening, but the gradual, instinctive response of her body slowly lessened, her body stiffening as his hand slid down the softness of her throat to caress her shoulder and the fullness of her breasts beneath. His hand had slipped over her ribcage, past her waist, and was slipping further down in a gentle, caressing motion as his mouth probed hers intimately, searching, demanding an answering need that was gradually being denied him. Suddenly she was fully awake and fighting his embrace, her body twisting and turning in a frightened rage as she fought to free herself. Her eyes snapping wide with fright, she twisted her mouth free of his as she said in a low, almost pleading tone, "You cannot do this. No, I won't let you. Let me free." But her struggles were to no avail when Damien quickly flipped himself over on top of her, pinning her to the bunk with the weight of his body, holding the flailing fists up above her head as he whispered softly, "Stop, Amethyst. Stop this hysteria. I won't hurt you, I promise you that." When her struggles continued he said again, "Stop and look at me. Listen to what I have to say, Amethyst. You needn't be afraid."

Catching her tearful gaze with his own, he held it fast until her struggles ceased, desperately trying to ignore the softness of her body beneath his and the wild longing to claim her completely as his own.

Lowering his voice to a whisper, Damien looked directly into her eyes, his lips grazing hers lightly as he spoke. "If I free your hands, will you promise to listen to me, Amethyst?" He could see the marks on her wrists where he held her fast, and had no desire to hurt her.

Unable to speak, Amethyst nodded her head lightly and swallowed hard, drawing his attention to her lips to stir anew his insatiable desire for her. Forcefully moving his glance away from her mouth, he said softly, "Amethyst, don't be afraid of me, darling. I won't force you into anything, you have my word on that. The idea of our being together is too new for you to accept right now, I realize that. But we were meant to be together, darling. Of that I could not be more sure. You just need more time . . ." Cupping her face with his hands, he covered her mouth with short, lingering kisses, until she turned her face aside to speak.

"No . . . no, Damien, please understand." Amethyst was frightened past guile and stammered uncertainly, "I couldn't ever . . . William and I . . . we . . . we're going to be married . . ."

His body suddenly rigid atop hers, Damien's hands slipped up to tighten in her hair, his face hardening as he said with threatening vehemence, "Never! William Sheridan will not have you! I tell you that now,

Amethyst, so you may get that thought completely out of your mind once and for all."

Again appearing to gain control of his emotions, Damien slipped to the bed beside her, drawing her toward him as he did. Kissing her lips lightly, he smiled gently. "I'm going to take you home now, Amethyst. Word has come that there will be a performance of Othello tonight in lieu of the aborted performance last night. You'll need some time to prepare."

Getting to his feet, Damien drew her up beside him. "Come," he urged softly, "Tillie will be worried."

Despite her expectations, the performance had gone extremely well. Having performed her various walk-on parts without a problem, Amethyst had left the stage at the conclusion of her intermission entertainment to thunderous applause. She had been a great success, and smiling gratefully at the enthusiastic audience, she raised her eyes briefly to the box at the side of the stage from which Damien stared inscrutably. He had had no reason to ruin her performance tonight . . . he was quite satisfied with the state of affairs between them at present. Suddenly realizing the turn her thoughts had taken, Amethyst took one last bow and walked off stage, her pulse hammering. She mustn't slip into the trap of believing that obeah nonsense. Damien himself had said it was poppycock.

"Well, no matter," she consoled herself with a small inner smile, "because tomorrow I will be with William and out of Damien's reach."

This time Amethyst did not sleep past daybreak. In all truth, she had hardly closed her eyes all night. Having made the decision while on shipboard to escape to William's plantation and claim sanctuary there, she had had all she could do to maintain an outward semblance of calm as she waited for the evening to end. Patiently enduring Damien's kisses and endearing words when he took her home after the performance, she had steeled herself against the wild response surging through her veins. He was a master at the art of making love, she was certain. So expert was he that the featherlight touch of his hands against her body was barely noticeable until the searing heat gradually building inside her stirred her desire for more; the increasing pressure of his broad frame seeming to envelop her completely in a cocoon of pulsating desire as it drew her in, closer, tighter; the hard maleness of him pressing against her in constant enticing promise as he seemed to swallow her completely in his embrace while making her yearn hungrily to be further consumed; the cool translucence of his light gray eyes burning with a strange, hypnotic light as they traveled her face with an unspoken yearning that tore viciously at her resistance, almost destroying it completely as he crushed her endlessly against him; his sensuous mouth working the final magic to complete the spell from which she had almost lost her desire to escape. The trembling of his massive frame as he released her at the door of her home had been the final test of her will, and had been matched only by her own trembling as she had closed the door behind her. She had to get away! There was no denying his power over her any longer, as well as there was no denying her waning resistance.

Dressing quickly as the first light of dawn creased the night sky, Amethyst snatched up the small bundle of clothing she had prepared the night before and walked quickly into the living room. Standing outside her door, Tillie urged quietly, "You ready now, missey? Best you get started before him wake and come looking fe you again."

Swallowing the small lump of fear Tillie's words had evoked, Amethyst responded in the same quiet tone,

"Yes, I'm ready, Tillie."

Handing her another small bundle, Tillie offered quietly, "This be some food fe the way, Amethyst. It be a long walk without breakfast."

Accepting the bundle, Amethyst tucked it into the larger one she carried and turned back to Tillie's concerned expression. "Don't worry about me, Tillie." Doing her best to smile despite the peculiar stiffness of her face, Amethyst continued lightly, "I'll be fine when I'm with William again. Just make sure you get word to me when Captain Straith has left port so I may return. I've told Mr. Douglass that I'll not be performing for a while, but I don't want to wait too long. It would not do to come back and find myself replaced in the company."

Suddenly stepping forward, Amethyst threw her arms around the motherly mulatto and laughed as the woman hugged her tightly in return. "Don't worry, Tillie. I've walked this road so many times I could walk it with my eyes closed. I'll be at the plantation well before noon and I'll try to send word with Quaco when everything is settled."

Her dark eyes bright, Tillie said in a low voice, "Tillie not be worried anymore, Amethyst, but best be going now before it gets any lighter."

Nodding her head, Amethyst walked to the door, and was moving quickly down the street within a few minutes, stopping only a moment as she turned the corner to wave a last farewell to the woman who watched from the doorway.

The rising sun brought the heat of day to the familiar road Amethyst traveled. She had not walked the distance to Sheridan Plantation in almost a year, since William had taken to bringing her supplies to town as an excuse to visit. She had almost forgotten the intensity of the sun as it beat on her uncovered head, the sensation of perspiration trailing down her spine as she walked, and the gritty taste of dust in her mouth. "And," she muttered softly as she stopped to shake out her shoe, "I had forgotten these nasty pebbles." Slipping her shoe back on her foot, Amethyst adjusted the bundle on her arm and continued on the road, her heart skipping a beat as the first glimpse of Sheridan Plantation came into view. As confident as she had tried to appear for Tillie's sake, she was uncertain about her reception at the great house. In all the years of her association, she had never entered the house itself, her visits confined to the outhouses in the rear where the cooking was done and the buttery was located. Despite his acceptance of her needed contribution to his household stores, William Sheridan, Sr. had always treated her courteously, but in a manner that left no doubt in her mind that he considered her a business acquaintance only. But today she would not go to the plantation out-houses. She intended approaching the great house by the front door, as disheveled and dusty as she was. She was not a servant and was coming to visit the son of the master of the house, and that fact alone afforded her the dignity she needed to approach as a guest. Her true trepidation lay, however, in her plans for the next few weeks. Was she not desperate, she would not put herself at such disadvantage as to ask sanctuary that would be extended at best grudgingly, but she had no recourse. And there was William . . . she was certain he was suffering countless agonies at his ignorance of her fate, and she did not wish to be the reason for his coming to any further harm.

Her mind thus set in the direction she was to take, Amethyst passed by the path to the buttery with her head held high, and continued on the grand roadway that approached the front door of Sheridan Plantation.

Making a last simple adjustment to her hair by lifting the tendrils stuck to her slender neck with perspiration and smoothing back the straying wisps that curled at her hairline, Amethyst lifted the door knocker and rapped, she hoped with authority. Dismissing the startled expression of the well dressed slave that answered the summons with a raising of her brow and as haughty an expression as she could manage, Amethyst stated firmly, "I'm here to see Master William, Jr. Please tell him Amethyst Greer is calling."

Nodding uncertainly, the old Negro showed only a moment's more hesitation before stepping back to allow her entrance. Leaving her standing in the hallway, he progressed up the elegantly curved staircase to the second floor. Within a few moments he had disappeared around the corner of the hall and utter silence reigned in the household until a familiar voice shouted joyfully, "Amethyst! Amethyst! Come up here right now, or I will get out of this bed and come down!"

The relieved tears springing to her eyes were silent testimony to the secret fear she had nourished during her long walk to Sheridan Plantation, and overjoyed at William's obvious impatience to see her, she started up the curving staircase hesitantly. Within a few seconds, the slave appeared at the top of the stairs, and preceded her down the hallway to William's room.

Her eyes moving quickly past those standing at bedside, Amethyst's glance moved directly to William. His pale face shining with delight, he held his arms out to her, urging softly, "Quickly, Amethyst, come quickly or I shall get up and come to you."

Her eyes filled with emotion, Amethyst made a small gulping sound deep in her throat as she rushed toward the great four-poster and into his waiting arms. Held tight against his chest, Amethyst was almost off her feet as William continued to hold her pressed against him, murmuring softly in her ear, oblivious to those surrounding them, "Amethyst, darling, thank the Lord you are here. I was so worried when I regained consciousness yesterday and found myself at home and realized I had abandoned you again to that madman. You are alright, aren't you, darling?"

Allowing her to pull away just enough to search her face, his deep mahogany eyes perused her expression fearfully, awaiting her response. Nodding her head with a brilliant smile stimulated by his obvious concern, Amethyst said softly, "I'm fine, William. My greatest fear was for you."

Glancing to the gray-haired gentleman standing at the bedside, William's response was cautious. "Dr. Martens assures me I will be quite well within a week, provided I stay in bed and rest until the headaches and dizziness pass. I was certain the treatment would be past endurance until I heard your voice, darling, but now that you are here to stay with me, my recuperation will be a pleasant idyll. Promise me you will not leave until I am well enough to accompany you to town, Amethyst." His dark eyes intense, William urged again, "Promise me you will not leave, darling . . ."

Grateful that William's concern had spared her the discomfort of asking refuge, Amethyst nodded silently, adding a few seconds later, "I will be happy to stay until you are well, William."

"Miss Greer," a thin nasal voice from behind drew Amethyst's attention to Dr. Martens's stooped figure, "you do understand that William is to have no excitement while he is recuperating. He is to keep his emotions at a very low level and must not have any undue stimulation."

His direct stare and the slight raising of his brow as he stressed "undue stimulation" brought a hot flush of color to Amethyst's face. Drawing herself out of William's arms, she stammered quickly, "I understand perfectly, doctor. You need not worry . . . I certainly should not . . . I do not intend to 'stimulate' William in any way!"

Laughing softly at her obvious embarrassment, William said lightly, "Then I'm afraid I shall have to keep my eyes closed for the duration of my confinement, Amethyst, because I'm afraid just to look at you stimulates me beyond measure."

"William!" The quick ejaculation by the slender gray-haired woman at bedside brought a hearty laugh from William, causing him to clutch his head suddenly as he winced with pain.

"Perhaps, Mother," William said softly as he slowly opened his eyes, "perhaps it would be best if I had a little quiet for a while. I would like to rest and you may be assured that I will take Dr. Martens's advice very seriously." Slowly sliding a meaningful glance toward Amethyst, he continued, "I have an all-consuming desire to be on my feet again."

"Certainly, dear," Sylvia Sheridan responded lightly, bestowing a loving glance on her only child just seconds before she quietly began herding those at bedside out the door. When she touched Amethyst's arm, William protested softly.

"I want Amethyst to stay, Mother. I will be better able to relax knowing she is here beside me."

Until that moment, William Sr. had chosen not to speak, his dark expression adequately conveying his distaste for the situation, but his son's request brought an instantaneous protest from his lips. "Certainly you cannot ask us to leave this woman here with you unchaperoned in your bedroom, William!" Shooting a quick glance toward Amethyst, he continued softly, "Think of Miss Greer's reputation, son."

"Father," William's voice was weakening, but his purpose was firm, "if you truly wish to comply with Dr. Martens's instructions, you will allow Amethyst to stay, and the hell with convention! I am, after all, Father, temporarily incapacitated."

Shooting her son a worried glance, Sylvia Sheridan said quietly, "William, please, let the girl stay."

His face reddening slightly with frustration, William Sr. finally raised his shoulders in helpless assent before turning on his heel and leaving the room, followed by his wife. Following closely behind, Dr. Martens paused briefly at the door as his glance moved between the two remaining. Raising his finger, he shook it warningly in William's direction, his wrinkled countenance adamant. "Remember what I said, William, no stimulation!"

Turning, he left the room, his departure bringing subdued laughter from the man in bed. Extending his arms in her direction, William said softly, "Come here, darling. I am truly fatigued, but I want to feel you in my arms before I sleep."

Moving quickly into his outstretched arms, Amethyst smiled at the soft groan of contentment in her ear as William quickly enclosed her in his embrace. "Now I will be truly able to rest for the first time in two days," he whispered against her hair as he pressed her tight against him. Within a few minutes his breathing was deep and regular, and Amethyst drew herself carefully from his arms. Kissing him lightly on the mouth, she whispered into his unhearing ear, "As will I, darling, as will I . . ."

Damien strode quickly down the street, his eyes intent on the small frame house, his mind intent on thoughts of the beautiful girl/woman inside who drew him so relentlessly to her. It was barely noon, but he had been unable to concentrate on his calculations for the visions of luminous purple eyes that invaded his thoughts. She was with him in everything he did, every place he turned until he was no longer able to think for the ache that had built inside him. He snickered lightly. Amethyst spoke of his reputed powers of obeah. That was a joke. He was the one who was truly possessed ... by a woman who professed she wanted nothing to do with him ... who claimed she loved another man. But she had not protested last night. He was certain had he pressed her a little further, had he told the driver to drive to his ship rather than her house, the evening would have had a far different conclusion. But he didn't want it that way. He wanted Amethyst to come to him freely, not in a moment of passion that might be regretted with the first light of morning. No, what he felt for her was too special, too beautiful ...

Mounting the steps in two quick strides, Damien pushed open the door, still unwilling to submit to a request for entrance. Slow footsteps from the kitchen brought Tillie to the doorway of the room, her strange expression causing a slight chill of apprehension to rush down his spine.

"Where is Amethyst, Tillie?" His voice was gruff, far gruffer than he had intended, but the woman was acting peculiarly.

"Amethyst not be here, Captain Straith."

"Where is she?" Walking quickly to the bedroom, he pushed open the door without waiting for a response. Finding it empty, he strode toward the kitchen, moving Tillie roughly aside as he surveyed the empty room. In a few quick steps he had pushed open the door to Tillie's room to find it also empty. Turning, he faced Tillie, his breathing heavy as tension knotted his huge hands into fists.

"I said, where is she, Tillie? Where did she go?"

"Gone, Captain. Amethyst gone where him be safe from you. Him free of you spell. Him not gowan ..."

Taking her roughly by the shoulders, Damien shook the woman hard, demanding in a voice deep with anger,

"Tell me where she's gone. Tell me now!"

"Amethyst safe at Sheridan Plantation now. Mr. Sheridan gowan take care of him . . . not gowan let you take him away."

His face blanching white under his tan, Damien muttered through clenched teeth, "When did she leave, Tillie? Tell me!"

"Him left at dawn. Him safe now."

Turning quickly on his heel, Damien left the house, walking back down the street in a quick stride that was almost a run. Within minutes he had rented a horse and was on his way out of town, urging the willing animal into a fast gallop as soon as he hit the open road. But he saw no one with the exception of a curious tinker and a few slaves returning home. Still he continued to press on, urging the horse to an even faster pace in the hope that Amethyst had not yet reached her destination. Finally reaching Sheridan land, he reined the horse to a slower gait. His eyes moving across the landscape hopefully, his heart pounding at each female figure he saw in the distance, he experienced with each disappointment deeper and truer frustration. Maybe Tillie had lied. Perhaps Amethyst was still in Kingston, possibly at the theater at this very moment! No, Tillie was too frightened of him to chance his displeasure. Amethyst had indeed headed for Sheridan Plantation as she had declared so vehemently only yesterday. But that was before—before last night when she could have been his, but for his reluctance to press her. Urging his animal slowly forward, Damien finally came to the main drive of Sheridan Plantation, his throat tight with despair. She had left . . . she was gone . . . there was no way he could get her back.

Her hand sliding lightly along the graceful molded handrail, Amethyst descended the staircase. She had been at Sheridan Plantation for three days and had yet to see the great house in its entirety. Her eyes scanning the first floor as she approached, she had to admit that it was indeed a beautiful home. Most impressive were the mahogany floors, bare except for an occasional reed mat, polished to a brilliant sheen that reflected almost as clearly as a mirror the graceful furnishings resting upon it. The rich mahogany glow was repeated in the paneling that ran to cornice height, covering all the walls and extending as far as the spacious verandas onto which all the rooms on the first floor emptied. Walking cautiously to the rear of the house in her search for a cool drink for William, she was amazed to see that although the house consisted of two stories above ground, on the north side, cleverly planned to take full advantage of the land contours, the house had a third lower ground floor on the south. As she walked out the rear toward the out-houses behind the house, a small gasp escaped her lips at the infinite beauty spread out before her. Set upon a rise of a few hundred feet above the cane fields, the rear commanded a spectacular view of the master's holdings, extending almost as far as the eye could see. She also realized that although it was not visible from her position, a few miles to the west lay the remainder of the estate buildings; a factory for refining the cane into sugar, and a lime kiln.

Suddenly understanding for the first time the extreme sense of pride the Sheridans had for their land, Amethyst took a deep, awe-filled breath and moved quickly toward the kitchen.

Within minutes Amethyst was quickly ascending the same staircase toward William's room, a small smile crossing her face as she heard William's voice.

"Is that finally you, Amethyst?" Hesitating a brief second, he repeated, "Is that you returning, Amethyst?"

Shaking her head as she walked through the doorway,

Amethyst said sternly, "What do you mean, 'finally returning'? I've barely been gone five minutes. You did say you wanted a cool drink, did you not?"

"Yes." Smiling as she approached the bed, William continued softly, "but I would rather someone else had gone to get it."

Taking the glass from her hand, he quickly emptied its contents and placing it on the night table, extended his arms toward her. "Come here, Amethyst." William's voice was a low purr that set Amethyst to laughing as she shook her head firmly. There was a definite gleam in his eye as he lay back against the pillows, his dark wavy hair spilling onto his forehead boyishly.

"Oh, no, William. I think are you feeling far too well today for your own good. I have the feeling you will overdo at the slightest opportunity, and you must remember. Dr. Martens said, 'no stimulation'!"

"Come here right now, Amethyst," William repeated firmly, "or I will far overdo by becoming frustrated and angry. You know I am to be pampered for a few days more."

Still laughing at his self-serving reasoning, Amethyst walked closer to the bed and was immediately taken into a tight embrace that all but carried her onto the bed beside him.

Squirming uncomfortably, Amethyst protested in a soft voice, "William, please, if anyone should walk in now, it would be a complete scandal, and you know very well the opinion your family already has of me."

His face suddenly sober as his dark eyes looked into hers, William inquired quickly, "Has anyone been discourteous to you since your arrival, Amethyst? If so, please tell me. I will set the matter straight."

Caressing his cheek with the palm of her hand, Amethyst interrupted his building anger. "No, William. Everyone has been quite hospitable, the little I've seen of them. You know I spend most of the day with you and take all my meals with you in this room. There has been very little opportunity for a clash of personalities."

"Then why did you say . . ."

"You really do not believe that opinions of long standing will be changed by my brief visit here, do you?"

"This need not be a brief visit, Amethyst."

Looking sincerely into William's sober face, Amethyst responded quietly, "I appreciate your extended hospitality much more than you realize, William."

As yet Amethyst had not considered it wise to advise William of the situation with Captain Straith, realizing it would serve only to inflame his anger and possibly worsen his condition. When he was fully recovered she planned to explain her predicament and her need for sanctuary.

"You could stay on, you know, Amethyst . . ."

Suspecting him of reading her thoughts, Amethyst pulled back in astonishment, only to have William pull her closer within the circle of his embrace. His expression intent, he lowered his mouth to cover hers, emitting a low groan as he suddenly tightened his embrace, increasing the pressure of his kiss. Basking in the warmth that always pervaded her senses with William's touch, Amethyst allowed the kiss to deepen until the frantic pounding of his heart against her breast stirred her guilt. Gently extricating herself from his embrace, she covered his lips with her hand as he sought to kiss her again, whispering softly as she did, "Please, William, there will be time for this later, when you are completely well."

Noting he had started to pale, Amethyst pushed him gently back against the pillows, imploring as she did, "Please, don't excite yourself, William. If my presence proves an impediment to your recuperation, I will have to leave."

"No! Don't leave, Amethyst. That is exactly the point I was trying to make, darling." Taking her hand, he turned her palm to his lips and kissed it lightly. "I want you to stay here, Amethyst. We can be married at the end of the week, when I am feeling better."

"What! William, you can't be serious!"

"Alright, within two weeks if you need the time and we wish to be absolutely certain I will be completely recovered. What is the point of waiting, darling? You know I love you . . . I have for a long time . . . and once you are my wife you will no longer be prey to the advances of madmen like Damien Straith."

"William . . ."

Reaching out to snatch her against him again, William attempted to press another kiss against her lips, mumbling softly as he did, "Amethyst, darling . . ."

The sound of an opening door and Sylvia Sheridan's shocked gasp did not deter William from his purpose as he continued softly, "Tell me you will consider staying, darling."

"Really, Miss Greer," a haughty voice from behind interrupted angrily, "I should think you would have a better sense of propriety than to be found in such a compromising position . . ."

Finally relinquishing his hold so Amethyst might pull herself to her feet, William still retained his grip on her hand as he turned to direct his next words to his mother.

"I'm afraid the lack of propriety is entirely my fault, Mother. I was trying to convince Amethyst to remain here so we might be married as soon as I am well."

Sylvia Sheridan's short intake of breath as he concluded his statement speaking far more clearly than words, Amethyst lowered her head, diverting her gaze from William's angry expression.

"I tell you now, Mother," William continued softly, his voice firm despite the signs of weakness beginning to show on his face in his loss of color and the small beads of perspiration that had formed on his forehead and upper lip. "I intend to press this issue with Amethyst until she agrees to marry me."

"I think we should discuss this some other time, William," Amethyst suggested quietly, "when you are feeling better. There is no necessity for haste."

"The necessity is that you are here now, Amethyst, and I do not want you to leave. Will you at least give me your word you will not leave until we have this settled between us?" His eyes beginning to droop with weariness, William urged again, "Do I have your word, Amethyst?"

Shooting a quick, furtive glance to the woman in the doorway who stared at her son helplessly, Amethyst said quietly, "You have my word, William. Now, will you please rest?"

"Only if you will pull your chair near the bed and sit beside me while I sleep." Looking up, he smiled a small, apologetic smile. "I am a selfish, inconsiderate beast, am I not, Amethyst?"

Pulling her chair close to the bed, Amethyst sat down and taking his hand, kissed the knuckles lightly, mumbling for his ears alone with a small smile, "Yes, you are, William, a darling, inconsiderate beast."

Running his hand through his thick tawny hair, Damien's brows knit into a dark frown as he stared unseeingly at the column of figures in the ledger. Abruptly throwing his pen against the page, he leaned back in his desk chair with a frustrated groan, finally jumping to his feet as a sense of utter despair overwhelmed him. What was wrong with him? He was no longer capable of adding a simple column of figures, so poor was his concentration. What had ever possessed him to come to Jamaica in the first place? Unbidden, the answer flashed before his eyes in the vision of the dark-haired, waif-like seductress that had stolen his peace of mind. Damn her! What was she doing at Sheridan Plantation anyway? She had been there almost two weeks. In less than two weeks he would be leaving Kingston, not to return for several months. Even then, he would probably not return legally. His preliminary figures showed that this trip would not be very profitable to him or his men and he had a business to run. But he could not seem to concentrate on business these past two weeks. Completely ignoring his old haunts he had begun to hang around the theater, hoping for some news of Amethyst, but none was forthcoming. All he had managed to do was to give that sultry little flirt Sally Warren the wrong impression by his rash of questions and his frequent appearances at the theater. As if that little baggage compared to his Amethyst. *His* Amethyst! He still could not think of her any other way, even though right now she was probably in the arms of that pampered plantation pup! Rumor had it that he wanted to marry Amethyst, but his parents disapproved. She wouldn't marry him. He was certain . . . almost certain . . . that the response he had felt to his lovemaking had not been feigned. He was too experienced to be fooled by acting . . . or was he? Suddenly remembering the warmth of her small body against his, the taste of her mouth . . . the scent of her breath upon his cheek, a rage of frustration swept over him. No! She would not marry Sheridan. She would return to Kingston and when she did, he would be waiting. . . .

Slowly pulling herself out of the downy mattress on the large four-postered bed she had occupied since her arrival at Sheridan Plantation, Amethyst walked to the window and gazed out thoughtfully. Situated at the rear of the house, her room overlooked the cane fields where work gangs already labored in the early morning sun. Turning around, she surveyed her temporary room casually. The room was moderately sized, really quite ample for her needs, with plastered walls painted a pale yellow and a floor boarded in rich mahogany that gleamed with true depth of beauty. The bed and the other well-carved furniture in the room were also constructed from the mahogany that was so abundant on the island, and gleamed with the same rich hue. Walking to the large wardrobe that dominated the corner of the room, Amethyst opened the doors, smiling at the ridiculous picture of two skirts and two blouses hanging so forlornly within its vast expanse. She quickly removed the blue skirt and one of the alternate white blouses which disappeared each night when she took it off to reappear mysteriously the next morning, freshly laundered. Laying them on the bed, she moved to the washstand to commence her daily ablutions. She was up a bit early this morning, but she wanted an opportunity to speak to William alone before breakfast.

A small frown creasing her brow, she recalled several days previous when she had donned her blue skirt for the first time since arriving at the great house. Noticing a small bulge in the skirt, she had reached into the concealed emergency pocket her mother had insisted she sew into her skirts, and drawn out the grisly charm Tillie had tried to force on her on so many occasions. Suddenly remembering Tillie's placid expression when she left as she had stated solemnly, "Tillie not be worried anymore, Amethyst," she was irritated beyond sizeable proportion at the well-meaning woman's interference. She considered her escape from Damien Straith a result of her own ingenuity and her present satisfactory, if somewhat uncertain position in William's household, a result of William's concern and generosity. She did not wish to put the credit for her improved circumstances on the powers of black magic. Also, during her short stay she had come to lay the blame for her mishandling of the whole affair with Damien Straith on the hysteria his imposing figure seemed to stir within her. To accept the charm would acknowledge his powers which she had recently refuted in her own mind. With a deep sense of purpose Amethyst had dressed and walked to the kitchen on the pretext of visiting Delsea that morning, and had thrown the charm unseen into the fire. Turning back, she had steadfastly ignored the slight chill of apprehension that had slipped down her spine and had returned to the house and William's room.

Now giving a last-minute check to her appearance, Amethyst followed her daily routine since arriving at the great house and walked down the hallway to knock on William's door. He had not recuperated from the persistent headaches and weakness as quickly as the doctor had expected, but in the last few days had made it a point to put on his robe and come down to breakfast with the family. On those occasions Amethyst assisted Amos in helping him down the stairs and sat on his right at the table with an honest attempt at being as unobtrusive as possible. The senior Sheridan's resentment of her presence was apparent from the black scowls he sent in her direction, as was his son's obvious irritation with his father's attitude. Sylvia Sheridan's nervous tittering through the tense meals did nothing to abate the growing hostility and in fact had the effect of rubbing tattered nerves raw. But William was adamant, speaking frequently of their forthcoming marriage, directing his comments pointedly to his stiff-faced parents, and Amethyst's heart went out to him. She had not actually agreed to the marriage, but each passing day only convinced her more of her love for William.

Cecily Hargrove had come to visit several times during William's convalescence. The hearty reception afforded her by William's parents was in such sharp contrast to the manner in which they tolerated Amethyst's presence, that William's pale face had flushed with embarrassment.

Completely frustrated by the perpetual dilemma her life seemed suddenly to have become, Amethyst knocked again, realizing William might still be asleep, but hoping to gently dissuade him from the marriage he had tentatively set for the following week. When there was still no response, Amethyst listened intently, her sharp ears detecting a low moan from the other side of the doorway.

Slowly opening the door, Amethyst saw William was still abed. He seemed to have taken no notice of her entrance and simply turned his head away with another small moan. Fear closing her throat, Amethyst rushed to his side, her voice hoarse as she said urgently, "William, what's wrong? Are you in pain?"

The face William turned back to her was flushed a bright red, the eyes glazed as he stammered thickly, "Amethyst . . . is that you? Damn, why is it so hot? Bring me a drink, will you?"

His dark hair was damp with perspiration, his nightshirt adhering to his chest like a second skin. Reaching out, Amethyst touched his forehead, gasping at the searing heat under her hand. Panic momentarily dulling her senses, she stared at William's flushed face, the knot of fear in her stomach tightening painfully as William began to mumble incoherently, turning his face away to stare at some imagined figure at the other side of the room. Suddenly spurred into action, Amethyst ran out of the room and across the hall to pound heavily on the master bedroom door.

"Damn! What is it? Amos, is that you? Are you crazy, man?" a deep voice bellowed irritably from the other side.

"No, it's Amethyst! Quickly, Mr. Sheridan, you must come! William is ill! I don't know what's wrong with him!"

Within a few seconds the door jerked open to reveal the senior Sheridan in his stockinged feet, hurriedly stuffing his shirt into his britches. His anxiety apparent, he began walking toward William's room. "William is sick, you say?" he mumbled under his breath, not pausing to hear her response as he pushed open the door to his son's room. With a few long strides he was at bedside, his hand moving to touch his son's forehead. His face blanched white with fear.

"My God, he has the fever!" he muttered desperately before turning on his heel and making for the door. He was shouting for the servants to get the doctor when William began retching violently.

Sitting quietly in the corner of William's room, Amethyst listened as Dr. Martens's voice lightly penetrated the mantle of exhaustion that had settled over her. She had been sitting with William day and night for three days as he continued to slip deeper and deeper under the influence of the fever that was sweeping Sheridan Plantation. Six slaves had already died, their bodies hurriedly buried to prevent contagion, and eighteen more lay twitching in their own excrement while the majority of the other slaves refused to tend them for fear of contamination. Low and mournful, the burial chants continued unceasingly, drumming into her brain, as did the soft pleas sung to Pucku to free them from the evil spell cast upon them. She herself could hardly think now, could hardly concentrate on the low conversation progressing between Dr. Martens and William's worried father. William had been vomiting blood for a whole day, his skin turned a pasty yellow color as he twisted and turned in the throes of the fever that appeared to be consuming him. He was incoherent most of the time, struggling out of his dark nether-world for only brief periods when he called her name, demanding that she come to his side when she had indeed never left it.

Dr. Martens was saying that William was not doing well. The course of his sickness was following closely that of the slaves that had already died, and Dr. Martens was extremely worried. Amethyst had only recently become aware, isolated in the great house as she was, that the fever had started in the slaves' quarters shortly after her arrival and had slowly progressed to the point at which it now stood. Only one other person at the great house had been stricken, a young house slave by the name of Juba, but she had been quickly removed to the slaves' quarters to pass the following stages of the disease in isolation.

"Amethyst! Come here! Where are you?"

The hoarse call from the bed raised Amethyst to her feet in such haste that she was momentarily lightheaded. Rushing to his side, she grasped the hand reaching out to her, bending forward to listen to William's fevered ramblings.

"Remember, Amethyst, you must not let them anger you. It is their ignorance that sustains their prejudice against you. You will see, they will change their mi . . . Mother!" Turning his head, William exclaimed loudly, beginning to laugh wildly as he pointed to a spot at the other side of the room. "Since when do you allow Nero in the house? Say, do you miss me, boy? Well, I will be down to ride you again soon. Father! Have Amos take him out of here. There is a stench in this room . . ." Turning back to Amethyst, William's expression was suddenly fervent as he pulled her hand to his lips, kissing it lightly. "You needn't worry, Amethyst. I won't have that thoughtless blonde stick, Cecily Hargrove, no matter what my parents say. I love you, Amethyst . . . she . . ."

Suddenly doubling up with pain, William turned his

head from her, mumbling as he did, "I'm sick, Amethyst . . . I'm sick . . ." The retching began again while Amethyst grabbed a basin, holding it with a sense of horror as William again filled it repeatedly with the dread black vomit.

It was the middle of the fourth night of William's sickness when Amethyst could no longer ignore the waves of guilt assailing her. She no longer doubted Damien Straith's powers of obeah, nor did she doubt that she was the cause of the disaster that had struck Sheridan Plantation. Twenty-four more slaves had come down with the disease . . . there had been six more deaths . . . William was dying . . . Oh, God . . . William was dying! How much longer could his body heave up those huge quantities of blood without expiring? Dr. Martens was helpless against the disease, his liberal doses of laudanum either being vomited up or doing little else but slightly relieving the wracking pain that tore at William's body.

Amethyst had found out that the sickness had hit the plantation almost to the day that she had burned the shriveled fowl's foot in Delsea's fire. If she but had the opportunity now, she would gladly put her hand into that same fire to retrieve the charm and sustain William's life, but it was useless to even think of it, now. It was too late.

Choking sounds from William's bed snapped up her head to see Sylvia Sheridan put the basin under her son's head as he gasped and sputtered up more of his life's blood.

But perhaps it was not too late! Glancing toward the window, Amethyst was certain she could see the darkness of night beginning to fade. It would be daybreak in a few hours . . . she would try . . . she would at least try . . .

Rising from her chair, Amethyst walked quietly toward the bed to stand staring wordlessly at William's momentarily peaceful face. Reaching out her hand, she smoothed the hair from his forehead, only too aware of the raging heat beneath her fingers. Bending, she pressed a light kiss against his cheek before turning to walk toward the door.

"Amethyst," Sylvia's voice was weary, "where are you going? William may awaken and look for you."

Without turning back, Amethyst reached for the door knob. "I'm going to my room."

Slipping noiselessly into her room a few minutes later, Amethyst walked directly to her washstand mirror and assessed her appearance, the reflection looking back at her another blow to her weakening spirit. "I look terrible," she mumbled desperately, raising her hand to cover her eyes for a few brief seconds of escape. The heavy humidity of the night was oppressive, causing her hair to cling wetly to her scalp, and hang from the neck down in a mass of tangled snarls. She was pale . . . she had had no sleep for days, and her face was gaunt, for she had lost her appetite and had been unable to eat since William was stricken. Oh, well, she would have to do the best she could, if only it was not too late.

Determined to make herself as presentable as possible, Amethyst slipped into the hall and walking silently down the staircase to the first floor, followed the winding hallway to the ground floor. Slipping out the back door, she made her way to the well. Drawing up the bucket, she lowered her hair into the water until it was saturated, and taking the bar of soap she had slipped into her pocket, worked up a good lather. Satisfied at last that the soap had lifted the grime of her recent ordeal, she carefully lifted the bucket and bending over to escape as much of the water draining off her hair as possible, cautiously dumped the cold water over her sudsy head. The water was terribly cold, sending a deep chill over her perspired body, but her hair was clean. Wrapping her dripping hair in the cloth she had carried from the house, she carefully made her way back to the house and to her room. Seated exhaustedly on the chair by her bed, she rubbed her hair dry. Dragging herself wearily to the washstand, she combed it carefully, grateful to see the natural sheen had returned, and tying it to the back of her head temporarily, she stripped to the skin and began to wash fastidiously. Within the hour she was dressed again, this time in her brown skirt and fresh white blouse. Carefully rolling her soiled clothes into a small bundle, she slipped her comb and brush inside, and surveyed the room critically. To the best of her recollection, it looked exactly as it had the day she had entered it, and satisfied that she had removed all trace of her presence, Amethyst slipped quietly out the door and down the hallway past William's room. Moving stealthily, she walked down the grand staircase and careful not to make a sound, out the front door. The first morning light had not quite penetrated the black sky of night, and grateful for the cover of darkness, she moved down the grand roadway and turned onto the road toward Kingston.

Glancing up into the morning sky, Amethyst noted absentmindedly that only the faintest trace of wispy clouds broke the endless expanse of brilliant blue. That probably accounted for the excessive heat of the day, and judging from the position of the sun, it was well into morning. Drawing her attention back to the dusty road ahead of her, Amethyst sighed, but maintained her forward pace. Her back ached fiercely and she was far more weary than she had expected. A wave of nausea rolled over her as the road stretched out in an endless wavering ribbon through the fields of growing cane. But tightening her hold on the small bundle in her arms that had seemed to gain incredible weight since the inception of her journey, she continued forward. She was extremely thirsty, and would have to look for a clear stream near town in order to drink and refresh herself. She did not wish to reach Kingston looking as bedraggled as she felt.

Within the hour Amethyst was walking through the streets of Kingston, her destination not the small frame house that had been her home for seven years, but the docks of Kingston Harbor. As she had planned, she had stopped outside Kingston at a small stream, drinking her fill and carefully refreshing her appearance, taking the time to withdraw her brush from her bundle and sweep her hair neatly off her face to secure the front two locks at the back of her head with a white ribbon. Careful to brush off the dust of her journey, she had entered town and could presently see the tall masts of the *Sally* as she approached the dock. Strange how they seemed to waver in the light of the brilliant sun, as did the very ground on which she walked. For a moment she staggered. Pausing to clear her mind, she ignored the throbbing pain in her head that had gradually increased over the past hour until she was forced to squint in order to ascertain the blurring figures walking around her. But she could not mistake the *Sally*. She was a beautiful ship, far too regal a vessel for her captain. She approached the gangplank with an inner trepidation that set her to shaking, and furious with her own fear, Amethyst increased her pace. The docks were dreadfully noisy today . . . what was that thunderous humming sound? If only it wasn't so very hot—she was certain her blouse was stained with perspiration. If only she could manage to put her feet down in the exact spot she desired, instead of weaving an uncertain path toward the gangplank. Well, it was not much further. Strange, she had not remembered the gangplank to be so steep, so difficult to climb.

Finally standing on deck, she was amazed to find it moving beneath her feet as if the ship were at sea, and grasping the rail for support, she turned her attention to the men on deck. Having unexpected difficulty in focusing her eyes, Amethyst's glance moved slowly across the three men on deck. No, none of them was Captain Straith. She opened her mouth to ask his whereabouts, but found herself strangely unable to form words past the incredible dryness in her throat. Watching the direction of the men's glances moving toward the cabin stairs, Amethyst turned to see a tall figure step onto the deck. His face was unclear, but the blond hair gleaming in the sunlight and the broad stature and erect carriage were unmistakable. Approaching him hesitantly, Amethyst noted that the heaving deck was not a problem for him as he stood, unshakable and unmoving, staring in her direction. Amethyst stumbled, grasping a rope for support, and suddenly Damien Straith was beside her, his strong arm supporting her against the swaying that made her almost unable to stay on her feet. His face was still blurred, but the penetrating translucence of his eyes came through the haze that seemed suddenly to surround her. Although his lips were close to her ear, his voice seemed to come from a distance as he said in a low voice, "Amethyst, what's wrong?"

Struggling to clear her throat of the terrible dryness that stole her voice, she said hoarsely, "I have returned, Damien. Your obeah is too strong for me to fight. You have won . . ."

But he was slipping away from her, his broad tanned face moving away in an ever-closing spiral of blackness that removed all light from her vision . . . And then he was gone.

Damien ascended the steps to the deck slowly. He had had enough of figures and calculations for the day, and the way he felt right now, he had had enough of them for the rest of his life. He had always enjoyed the bookeeping aspect of his voyages before, but he seemed to get no pleasure at all from any part of this voyage. He came eye level with the deck, his eyes becoming fixed on the three men who stood motionless, staring toward the gangplank. Hell! All he needed now was to have his crew get lazy on him. This was the last straw! Stepping onto the deck, Damien turned his eyes in the direction their glances followed, his heart leaping in his chest as they touched on Amethyst, the indescribable joy surging through him turning abruptly to apprehension. Something was wrong. She was swaying visibly, suddenly grasping for support at a rope hanging lankly from the mast. Within moments he was at her side, holding her in his arms, stunned at the heat emanating from her small body. Her face was flushed, her eyes glazed. She seemed to be having trouble speaking.

"Amethyst, what's wrong?" He pulled her tight against him as he strained to hear her barely audible whisper.

"I have returned, Damien. Your obeah is too strong for me to fight. You have won."

Gradually fighting her way back from the blackness that had swelled over her, Amethyst struggled to open her eyes. Her head was throbbing with a vicious ache, her back so full of pain that she hardly dared move, but William was so ill. She could not waste a moment's time. Steadfastly battling the weight of her heavy eyelids, she finally forced them open to gaze dully around her. The surroundings were familiar. She was in her own room, and Tillie was beside her bed, a worried expression marring the beauty of her ageless features. She opened her mouth to give the concerned mulatto a word of comfort, but was startled to find her voice a hoarse croak as she attempted to speak. She was still attempting to find her voice when Tillie was moved firmly from her bedside as a deep voice ordered, "Tillie, find out why the doctor is so long in coming. I sent one of my men for him almost an hour ago. You are more familiar with these people. Perhaps you will be able to locate him more quickly. Hurry now!"

And then Tillie was out of her line of vision, taking with her the wordless consolation of her presence. Alone with the man whose broad frame crouched over her bed as he gazed searchingly into her face, Amethyst swallowed hard and again attempted to speak. Finally managing a small whisper she began hesitantly.

"Captain... Damien... William is ill... he is dying... you must allow him to get well... please..."

There was a moment's hesitation before Damien responded in a strangely tight voice, "Don't excite yourself, Amethyst. Just lie quietly. The doctor will be here soon."

"But you don't understand," she continued, her voice cracking again as she gripped his hand in a frantic gesture. "There is no time to waste. You must rescind your obeah now or it will be too late. William will die!"

"Amethyst," covering her clutching hand with his own, Damien said quietly, "there is nothing I can do."

The sober tanned face above her blurred almost unrecognizably as Amethyst fought to retain consciousness. Finally able to speak again, Amethyst begged softly, "Please, Damien... you have nothing to gain by allowing William to die. You have won. I give you my word I will not run away again. It will be just as you say... I will stay with you as long as you want me." When still he did not respond, Amethyst continued hoarsely, "Please, Damien, I beg you... please..."

Suddenly grabbing her shoulders, Damien gave her a hard shake, his voice heavy with anger as he exploded heatedly, "Are you so crazed with fear for William Sheridan that you cannot hear the words I speak? I tell you, Amethyst, I have no magic powers. I did not make

William fall ill. I cannot cure him by simply waving my hand!"

But she was not listening, her eyes slowly closing as her voice trailed off weakly, "Please, Damien ... please ..."

His face flushed with frustration and anger, Damien stared helplessly at the small woman lying before him. Reaching out, he touched her forehead, his stomach tightening at the searing heat under his hand. Quickly reaching to the basin beside the bed, he wrung out the cloth carefully and applied the cool compress to her forehead. The cloth warmed almost immediately, a frightening indication of her escalating temperature and frowning darkly, Damien removed it to repeat the same procedure again and again to no avail. She grew no cooler and began twisting and turning in bed, soft moans escaping her lips as she drew her knees to her chest in pain under the light coverlet.

A sudden sound from behind snapped Damien's head around to see a small, slovenly man entering the room beside Tillie. His unkempt gray hair was plastered wetly to his head, his wrinkled face blotchy and unclean. He reeked of liquor and observing the man's unsteady step as he approached the bed, Damien rose immediately to his feet and shot an angry glance to Barnes who had followed the man to the doorway.

Anticipating his Captain's next remark, Jeremy Barnes protested quickly in self-defense, "We had the devil's own time finding him, Captain, and when we did, we had to sober him up enough to walk." Lowering his voice, the earnest sailor continued, "He may not be much, but he's the only doctor available in Kingston right now. Dr. Martens is out at the plantations where the fever has hit the hardest."

Signaling his first mate into silence with a small wave of his hand, Damien turned his attention back toward the bed, only to find himself being firmly ushered to the door by a determined Tillie.

"Best you leave the room now, Captain. Tillie keep him eye on this man while him take care of Amethyst."

"I will not allow that old drunk to touch her with his filthy hands," Damien protested stiffly, refusing to be budged.

Her expression adamant, Tillie responded softly, "Him all we got, Captain, and him we got to take now. Don't worry, Tillie make him wash him hands."

Staring wordlessly into the woman's face for a few long moments, Damien turned abruptly and left the room, closing the door behind him. Dismissing Barnes to return to the ship, Damien turned to stare at the closed door for a few brief seconds before his pacing began.

Watching wordlessly as Amethyst twisted restlessly in bed, Damien felt a strong sinking sensation in the pit of his stomach. Her fever had been raging for three days and her physical deterioration was obvious. Wretchedly thin, her face was a pasty yellow color that did not speak well. She had begun vomiting a deep black yesterday, indicative of internal bleeding, and Damien's heart had almost stopped at the sight. She was hallucinating more and more frequently despite the brief moments of lucidity during which she continued to plague him relentlessly about William. Torn between a sickening jealousy and a growing fear for her life, Damien was filled with anxiety. Shaking his head helplessly, he was again filled with anger. "She has no concern for her own health. The only person she can think of is that pampered lout on Sheridan Plantation who is probably receiving the best of care!"

And Dr. Clarke seemed absolutely useless, hardly able to maintain sobriety long enough to conduct a daily visit.

At a small familiar sound from the bed, Damien moved

quickly to hold the bucket as Amethyst prepared to retch again, his expression filled with anxiety.

Her frail body having completed its heaving spasms, Amethyst fell back against the pillow in exhaustion. Moving to sit on the side of the bed, Damien eyed her in frustrated helplessness against the fever that was slowly consuming her. Reaching to the basin beside the bed, he took the cloth and commenced sponging her face gently, running the refreshing coolness across her forehead, cheeks and lips before continuing down the slender column of her neck. It was night and Tillie had retired for the first few hours of rest since Amethyst had returned. He had not slept for three days. Remaining diligently by Amethyst's bedside, he had left the *Sally* temporarily in Jeremy Barnes's care. He dared not leave . . . he had made that mistake once before and had lost her. Now that she had returned, he could not risk the same thing happening again.

Her fevered ramblings growing suddenly louder, Amethyst's eyes abruptly snapped open, her hoarse voice unexpectedly cutting the silence of the room.

"William . . . is he well? Tell me . . . you must, Damien."

Catching the hand that sponged her face, Amethyst directed her frenzied glance into his eyes to continue her frantic appeal.

"Damien, please, William is so ill . . ."

The croaking whisper faded from Damien's ears as his eyes perused Amethyst's fervent expression. He had been denying any responsibility for Sheridan's illness for three days to no avail. Amethyst's fevered mind still refused to accept his adamant protests of innocence. She was beyond reasoning. Having convinced herself he was responsible for Sheridan's illness, she was also convinced he was the only person who could save his life. Heartily tired of hearing William's name on Amethyst's pale lips,

Damien could bear her frenzied pleas no longer. Gently prying her clutching hand from his, he held it gently in his palm as he tilted her chin so she looked directly into his eyes.

"Listen to me now, Amethyst, and remember what I am saying. You may set your mind at rest. Because you have returned to me, I will free William Sheridan from my obeah. He will get well."

Blinking briefly as the import of his statement penetrated her confused state, Amethyst stared expressionlessly into his eyes for a few brief moments before relief moved slowly across her features. His jealousy flaring unreasonably, Damien was unable to keep the harshness from his voice as he continued, "But you must also understand this, Amethyst. You must make every effort to get well now. I will not be cheated in our bargain. Is that understood?"

Appearing completely lucid, Amethyst swallowed tightly, nodding as a weak whisper escaped her lips, "Yes, I understand, Damien. It will be as you say."

So strong had been Amethyst's faith in his powers of obeah that Damien had almost become convinced she would immediately begin to improve once he had set her mind at rest, but the following days during which Amethyst grew steadily weaker soon destroyed his optimism.

The sixth day of her illness found a frail, emaciated Amethyst who lay in restless unconsciousness most of the time, awakening only to retch violently at frequent intervals. Almost beyond despair, Damien again assumed the night watch, allowing Tillie a few hours reprieve from her nursing chores.

Taking the delicate hand lying motionless on the coverlet into his, Damien held it gently for a few wordless minutes. So fragile was it between his work toughened palms that he almost feared he would crush it should he clasp it any harder. His eyes moving to Amethyst's face, he slowly perused her still features.

Even in her wasted, critical state of health, she was beautiful. The black hair streaming across her pillow, tended unfailingly by Tillie during her illness, still retained a portion of its former beauty. Her small, perfect features, refined to the point of fragility by her illness, gave her an added air of vulnerability which drew him more strongly still. Her eyes always large and expressive, seemed to dominate her face in her few waking moments, her full sweep of black lashes in repose appearing longer, more luxurious. The clear skin drawn tightly over her splendid facial structure emphasized the magnificent planes of her face and the delicate line of her jaw; her lips wan and lifeless, appeared too perfect to be real. Always of small stature, her illness had stolen the softness from her frame, leaving a fragile shell of her former self, dainty and doll-like as she lay sleeping.

The violent stomach spasms had stopped early in the evening, allowing her to lapse into a deep sleep. Slowly lifting the small white hand to his lips, Damien kissed it lightly, realizing as his lips touched her pale skin that it was cooler to the touch. No sooner had that thought crossed his tired mind then Amethyst began to stir, her eyelids fluttering lightly before opening wide to look clearly into his.

Her eyelids were heavy. The light from the small lamp at bedside hurt her eyes with its dull glow as she struggled to raise them. The room was momentarily blurred and attempting to focus her gaze, Amethyst was startled to find the small effort almost beyond her strength. Her body ached desperately, with the main concentration of pain in her stomach and throat. She must have been ill . . . yes . . . Abruptly bringing the room into focus,

Amethyst was startled to see Damien sitting at her bedside, his hand holding hers as he gazed at it speculatively. With sudden clarity their conversation of a few days before returned to her mind. Damien had finally agreed to release William . . . William would soon recover . . . and in return she had promised herself. Closing her eyes for the briefest second as the full magnitude of her commitment washed over her, Amethyst took a deep breath. She dared not renege for she was certain that to do so would mean William's life.

Opening her eyes again, Amethyst's gaze met clear, translucent gray eyes as Damien bent toward her. Within a moment a large tanned hand touched her forehead, and a tentative smile grew on his weary face.

"Your fever has broken, Amethyst. You will soon be better, darling." The broad hand on her forehead slipped down to gently touch her cheek as his eyes moved caressingly over her face.

A small frown slipping across her brow, Amethyst was puzzled at the pale beneath Damien's tan and the stubble on his normally cleanshaven face. Apparently he had not shaved for several days. There were dark circles under his eyes . . . his hair was disheveled as if raked by a nervous hand . . . his clothes were untidy and wrinkled . . . his appearance in general so unlike his usually meticulous grooming that Amethyst was momentarily confused.

"Have you been ill, Cap . . . Damien?" Amethyst offered hesitantly, realizing her weak voice was only audible because of the absolute silence of the room.

"I?" Momentarily puzzled, Damien stared into her face for a few moments before a small smile slipped across his bold, even features. "Not I, Amethyst. You are the one who has been ill. But you will soon be better, darling, and we will . . ."

Interrupting dully, Amethyst strained to speak again,

"And William . . . he is recuperating?"

The smile dropping from his face as it slowly assumed a stiff, emotionless mask, Damien answered quietly, "Yes, he is recuperating."

Nodding her head briefly in acknowledgment, Amethyst slowly drifted back to sleep, unaware of the angry tightening of Damien's lips the moment before he turned from the bed in frustration.

"Damn!" Taking a few short strides toward the doorway, he paused with his back to the bed. "Damn her!" he cursed again under his breath, turning back abruptly to direct a heated glance toward Amethyst. "William, William, William! She can think of no one else! Well, it will do her no good to think of him any longer. She belongs to me, now. Only to me."

Wearily rubbing the back of her hand across her forehead, Tillie paused momentarily to lift her head from her washing and stare unseeingly into the distance. She could not seem to concentrate on her work. Amethyst had been free of fever for almost five days now and although she was still weak, she was definitely on the way to recovery. Quaco had been sent to them several times within the last week inquiring as to the state of Amethyst's health for a worried and recovering William. At William's request and Tillie suspected for an outrageous price, Dr. Martens had also come to examine Amethyst, pronouncing her free of the disease that was still sweeping the island. Amethyst was indeed feeling better. She had begun eating again and some of her natural color had returned. Captain Straith had coaxed her into walking with his support several times in the last few days, despite her lingering weakness, although she was still confined to her bed for the greater portion of the day.

Captain Straith . . . Tillie had considerable difficulty

in sorting out her conflicting impressions of the tall, fair-haired man with Obeah eyes. Obviously affected by Amethyst's illness, he had not left her side since she had fallen ill except for occasional brief outings in the back yard for fresh air. He seemed obsessed by Amethyst, spending as much time nursing her during her illness as Tillie herself. And Tillie was fully aware she probably could not have managed the round-the-clock care demanded by Amethyst's illness without him. Strange . . . where at first she had believed Amethyst under the Captain's Guzu, it now appeared that it was Captain Straith who was bewitched. Whatever the case, it was clear that he did not intend to allow William Sheridan to spirit Amethyst away at any cost and Tillie silently feared the confrontation to come when the young man was once again well enough to travel. In an effort to put off the inevitable, she had strictly forbidden Quaco to tell his master of Captain Straith's presence in the house. The trouble would start soon enough and neither Mr. Sheridan nor Amethyst was yet strong enough to withstand the stress.

But Amethyst would recover, and from all indications Captain Straith would be sailing within a short time. Time was in their favor.

Having dismissed that worry from her mind, Tillie faced at last the nagging fear that had grown until it gave her no peace. Three days before she had received word that the fever had struck Conway Plantation, with the slaves' quarters particularly hard hit. Almost half its slave population had come down with the disease in varying degrees. There had been rumors of at least 20 deaths. Tillie allowed herself to think no further. Her throat closing with emotion, she once again lifted her hand to brush away the frightened tears that had gathered in her eyes. Raymond . . . she prayed to the great Pucku that he had not been stricken. Her heart pounding heavily within her breast, Tillie raised both hands to wipe away the tears now cascading down her cheeks. Raymond . . . she could bear ignorance of his fate no longer.

Carefully hanging out the few clothes she had washed, Tillie absentmindedly dumped the pail of water into the yard and turned back to the house. She would go tonight to Conway Plantation and return at dawn. Captain Straith had spent the last week and a half sleeping in their living room and was not likely to leave now. She had left Amethyst in his care before and was certain she could depend on him should Amethyst feel ill. Yes, she would go tonight . . . she would have to hurry . . . it would be twilight in a few hours, and she had much to do.

With a deliberate effort to appear casual, Tillie walked leisurely to the opposite edge of town, her heart pounding heavily in her breast as she finally slipped into the woods to reverse her trail to Conway Plantation in the usual manner. She, also, had lost considerable weight in the previous two weeks, anxiety having inhibited her normally hearty appetite. Slimmer in the cheek, shoulders, and waist, her loss of weight seemed to add to the natural grace of bearing obvious even as she traveled the rough trail. Having taken pains with her grooming in spite of her haste, she was a strikingly handsome woman in the inconspicuous dark skirt and white native blouse she had chosen to wear. But her mind lay on the path ahead, each step bringing her closer to relief or realization of her fears as she picked her way cautiously through the damp forest, unconsciously swatting the annoying insects heavy on the night air.

Within the hour the dwindling light of day revealed the familiar landscape of Conway Plantaton, and swallowing tightly, Tillie turned onto the trail on which Raymond had led her so proudly a few weeks previous. A few steps more and the small clearing was within sight. If Raymond was well, he would be done with his work for the day and would be waiting as he had promised he would each night for her to come to him again. It had been a long time, but Raymond would not forget. He . . .

An abrupt movement at the doorway of the hut caught Tillie's eye and slipping back into the shadows, she waited cautiously for someone to emerge. Abruptly stepping from the dimness of the hut into the rapidly fading light, a young Negress stopped a moment as if sensing her presence, before turning to direct her words into the hut behind her.

"Alright, Raymond, I'se gowan now, but I'se come back when Raymond call. Quasheba ready fe Raymond . . ."

The young woman stared expectantly into the dark hut, waiting until a tall, massive shadow came to stand behind her. Were it not for his size, Tillie would have found it impossible to distinguish Raymond's black form in the growing darkness, but his unusual height could not be mistaken. Waiting a few more minutes for a response that was not forthcoming, the young Negress turned and walked slowly in the direction of the slaves' quarters.

The burning ache inside her rapidly growing into a violent rage, Tillie waited until the woman had disappeared into the blackness before stepping into the open, her eyes flashing with anger.

"So, 'Tillie the only woman fe me,' be that true, Raymond?" Tillie hissed, mocking his ardent declaration of their last meeting as she trembled with fury at the scene she had just witnessed.

Momentarily startled into immobility, Raymond stared in Tillie's direction, his expression unclear in the waning light. Abruptly in motion, he was at her side within a few seconds, a low moan escaping his throat as he wrapped his strong arms around her, straining her roughly against his massive chest.

"Tillie... Tillie Swann..." Mumbling tenderly against her hair, he was seemingly unaffected by Tillie's violent struggles to free herself.

"Turn me loose, Raymond," Tillie ground out warningly from between gritted teeth as she realized her struggles were to no avail. "How many women Raymond want this night? Tillie want no part of black man who take plantation women like old plantation bull! Tillie get him own man... nice mulatto man like Chauncy Worth, and..."

His arms tightening warningly, Raymond muttered softly against her ear, refusing to relinquish his hold despite her protests, "Tillie take no mulatto man. Tillie woman fe me like Raymond man fe Tillie."

"Tillie see that woman... him come out from him wappen-bappen. Tillie no fool..."

His full lips moving knowingly against her cheek, Raymond whispered softly, "Raymond tell Quasheba gowan home. Not woman fe Raymond."

"Humph!" Tillie scoffed loudly, a burst of hope she could not suppress lightening the weight in her chest despite herself. "No black man turn away black streggah when him come."

"Tillie be hard ears t'night." Raymond's voice was patient, his joy at Tillie's appearance overpowering his anger with her surly mood. "Quasheba come 'n Raymond make Quasheba go. Raymond got no time fe him when him wait fe Tillie Swann."

Noticing her struggles had all but ceased, Raymond loosened his hold and slipping his arm around her shoulders, gently urged Tillie toward his hut. "Tillie come now... lie with Raymond 'n Raymond tell Tillie how long days be since Tillie come see him."

Touching his mouth to her temple as Tillie slowly began moving alongside him, Raymond continued softly,

"Raymond prove him save himself fe Tillie..."

Within minutes they were inside the dimly lit hut, its damp scent pleasingly familiar to Tillie's heightened senses. Raising her hand, Tillie touched the broad dark cheek, inwardly delighting in the touch of his skin as she avidly searched his face in the light from the single candle.

"You be truthful, Raymond? Tillie Swann share no man..."

"Raymond tell Tillie true."

Studying him silently, Tillie's heart began a rapidly accelerating beat as she felt his body's eager swelling against her. Satisfied by this final proof that Raymond had indeed been true, this night at least, she firmly wiped away all thoughts of other nights when she had not come and slid her arms slowly around him to caress the back of his neck as she spoke.

"The fever... my Amethyst, him almost die. Tillie worry Raymond be sick and be all alone, with no one fe care fe him."

"Raymond fine, Tillie." His voice heavy with passion, Raymond continued softly, "Tillie be medicine Raymond need... keep him well... keep him happy..."

Moving his hands to his waist, Raymond quickly undid his rough britches, tossing them to the chair as he drew her down to the sleeping mat, still clean and neat as Tillie had demanded. His voice a soft command, he drew her against him, whispering in her ear as his hands eagerly caressed her light cocoa skin, "Forget fever now, Tillie. Remember only Raymond... think only Raymond..."

His touch fanning the embers smouldering within her, Tillie turned willingly toward him, and for that night at least she did think only of Raymond...

Her hair streaming out behind her, Amethyst's feet barely touched the ground as she ran wildly through the dark Kingston streets. The heavy night air lay against her skin like a smothering blanket, but the perspiration soaking her clothes, causing them to adhere to her body in dark, sticky patches, was the cold sweat of fear. Turning a corner, she came to a part of town with which she was strangely unfamiliar. More lost with each step she took, she became frantic with fear and again began to run. Finally reaching another corner, she stopped abruptly. Her chest heaving with exertion, she glanced first left and then right, in an attempt to regain her bearings, but the effort was in vain. Noticing a small group of men gathered midway down the street, she slowly advanced toward them, but was startled when their heads suddenly snapped toward her. Their pale, yellowed skin glowed eerily in the light of the street lamp overhead as their gaunt, wasted faces stared in her direction with a strange fascination. Revulsion overwhelming her senses as the sickly skeletons continued their steady perusal, she abruptly turned around in an attempt to escape their intense scrutiny. She had just begun running in the opposite direction when she saw a person standing at the end of the street. The man's back was toward her and slowing to a halt, she strained to identify the familiar stance. She was still staring steadily in his direction when the shadow turned to reveal William's boyishly handsome face.

"William!" Her relieved shout echoing in the street, she sobbed joyous tears as she began running in his direction only to be jerked to an unceremonious halt by a strong hand reaching out of the darkness. Turning, Amethyst saw a tall, broad figure step out of a hidden doorway. The thick, sun-streaked hair glinting in the meager light set her heart to racing moments before he moved fully into the open to reveal the sober expression and pale accusing eyes of Damien Straith.

Meeting his cold stare for a few brief moments,

Amethyst suddenly attempted to pull herself from his restraining hand in an effort to escape, but the other heavily muscled arm snaked out to secure his grip and pull her tight against him as he muttered angrily, "We have a bargain, Amethyst . . ."

"Yes . . . yes, I know, but," her voice a tremulous whisper, Amethyst pleaded desperately, ". . . but I just wanted to talk to William . . . make certain he is alright . . ."

"No!" The deep-throated response emphatically denied her request.

"But," she continued hoarsely, "I must talk to him, please."

"No!" Adamantly shaking his head, Damien held her more tightly still as he turned in the direction of the group still observing the proceedings from midway down the street, and gave a short nod. Acknowledging his signal, the men moved quickly toward William, and within seconds had taken him prisoner. Struggling violently as they dragged him away, William repeatedly called her name, but within moments the entire group was swallowed up by the darkness.

Turning to Damien, Amethyst begged hysterically, "Stop them, please! They're taking him away! Damien . . . you cannot allow them to hurt him . . . please . . . you promised . . ."

His ice gray eyes suddenly boring into hers with an intensity that set her to trembling, Damien responded pitilessly, "And *you* promised *me*, Amethyst."

Shaking her head wildly, Amethyst's voice was a raspy whisper as he strained her closer still, "No . . . no . . ."

His voice an insistent command, he demanded harshly, "Yes . . . you promised, Amethyst . . . Amethyst . . ."

He was shaking her roughly by the shoulders, his voice demanding insistently, "Amethyst . . . Amethyst . . ."

jarring her cruelly when she snapped open her eyes to see the dark street had disappeared. She was in her own room, in bed, and Damien was shaking her, a deep frown darkening his expression as he searched her face worriedly.

"Are you finally awake, Amethyst? Damn that doctor and his laudanum. I told him he uses too liberal a dosage. I could hardly wake you. Are you alright now, darling? You were having a nightmare."

Gently wiping away her tears with his broad palm as Amethyst struggled to regain control of her emotions, Damien continued softly, "You were tossing and turning in your sleep and cried out. I was afraid your fever had returned, but you are cool to the touch."

But she was still trembling, and overwhelmed with tenderness, Damien gently gathered her thin body against him, a trembling beginning inside himself as he held her close. "Don't worry, darling. You're safe with me. I won't let anyone hurt you . . ."

But she moved uncomfortably in his arms. Her night rail was soaked with perspiration from her frantic dream, and realizing her discomfort, Damien released her. His eyes flicking assessingly over her person, he rose abruptly to take the basin from beside the bed and left the room. Within minutes he returned, balancing the basin carefully as he replaced it on the nightstand.

Moving familiarly to the dresser, he removed a fresh night rail and laid it across the foot of the bed. Turning back toward her, he said softly, "You must take off that damp gown, Amethyst. And then I'll help you bathe so you may relax into a sound sleep."

"No, I'm alright, Damien. You needn't bother," Amethyst protested, drawing a frown from the strong face that towered above her.

"Is this more maidenly modesty, Amethyst? I'm afraid I cannot wrap you in a blanket and allow you to remove your clothes this time." Raising his brow, Damien continued with authority, "And I can assure you, I bathed you on several occasions while you were ill. I have seen you in your entirety several times, Amethyst. Your nakedness will not be a new sight to me."

Flushing brightly, Amethyst mumbled through tight lips, "But it is not necessary that I bathe. I have already bathed this evening."

"And you are about to be bathed again!"

Moving determinedly toward her, Damien sat lightly on the side of the bed and began to unbutton the top of her gown. Quickly brushing away his hands, Amethyst snapped tightly, "I can do that!"

Within moments Damien was lifting her gown. Rolling her slightly from side to side to free the garment and slipping her arms free, he pulled it gently over her head and dropped it casually to the chair. As he turned back to face her, Amethyst avoided his eyes, her own gaze darting to the far corner of the room where it remained fixed with resolution. Suddenly grateful not to face her discerning eye, Damien felt himself flush hotly as his eyes moved slowly over Amethyst's naked form. He truly had bathed Amethyst's fevered body several times during her illness, his anxiety removing all thought but the business at hand from his mind, but tonight was another matter. Mesmerized by the beauty of the small woman lying in front of him he could not seem to tear his eyes from her. His heart racing in his chest, he felt a revealing tightening in his groin and groaned inwardly as he took up the cloth and vigorously worked up a lather with the lavender-scented soap. This was going to be far more difficult than he had anticipated, but he had insisted and was determined to follow the course of action through to the finish.

Moving the cloth slowly across her brow, Damien commanded hoarsely, "Close your eyes, Amethyst."

Complying with his terse command, Amethyst snapped her eyes shut, allowing him to run the cloth across the narrow dark brows and thick fringe of lashes before moving across the smoothness of her cheeks and the delicate lips compressed into a tight line. Taking another cloth, he rinsed her face clear of soap, noting with an odd fascination the manner in which the dark lashes curled upward against her velvet cheeks, the way the little tendrils at her hairline curled appealingly, the perfection of her profile as he ran the cloth gently across her lips. He had patted her face dry when Amethyst's eyes snapped open again to resume her adamant scrutiny of a point in the far corner of the room, but this time Damien was grateful for her stubbornness. He was not certain he could maintain a casual facade as he ran the soapy cloth down her throat, onto her gently curving shoulders, and lower to circle the white smoothness of her breasts. Even in her thinness, Amethyst was beautiful . . . her breasts smaller than before, but perfectly shaped, the pink crests bright and appealing against the stark whiteness of her skin. Lifting her arms, one at a time, he washed them gently to her slender fingertips, repeating the whole process as he dried her with a soft cloth.

His hands were trembling noticeably now as he worked up a fresh lather and turned to move the cloth below the soft breasts to the slender waist; on to the flat stomach and slightly rounded hips. Taking a deep breath, he moved the cloth slowly among the dark curls nestling between her thighs, the pounding in his chest echoing deafeningly in his ears as he separated them gently to run the cloth between her legs. When he had completed drying the area he had just cleansed, Damien could feel the perspiration on his forehead and upper lip, and quickly brushing it away with the back of his arm, he ran the soapy cloth down the lengths of her slender legs and on to the dainty feet, making sure to cleanse between each perfect toe as he did. He was breathing heavily now, the task he had unwittingly chosen for himself playing havoc with his senses. Barely managing an even voice, he commanded harshly, "Alright, now roll over, Amethyst."

Her eyes returning to his for the first time, Amethyst protested once again, "Surely you are done now, Damien."

"I have not washed your back."

"But it isn't necessary. I . . ."

"Roll over, I said!" Unsure how much longer he could maintain the cool facade he had managed for Amethyst's benefit, Damien's command was curt, serving his purpose well as Amethyst flopped over angrily, her face almost buried in the pillow in angry embarrassment.

The silky white back was a further test of his control as Damien circled it gently, moving slowly to the base of her spine and on to the small buttocks, faultlessly lovely to his eye.

He had never seen such a beautiful woman, flawless in every detail. Almost overcome, Damien dried her slowly in an attempt to stretch out the time remaining during which he could feast his eyes on Amethyst's inordinately sensuous appeal. Running his eyes over her back, Damien's gaze caught on a small beauty mark below her shoulder blade, and lowering his head unthinkingly, he kissed it lightly. The coolness of her skin against his lips sending a sharp electric tingle through his body, he gently ran his palms across her shoulders, smoothing, caressing, as his mouth covered the narrow expanse of her back, touching, tasting, breathing in the sweetness of her. Taking the heavy black curls on her neck into his hand, he lifted them gently to reveal the vulnerable nape of her neck, and leaning forward, circled it with soft, tender kisses. Trailing the line of his caress down her spine, he pressed his cheek against the base for a few long moments, before moving to spread a tender barrage of kisses on the firm, round buttocks that fascinated him so completely, continuing on down her legs to the hollow at the back of her knees, where he stopped for a lengthy, fervent caress.

Moving upward once again, he took the small hand lying limply at her side, kissing the palm again and again, the roaring in his ears almost deafening as he trembled with desire for the woman who lay so vulnerable to his touch.

Realizing he was almost past coherent speech, Damien swallowed hard in an attempt to regain some semblance of control and gently turned Amethyst around to face him.

The deep lavender eyes that met his were dazed, searching his face expectantly, the soft lips parted with irresistible appeal. Cupping her cheeks with his hands, his eyes caressed her, her sublime magnificence robbing him of words as he mumbled hoarsely, "Amethyst . . . Amethyst, my darling . . ."

And then his mouth was on hers, the innate sweetness triggering the raging emotion he had held in check so long. Parting her lips even further, his tongue probed gently at first, passion soon driving him past caution as he pressed deeper and deeper into the beauty opened to accommodate the caress of his tongue. Tearing his mouth finally from hers, he trailed moist, heated kisses down the column of her throat to the hollows at the base of her neck, thrilling wildly at the small moan of pleasure his caresses raised from her throat. The graceful curve of her shoulders then knew his passionate touch and lowering his head, he continued to caress them gently with his palms as he circled the rounded mound of her breast with his mouth, his tongue licking out occasionally to taste the tender flesh in his slowly narrowing circle to the erect pink crest that awaited his kiss. His mouth closed over it eagerly, the breathless gasp issuing forth from between Amethyst's soft pink lips pushing him over the edge of passion as he continued to kiss, caress and fondle the inviting peaks again and again, mindless in his desire for her. But they were too sweet . . . he could not leave the delicate mounds just yet. Continuing his ardent caresses, his hand slipped down to find the shining nest of dark curls, his fingers tightening convulsively in them for a few short seconds before slipping into the moistness beneath.

Suddenly he could bear no longer the impediment of clothing between them and standing abruptly, he stripped off his clothes and dropping them to a chair, turned to see Amethyst watching him with a bemused, half-lidded gaze. Moving her glance slowly across the broad planes of his face, her eyes traveled to the expanse of his shoulders and chest, massive and heavily muscled; and progressed slowly down to the narrowness of his waist to follow the faint line of golden brown hair to his groin where the full extent of his passion was exposed to her gaze. Her eyes, widening slightly, showed the first trace of fear, and a flush of tenderness suffused him. Lowering himself to the bed beside her, he took her gently into his arms. Almost breathless as their flesh truly met for the first time, Damien whispered against her hair, "Don't be afraid, darling, I won't hurt you . . . I only want to love you . . ."

His hand moving steadily downward, slipped into the warm crease to resume the caress interrupted only moments before as his mouth plundered hers hungrily, eagerly, with a growing tumult that could lead in only one direction. Moving quickly, he was atop her, easing his weight down gently for fear of crushing the fragile beauty that lay beneath him. He probed her gently as his mouth ravaged hers, seeking, drawing, demanding more and more with his escalating passion.

And then he was inside her, her sharp intake of breath simultaneous with the rigid stiffening of her frame as her body closed completely around him for the first time. A blinding wave of exaltation swept over Damien as he came to rest inside her, the sweet singing in his blood rising to a deafening pounding in his ears as he savored the heady feeling of complete possession.

Suddenly conscious of her rigidity, Damien slipped his arms under and around her, holding her tight in the circle of his arms as he lay motionless inside her. His hand moving up to tangle gloriously in the long dark curls at her neck, he whispered softly into her ear between intermittent kisses, "Don't be frightened, darling. Just relax and let me love you."

Moving slowly inside her, he continued his kisses and soft encouragement until he was moving freely within her, her own body's response eliminating the need for any further words as he plunged deeper and deeper with each thrust. Abruptly he was there, poised at the ultimate summit. Hesitating briefly, he glanced down into Amethyst's face, drinking in the passion displayed in the glow of her eyes and her short, gasping breaths. His voice deep with emotion, he whispered against her lips, "It is beautiful, isn't it, Amethyst? Together, you and I . . . it was meant to be . . ."

And then it was there, the crashing finale of the violently loving act that had brought them to the breathless pinnacle of love, to send them careening in a bursting spiral of ecstasy from its glorious heights.

Moments later they both lay motionless, bodies still joined. Raising his head, Damien cupped Amethyst's face between his palms. The heavy lids raised slowly, exposing the deep violet of her eyes as they looked silently into his, and Damien felt a sense of wonder totally foreign to his experience sweep his senses.

His voice breaking with emotion, he said simply and sincerely, "And that, my darling, is why I could not and will not let you go . . ."

Chapter 6

Awakening suddenly from a restless sleep, Damien anxiously clutched the small woman sleeping within his embrace. Lifting his head from the pillow, he stared into Amethyst's sleeping countenance, reassuring himself for yet another time that night that he had not truly been dreaming . . . that Amethyst was finally his own. The soft naked body pressed tightly against his tantalized him pitilessly, but extremely conscious of her fragile health, he controlled by sheer strength of will the overwhelming desire to kiss open those glorious violet eyes, to taste again the moist sweetness of her mouth. She was not yet well . . . he dared not make love to her again this night. But, God, he wanted her! The velvet skin moving so subtly against his seared him with its touch until his desire was a living, palpable force.

Suddenly frowning in her sleep, Amethyst uttered a soft moan and turned uncomfortably in his arms. Feeling a prick of conscience, Damien loosened his hold. Had he been more considerate, he would have waited until she had fully recuperated. But somewhere along the way he had lost control and succumbed to his own defenselessness against her. Moving his hand gently in the long, black spirals of hair stretched across the pillow, he luxuriated in the sensation of the silky strands moving against his palm while he strained to see her face more clearly in the weak light, suddenly wishing it was morning so he might peruse the flawless countenance more easily. God, would he never tire of looking at her? Would his mind never be free of her? From the moment of his return to the island, he had been able to think of nothing else but the gleam of her hair as it bounced against her slender back, the heavy black lashes shading those glorious eyes, the glow of her skin, those full, sensuous lips that promised so much, only to succeed in surpassing his wildest expectations the moment of their contact with his. "No," he thought, a sudden clarity of mind abruptly banishing the last trace of guilt. He wasn't sorry he had taken her tonight. God, no! This wasn't remorse he felt pounding through his veins, and he would not waste time berating himself. He was glad she was finally in his arms! His only regret was the need for caution . . . that he could not fully indulge his passion until she fully recuperated. "But then . . . then . . ." lying back against the pillow he gently moved her close again, "then when you are well, my darling, then we will see . . . then we will see . . ."

The first gray light of dawn slipped soundlessly through the window, its pale glow nudging Amethyst into wakefulness as she moved uncomfortably. Her body ached and a peculiar sense of unrest nagged persistently at her subconscious mind, urging her awake. But she did not wish to awaken yet . . . she was strangely afraid to open her eyes, to ascertain if her dreams of the previous night were indeed a reality. Steadfastly resisting the urge to raise her heavy lids, she heard a deep voice whisper in her ear as a broad hand slid familiarly across the bare skin of her stomach to pull her against a warm, hard body, "What's wrong, Amethyst? Aren't you feeling well? I can feel your whole body tensing."

The hand moving up her arm turned her face toward the voice that urged softly, "Open your eyes, darling. Look at me . . . Amethyst . . ."

Unable to bear the suspense any longer, Amethyst snapped open her eyes to see Damien Straith's handsome face, his expression concerned as he stared down at her. A hot flash of shame flooding over her, Amethyst reached up to cover her face momentarily with her small hand. Her voice a forlorn whisper, she mumbled almost incoherently, "It's true . . . it's true . . . I thought . . . I hoped it was just a dream, that I would awake this morning and laugh at my fears, but it's true . . . Oh, God, it's all over . . ."

Firmly removing her hand from her face, Damien raised her chin until her eyes were level with his, his lips only inches away. "No, darling, it isn't all over. It's just begun." Gently smoothing the warm tears from her cheeks, his voice was a reassuring whisper. "You mustn't cry, darling. I hadn't intended last night to happen so quickly, but I'm glad it did. You will become adjusted to the situation shortly, and will come to realize that we were meant to be together, just as I have known from the moment I saw you again."

He was kissing her lightly, his lips following a wide, erotic trail across the smooth skin of her cheek as her lavender eyes stared hopelessly into his. "You'll see, darling. This strangeness will pass and you'll realize just as I," his words were becoming blurred with the increasing warmth of his kisses, "that this was meant to be."

Suddenly he was past speech, his mouth devouring hers with an intensity that set her to quaking, his hands moving familiarly on her body, urging her closer still until she was pressed against the full, naked length of him, her face flaming hotly as she felt for the second time the hardness of his desire pressed so intimately close. She was trembling violently, the true cause of her shame the confused realization that as he continued kissing her, his hands stroking her with increasing passion, she was uncertain if she truly wanted him to stop. Her body seeming to come alive under his touch, Amethyst moved restlessly, resisting the wild urge to pull him closer against her, to separate her lips under his kiss, to feel the caress of his tongue against hers as his hands roamed her body freely in enticing, heated promise. Almost unable to suppress her surging response, Amethyst stiffened noticeably, jarring Damien from his impassioned course.

"Amethyst, darling," his voice hoarse with emotion, Damien pulled his mouth reluctantly from hers to whisper appealingly, "I must have you again, darling. I had wanted to wait . . . to give you a chance . . . but I must have you darling . . . I must . . ."

Quickly shifting his weight, Damien moved atop her, the crush of her body under his sending a jolt of ecstasy through him that caused a low groan to issue from his throat as he buried his face in her soft, warm neck momentarily. Lifting his head, he pressed light kisses against her ear, whispering softly, "I won't hurt you, darling. Don't be frightened. Just relax and let me in . . . darling . . ."

Suddenly his mouth was covering hers, his lips forcing hers apart as his tongue savored the moist sweetness, fondling, searching, drawing her with him to a height of passion where she was hardly aware of his probing manhood until it was abruptly inside her. Gasping at the first penetration, Amethyst stiffened, snapping her eyes shut in mortification at her body's greedy acceptance, and misconstruing her reaction, Damien whispered gently, "Open your eyes, darling. I want you to look at me. Open your eyes," he urged again, his body remaining a still, unmoving part of her as he waited patiently.

Reluctantly following his urging, Amethyst stared into clear silver eyes, her breath catching at the strange, stirring glow in their translucent depths.

"Yes, darling," he said tenderly as he began moving sensuously within her once again, "I want you to see who it is that is loving you, who it is that possesses you . . ."

But the drug of ecstasy was too strong, weighing her heavy lids until they dropped closed over the luminous lavender orbs, causing Damien to urge, his voice thickened with passion, "Open your eyes, Amethyst, and look at me." Once again he paused, waiting for her to comply with his soft command, and suddenly unable to bear the cessation of the sweet, heady languor which gained greater control of her senses with each heavy thrust, Amethyst opened her eyes to Damien's impassioned face. And still he paused, inciting in Amethyst a desire to cry out, to plead with him to continue his loving penetrations.

"Say my name, darling . . . tell me who possesses you now . . . who is loving you so completely that your body is no longer yours alone. Tell me, darling . . . Amethyst . . . say my name . . ."

But she did not speak. Mesmerized by the silver glow of his eyes, she continued to stare into his face, unwilling to submit to the final subjugation to his will.

Refusing to concede even to himself that the burning need to have Amethyst acknowledge him stemmed from his fear that Amethyst closed her eyes to block out his image and substitute the face of William Sheridan, Damien urged more strongly, his voice a throbbing command that could not be ignored, "Tell me, darling. Who possesses you now? Say my name, Amethyst . . ."

There was a brief silence before Amethyst heard her own voice, hardly recognizable in its hoarse, breathless gasps, "It's you . . . Damien . . . you are the one. You possess me now, Damien . . . you possess me . . ."

The tension building in the broad planes of his face relaxing suddenly, Damien lowered his mouth with a low groan to cover her lips with a long, demanding kiss. Thrusting inside her again and again, Damien raised her rapidly, with growing exhilaration to a peak of mindless glory, brilliant in a beauty so intense that it was almost pain. With one last heaving thrust he carried her breathlessly to the summit for a brief, rapturous eternity before plummeting mercifully to complete, magnificent release.

Quickly dropping to his side to allow Amethyst's frail body freedom from his weight, Damien pulled her with him, rolling until their positions were reversed, Amethyst lying atop him . . . small, warm . . . relaxed . . . their bodies still joined. Reluctant to separate from her, Damien reached down to pull the light coverlet across them, whispering against the glowing curls tucked so comfortably beneath his chin, "Sleep now, darling . . . my little darling. I'll take care of you . . . you needn't worry. You belong to me now, darling. You belong to me . . ."

The sound of a light step passing the window a short time later aroused Damien the second before the front door of the house clicked open. Glancing toward Amethyst as she lay beside him, sleeping in the circle of his embrace, her face resting lightly against his chest, he reached over to tuck the coverlet more securely against her, shielding her naked body from the confrontation to come. Listening intently, he raised himself to his elbow as the step stopped in the living room in a spot he gauged to be near his abandoned pallet. After a brief pause, the step moved rapidly to the bedroom door. Within a moment the door swung open to reveal Tillie, her eyes widening in momentary shock which swiftly turned into heated fury.

"You!" she hissed softly, realizing Amethyst was just beginning to stir and not wishing to frighten her with the anger she directed into his self-possessed expression. "You! What you do in my Amethyst's bed? Amethyst be good girl . . . virgin . . . not plaything for whoring captain!"

"Be still, Tillie!" Damien's voice whipped out to quiet the angry woman's words, as he glanced anxiously in Amethyst's direction. Turning back, he answered coolly, "My presence in this bed is none of your concern. I owe you no explanation, but to set the matter clear once and for all, I will restate what I have said before. Amethyst is mine. She belongs to me, and nothing you do or say will change that simple fact. I have simply sealed my possession of her."

The soft moan issuing from the mulatto's lips and the tears filling her dark eyes at his declaration causing him a moment's remorse for his bluntness, Damien stopped momentarily, his glance moving once again beside him to Amethyst, who, eyes averted from his, swallowed tightly. Turning back toward the woman who still stood in the doorway, he said in a softer tone, "You needn't worry, Tillie. I will take care of Amethyst. I haven't hurt her."

"But . . . but . . ." Tillie stammered, interrupting his words uncertainly, "Amethyst be a virgin . . . Mr. William Sheridan . . . him want Amethyst for him wife . . ."

The Sheridan name inflaming his anger, Damien snapped curtly, "Well, she is a virgin no more! And now if you will kindly leave the room, you may prepare Amethyst's breakfast!" At the angry glance his command aroused from the imposing figure in the doorway, he responded with growing heat, "And if you do not wish to make breakfast, you may leave this house and I will care for Amethyst myself!"

Turning in a huff, Tillie closed the door emphatically behind her. Listening as her angry strides moved toward the kitchen, Damien waited only until he heard the irate slamming of the kitchen utensils before looking again in Amethyst's direction. Gently turning her averted face toward him, he saw tears filled the huge luminous orbs that studied him intently. Overcome with tenderness, he gathered her slowly into his arms, the touch of her breasts against his chest sending a jolt surging through his blood which he struggled to ignore. His voice was low and husky when he was finally able to speak.

"Darling, Tillie will soon become accustomed to our being together. You must not allow her anger to affect you."

Nodding her head, Amethyst swallowed again, finally allowing herself to relax against him as he stroked her hair gently. Suddenly realizing the warmth of Amethyst's small body against his was affecting him far more than he desired, he released her gently. Lifting the coverlet, he got out of bed and reached for his britches.

Turning unexpectedly, Damien caught Amethyst's gaze as it wandered over him openly, seemingly mesmerized by the play of muscles along his powerful thighs, the turn of his firm buttocks, the narrow flatness of his waist, from which his frame shot upward in a sharp "V" to a broad, powerful chest furred lightly with golden brown hair and massive shoulders that gave the final touch to his impressive appearance. Her eyes moved along his strong neck and chin and his full, sensuous mouth . . . Suddenly Amethyst's eyes were in contact with his, causing heat to surge recklessly through his veins.

"If you continue looking at me that way, Amethyst," Damien's voice was a husky whisper, "it will be extremely difficult for me to leave this room as I had planned."

The revealing swell of his body leaving no doubt as to the significance of his words, Amethyst flushed hotly and turned her glance away. Turning back as his step neared the door, Amethyst watched him leave the room, only to see him return within a few minutes with a basin filled with water and fresh cloths. At her questioning glance, Damien stated brusquely, "I'm going to help you bathe, Amethyst."

Reacting with spontaneous anxiety to his statement, Amethyst flushed hotly as she stammered uncertainly, "No . . . no, Damien. Tillie is home now. She can help me. It isn't necessary that you . . ."

Carefully placing the basin on the nightstand, Damien sat on the side of the bed and reached out to cup her cheeks in his hands.

"You needn't worry, Amethyst." His voice soft, he continued reassuringly, "If you wish, Tillie may help you bathe after today, but I think it best that I help you this one more time, darling."

Suddenly comprehending the reasoning behind his statement, Amethyst glanced away and within moments Damien was lightly sponging her face.

Steeling himself against his body's weakness, Damien continued his loving administrations, moving down the graceful column of her throat, across her slender shoulders and arms, those small, perfect breasts, the pink, appealing nipples firm and erect under his touch. Taking a deep breath, Damien moved lower, the soapy cloth finally coming into contact with the tight curls between her thighs. Gently separating her legs, Damien cleansed Amethyst meticulously, carefully removing the last traces of the virginity lost in the raging passion of the previous night. Suffused with tenderness as he completed his intimate chore, Damien raised his eyes abruptly, catching in Amethyst's glance an expression of vulnerability and loss that moved him beyond words. Sweeping her into his arms, he held her almost painfully close, his heart throbbing in his chest as he whispered against her silky curls, "Don't look so sad, darling. I'll make you happy, I promise you."

A now familiar heat surged through his veins as Damien covered her mouth briefly with his, but realizing their privacy was limited even if he could dare another loving assault on the small woman lying so helpless in his embrace, Damien pulled himself away with an obvious effort, his smile apologetic as he reached for the fresh nightshift lying on the chair beside the bed.

"I'm afraid I sometimes overestimate my willpower, Amethyst."

Carefully slipping the delicate garment over her head, he assisted her in slipping her arms into the sleeves as he would a child, a strong sense of relief flooding his senses as the voluminous garment covered the slender body that drew him so relentlessly. Sliding his arms beneath her abruptly, he lifted Amethyst into his arms. Holding her tight against him for a brief second, Damien experienced a peculiar thrill as he held her so possessively. Her questioning expression finally penetrating his bemused state, he stated softly as he lowered her into the chair beside the bed, "I'll put some fresh bedclothes on the bed so you may rest comfortably."

Turning his back, Damien proceeded to strip the bed in quick, sweeping movements, but not before Amethyst's eyes caught the bright red stains marring the whiteness of the cotton sheeting. Her face paling at the reminder of her loss, Amethyst closed her eyes weakly for a few brief seconds as Damien swiftly redressed the bed. Turning back in her direction, Damien deliberately ignored her pallor as guilt began to gnaw at his increasingly active conscience, and sweeping her back into his arms, he held her only briefly before laying her gently against the freshly fluffed pillows. Carefully pulling the light covering up to her chest, he said in a tone that belied the heavy hammering of his heart, "I'll go now and see what is keeping your breakfast."

Within the hour Amethyst had eaten and was once again reclining in bed, her eyelids growing heavier with each passing minute. Walking to the window, Damien lowered the blind, turning in time to catch the sudden widening of Amethyst's eyes as she nervously averted her face.

"Damn!" Damien was suddenly irritated. "Does the little chit think I will attack her each time the room is darkened?" Walking to the bed in two swift strides, he frowned unreasonably, stating in a cold voice, "You may sleep now, Amethyst. I shall be going to my ship for a few hours."

He was stomping down the street toward the harbor, an angry scowl on his face, when he admitted to himself for the first time the true reason for his flaring irritation lay in Amethyst's accurate reading of his unconscious intentions, and her all-too-obvious reluctance. Suddenly slowing his stride, Damien heaved a small sigh as he mumbled to himself, "Straith, you surly bastard, what else could you expect from the child? Twice you assured her of your platonic intent, only to end up making love to her each time. She trusts your good intentions no more than you trust them yourself! Give her time, man! She's barely well, yet each time you make love to her you can feel her response . . . the fire burning just below the surface. You must be patient, man, patient. It will be worth the wait . . ."

Damien's tall, broad figure had barely cleared the doorway before Tillie was at Amethyst's door, her face clearly showing the anxiety she had suppressed in Damien's presence. Advancing slowly into the room, she stared silently in Amethyst's direction for a few long minutes, hesitant to speak. Doing nothing to alleviate her discomfort, Amethyst avoided the worried mulatto's discerning eye, glancing toward her only once to quickly move her gaze back again to the window.

Tillie's soft, rich tone finally broke the silence of the small room, her voice trembling noticeably as she inquired softly, "Amethyst, you be alright, child? There be anything Tillie do fe you before Captain Straith come back?"

Waiting anxiously for a signal from Amethyst to voice her condemnation of the man who had just left the house, Tillie's heart plummeted in despair as Amethyst replied quietly in a tone that invited no comment, "No, thank you, Tillie. I'm really quite tired. I think I'll rest for a little while."

Her throat tightening unmercifully at her exclusion from Amethyst's confidence, Tillie could do no more than nod dumbly before turning to leave the room, closing the door quietly behind her.

Once again alone, Amethyst closed her eyes tightly, the tears she had hidden from Tillie with her averted gaze slipping needlessly out of the corners of her eyes as she struggled to suppress the deep sobs she felt building inside her. She had been such a fool . . . and now she was paying the price of her own stubbornness. She should have listened to Tillie from the beginning. Damien Straith truly was an obeah-man. There was no longer any doubt in her mind that the infamous Captain held a strong power over her which he exerted at will. What other reason could there be for the malady that was slowly consuming her . . . the complete loss of will that overtook her each time Damien took her into his arms . . . the weakness that assailed her each time his lips touched hers, a weakness that had no relation to her recent illness . . . the burning desire that surged within her each time his strong male body pressed intimately against hers, urging her to strain him closer still while she ached with the need to feel him moving freely inside her? Oh, she had been a fool!

A stubborn, childish fool! Had she not been too proud to openly accept the charm Tillie offered her, she would still be at the great house of Sheridan Plantation; William would be well; and she would be safe in his arms.

William . . . oh, William! Unable to suppress the soft sob that escaped her lips at the picture of William's handsome, loving face, Amethyst turned into the pillow to bury the heartbroken sound. Tillie was right . . . William would not want her anymore, and even if he did, his parents would never accept her now. He deserved more in a wife . . . far more . . . In a few weeks Damien Straith would sail again for America, but Amethyst's life would remain immeasurably changed, for William was irrevocably lost to her. And the truth of that knowledge hurt, hurt more deeply than physical pain and, she feared, was a pain that would be far more enduring.

His attention wandering from Jeremy Barnes's efficient recitation of the business conducted in his absence, Damien breathed deeply of the fresh breeze blowing off the ocean, awaiting the sense of contentment that usually accompanied the sensation of the *Sally*'s deck beneath his feet and the scent of salt air in his nostrils. But the peculiar unrest remained. A few hours before he had returned to the ship, bathed and shaved leisurely for the first time in over a week, and donning a fresh set of clothes, had come up on deck to assess the progress made during his absence. It was obvious to his discerning eye that Jeremy Barnes had done his job well in keeping the men in hand and preparing the ship for the return voyage to America due to commence within a fortnight. Obeying his orders to the letter, Barnes had continued contracting for return cargo, and had, in fact, done the job as well as Damien could have done. Due to Barnes's efficient handling of the time since his absence, the option to sail earlier than planned would certainly be open to him, but somehow the thought did little more than increase his discomfort. He and his men had been in Kingston for a considerable time, but he had no desire to quit the island.

His frown deepening considerably, he was forced to

admit that his reluctance was due entirely to the fragile woman whose bed he had left only a few hours before. Nodding absentmindedly as Barnes's low recitation droned on, Damien rationalized silently, "It's too soon to leave now. I've not yet had my fill of her, but within the fortnight I will have become sated, and will be anxious once again to be free on the open seas."

Shaking himself mentally, Damien made a supreme effort to devote his full attention to the earnest first mate and draw his wandering thoughts back from the picture of deep violet eyes that seemed determined to interrupt his concentration. Within the half hour, no longer able to deny a vague apprehension building inside him, Damien gave his bewildered first mate terse instructions before striding back down the gangplank. His apprehension growing with each step he took, Damien approached the front door to Amethyst's house in a stride that was just short of a run. Pushing the door open abruptly, Damien was faced with Tillie's startled expression. Instantly suspicious, Damien glanced briefly toward Amethyst's door before moving unhesitantly in its direction. Within minutes he was in the darkened room. His eyes finally adjusting to the dim light, Damien saw the petite figure lying motionless in bed. Closing the door lightly behind him, Damien walked quietly toward the bed, noting the slow, even rise and fall of the small breast beneath the light covering. His heartbeat gradually returning to normal, Damien allowed his eyes to move slowly over the small, perfect face outlined by a halo of deep, black curls against the pillow. Moving closer, he saw tear stains on the smooth cheeks and suddenly immeasurably saddened to see evidence of her unhappiness, Damien crouched by the bed to brush the shining curls lightly with his lips. The need to hold her close more than he could withstand, Damien moved to lay beside her atop the coverlet, careful lest he disturb her slumber. Turning on his side toward her, he moved closer until his face lay only inches from hers on the pillow. Slowly sliding his arm across her waist, Damien fitted himself as closely against her as he dared without disturbing her sleep. Closing his eyes, he breathed deeply of Amethyst's fragrance, effectively dismissing in that short moment the guilt that had begun to eat at his mind in the sudden, absolute confirmation of his belief that this indeed was the way it was meant to be. . . .

The following days moved in a steady, easy pattern for Damien, the leisurely pace belying the speed with which the week slipped past. Strangely reluctant to abandon Amethyst for even one night, he scornfully ignored the pallet Tillie prepared in the living room and returned to Amethyst's bed each night, secure in the knowledge that Amethyst would not refuse him. Nagging relentlessly at his conscience however, was his realization that Amethyst's acceptance of him was due mainly to fear of his retaliation should she ultimately refuse him. But the warmth of her response to his lovemaking was not due to fear, of that he was certain. There was no denying the spontaneous spark that ignited each time their bodies touched and the growing warmth of Amethyst's acceptance, despite the reluctance with which it was given.

Fiercely possessive, he watched with great personal satisfaction the slow return of Amethyst's strength and color, personally supervising every facet of her recovery to Tillie's obvious but unexpressed annoyance. In truth, sorely conscious of his own growing obsession with the small violet-eyed woman around whom his life suddenly seemed to revolve, Damien firmly refused to consider the situation beyond a day at a time while the *Sally*'s scheduled sailing date the following week nagged persistently at the back of his mind.

Forcing himself to attend to business matters in the

morning hours of the day, Damien returned to the house punctually each noon to assist Amethyst in her daily exercise, carefully lengthening its duration so she might gradually strengthen her weakened muscles. But however long the daylight hours, night brought Amethyst into his arms again, allowing him to gently explore the depths to which the reluctant lavender-eyed waif stirred his boundless passion.

Slowly opening her eyes, Amethyst allowed her sleep-drugged gaze to drift around the small room. Suddenly looking to the bed beside her, she was relieved to find it empty. Shaking the fogginess from her mind, Amethyst recalled impatiently that it was afternoon and she was merely awakening from the nap which Damien had insisted she take. A small frown creasing her brow, Amethyst mumbled under her breath, "My life is no longer my own since Damien Straith has become concerned with it, damn him!"

"You must get ample rest, Amethyst, if you are to get well. You must eat more, Amethyst, if you are to regain your strength. You must not attempt to walk by yourself yet, Amethyst. You aren't strong enough. Do this, Amethyst . . . do that, Amethyst . . ." Damien's steady stream of commands echoed in her brain even during his absence. Sorely tired of the level steel-gray gaze and the endless orders accompanying it, Amethyst had all she could do to maintain her composure. But she dared not oppose Damien in any way. Her mind moving unconsciously to William, she shook her head. No, the result of outright opposition could be disastrous. She must be patient a little longer . . . especially now. From the few remarks Damien had dropped and the occasional visits from his first mate when business matters had necessitated the call, she had gathered she would not have to tolerate his presence in her life much longer. The *Sally* would soon be ready to sail . . . perhaps within the week. The realization that she would soon be free of her bondage shook her with a tremor of inexplicable emotion. Taking a deep breath to shake off her momentary weakness, Amethyst continued her silent plans. Damien would soon be sailing for America and she would resume her life. She would allow these few weeks to assume no more significance in her life than they would in Damien's. When she was strong again she would return to the theater, and when the troupe returned to America, she would accompany them. She no longer had any ties on the island. William's and her future together had been shattered the day she left Sheridan Plantation.

Firmly refusing to succumb to the sorrow that thought evoked, Amethyst threw back the coverlet and prepared to rise. "No matter what Damien says, I shall walk unaided today!" she mumbled adamantly, the small rebellion lifting her spirits immeasurably as she pulled herself to a sitting position on the side of the bed. Suddenly conscious of the full extent of her debility as the room appeared to rock unsteadily around her, Amethyst took a firmer grip on her resolution and inhaled deeply. A bit more secure as the room ceased moving, she pulled herself gingerly to her feet, leaning heavily on the bed as she fumbled with her slippers. Satisfied at last that she was standing reasonably steady, she attempted her first step. Her knees wobbling weakly, she took another, and another, until she was standing before the bedroom dresser. Still trembling, she lifted her eyes to the mirror, her own reflection eliciting a shocked gasp.

"No! That cannot be me!" Raising a tentative, exploring hand to her face, Amethyst stared wide-eyed into the mottled glass. She looked ghastly! Thin to the point of emaciation, her face was small and white, the skin drawn tightly over her cheekbones, further emphasizing the deep lavender of her eyes, which indeed appeared to overwhelm her face. Thick black curls tumbled in wild disarray to shoulders that poked out sharply through the voluminous night rail in which her thin body appeared decidedly lost. Even her hands had a wan, skeletal appearance, and assessing herself critically, Amethyst silently marveled that Damien Straith could bear to look at her, much less desire to share her bed.

Taking a firm grip on the dresser with one hand, Amethyst reached for her brush with the other. She had only been able to give her riotous curls a few short strokes before her strength began to fade, but unwilling to admit defeat and return to bed, Amethyst relinquished the brush and prepared to walk to the doorway. One step, two and then three and she was at the door, experiencing a tremendous burst of pride in that small accomplishment as she grasped the doorknob tightly. She still swayed uncertainly, but taking another deep breath, Amethyst turned the knob and walked unsteadily through the doorway into the living room.

Her sudden appearance brought a low gasp from Tillie and an angry snort from Damien as both heads snapped in her direction. At her side within seconds, Damien steadied her faltering step as he scowled blackly.

"What do you think you're doing, Amethyst?"

"It should be fairly obvious, Damien." Angry that her voice lacked the strength to carry the proper sting, Amethyst continued as arrogantly as she could manage, "and I do *not* need your assistance to get to the other side of the room!"

His scowl darkening, Damien dismissed her words with a small deprecating glance. Swinging her up into his arms, he held her tightly against his broad chest as he carried her effortlessly toward the couch.

Incensed by his high-handed manner, Amethyst's pale

face flushed brightly as she insisted through clenched teeth, "I said I am quite well enough to walk across this room. Put me down, I say!"

His expression softening only briefly as his glance traveled the small furious face staring up into his, Damien mumbled begrudgingly as he lowered her to the couch, "I admit you must be feeling somewhat better since you appear to be reverting to your usual bellicose manner, but you are not at all strong enough to walk unaided, Amethyst. I have no intention of allowing you to effectively negate all the hard work I have put into your recuperation by . . ."

"And who gave you authority for absolute control over my recuperation *and* my life, Captain Straith?" Amethyst burst out heatedly, anger effectively dismissing her former caution.

Translucent gray eyes regarding her with a maddening assurance, Damien responded without hesitation, "You did, Amethyst, the day you walked back aboard my ship."

Words of denial choking her throat, Amethyst swallowed hard before retorting fervently, "But I did not turn myself over to you body and soul, Damien Straith. I . . ."

Not bothering to allow her to finish her statement, Damien interrupted softly with an intimacy that darkened the flush on her cheek, "When it comes to you, Amethyst, I find I can accept no less a commitment."

Her expression tightening in anger, Amethyst deliberately withheld her instinctive response in deference to caution. Jerking her glance from his, she stubbornly fastened it on an object in the far corner of the room, continuing to ignore him as she sensed the heat of his glance slowly moving over her prone figure.

When he finally spoke, Damien's voice held an oddly cautious ring. "At any rate, Amethyst, you will not be bothered by my interference much longer . . ."

Lavender eyes snapping back to his face revealingly in an unguarded moment, Amethyst whispered hopefully, "What do you mean, Damien?"

"The *Sally* will be sailing within a week's time . . ." Damien's voice trailed away as he scrutinized her classic features.

Reacting with instinctive caution to his assessing glance, Amethyst glanced away, struggling to hide the elation surging through her veins as a small voice echoed over and over in the back of her mind, "I will be free . . . I will be free!"

Finally in control, Amethyst raised her eyes. "You will be returning to Charleston, Damien?"

"No, our destination is Philadelphia. Our merchandise will be well received in that port."

Nodding her head in silent acknowledgment, Amethyst once again averted her gaze, the tight rein kept on her raging emotions all but consuming the last of her waning strength.

Unconsciously frowning, Damien pulled his powerful body to its full height to speak in a warning tone. "I must return to my ship for a few hours. You may rest on the couch if you wish for a while longer, but you will not attempt to walk back to bed unaided, is that understood, Amethyst?" When she did not respond, choosing instead to continue her perusal of an unknown object in the corner, his deep voice boomed angrily in the room, snapping her eyes back to him as he repeated with added emphasis, "Do you hear me, Amethyst?"

Her gaze filled with disdain, Amethyst replied quietly, "My illness did not affect my hearing, Damien."

"Yes, it would appear your hearing is intact, leaving only your common sense impaired, Amethyst! You will allow Tillie to help you return to bed when you tire."

Suddenly unable to bear his autocratic tone a moment longer, Amethyst snapped heatedly, "And what would you do should I refuse to obey your 'request,' Damien? Punish me? Send me to bed without supper?"

Silence followed Amethyst's haughty challenge, during which the fury in Damien's penetrating stare seemed to seep into her very soul. The power of its translucent glare was overwhelming, slowly draining her rebellion, leaving her small and defenseless as she struggled to restrain the violent tremors of fear suddenly shaking her body.

A small, confident smile growing on his lips, Damien responded softly, "Would you like to test me and see, Amethyst?"

The last of her courage deserting her, Amethyst's glance finally fell from his. Attempting to talk with a mouth that had suddenly gone dry with anxiety, Amethyst stammered uncertainly, "N . . . No, Damien. I . . . I will call Tillie when I'm ready to return to bed."

Her face was still averted when he turned and moved toward the doorway, leaving to slam the door loudly behind him. Turning to stare with blazing hatred in its direction, Amethyst mumbled heatedly under her breath, "Enjoy your domination while you can, Damien Straith! I am too weak to fight you now, but you will soon be gone and then I will be free of your insufferable demands! And you may rest assured you will never find me vulnerable to your wants again!"

Amethyst was shaking violently and fearful for her health, Tillie moved swiftly to her side. Stroking her cheek gently, the worried mulatto crooned softly, "Him not worth you anger, Amethyst. Amethyst soon be free of that obeah-man, and Mr. Sheridan . . . him take you back with . . ."

Tears welling in her eyes at the mention of William's name, Amethyst snapped sharply, "I don't wish to discuss it, Tillie!"

Immediately regretting her harsh words, Amethyst turned apologetic eyes to Tillie's hurt expression.

"Tillie . . . please . . . I find Captain Straith was right after all. I am far weaker than I realized. Would you help me back to bed?"

Unable to respond past the lump in her own throat, Tillie nodded dumbly, gently helping Amethyst to her feet.

Settled once again in bed, Amethyst snatched Tillie's dark hand as she turned to leave the room. In a voice filled with remorse, Amethyst whispered softly, "Please don't be angry with me, Tillie. You know I love you, don't you? You're all I have left now . . ."

Her rich voice deep with emotion, Tillie returned the pressure of the thin white hand, her own eyes bright with tears. "Tillie knows. You not to worry, Amethyst. Tillie knows . . ."

Pulling his tall, gaunt frame tentatively to his feet, William ran a nervous hand through his tousled mahogany hair. His face creased in concentration, he advanced slowly toward the window of his room, straining to overcome the weakness that caused his knees to wobble uncertainly. Finally at the window, he grasped the pane for support, the thin veil of perspiration covering his forehead and upper lip silent testimony to the effort expended by the small exertion.

"Damn! Damn!" he muttered beneath his breath. "How damned long will it take me to regain my strength?" Determined to test his endurance further, William took a deep breath and advanced in the direction of the doorway. This time he smiled as he appeared to regain a bit more stability with each step, his spirits soaring. He was doing better already! He was certain he had remained in a weakened condition because Dr. Martens's caution and his parents concern had kept him confined to his bed. But the fever and retching had been gone for well over a week. Strange how Amethyst's departure had seemed to signal a turn for the better in his condition. He realized he still had a way to go before complete recovery, but he was definitely on the mend. Even his dizzy spells had ceased, and he was now certain he would be fit to travel within the week. Yes. He would set the date a week from today . . . a week from today he would be on his way to Kingston to see Amethyst!

Amethyst! Lord, how he missed her! He had not gotten a proper explanation for her abrupt disappearance from Sheridan Plantation while he was ill, but he had not believed his parents when they said she had become tired of nursing him and returned home. Amethyst would never have behaved so selfishly knowing how dependent he was on her presence. No, his own reasoning was more feasible. He now knew that Amethyst had been dreadfully ill with the same fever that had almost taken his life, and reasoned that she had left Sheridan Plantation in her delerium to return home. At any rate, Quaco had found her at home, dreadfully ill but recuperating, with Tillie her devoted nurse. Tillie . . . Tillie loved Amethyst almost as much as he. He would have to reward Tillie for her diligence after Amethyst and he were married. And that would be soon . . . as soon as Amethyst was well enough to stand beside him at the altar.

His excitement dissipating the last of his strength, William turned once again toward his bed and within seconds was sinking gratefully onto its welcome softness. It would not do to push too hard. He would walk again later and gradually build his strength without his parents' knowledge. There was no sense in worrying them any further. He knew what he had to do and would do it, and when he saw Amethyst again . . . Lord, his heart was singing . . . he would never let her out of his sight!

At least he was certain Captain Damien Straith was out of the picture. Quaco had told him the cowardly bastard had been afraid to risk the fever by seeing Amethyst. He also had it on good report that the *Sally* was fit to sail again within the week and it was obvious the good captain had not wasted any time in readying his ship for a quick departure from the island. The next time Damien Straith returned to Kingston, if indeed he ever did return legally, Amethyst would be his wife and safe with him at Sheridan Plantation. A familiar elation filled his being, causing William's boyish countenance to flush in anticipation. "Amethyst, darling," he whispered to the silent room, "I will see you within a week. Quaco will bring you messages of my love each and every day until the time that I can hold you in my arms again. And this time, darling, I will not let you go."

The warm scent of her hair teased his nostrils as Amethyst lay close against him in sleep. Pulling her closer still, Damien breathed deeply of her fragrance. Lord, he could not hold her close enough! Slowly moving his hand, Damien tangled it gently in the tumble of curls on the pillow beside her head, tightening his grasp as the silky strands seemed to slip through his searching fingers. Her hair was heavy . . . warm . . . sensuous to the touch, stirring him deeply as did every facet of the small, beautiful woman in his arms. Tall, impressive women, almost matching him in size, their personalities warm and compliant to his wishes with just enough spark to keep his interest had always been his preference in the past. But Amethyst was small, dwarfed by his broad, muscular frame, so delicate that he sometimes feared he would crush her in the boundless passion she inspired within him. And although she was still in a weakened condition, she was far from compliant. At times he believed she barely controlled the volatile personality bubbling just below the surface calm she maintained, but he suspected she played a waiting game. He had not been fooled by the facade she had assumed for his benefit a few days before, when he had informed her of his imminent departure. She had been a few seconds too late to conceal the relief in her eyes, and that knowledge ate at his vitals like a festering, malignant wound.

Suddenly acutely aware that the nights during which he would be able to hold Amethyst so intimately in his arms were quickly drawing to a close, Damien clutched her tightly, a wave of panic engulfing him. Squirming uncomfortably in his arms, Amethyst stirred, her eyes opening sleepily. Her mumbled words were slurred. "Damien . . . you're hurting me. You're holding me so tight . . ."

Immediately loosening his grasp, Damien caressed the velvet cheek, the corners of his mouth picking up as her eyes fluttered closed again and again while she struggled to remain awake.

"I'm sorry, darling." Lowering his head slightly, he covered the parted lips briefly in a lingering kiss. "Go back to sleep. Everything is alright."

The heavy lids fluttered closed and within a few minutes Amethyst's breathing was slow and even. Staring for long, sober minutes at her face, vulnerable, appealing, unbelievably beautiful in the dim light of the room, Damien felt for the first time the weight of complete realization. His throat tightening painfully, choked his voice into a small, hoarse whisper as he confessed softly into her unhearing ear, "Darling . . . Amethyst . . . my problem is a simple one . . . I do not want to leave you . . ."

With long, anxious strides Damien retraced the path he had walked so many times within the past weeks from his ship to Amethyst's home, his broad impressive figure exuding a confidence he did not feel. His brows drawn into a pensive frown, his mind was far from the street on which he walked. It was already late afternoon and the *Sally* was due to sail on the next morning's tide. When he returned to his ship tonight, he would not see Amethyst again for many months. The thought produced a familiar tightening in his stomach, slowing Damien's step as anxiety returned with nagging persistence. Amethyst would have no worries during his absence. He had made provisions for her welfare that were more than adequate. Having paid the rent on her house for a full year in advance and filled her larder to bursting with supplies, he had assured her security by leaving a generous draft in her name for her own personal use. But his concern had been treated by Amethyst with a cool indifference that managed to convey without words that she cared not a damn what he did! Infuriated by her attitude and immediately suspicious, he had demanded her plans for the future. Lifting her chin a notch higher, she had responded in a clear, arrogant tone which effectively raised his anger to greater heights, that what she did after he left was none of his concern!

Eyes blazing with anger, he had bent low over her bed, taking her shoulders in a grip which later produced startling bruises on her perfect white skin. His voice had been menacingly low.

"Amethyst, make no mistake about this. You belong to me! I am concerned with everything you do now or *will* do during my absence from this island! I will return within a few months and will expect to find you waiting here for me. And I warn you now," his growling whisper had shaken for the first time the cool facade she had assumed, "if you are not here when I return, no force in Heaven or Hell will stop me from finding you again and reclaiming you any way I can! Do not make the mistake of taking another man, Amethyst, for his death will be on your head! I will suffer no trespassing on that which is mine, and *you* most definitely *are* mine, Amethyst, and will *remain* mine until I give you your freedom. For your own sake, I pray you do not forget what I say to you today!"

Her face a bloodless color that had sent a momentary jolt of anxiety through his veins, Amethyst had nonetheless succeeded in rendering one last jibe.

"You may rest assured, Damien, during your absence, I will attempt to be as true to you as you will be to me . . ."

The small smirk on her lips at the conclusion of her remark and the hint of ridicule in her eye pushing him over the edge of restraint, he had reacted in the only manner remaining to him by sweeping her against him in a bone-crushing grip, his mouth plundering hers savagely until the warm taste of blood filled his mouth. Pulling his mouth from her bruised and bleeding lips, he had stared with strange fascination at her tear-streaked face for long moments as his anger drained away. He then lowered his mouth to hers gently, lovingly, with a rising passion which excluded rage, leaving only the deep loving tenderness that endured for the infuriating termagant in his arms. Desire and passion overcoming reason, they had concluded their conversation with an intimacy that left no room for words.

But nothing had been truly settled, and the cold fear welling inside him as he turned off Port Royal Street was that he would be no more successful this night in obtaining an answer to his questions than he had been previously. And he desperately needed peace of mind . . . a word from Amethyst that she . . .

But who was that? His eye catching the tail end of a familiar wagon as it turned the far corner of the street set his heart to racing. Darting quickly into a small alleyway, he ran at breakneck speed to the connecting street and down another alley, emerging at last to stand waiting at the spot where the wagon would move onto the road leading out of town. Within moments the wagon turned the corner and rambled slowly toward him. Immediately confirming his tentative identification, Damien felt anger build inside him. The heavy heaving of his broad chest not due solely to his recent exertion, Damien raised his hand to signal the old Negro to halt.

"I thought it was your wagon I saw leaving John's Lane just now, Quaco. It has been so long since we've seen you at the Greer household that I feared you had forgotten us." Noting the guilty expression that stole across the old slave's face, Damien continued, "How is your young master faring?"

"Him be well, Massa . . . him be well . . ." The old Negro was obviously agitated, surprised by his sudden appearance, and taking advantage of the man's uneasiness, Damien pressed harder, "It seems your master wishes to send a message to Amethyst that you cannot deliver in my presence, Quaco."

Showing a spark of resentment at Damien's snide reference to his master, Quaco answered quickly, "No, Massa! Massa William, him be honest man! Massa Sheridan Sr. tell Quaco not tell Massa William 'bout you 'n Miz Amethyst, 'n dat be what Quaco do! Tillie tell Quaco de time t' come when de Cap'n be 'way 'n Quaco come ever day, 'n leave 'fore de Cap'n come back."

"So, you have brought messages every day to Miss Amethyst from Master William . . ." His blood pumping heatedly at the deception that had been practiced right under his nose, Damien continued tightly, ". . . and I suppose you have carried Miss Amethyst's loving messages back to your master each day also . . ."

Shaking his head emphatically, Quaco declared ardently, "No, Massa, Miz Amethyst, him say nothin', but Massa Sheridan make me tell de young massa dat Miz Amethyst send him love. Dey be 'fraid de young massa get right up frem him sickbed 'n gowan see Miz Amethyst if him think anythin' wrong. Dey make me tell him you be 'fraid of de fever and stay 'way frem Miz Amethyst all dis time!"

"And does Master William know I'm about to leave Kingston, Quaco?"

"Yessuh! And him tell me t' tell Miz Amethyst dat de doctor say him 'lright t' come t' town tomorrow.'n him gowan come 'n take Miz Amethyst back home wid him!"

"Back to Sheridan Plantation with him?"

"Yessuh! Him gowan take Miz Amethyst back wid him 'n him tell Quaco him gowan marry Miz Amethyst as soon as him be well!"

His body growing taut with anger, Damien inquired levelly, "And what was Miss Amethyst's response?"

"Quaco tell Miz Amethyst and him say nothin', Massa. But Tillie say him have Miz Amethyst ready t' go wid Massa William when him come in de mornin'."

His eyes turning to ice, Damien said tersely, "Thank you, Quaco. You may go home and deliver the message as you were told, but," directing the power of his translucent gaze into the old Negro's eyes, Damien continued in a tone that set the old man to trembling, "you will tell no one of our discussion, do you understand, Quaco?"

His grizzled old head bobbing in assent as he shook visibly with fear, Quaco mumbled, "Yessuh, yessuh, Massa, I'se understand."

Dismissing the trembling Negro with an absentminded gesture Damien turned, his mind racing. "So, the deceitful little witch intends to run off with her lover tomorrow as soon as I leave. Well, I'll see about that . . ."

A sound at the front door turned Amethyst's head in its direction the second before Damien stepped through the entrance. Standing motionless in the doorway, his unmistakable frame silhouetted by the light at his back, his expression was unreadable, but something about his stance, the manner in which he hesitated as she felt his eyes move over her, set her nerves to prickling. A small frown covering her face, she felt only the tension of the moment, unaware of the effect her consummate beauty had on the tall man regarding her so intently.

Unable to draw his eyes from Amethyst as she lay propped with two large pillows behind her back on the low, well worn couch in the living room, Damien's eyes raked her savagely. Amethyst was frowning, her graceful winged brows drawn together with a small pucker over her slender, perfect nose, causing the long sweep of black lashes to almost touch her brow as she regarded him steadily. Lavender eyes dark with concern, she strained to make out his expression, her fine, well drawn lips in a straight line that finally quirked impatiently in the corner, displaying a fleeting dimple in her smooth cheek. The sallow color of sickness had disappeared during her short convalescence, not quite restoring the full bloom of health, while still managing to preview a glimpse of the beauty yet to return. Stringent attention to her diet had put a few pounds back on her fragile frame, smoothing the sharp contours of her cheek and shoulder, where the glorious mane of curls moved impatiently to spill in heady profusion down her slender back. His heart wrenching tightly in his chest, Damien swore silently. She was a magnificent creature, his Amethyst . . . damn her!

Her nerves stretched to the breaking point, Amethyst had awakened that morning at dawn, instantly alert to the fact that the *Sally* was to sail the following day. This was to be the last morning she would awaken to find Damien Straith sharing her bed, and unconsciously breathing a brief sigh of relief, she had quietly studied the unfathomable man lying beside her.

With an impatient shake of her head, she had come to the conclusion that she would never understand the personality which vacillated among loving tenderness, harsh criticism, wary aloofness and an obsessive, smothering possessiveness that drove her to the brink of distraction. But it would not be much longer. He would be leaving soon. Unconsciously moving her eyes across his strong, handsome features, Amethyst had allowed them to linger for a moment on the bright tawny hair hanging boyishly on his forehead, the thick stubby lashes on the lids covering those startling eyes. Thankful those same eyes were not open to observe her perusal, she had swept her glance along the firm, square jaw which only hinted at the stubbornness to which it could set, her eyes flicking momentarily to the sensuous mouth that set her soul to quaking. Damien slept naked, the light covering pulled across his waist exposing a vast muscular chest lightly peppered with golden brown hair and on one long leg, the strong, well muscled thigh blatant evidence of its power. Yes, she had to concede that Sally Warren had been right. Damien Straith was a wildly appealing man. And frightening herself most of all was her recognition that a level look from those compellingly sensual eyes set her blood to racing. Despite herself, she also had to concede that Damien's lovemaking often carried her past logical thought, to the point where only they existed in the heady realm of intoxicating sensation and brilliant emotion. But reality inevitably returned with all its memories, dropping her beyond despair for her body's betrayal. She could not take much more of the emotional teeter-totter Damien practiced on her heart. She desperately needed relief . . . needed to be free . . .

As if sensing her thoughts, Damien had muttered softly in his sleep, turning on his side toward her to slide a long, muscular arm possessively across her body. Clutching her instinctively, he had fitted the full length of his body against hers, moving to slide his face into her hair, effectively holding her prisoner in his grasp even as he had slept. Closing her eyes, Amethyst had resigned herself to his possession. Realizing his power over her was so complete that she had neither the strength nor the desire to resist, she had silently consoled herself with the fact that in one more day she would be free at last from his domination.

But she could sense something was wrong now. Tension hung heavily on the air as Damien stood observing her from the doorway, sending a prickle of apprehension down her spine. Swallowing hard, Amethyst asked cautiously, "What's wrong, Damien? Have you run into some problem with the *Sally?*"

There was a moment's hesitation before Damien walked slowly forward to stand towering over the couch, his glance steady and unrevealing. A small cold smile curling his lips, he said smoothly, "No, darling, what could possibly be wrong? The *Sally* is set to sail and will leave on the morning tide as planned. You need not disturb yourself that I may remain another day in Kingston."

Suddenly dropping to his knees beside the couch to bring his face level with hers, Damien slid his fingers into the hair at her temples, his wide palms cupping her cheeks, holding her face steady as he whispered softly against her lips, "You will miss me tomorrow, will you not, Amethyst, when you lie here all alone with only Tillie to care for you?" When she did not respond, he continued in a low, throbbing voice, "You will miss my arms around you at night . . . the touch of my hands on your body . . . the beauty we create when I am deep inside you . . ."

Amethyst felt the flush on her cheeks as his glance moved heatedly across her face, and unable to look away, experienced once again the lethargy his steady gaze evoked as it seemed to sink into her very soul. Mesmerized, she held his glance as his passionate whisper droned on. "You will miss me, Amethyst, tomorrow when my ship sails and you are all alone. You will miss my loving..."

Unable to bear his glance a moment longer, Amethyst closed her eyes, unmindful of the lone tear that slipped down her cheek as Damien's soft voice continued in her ear, "But we have some time left, darling until I leave you tonight. We have a few hours left for me to love you..."

The bright light of morning hurt her eyes as Amethyst squinted against its glare. Her head was throbbing dully, her mind foggy, barely functioning as she moved her eyes slowly around her. Dazed and disoriented, she stared for long moments at her surroundings in an attempt to ascertain her whereabouts, not quite certain if she was indeed in the midst of another dream or truly awake. The room was familiar, certainly, but it was not her own room. And the floor was rocking beneath her, a gentle steady motion, soothing to her senses...

Sudden realization flashing across her mind, Amethyst snapped to a sitting position in bed, her hands reaching up to grasp her throbbing head as she glanced to the window! She was on a ship... this was Damien's cabin... and the blue sky outside the porthole was moving... moving! What was she doing here? It could not be morning... Damien was to sail in the morning! Trembling as she fought the fear rising within her, Amethyst slid her legs over the side of the bed and stood up. Too upset for caution, she stumbled weakly toward the porthole, one hand holding her throbbing head, the other reaching out to grasp the furniture in her path for support. Finally at the porthole, she looked out to see only sky above and tranquil turquoise sea below.

"No! It can't be true!" she gasped, her hand pressing

hard against her lips in an attempt to stifle the sobs choking her throat. "He could not have done this! He could not have taken me from my home without my consent!"

Unwilling to accept the evidence of her own eyes, Amethyst stared hopefully around the room. But this was Damien's cabin . . . and they were under sail. Closing her eyes for the briefest moment, Amethyst swayed weakly, her hand moving up to still the steady pounding in her head that seemed to deaden her brain. Opening her eyes once again, she staggered back to bed, collapsing against the spotless linens in unbelieving bewilderment. But where had the evening of the previous day gone? She remembered Damien's return to her house in a strange mood, his eyes cold and angry while he spoke intimately of wanting to make love to her. Completely ignoring Tillie's presence, he had swept her into his arms and carried her to her room where they had spent what was to be their final hours together before he was to leave at nightfall to return to his ship. But memory faded after their light supper in her room when Damien had brought her the milk she detested and which he had insisted she drink as a nightly ritual until she regained her strength. With a slow dawning of realization, she remembered she had remarked the milk tasted curiously bitter, but Damien had been adamant that she drink all of it, waiting deliberately beside her until she had drained the glass.

It was at this point that memory began to blur and then ceased completely. Amethyst raised herself to a sitting position in bed, anger replacing the myriad of emotions overwhelming her since awakening. How could he! How could he kidnap her so coldly, without the slightest regard for her wishes! And where was he now when she was ready to face him? She would not allow him to get away with this! She would find him immediately and make him turn the ship back to Kingston!

Suddenly glancing down, Amethyst realized she wore only her night rail. Quickly scanning the room, she saw none of her clothing in evidence. She could not afford to waste time in searching. Standing unsteadily, Amethyst yanked the light coverlet off the bed, and holding her aching head as high as she dared, started for the door. Knowing a moment's panic as her hand touched the knob at the thought that the door might be locked, Amethyst breathed a small sigh of relief when it turned easily under her hand.

Once in the familiar passageway, Amethyst moved uncertainly toward the ladder to deck. The sooner she faced Damien Straith and made him turn back to Jamaica, the sooner she would be home in her little house on John's Lane and away from him!

Her weakened muscles already feeling the strain, her painful headache adding immeasurably to her distress, Amethyst made an uneasy ascent to deck. Finally arriving atop, she stood squinting in the bright sunlight as her eyes adjusted to the light. Swaying uncertainly, she glanced around her to find herself in the midst of a group of men of varying ages and appearances, the solitary common bonds apparent between them at first glance the fact that they all wore peculiar britches that belled out awkwardly at the knee, and they all stared at her in open-mouthed amazement. Boldly returning their stares, small bare feet poking out from beneath her full white night rail, Amethyst stood clutching the light coverlet around her shoulders. A stiff ocean breeze succeeding in flaring the light wrapper out behind her like a floating cape despite her efforts to restrain it, molded the fine material of her gown against her body revealingly. The long black ringlets tumbling almost to her waist blew back from her face to flutter rapidly in the breeze, clearly displaying the small perfect face in which large purple eyes glowed in purposeful anger.

Padding up to a young, red-haired fellow who gaped in an almost ludicrous fashion, she demanded imperiously, "I want to see your captain. I demand to see him immediately!"

Gulping inwardly, the fellow flushed, stammering weakly, "He . . . he's over there, ma'am."

Turning in the direction the fellow pointed, Amethyst was in time to see the object of her quest striding toward her, anger drawing his face into a tight mask.

Refusing to allow the frightening specter to intimidate her, Amethyst began haughtily, "Captain Straith, I demand . . ."

Ignoring her as if she had not spoken, Damien swooped her up into his arms with barely a break in stride, and was carrying her down the steps toward his cabin before Amethyst could recuperate enough to gasp indignantly, "How dare you! Put me down this instant! I demand . . ."

His expression frightening to behold, Damien looked directly into her face for the first time, his voice a low growl. "Shut up, Amethyst, or I will accommodate you by dropping you where we now stand!" When she still sputtered ineffectually, Damien hesitated once again in his descent to repeat his warning, "I warn you, woman, you try my patience too far. If you speak another word, I will not be responsible for my actions!"

Courage momentarily deserting her in the face of her helplessness against his fury, Amethyst abruptly snapped her mouth closed. She would hold her tongue until she was in a safer position, with her feet on the floor.

In long, angry strides Damien walked down the corridor, roughly pushing open the cabin door with his shoulder. In another few steps he was at the bunk, and in a quick, unexpected movement, dropped her abruptly onto its surface.

Gasping at his ungentlemanly treatment, Amethyst managed to pull herself together enough to shoot a disdainful look in his direction the second before Damien exploded angrily, "I ought to beat you within an inch of your life! What do you mean by coming on deck in that manner . . . barefoot and . . . undressed!"

"Undressed!" Indignation flaring, Amethyst repeated heatedly, "Undressed! You surly beast! How dare you insinuate that . . ."

Apparently deaf to her words, Damien bent down to rest his hands on either side of her shoulders, looming large and threatening over her, succeeding in cowering her back against the bedclothes as he demanded icily, "You will never come on deck again without my permission! And you will *never* appear in the presence of my men again unless suitably attired! I will set the rules for your conduct aboard this ship, and you will obey them to the letter, or so help me God, I will . . ."

"You need not worry about setting rules for my behavior, Captain Straith!" His dictatorial tone sending the blood rushing to her head, increasing the pain that throbbed unceasingly through her brain, Amethyst managed to continue, "For I will not be on this ship long enough to abide by them!"

"Oh, is that so, your ladyship? And do you expect to swim all the way back to Jamaica?"

"No! You will turn this ship around and take me back immediately! I demand that you . . ."

"You may demand all you wish, but I am captain of this ship and my word is law here!" Pushing his face closer still until she pressed tightly back against the hard mattress in an attempt to avoid his furious stare, he continued softly, "You will obey me and will live by every rule I set for you on this voyage for I will stand for none of your nonsense! I warn you now, Amethyst!"

His frightening visage was demoralizing, the power of his massive frame overwhelming her with its sheer proportions, and suddenly unable to think beyond the fierce pounding in her head, Amethyst whispered bewilderedly, "But . . . why . . . why did you do this? Was it just for the sport of . . ."

His handsome face contorting into an angry sneer, Damien hissed heatedly, "Don't play the innocent, Amethyst! Did you think me such a fool that I would not discover the little deception you practiced?"

"Deception . . . ?"

"Did you think I would allow you to go running into Sheridan's arms the moment my ship left shore?" At her surprised expression, he continued snidely, "You should have realized that no secrets could prevail against my obeah!" Damien's short bark of laughter was directed mainly at himself as he silently groaned under the weight of his own ironic bewitchment with the small girl/woman cowering with fear beneath him. "You belong to me, Amethyst. I told you I would allow no one a part of that which is mine and you most assuredly are mine! It is unfortunate you chose to ignore my warning, but I am not at all certain I will not come to enjoy your presence on my ship. I may now, after all, look forward to many long, full nights that otherwise would have been spent . . ."

Damien's furious tone droned on as Amethyst began to lose the drift of his angry words. The pain in her head was increasing rapidly, interfering with her ability to distinguish between one sentence and the next as Damien's violent tirade continued. Suddenly unable to bear the hot, searing jabs of pain piercing her brain with maddening precision, Amethyst closed her eyes, simultaneously raising her hand to her temple with an unmistakable grimace of distress.

Stopping abruptly in mid-sentence, Damien's anger drained away as Amethyst emitted a soft groan, clutching her head in pain that was obviously not feigned. He had noticed her face paling rapidly, but had put her change in color to fear. Angry with his own stupidity, Damien reached out to lay his palm against Amethyst's forehead, breathing a quick sigh of relief when he felt it cool to the touch.

"Amethyst . . ." His voice an anxious whisper, bore no trace of its former hostility, "What's wrong, darling? Are you in pain? You must tell me so I may help you, darling."

Her own anger conquered by the pain stabbing unceasingly through her brain, Amethyst stammered weakly, "Damien . . . my head . . . it hurts so badly . . . It was painful when I awakened, but now it is . . ."

The laudanum! Damien started guiltily. He had given her a heavy dosage last night so she might sleep straight through until morning. She had probably not had enough time to recover completely but had pushed herself despite the effects of the drug until her body could no longer withstand the strain. His anger dissipated, he knew only the desire to relieve her pain. All other thought swept from his mind, Damien sat on the side of the bed, and leaning forward, pulled Amethyst onto his lap. A flood of warmth rushing through his body as her softness pressed against him, he rocked her as he would a child, laying his head atop hers as he whispered soothingly, "You will be alright, darling. Just close your eyes and sleep. You have pushed yourself too hard today. You will feel better after you have rested. Sleep, darling . . . I'll stay with you . . . I'll take care of you, darling . . . my darling Amethyst . . ."

A soft, gentle touch on her cheek awakened Amethyst from her dreamless sleep. A sober-faced Damien still sat on the side of the bed, his glance pensive as it moved slowly across her face. His deep whisper finally breaking the prevailing silence, Damien said huskily, "How are you feeling now, Amethyst?"

Amethyst hesitated in responding, tentatively moving her head on the pillow as she held her breath in anticipation of a recurrence of pain. But there was none. "The pain is gone, Damien."

Immensely relieved, Damien smiled for the first time, leaning down to cover her lips lightly with his own as he said softly, "You must remember that you are still recuperating, Amethyst, and not push yourself too hard. If you wish to go on deck, I will take you, but you must first . . ."

"Why did you do this, Damien?" Blurting out the question that still plagued her mind, Amethyst continued haltingly, "Why? You most assuredly have a . . . a . . . woman waiting for you in Philadelphia who can more than adequately fill your needs. And you certainly have become accustomed to doing without a woman's company for the duration of the voyage. Then why the need to take me from my home . . . the life I have made for myself . . ."

A hint of his former anger stealing back into his countenance as his lips tightened convulsively, Damien strove to control his emotions. "I have already answered that question, Amethyst, and do not feel the need to discuss it further."

"No matter what you think, Damien," Amethyst persisted, "your obeah has failed you this time. Quaco did come to my house yesterday with a message from William, but I had no intention of returning to Sheridan Plantation with William. I was going to tell him so when he came . . ." Her words trailing off significantly, Amethyst lowered her eyes as she continued indistinctly, "I felt I should tell him myself . . . face to face . . . to try to explain . . ." Finally lifting her face once again, she read the skepticism in Damien's expression. Barely restraining the flash of anger that restored the color to her cheeks, Amethyst continued with a hint of her old *hauteur*, "I would not have you believe I intended to refuse William out of any misguided loyalty to you, Damien. It was merely a matter of a change of circumstance. I was and am no longer the person William wanted to marry, and he was ignorant of that fact when he proposed to come. Even should he choose to overlook the fact that you . . . I . . . we have . . . been intimate, I could not allow William to accept less in a wife than he is worthy of receiving."

Her thoughtful consideration of the "worthy" William's feelings only serving to further tighten the knot forming in his chest, Damien cut ruthlessly into her statement, his voice harsh with suppressed anger. "I have not released you from our bargain, Amethyst."

"Our bargain!" Her eyes widening expressively, Amethyst responded incredulously, "I came to you, Damien, simply because I was no longer strong enough to oppose you and feared for William's life. But he has recovered and our bargain is finished!"

Abruptly pulling himself back, Damien's voice was low with suppressed menace. "I will be the one who ultimately releases you from our bargain, Amethyst, and I say our bargain is not absolved!"

Angry tears sparkling in her brilliant eyes, Amethyst swallowed hard, lifting her chin to continue purposefully, "And when you *are* finished with me, will you abandon me in Philadelphia, far from my home and friends, my reputation ruined, fit for no other work than that of a . . . a . . ."

Never having considered the thought, Damien was struck by its idiocy. That he should abandon her at all . . .

"You are talking like a fool, Amethyst!"

Her tone insistent, Amethyst continued, "I will know now what you intend to do with me . . . how I am to return home when I am once again free to do so. I have no clothes, no money... I know no one in Philadelphia..."

Resentful and unaccustomed to being pressed for a future commitment, Damien frowned darkly, his expression growing more ominous by the second as he pulled back even further to eye Amethyst coldly. Somehow the little termagant had turned the tables on him and he was on the defensive, a position he did not enjoy playing. But the damned little brat was not well yet, and he feared for her health should the uncertainty of her future prey on her mind. He had to give her some sort of answer.

His expression stiff, he began cautiously, "I will make one thing clear to you from the start, Amethyst. You force nothing from me which I am not prepared to give. I speak only to demonstrate that I am keeping our bargain in good faith. These are my terms. We shall have a truce for the duration of the voyage, Amethyst, a *loving* truce. Since your good name is so important to you, when we arrive in Philadelphia you will come to my house and live as my ward, with all the privileges and conveniences entitled to your position."

Amethyst's scoffing expression drew his words to a premature halt. "Who would believe such an unlikely situation, Damien? I would be the laughingstock of the city should I try to pass off such a ridiculous farce!"

His jaw hardening as he fought to retain control, Damien said tightly, "I am a very well respected man in Philadelphia, Amethyst. My word will not be challenged unless your behavior reflects negatively on my claim."

Her expression still disbelieving, Amethyst lifted one slender brow to say softly, "And then, Damien, when you are finished with me?"

Her question striking a discordant note in his mind, raising his ire to a volatile level, Damien spat out from between clenched teeth, "When that time comes,

Amethyst, I will see that you are returned to Jamaica, if that is still your wish, to pursue whatever life you feel will suit you!"

Her wide lavender eyes blinking hard at his final barb, Amethyst could do no more than stare without expression into his face for long moments. Taking the opportunity to press his advantage, Damien continued emotionlessly, "However, I will give you one assurance. On my honor as Captain of the *Sally*, I will not turn you out penniless and destitute as you are wont to believe. I will provide you with the passage home and funds sufficient to hold you over until you have reestablished yourself."

There was a brief pause as Amethyst appeared to consider Damien's statement and suddenly infuriated that the little twit should have succeeded in putting him to such disadvantage that she now appeared to be mistress of the situation, Damien exploded vehemently, "And that is all I will guarantee you, Mistress Greer! You do realize I do not *need* your consent to do whatever I will with you? You are on my ship and I am master here! You are dependent entirely on my good will! I will have you remember that! The assurances I have given you I give only out of consideration for . . ."

"Consideration!" Amethyst's outburst was followed by a shrill, mirthless laugh. "You are not capable of con . . ."

"Amethyst!" Damien's face a frightening red as he leaned forward to peer threateningly into her face, seriously damaged her shaky confidence, as he growled further, "I will hear nothing else from you except acceptance or refusal of our bargain as I propose it!"

Staring wordlessly into the handsome, wrathful face as it hovered above her in blatant intimidation, Amethyst's mouth tightened stubbornly. "The heartless beast," her mind raged. "He knows no need or desire save his own, yet still professes consideration and generosity to his captive. Well, if he will give me no assurance save the pitiful commitment for the future he has just declared so magnanimously, then I will see he receives the same from me! No commitment past the present day ... no affection past the present moment. As he uses me, I will use him, to gain all I can while I am able, to finally conclude our 'arrangement' in a far more satisfactory position than he!"

Her voice when she finally spoke was low, its tone steeled with a determination that was not lost on the angry man peering savagely into her face. "Alright, I accept your bargain, Captain Straith. We will have a truce..."

Suddenly more relieved than he dared show, Damien's anger began to dissipate, to be replaced with a glow of victory and anticipation immediately obvious to the woman who lay stiffly beneath him. His lips finally softening into a small, rakish smile, Damien stated in persistent clarification, "I said a 'loving' truce, Amethyst..."

Tillie's words flashed fleetingly across her mind... "Him be obeah-man... him steal you soul..." The curving of his sensuous mouth sent little shivers chasing up her spine. Abruptly, Amethyst realized further resistance would be futile while her own body played traitor to her mind. Her body's will to oppose Damien Straith was dangerously short-lived however determined her mental resistance. It was useless ... she would not be free until he chose to withdraw the obeah he practiced upon her. There was no other sensible explanation for the strange fascination she felt for the man she had despised since childhood and who now seemed to control her emotions at will. She would have to be patient ...

use her time well . . . reinforce her resolve with each day that passed . . .

All other thought slowly drifting from her mind, Amethyst became totally engrossed in the strong, firm lips slowly descending toward hers. Her only response the sensual lowering of heavy lids over deep purple eyes as her own lips parted invitingly, Amethyst's ultimate capitulation was unmistakable and complete.

The rapid quickening of his pulse as desire effectively eliminated the last remnant of his hostility rang a warning bell in Damien's mind. Damn her! Why was he feeling so smug? He had committed himself despite his best efforts to an indefinite period of subservience to a passion that consumed him more with each passing day. Even as her slender body yielded under his, sending the blood rushing through his veins in unmistakable prelude to the tumultuous emotion only she stirred within him, his mind nagged relentlessly, "You fool, who is the victor here? And who the vanquished?"

Endless green fields of creole cane stretched out on either side of the road, the bright sun overhead gleaming brightly on the perspiration-covered black backs bent laboriously between the narrow rows. The morning air hanging in a heavy humid cape around William's shoulders increased the discomfort of glaring sun and buzzing insects as he rode silently toward Kingston, but he was oblivious to all but the meeting soon to come. Even the furtive glances sent in his direction by Quaco from his position in the driver's seat of the black-and-gold Sheridan carriage went unnoticed. Still staring unseeingly to the side, William closed his eyes briefly in a supreme effort to control his soaring spirits. It had been so long since he had seen Amethyst . . . almost three weeks . . . and so much had happened in that time! But

Quaco had assured him that Amethyst was recuperating nicely, and if she was still weak, the carriage would certainly be comfortable enough to transport her back to the plantation in complete safety. At any rate, he had made up his mind that he would not leave Kingston without her. No! He was tired of separation . . . had had his fill of endless days without the spark of Amethyst's presence.

Shaking his head lightly, William smiled to himself. Strange, he had considered his life quite full and satisfying before meeting that small, lavender-eyed unpredictable sprite, and now having come to love her, found his life quite empty in her absence. Lord! He loved her with an intensity that was at times frightening, and acknowledging the power of that emotion over him, William felt the first prick of uneasiness. Amethyst would not refuse to return with him . . . she could not . . . he would not accept refusal. Damn his parents' foolish pride! Amethyst was too sensitive to their unspoken disapproval, despite the fact that they would do nothing that would turn their only son against them. They would accept her in time . . . he would explain that to Amethyst. Once she left the stage and became his wife they would be able to see her without their prejudices blinding them to her many virtues. At any rate, he was determined not to accept No for an answer this time. She would accompany him back to Sheridan Plantation today, and they would be married as soon as she was strong enough to stand beside him at the altar!

Having reviewed his plan again in his mind to his complete satisfaction, William smiled to himself and pulled restlessly at his shirt collar. It was particularly humid today, and he did not want to reach Amethyst in a dishevelled state. He had taken particular care in dressing this morning, amused at his own preoccupation with his appearance, but he wanted to look his best. It had been difficult to disguise the marks of illness that had not yet completely left his person, manifesting themselves most appreciably in the thinning of his already slight frame and the vague circles under his dark eyes. He had surveyed himself with particular discomfort in the mirror this morning after having dressed meticulously, if not casually, in light tan britches that previously had been much too small and now were fashionably tight; and a fine lawn shirt buttoned only to mid-chest in deference to the heat of early morning, exposing a ruff of dark curling hair, the full sleeves that ballooned to the wrist concealing any further loss of weight that might be evident upon first glance. Gleaming brown boots polished to a high sheen and reaching to his knee lent an aura of trim masculinity, effectively disguising his otherwise obvious weight loss. His face, still a bit gaunt, had regained most of its former color, and his freshly trimmed wavy hair gleamed a rich mahogany, matching the color of his pensive stare as he frowned at his reflection with dissatisfaction. Consoling himself that Amethyst would certainly not expect him to look his best after such a severe illness, it occurred to him that Amethyst had probably suffered much the same temporary physical deterioration, but instead of affording him relief from anxiety, the thought had only increased his concern.

"No," he thought, in an attempt to regain control over his rioting emotions once again, "no matter the physical condition in which I find Amethyst, I will bring her home with me today and nurse her back to health." Then she would become his, and he would spend the rest of his life making up for the hardships she had experienced. He had had no control over her destiny before, but from this day on she would live a beautiful, safe existence; become his wife; and then nothing would ever come between them again.

Sensing for the first time Quaco's furtive glance, William turned in his direction, only to have the old Negro snap his head quickly forward. With a small frown he considered the old man's unusual behavior silently. His mother had insisted he was not yet well enough to go to Kingston . . . perhaps she had instructed Quaco to keep a watchful eye on her son. Feeling a prick of annoyance, William shrugged the thought away. Mother was going to be a problem for Amethyst and himself, but it would work out. He would make it work out.

Glancing impatiently at his pocketwatch as the carriage turned with maddening slowness into John's Lane, William frowned. It was nearly ten o'clock. The trip had been excruciatingly slow, but it would not be long now. A gradual giddiness building inside him, William suppressed the sudden urge to jump from the carriage and run the rest of the way down the street. His heart pounding in his chest, he could not suppress the small smile growing on his face as he pictured Amethyst's welcome. He remembered little that happened during his illness, but the picture that had returned again and again to his mind was Amethyst's worried face at bedside, and the comforting sound of her voice, even if the words she had spoken were now a complete blur in his memory. She had spent many long nights beside him, and he knew she would be relieved to see him well again.

Hardly waiting for the carriage to pull to a complete stop, William jumped to the ground, and with two long strides was pounding at the door to Amethyst's house. Surprisingly, there was no answer and ignoring the prickle of apprehension flicking down his spine, he knocked again, this time calling loudly, "Amethyst . . .

Amethyst, are you awake? Tillie . . . are you there?"

When there was still no response, William pushed open the door, squinting as his eyes adjusted to the dimness of the room to ascertain the identity of the figure he saw sitting motionless in the corner. Taking a tentative step foward, he said slowly, "Tillie, is that you? What's wrong? Where's Amethyst?"

A sudden fear gripping his throat, William did not wait for a response but strode quickly to the door to Amethyst's room and pushed it open. It was empty! The bed had been made up and a coverlet carefully arranged over it. Panic turning his blood to ice, William turned and within seconds was standing in front of Tillie.

"Tillie, where is Amethyst?" When the dazed woman did not answer, roughly grabbing her by her broad shoulders, he pulled her to her feet. With a hard shake, he demanded again, "Damn you, woman, tell me! Where's Amethyst?"

Her voice filled with pain, Tillie responded softly, "Amethyst be gone, Mr. William. Him be gone . . ."

"Gone!" Beginning to tremble, William stared disbelievingly into Tillie's tortured expression. Lord! She could not be dead! No! She was almost well . . . "Where? Where has she gone, Tillie? Tell me, damn you, before I . . ."

"The obeah-man . . . Captain Straith . . . him take Amethyst away . . ."

"Straith! But how . . . ? Quaco told me he was afraid to come near Amethyst because of the fever . . . that he was preparing to sail . . ."

"Him come and take Amethyst with him last night. Amethyst fall asleep, and him pick her up and take him back to him ship."

A sudden rage filling his being, William whispered disbelievingly, "The bastard! I'll go to the ship right now and get Amethyst back, and then I'll kill him!"

He was about to turn away from Tillie when her hand stayed him, her soft words snapping his attention back in her direction. "No, Mr. William. It be too late. Him sail away with Amethyst this morning. Amethyst gone . . . him gone . . ."

His youthful countenance draining of color, William violently shrugged off her restraining hand. "No! He will not have her! I will get her back, and when I do, I will kill Damien Straith! No, she is not gone!"

William was out of the door within a second. Giving not a thought to the carriage awaiting him outside, he turned to race in the direction of the docks, unmindful of the curious stares that followed him as he ran. His breath coming in deep, uneven gasps, he turned the corner into Port Royal Street, his frantic pace continuing until he arrived finally at the docks. His eyes anxiously scanning the area for a glimpse of the *Sally*, he refused to believe the evidence of his own eyes and approaching an old salt who eyed him curiously, he demanded breathlessly, "The *Sally* . . . where is she docked? I must talk to the captain . . ."

Squinting up from a weather-toughened face, the old sailor replied slowly, "Well, you're a bit too late, mate. The *Sally* sailed this morning with all hands."

Unwilling to believe the man's response, William gripped him by the shoulders, his anxious face paling as he demanded, harshly, "Tell me the truth, man! I must know. Where is the *Sally*?"

"I told you, damn you. She sailed this morning! Now take your hands off me before I split your ruddy skull!"

Allowing the man to shake off his restraining grip, William stood momentarily stunned. Lord! It could not be true! Amethyst . . . she could not have been taken from him by that . . . that . . .

Turning back in the direction of the sea, William stared unseeingly at the empty spot where the ship had been docked, his eyes seeing only the mental image of Amethyst's beautiful face, gradually replaced by the picture of Damien Straith's victorious expression as he gathered Amethyst slowly into his arms.

"No!" Closing his eyes against the horrendous thought, William stood trembling with rage as he sought to eject the image from his mind. Slowly opening his eyes, he was once again in control of his emotions. With eyes blazing, he stared bitterly at the open sea, the pain of his loss growing deeper with each second. His voice low, he muttered softly beneath his breath, the fury in his expression lending full credence to his solemn vow.

"With God as my witness, I swear this day I will find Damien Straith, and as surely as I stand here, I will make him suffer for this crime he has committed against Amethyst, and once she is safely returned to me, I will see him dead!"

With a dull, bemused expression, Tillie stared at William Sheridan's back as it disappeared through the doorway. Unable to feel sympathy for the young man's plight, she knew only the gnawing void in her own heart that had numbed her as she had watched the *Sally* sail that morning. The pain of her loss deep and excruciating, she muttered incoherently, "Amethyst be my child . . . my soul-child . . . that obeah-man, him steal my child . . . take him from me . . . My child . . . she be lost . . . lost . . ."

She had gone to the docks that morning in an attempt to dissuade Captain Straith from taking Amethyst with him, but had been refused entrance to the ship. Reduced to standing by helplessly as the sailors prepared to lift anchor, she had watched the ship sail away until it disappeared into the horizon. What would become of

Amethyst now? Would she ever see her again? Would Captain Straith desert her in Philadelphia, penniless and friendless when he tired of her? The obeah-man had ruined Amethyst's chances for a respectable life... had stolen her only valuable possession, her good name. What would become of her Amethyst... her darling soul-child? Filled with despair, Tillie had returned to the small house on John's Lane to sit unmoving in the same spot William Sheridan had found her just a few minutes before.

Slowly rising, Tillie walked listlessly to the door of the house. Not sparing a glance for the frantic figure that could still be seen running down the street as his man followed in the carriage a discreet distance behind, Tillie turned in the opposite direction. Moving more by instinct than by any conscious direction, Tillie turned toward Conway Plantation. Stepping from the Kingston streets to the heavily foliated trail to the plantation, Tillie made her way to the only person in the world who could ease her grief.

The sun was setting when a tall shadow darkened the doorway of the small hut for the first time that day. Averting tear-filled eyes, Tillie did not see Raymond's anxious expression as he saw her slumped figure seated on the low mat in the middle of the room.

Moving quickly to sit at her side, Raymond's deep voice was filled with anxiety. "Tillie, somethin' be wrong? Look at Raymond, Tillie." Raising her chin with his hand, Raymond stroked the light cocoa skin of her cheek, his voice soft and coaxing. "Tell Raymond what be wrong, Tillie."

Finally raising her moist, dark eyes to his, Tillie whispered hoarsely, "The obeah-man take my soul-child, Raymond. Him take Amethyst far away, away from Tillie. Now Tillie never see him child again...

never again . . ."

Her voice cracking on her last words, Tillie threw herself forward against Raymond's chest, her body heaving with the sorrow she had suppressed through the day. His strong black arms closing around her, Raymond pulled her close, mumbling softly against her cheek, "Tillie stay wid Raymond t'night. Raymond mek Tillie feel better." Swaying slowly back and forth in a rocking motion as he held her close against him, Raymond mumbled soft words of consolation as he gently massaged her back, easing the tenseness out of her ample body with the gentleness of his touch. Gradually, her sobbing ceased, but he continued to hold her in his arms, humming a low, haunting melody familiar to both from their childhood, lulling Tillie into a sense of peace and comfort despite the aching voice in her breast. Her heart filled to bursting, Tillie raised her ageless face to Raymond, the loving tenderness in her expression stealing Raymond's breath as he returned her intense stare.

Her deep voice tremulous, Tillie whispered, raising her full lips to his, "You be all Tillie have left in this world to love, Raymond, and love you Tillie will till the day him die . . ."

Speechless with the emotion Tillie's soft confession raised inside him, Raymond clasped her tight against him, his former gentleness disappearing with the strength of his emphatic embrace as he wondered at his amazing fortune that he, a simple field slave, could hold the love of a woman as beautiful and spirited as his Tillie. His own voice husky and broken, Raymond whispered in return, "Tillie be de woman fe Raymond . . . fe all him life . . . all him life long . . ."

Standing silently outside the wall of the small hut a slender figure listened to the halting words of love, her dark face tight with jealousy. Slowly turning away, she followed the darkened trail back to the slaves' quarters. Her expression grave, she mumbled venomously under her breath, "It be Tillie Swann t'night, Raymond, but Quasheba be ready fe Raymond, 'n him be Quasheba's man soon."

The *Sally* sailed steadily northward, leaving behind the clear turquoise water of the Caribbean Sea in staunch progress toward her home port of Philadelphia. The balmy tropical breezes moving her unerringly toward her goal turned cooler as the days moved on, the bite in the air bringing a bright color to Amethyst's cheek in the endless hours spent in total infatuation at the rail. The sea was glorious! Why had she not remembered the beauty of the sun as it rose and set, reflecting its myriad of breathtaking colors against the endless shimmering surface? There was beauty everywhere . . . in the graceful flight of the gulls as they swooped into the churning waves, dipping and diving in a graceful aerial ballet of infinite diversity; the great schools of fish that often moved below the ship, darkening the brilliant water with the mere power of their number as they passed in a vague, single shadow beneath and around them until they were gone. There was even a beauty in the manner in which the *Sally*'s sailors scaled the masts, responding with skilled precision to the orders barked from below as they released the limp sails to fill and puff against the brilliant blue of the cloudless sky.

Ah, but the fact was that the last time she had sailed these waters she had been a child, entirely preoccupied in nursing an ailing mother whose precarious health was her sole consideration. How different were her circumstances this time. While in fact kidnapped onto the ship, she was treated as a cherished guest whose smallest wish was the crew's command. Lassiter, bless his rusty old heart, had not changed since their first meeting, resuming the friendship he had extended to the stubborn child of nine, seven years before. The remainder of the crew, after recuperating from their astonishment at her presence, rapidly moved from an aloof wariness to a keen appreciation of her presence, with each man among them going out of his way to accommodate her.

Amused once again, Amethyst recalled to mind Damien's sneering disgust at the crew's behavior when he had angrily declared in a surly moment that she had turned a group of respectable, hard-working tars into a sorry lot of fawning imbeciles who would suffer all manner of degrading chores just for the pleasure of one dimpled smile! And that furious hour-long tirade inspired by poor Ezekiel Bellows, who sought to do her bidding by hanging a line on deck so she might dry her laundered clothing more quickly in the sun! Well, it had been no different when he had caught Lassiter lashing empty barrels to the mast in the midst of a howling rainstorm in the hopes of collecting enough water for her first freshwater bath since the inception of the voyage. Of them all, only Jeremy Barnes still retained Damien's respect by treating her with faultless courtesy and concern without, as Damien so colorfully put it, ". . . making a complete ass of himself!"

But where she could honestly fault no one for her treatment, not even the cryptic, overbearing captain of the *Sally*, and found all manner of surprising glory in her first true experience with the sea, her heart was in Jamaica. She sorely missed the great handsome woman whose deep Jamaican drawl shared a place in her heart with her own darling mother's light, precise tones. Having spent a large portion of her life entertaining in the theater, she also missed her work and her short-lived success in her role as songstress *extraordinaire* of the American Company. And even as she refused to allow thought of him to enter her mind, she realized she missed William and still ached for the pain he must have suffered when he had arrived at her home on John's Lane and found her gone. She had been a fool not to marry William when he had pleaded. In retrospect she could find no valid reason for her hesitation. But it was too late for regrets . . . too late for many things . . . most of all too late for William and her.

Her eyes stared unseeingly into a darkness broken only by the brilliance of a great full moon, its silvery light lending a mystic glow to a night sky already radiantly filled with endless twinkling stars. Momentarily startled as two strong arms stole past to grasp the rail firmly on either side of her, effectively holding her prisoner between them, Amethyst felt no need to turn to identify her captor. The clean, manly scent of his body strong in her nostrils, Amethyst spoke quickly before the night could work its magic, stealing her tongue to allow the inevitable its due course.

"What is your prediction for tomorrow's weather, Damien?" In the first week of their journey toward Philadelphia, Damien had made a nightly ritual of predicting the weather for the following day. Ever a master of the unexpected, he was surprisingly accurate each time, even in such minute details as temperature change and wind velocity, and she continued to play the game, its diversion suiting her purpose. Their truce was working well. Damien was well pleased with her acceptance of the situation, of that she was certain. The days were passing smoothly, with surprising amicability. Taking all his meals in his cabin with Amethyst, Damien was at most times a charming companion who spared no effort in explaining the complicated duties of ship's master, only occasionally raising her ire with a supercilious expression when her questioning touched on a matter he deemed too personal an intrusion for a reply. The sound of the ship's bell marking the half-hours and hours had become an accepted ritual of her daily life, its clear, echoing tones in the darkness of the night giving solace to troubled dreams.

Although at times finding it difficult to put up with Damien's autocratic, possessive manner, she found with her rapidly returning strength also came a renewal of her determination that he would not conquer her mind as he had her body. She would survive to achieve her ultimate independence from him, would return to Jamaica, and was thoroughly committed to emerge the victor from their association.

But Damien's response, tinged with sharpness, snapped her around to face him as he said impatiently, "I'm not in the mood for that idiotic game tonight, Amethyst. I have far more important things on my mind. And why are you up here on deck with only a light shawl? Are you seeking to become an invalid again? Will you never learn to care properly for yourself? I . . ."

Interrupting the building tirade, Amethyst frowned into his irritated expression. "I am wearing this light shawl, Damien, because it is all I have to wear. Somehow, on the tropical island of Jamaica, I did not feel it necessary to purchase a heavy cape to protect me from the broiling sun! And since I did not anticipate taking this voyage, my wardrobe is decidedly inadequate! But I do apologize," she continued sarcastically, "for not consulting you as to what I should wear on my short sojourn on deck this night, but, in truth, I had not realized you so much enjoyed dressing me each evening!"

His sullen expression lightening for the first time, Damien responded with a hint of humor, "If I am to be entirely candid, I would have to admit, Amethyst, I do not derive as much pleasure from dressing you as I do from the reverse procedure, but since it seems you need a guiding hand in matters involving a little common sense..."

Stiffening at his calculated insult, Amethyst stifled her response. It was obvious Damien was looking for an argument, and she had no intention of accommodating him. He would not take his ill humor out on her! Attempting to free herself, Amethyst pushed firmly at the brawny arm to the side of her as she responded stiffly, "Somehow the beauty of the night has paled for me, Damien. I would like to go below now." When Damien's wide hand still retained its grip on the railing, Amethyst raised haughty eyes to his. "I should think my desire to go below would please you, Damien, since you have broadly hinted at my stupidity at being up here in the first place!"

But her mistake had been in raising her eyes to his, to become lost in the silver depths that scrutinized her so deliberately. The weeks at sea had not eroded the power of his glance over her will, but had, in fact, only deepened its claim. Their glances locked, Amethyst once again experienced the slow draining of her opposition, and her body's final betrayal as Damien's hand moved up in slow deliberation to slip into her hair, his thumb caressing the line of her cheekbone as he held her mesmerized with effortless mastery. Her lips parting, she heard her own small intake of breath as his lips touched hers, his victory complete as her mouth opened to accept his tongue, her arms stealing around his back to return his crushing embrace. Sinking into the abyss of blazing emotions, Amethyst suddenly knew no other thought but the glory of his deepening kiss and the pleasure of his broad knowing hands against her body. Swaying weakly when deprived of his embrace for the briefest second, Amethyst succumbed completely, laying her head against his chest as Damien swept her up into his hungry arms to carry her downstairs in long, anxious strides to the cabin below.

She could not summon the slightest resistance as Damien kicked the door closed behind them and in a few swift steps placed her gently on the bunk. Kneeling on the floor beside her, he gazed for endless moments into her clear lavender eyes, frowning, his expression disturbed. Reaching out, he gently touched her lips with his fingertips, a small muscle twitching in his cheek as he obviously strove to maintain control.

He seemed about to speak, and then thinking better of the situation, merely trailed his fingers down her throat to the buttons at the top of her bodice. Slowly unfastening them one by one, he separated it at last to expose her shift. His hands trembling, he lifted her slightly to free her arms, exposing the fullness of her perfect white breasts, the pink crests erect, inviting his caress. Would he never tire of looking at her . . . touching her? There was no doubt in his mind that Amethyst was the most beautiful woman he had ever seen, and suddenly anxious to view her in her breathtaking entirety, he worked quickly and effectively to free her of the remainder of her clothing. At last she lay naked before him, her face exquisitely sculptured, high cheekbones, slender nose, firm pointed chin; those magnificent eyes, now heavy-lidded with passion as she trembled beneath his touch. The splendid faultless symmetry of her body exposed to his glance grew more beautiful each day with her returning health. Having regained most of her former proportions, the angular slimness of ill health was gone, returning the smoothness to her frame that flowed in graceful perfection from the glorious black curls over her high, clear brow, to the tips of her delicious toes. Having seen her thus countless times, Damien still marveled at her sheer perfection, and her ability to continually excite him without exerting the slightest effort.

Drawn by the allure of the small pink tongue barely visible behind perfect white teeth in a mouth that set his pulse racing, Damien lowered his head, at last covering the warm, red lips that drew him so mercilessly. Soft and pliable under his searching mouth, her lips separated to accept his tongue, meeting his with her own as he probed and drew greedily of the deep, inner reaches abandoned so completely to him. Deeper and deeper his kiss pressed, seeking, demanding, eliciting an abandon that was second only to his own as his mouth ravaged hers. Her heart pounding in her ears, Amethyst sensed Damien's withdrawal moments before he reluctantly drew back, his sober expression staring unblinkingly into hers. With great deliberation he moved the hands cupping her chin down the slender column of her neck. His fingers splaying widely to encompass as much of her warm perfection as they dared, he ran his palms smoothly along her body. Leaving no area untouched, his seeking, caressing hands roamed the gentle curve of her shoulders, to slide down the entire length of her slender arms to her fingertips. Moving from there to the perfect mounds of her breasts, he caressed them lovingly, smoothing, touching, fondling, the ever narrowing circular motion of his caress finally touching the tender crests awaiting him. Deliberately withholding his lips from their appealing tips, he slid his hands searchingly, caressingly across her ribcage, her narrow waist, along the rounded curve of her hips and the flatness of her stomach. Continuing his erotic quest, Damien moved his caress down the long slender legs, shapely and graceful in their former fullness, to the small delicate ankles and pink perfect feet. Lowering his head, Damien kissed each toe slowly, tenderly, continuing the line of his kisses up to her ankles, the slender calves now firm and strong, the delicately turned knees, the well shaped thighs. But the sweetness grew increasingly more intoxicating as he neared the triangle of dark shining curls nestled between. Spreading a rash of warm, moist kisses on the tender flesh of her inner thighs, Damien was drawn relentlessly by the sensuous lure of other lips awaiting his caress.

Her senses rioting, Amethyst knew only the deep, all-encompassing euphoria to which his caress transported her. Existing in the world of brilliant sensation and searing desire Damien had created within her, she relaxed completely under his loving administrations, experiencing little shivers of delight as his kisses moved along her feet and ankles, up her legs, the trembling within her escalating to frightening proportions as his lips and tongue moved sensuously upward. His searching caresses moved to the dark triangle of curls, kissing, nudging, coaxing, eliciting a sensation and anticipation within her that set her to trembling wildly, violently, in a realm of sheer aching desire she had never before experienced. Suddenly his lips were pressed tightly against the tender slit, his tongue moving quickly to taste the moistness between in a supreme intimacy that exploded a wealth of sensation inside her. A low groan issuing from her lips, she clutched Damien's head, attempting to stay him from his ultimate caress.

"No . . . Damien . . . no, please . . . I'm frightened. I've never . . . please, Damien . . ." Directing a pleading glance into the translucent eyes lifted to hers, she trembled violently. "You mustn't . . . you can't . . ."

Moving to cup her smooth, firm buttocks in his hands, Damien whispered softly, assuringly, "Yes, darling, I must . . . I must have all of you."

Shaking her head violently, Amethyst muttered softly, "No, Damien . . . no . . ." But Damien was deaf to her protests as he spread a warm spray of kisses along the tender curls. Somewhere, somehow, Amethyst's restraining hands lost their strength, the warm sensation of his tongue again slipping inside the tender crease transporting her past the realm of reasonable thought. She was floating, drifting in a world of breathless sensation, transported higher and higher out of herself to groan loudly, pleadingly for release from the ecstatic aura that held her suspended while each nerve in her body screamed for more and more and more . . .

Lost to his own passion, Damien pressed deeper, more lovingly, drawing, seeking, devouring the sweetness within. He would not stop, he could not stop, driven by a wild desire to know every part of Amethyst, experience every facet her beautiful body had to offer, to taste her, to titillate her, to consume her completely . . . as completely as his passion for her was consuming him . . .

Amethyst was shaking now, trembling violently under his touch, her low, pleading groans and cries turning to moans of pleasure, the intoxicating sounds exciting his senses, driving him to even further excesses of loving assault. The soft, ecstatic cries continued on, only to stop abruptly as Amethyst's slender body began a deep shudder of ecstasy to release in throbbing, convulsive spasms the final, ultimate tribute to his lovemaking. Accepting it gratefully, greedily, Damien swallowed deeply of its sweetness, basking in its splendor, drawing deeply again and again and again . . . until she could give no more.

In a few moments he too was naked, sliding his long, powerful body against hers in an intimate caress, his manhood pressed heavily against the tight black curls as he cupped Amethyst's chin lightly in his palm.

The flush of passion had left her face. Her eyes were closed, the thick fan of black lashes resting lightly against her ivory cheeks. A surge of familiar emotion overwhelming him, Damien whispered huskily against her lips, "You belong to me . . . only me, Amethyst. Tell me, darling. I want to hear you say it. Tell me you belong to me . . ."

When she did not respond, Damien insisted lightly, "Amethyst, answer me, darling . . . Amethyst . . ."

There was no response from the beautiful lips so close to his. His anger flaring, Damien lifted himself slightly, moving to slide his manhood within her in a quick, smooth thrust. Her eyes snapping open, Amethyst gasped as he came to rest inside her, the deep purple gaze meeting the silver glow of his eyes to be held hypnotically as Damien began moving slowly within her. The rhythm of his impetus gradually increasing, Damien watched as the soft light of passion gradually returned to Amethyst's gaze, escalating until she was gasping in the throes of the brilliant emotion, her lids fluttering almost closed again and again as ecstasy mounted, assuming control of her mind and body as it responded to his searching thrusts, meeting and returning their force boldly. Steadily taking her higher and higher onto the euphoric plane in an unaltering course to the pinnacle of passion, Damien led her to the brink, pausing to hold her breathless, her body screaming, demanding relief from the flaming emotions he had raised within her.

His throbbing voice low and demanding, Damien whispered softly against her lips, "Tell me now who owns you, Amethyst . . . who owns you more completely than you own yourself." When still she did not respond, Damien demanded angrily, "Now, Amethyst! Tell me . . . to whom do you belong? Tell me now, damn you," he continued, his voice a low growl, "Tell me now or I swear I will leave you here as you are now and walk away never to return to your bed again!"

His heart pounding violently at the scope of the commitment he had uttered in anger, Damien searched her face for sign of a response, but there was none. His eyes closing briefly in defeat, Damien made a small movement to withdraw when Amethyst's hand snapped to his shoulder to stay him.

In a voice hardly recognizable as her own, Amethyst heard herself whisper, "No . . . don't go, Damien, please. You . . . I belong to you, Damien . . . I belong to you . . ."

Exaltation swept over him, exploding into a supreme joy that held Damien speechless, his eyes devouring her exquisite face as her words echoed in his ears. ". . . I belong to you, Damien . . . I belong to you . . ."

No longer able to restrain the motion filling his being, Damien began thrusting deep and hard within her, his low passionate groans carrying them faultlessly, unerringly over the summit of passion to careen simultaneously in a long, brilliant spiral of glory to the breathless, ecstatic conclusion of their act of love.

His body spent, but unwilling to separate from her, Damien lifted himself to his elbows, his hand moving to caress Amethyst's cheek as he leaned forward to whisper hoarsely against her lips, "Ours is a magnificent joining, Amethyst . . . a splendor beyond . . ."

Inexplicably unable to go on, Damien buried his face in her ebony tresses, his arms slipping under and around her to draw her tightly against him, the strength and intensity of his embrace speaking far more loudly than words.

The cabin floor pitched beneath her, rolling and

dipping violently as Amethyst strained to retain her grip on the bunk on which she lay. The world outside the porthole had gone suddenly dark. A violent winter storm had descended, driving the freezing sleet of the January Atlantic against the *Sally*'s hull to prove the small iron stove bolted to the floor pathetically inadequate in relieving the frigid temperature of the cabin. Bracing herself in her bunk, fully dressed with a blanket wrapped around her against the bone-chilling dampness that had pervaded the room, Amethyst watched with horrified fascination as the great lantern over the desk swayed wildly from side to side as the ship rose and plunged on the raging sea. Her panic so complete that she was past tears, Amethyst prayed dry-eyed to the Lord above that he would greet her kindly when she met her end.

But she did not want to die! She was not ready to give up her life! Suddenly enraged, Amethyst muttered furiously under her breath as she strained to hold herself upright on the bunk, "Where is he, damn him? It is all his fault that I sit here with eternity clearly in sight! It has been hours since the storm started, and he has sent me not a word of encouragement, extends not a grain of consideration. Damn him!"

Damien's disposition had seen a marked deterioration during this, their last week at sea, his former victorious air of satisfaction with their arrangement changing to an attitude of moody irritation. Countless times she had turned to find his dark glance resting on her person, only to be diverted when her questioning eyes met his. Still stunned and bewildered by his changing moods after many hours spent in contemplation of his confusing conduct, she had merely laid his attitude to the fact that their journey was near its end, and the responsibilities of a stormy winter sea weighed heavily on his mind.

But this time there was no excuse for his blatant

disregard for her feelings! What had begun as a small winter squall had now evolved into a raging storm, subjecting the *Sally* to long hours of battering blows by the giant, angry waves Amethyst had seen through the porthole. Creaking and groaning under the devastating beating, the *Sally* was lifted effortlessly again and again to the crest of the waves, only to be plunged into the deep, dark valley between that preceded each smashing upsurge to follow. How long could the ship hold out against such battering? Would she break apart in the sea, abandoning her people to unmarked graves? Why had she not heard from Damien? Were circumstances so dire that he could not spare one man to bring her a word of comfort? Damn him!

Her anger escalating with the violence of the storm, Amethyst found the confines of the room too small to contain her fury with the man who so selfishly was sending her to a watery grave! Struggling to her feet, Amethyst dodged the desk chair as it careened across the room, thankful that most of the other furniture was bolted to the floor, providing her a less hazardous path to the doorway. She would show him! She would not sit below like a frightened child while Damien Straith ignored her existence!

Abandoning the inadequate blanket on the bunk, Amethyst made a wavering path to the chest. Struggling to maintain her balance, she lifted the top and removed Damien's cape. Wrapping it securely around her she fastened the front, completely ignoring the fact that she was all but lost in its ample folds. Paying no attention to the creaking groans of the ship and the howls of the January wind as it screeched its fury overhead, Amethyst jerked open the door to the passageway. Bounced roughly from side to side, she made her way with single-minded determination down the narrow corridor that led to the stairway. The screech of the storm grew louder with each step she ascended, sending chills of apprehension down her spine, but her resolve was firm. She would see Damien Straith and confront him with his sheer disregard for her life by taking her on this ill-fated voyage.

Amethyst had taken but two steps on the slushy, frozen deck of the *Sally* when the full folly of her actions hit her for the first time. Gripped by a powerful gust of wind, she was slammed against the rail, only to be knocked from her feet by the next wild plunge of the deck. Breathless with a severe pain in her ribs where she had struck the rail, Amethyst could do no more than grip the ropes hanging from the belaying pins, to be swung effortlessly back and forth with the violent motion of the deck beneath her. She could hear nothing over the screaming of the wind, nor see anything past the deluge that beat into her face, freezing her, numbing her, turning the hands that held the rope into inefficient, clutching fingers of ice. She could no longer feel the rope in her hand, nor the frozen deck against her legs, and straining to see past the rivulets of freezing rain that blurred her vision, she fought to regain her feet. Finally achieving her goal, she held tight to the rail, noticing for the first time the group of sailors swaying on the opposite side of the deck, their attention riveted on the main mast as they firmly supported their footing with the yards of hemp on the rail. Her eyes following the direction of their gaze, Amethyst gasped incredulously. High above them a man swung precariously on the shrouds as he struggled to free a clew that had become hooked on the yardarm, causing the main sail to flap wildly in the raging wind. Unable to take her eyes from the swaying figure high above them, Amethyst failed to take into account the reason for the deep lurching of the ship the moment before a giant wave crashed over them, its tons of freezing fury efficiently dislodging her stiff fingers to send her crashing painfully against the spar opposite her. Striking her head with a resounding crack, she was momentarily disoriented, long enough to slide with the next deep plunge to the far side of the deck. But there was no time to reach for support, to clutch for life before the following wave crashed on deck, lifting her in a swirling, frozen fury, carrying her, she was certain in a moment of blinding clarity, into the raging sea that awaited her. Unable to see or feel past the swirling darkness engulfing her, she gave herself up to the raging elements so bent on taking her life.

But a powerful force interrupted her seemingly inevitable passage into the sea, jerking mercilessly at her hair, staying her only to grasp painfully at her shoulders, to hold her swaying tightly against a totally human force. Opening her eyes, she strained to see through her water blurred vision, finally coming into contact with dark eyes as a familiar voice demanded, "Are you alright, Miss Greer? Can you walk?"

Jeremy! Jeremy Barnes! Recognition sent a thrill of hope through her veins, but unable to summon her voice, she nodded dumbly into his face the second before her eyes moved upward again to spot the figure that still swayed high overhead. How was it the man had not been washed into the sea by the last crushing wave? How had he still retained his hold on the frozen ropes? What divine providence still allowed him his life?

Noting the direction of her glance, Jeremy shouted over the howling wind, "You needn't fear, Miss Amethyst. The Captain will be alright, but you must go below now."

The Captain! It was Damien swinging so tenaciously overhead, his tenuous grip on life a matter of raw courage and supreme determination. But she had no more time to speculate as Jeremy Barnes drew her with him in a steady, sure path to safety while the elements raged around them.

Hardly cognizant of her descent to the berth deck, Amethyst felt completely conscious only when her feet touched the floor of the captain's cabin. Leaning over to jerk a chair behind her, Jeremy Barnes pushed her down gently. His voice hoarse from hours of shouting above the roar of the storm, he said quietly, "Will you be alright now, Miss Greer? I am needed on deck and . . ."

Swallowing tightly, Amethyst nodded, her voice a raspy croak as she whispered softly, "But the Captain . . . he must come down . . . he will be killed . . ."

A note of confidence entering his voice, Jeremy responded quickly, "You needn't worry about the Captain, Miss. He has almost freed the sail. If he allowed it to remain almost unfurled in that manner once it had broken loose, he ran the risk of having the ship capsize or splitting the main mast before this storm blows itself out."

Nodding dumbly as her eyes widened in fear, Amethyst sat shivering in the chair, causing a frown of uncertainty to slip over the young mate's frozen countenance.

"You must get out of those wet clothes, Miss Greer. If you were to become ill again the Captain would be very angry."

Nodding even more emphatically as her teeth chattered with cold and shock, Amethyst finally found her voice. "Yes, Jeremy. Please return to deck. I can take care of myself."

Obviously thankful for her permission to leave, Jeremy Barnes smiled briefly before turning on his heel and moving quickly out of the cabin to close the door tightly behind him. The picture of Damien's form swinging precariously above the churning sea still vivid in her mind, Amethyst finally arose and began to undress. Her frozen hands fumbling inefficiently at the closures on her sodden clothing, Jeremy Barnes's words resounded in her mind, accompanied by the vivid mental image that haunted her. "You needn't worry about the Captain, Miss . . . if you were to become ill again the Captain would be very angry."

The mental vision of Damien's fury replacing all else in her mind, gave speed to her frozen fingers, and within moments she was free of her wet clothing and shivering in the bunk, prey to the horrifying vision of Damien swaying high above the deck which would not leave her mind.

It seemed to Amethyst the storm was abating. The screeching of the wind gradually turned to a dull roar as she huddled beneath the coverlet, her body aching from her recent ordeal. She had received no word from the main deck and felt a deep dread of the events progressing above her. To divert her mind as her world swayed and dipped incessantly with the raging sea, she had a short time before stumbled from the safe cocoon of the bunk and braved the cabin's cold to slip into a fresh night rail, and quickly wrapping herself back in the blanket, had sat by the stove to thoroughly dry her matted hair. When all else failed to remove the image of Damien's figure swaying high above the deck from her mind, she had begun to brush her hair with a vehemence that set her scalp to tingling and transformed the snarls caused by the angry sea into a shimmering ebony cascade that gleamed vibrantly down her shoulders and back. Still shivering from the cold, she had climbed back into the bunk to wrap herself tightly in the extra coverlet while her mind totally avoided the possibility of an accident. Damien was an obeah-man, was he not? What else could account for his retaining his grip on the icy hemp in the midst of a howling gale? Yes, he would be fine . . . she was certain . . . almost certain . . .

With a startling abruptness the cabin door snapped open, interrupting her thoughts to bang loudly back against the wall. Damien stood in the doorway, his apparel stiff from the freezing rain, his face blanched white with cold, the frost on his eyebrows and hair silent testimony to the grim situation topside. Until the moment of his appearance, Amethyst had not realized fully the depth of her fear for his safety. A wild surge of joy sweeping over her, she was about to jump to her feet to embrace him when the brutal fury in his glance jerked her to a stop. Advancing slowly into the room, Damien stripped off his knit hat and dropped it carelessly to the floor. His heavy pea coat followed, as did the rest of his sodden apparel, until he stood unashamedly naked before her. The rage in his glance did not waver, and Amethyst was momentarily relieved when he turned to reach for the robe lying on the chair. Obviously frozen to the marrow, his tall, massive frame shook noticeably, but somehow the quaking of his strong body did not dilute the wrath burning in his light, clear eyes. Moving slowly toward her, he bent to grasp Amethyst by the shoulders and jerk her upright. When that did not seem to satisfy his anger, he pulled her roughly from the bunk to stand in her bare feet beside him. The mask of rage tightening as he stared unblinkingly into her face, he finally rasped, "You will *never* . . . NEVER come topside in a storm again, Amethyst, do you hear me? You will stay below in your cabin as you are told, and will not stray one inch from the area in which I have instructed you to remain!"

Suddenly infuriated with herself that she had spent the past several hours in quaking fear for Damien's safety when the main point of his concern was purely her disobedience of his orders, Amethyst glared back into his angry glance, her mouth tightening. She had made a mistake, yes, but his manner was insufferable. She had fully intended to apologize for the trouble she had caused his first mate, but now, faced with his overbearing attitude, Amethyst abandoned all thoughts of an apology. He could command her all he wanted, but he could not force her to . . .

"Amethyst!" Sensing her resistance, Damien shook her violently. "You are a damned fool . . . an idiot . . . risking your life for a whim! Did your curiosity get the best of you, Amethyst? Did it?" he demanded shaking her emphatically, "Did you have to see the full force of the storm for yourself?" His hands were biting cruelly into her shoulders as he shook her repeatedly, and Amethyst bit her lip against the pain, refusing to give him the satisfaction of pleading for release.

"And did it never occur to you," Damien continued furiously, "that you could have been killed . . . could have been swept over the side so quickly that no one would have realized you were gone?" His words suddenly choking off, he stared into her face, his expression inscrutable as he swallowed hard. When he resumed speaking a few moments later, his voice was controlled, but rage still seethed beneath the surface of his words. "You owe your life to Jeremy Barnes's bravery and quick thinking. In the event you are not aware, Mr. Barnes was almost swept over the side with you in his unselfish heroism . . . but that is surely one thing we can never accuse you of, Amethyst . . . unselfishness!"

Jeremy Barnes had almost lost his life trying to save her! She had not been aware of anything in that moment of soul-freezing terror when she had felt herself slipping over the rail, but the knowledge now shook her to the core. Still, she could not accept this man's blatant criticism of her actions. She had been foolish, yes, but selfish? She had had no thought of risking another person's life. He could not speak to her that way!

Stubbornly ignoring the numbness in her feet, Amethyst stood rigidly in Damien's fierce grip. "How dare you, of all people, accuse *me* of selfishness? Perhaps you feel yourself the master of the trait and well able to recognize it in others, but you are *wrong*, Captain!" Her glance filled with loathing, she continued venomously, "And if I am the ignoble person you make me out to be, Captain Straith, I do not see why you should be so upset by my behavior. Would it not be far better to allow me to continue my foolish conduct and next time instruct your men to ignore me while I am swept over the side? After all, who would know? And you would be spared the annoyance of my company as your ward once we reach Philadelphia. There would be no explanations demanded by outraged mistresses, and you could continue with your life as if I had never existed!"

The small twitch at the corner of his mouth at the conclusion of her remarks the only indication that he had heard her venomous tirade, Damien's grip slipped from her shoulders. Raising his hand in a quick, unexpected movement, he slapped her hard across the face to send her staggering backwards across the bed with shock. Taking a short step forward, he leaned over her, his hands on either side of her shoulders supporting his intimidating stance as he glared into her eyes.

"Bitch! You will never speak to me so heinously again, or I swear I will . . ."

A short rap on the door snapped Damien's attention in the other direction, interrupting his heated declaration. Slowly straightening up, he said hoarsely without looking back, "Cover yourself!" Then in a louder voice,

"Come in!"

Lassiter's gray, grizzled head appeared around the door within a few seconds. His glance moving uncertainly from one to the other, he advanced toward the table, carefully balancing the contents of his tray. A small covered pot steamed invitingly, and placing cups on either side of the small table, he commenced completing the remainder of the table setting. A loaf of dark bread, a bottle of rum, cheese and he was finished, looking up to shoot a questioning glance between the two tense figures.

"It be a light meal tonight, Captain," the old man ventured hesitantly, "but the hot tea should take the chill out of yer bones."

When there was no response from the tall man glaring coldly in his direction or the small pinched face in the bed, Lassiter lifted his shoulders in a slight shrug of acceptance and turned away. Damien stood staring at the door for long moments after it had closed, finally turning abruptly to send a short glance in Amethyst's direction.

"Come and eat now before the tea cools." His terse command left no room for argument even should Amethyst feel the inclination, which was hardly likely as her empty stomach gurgled in appreciation of the mere sight of food. Too hungry to pretend otherwise, she ignored the stinging on her cheek and scrambled to her feet, wrapping the blanket tightly around her. Within moments she was seated at the table, haughtily avoiding the light-eyed stare seldom lifted from her person. She would not give him the satisfaction of knowing his blow had shook her. However, finding midway through the meal that Damien's deep scrutiny was proving a severe hindrance to her enjoyment of her meal, Amethyst finally placed her cup on the table and raising her eyes boldly, stated in a determined tone, "If you would devote as much time to eating as you are devoting to sending black looks in my direction, we could have been finished here and tucked warmly in bed by now."

A small smile playing across his lips for the first time that evening, Damien directed a knowing look into her eyes, successfully raising a full blush to her cheek as she stammered ineffectively, "I didn't mean... I only meant to say..."

"Don't try to explain, Amethyst." Damien's tone bore a slightly taunting ring, "I do understand quite well what you meant, and I do agree. Certainly you owe me something for the trauma I experienced when I saw you slipping over the rail the second before Barnes grabbed you, and you have my assurance you will pay. But perhaps not tonight. I find I am quite fatigued and unfortunately my bed is far more appealing right now than the comforts you so willingly offer. But you needn't worry. My baser instincts are sure to revive once I have had some rest. You may console yourself with that thought."

Her eyes flaring wide at his insinuation that he was turning down her sexual overture, Amethyst angrily slammed her napkin down on the table. "You are a truly insufferable man, Damien Straith!" Abruptly jumping to her feet, Amethyst had only stomped two steps toward the bunk before she stopped just as abruptly, to turn, retrace her steps and resume her seat at the table. "And," she continued, her eyes narrowing with emphasis as she directed what she hoped was a deadly look into his now openly amused expression, "your insidious jibes will not stir me from this table one moment before I am ready to leave!" Finally dismissing him with as haughty a glance as she could muster, Amethyst turned her attention back to the food.

Within the hour the storm had abated to a low moan and the remains of the meal had been cleared away.

Feeling the bunk sink with Damien's weight as he slid in beside her, Amethyst curled tightly in the corner. Her back to him, she stiffly resisted as he attempted to pull her into his arms, only to jump as Damien hissed sharply, "Behave yourself, Amethyst. I have not totally forgiven your reprehensible conduct of this afternoon, and will stand for no more of your foolishness!"

Finally allowing herself to be drawn into his arms, Amethyst looked up as he turned her to face him. His expression unreadable, he lightly touched the almost indistinguishable mark of his blow on her cheek, wincing lightly as if he himself felt the soreness of the bruise. His quiet voice was solemn.

"Amethyst, you will never again behave as thoughtlessly as you did today, with complete disregard for your safety, for I warn you, I will not take another such incident lightly." When she did not respond, he insisted quietly, "I would like your acknowledgment now, Amethyst."

His intently serious, concerned expression draining the last of her defiance as his mouth hovered only inches from hers, Amethyst felt something akin to shame for the trouble she had caused that day. With a faint, barely perceptible nod, Amethyst stammered slightly, "You . . . you have my word, Damien."

His expression unreadable, Damien's eyes moved slowly over her face to settle warmly on the soft, parted lips only inches from his moments before he lowered his head for a deep, searching kiss. The clinging pressure of his mouth leaving hers at last, Damien adjusted her slight body to fit intimately against his own massive frame before closing his eyes to sleep.

Amethyst had been up since dawn, excitement charging the adrenalin through her veins as Philadelphia harbor came into view. Anxious to stay out of the crew's way, she stood quietly at the rail as the activity surged around her. From his position on the quarterdeck, Damien barked quick, concise orders to his men as they prepared to furl the mainsail. Tugging expertly at the halyards, a dozen sailors lowered and steadied the yardarm, securing it quickly on the belaying pins before moving to work the braces. Spilling the wind from the canvas by pivoting the yard until it pointed into the wind, they secured the braces, relinquishing the next portion of the task momentarily to the men manning the sheets. Once positioned, the square sail was hoisted to the yardarm by the clew and buntlines as the top men scrambled up the ratlines on the windward side. Moving cautiously across the yardarm, their feet balanced precariously on foot ropes, the crew worked precisely, securing the middle of the sail with gaskets, moving to the weather side, and concluding on the windward side. That portion of their job complete, the men nimbly descended the shrouds, moving immediately to accomplish the next orders being issued from the quarterdeck. In the frantic bustle of activity, Amethyst was all but unnoticed, and suddenly feeling a useless, unnecessary part of the lively scene, she turned to gaze toward the shoreline.

Despite Damien's word given at the inception of the voyage, Amethyst was uncertain as to her fate once they dropped anchor in Philadelphia. The last week of the voyage had found Damien becoming more and more pensive, the former lively manner he exhibited at mealtimes replaced by long bouts of silence that wore on her nerves. Unwilling to question his long silences, Amethyst remained as silent as he, her mind conjuring up wild, frightening visions of her fate should he decide to renege on his word. But the time was fast approaching when she would no longer be in doubt.

Gliding smoothly into berth, the *Sally* touched the dock, Amethyst's heart hammering as the men rushed to secure her lines and perform the last minute details of docking. Realizing they would soon be going ashore, Amethyst turned to go below. She had packed her few possessions the previous night, laughing at the supreme inadequacy of her wardrobe in the chill climate of a Philadelphia winter. Her lightweight cotton skirt and blouse, and her one cotton dress had proved small protection against the chilling ocean breeze, and she had taken to wearing Damien's heavy woolen sweater over her attire while in the cabin. Aware that she was a ludicrous sight in the dark sweater that reached almost to mid-thigh, the shoulders of the huge garment reaching almost to her elbow, allowing the cuffs to hang a good five inches past her fingertips, she had determinedly rolled back the cuffs deciding her vanity would have to suffer in deference to her health. Her costume for topside was even more ridiculous, consisting of Damien's much-abused cape, the ample folds of which provided heavy insulation against the biting wind, and Damien's peculiar woolen stocking cap, which she wore pulled down tight around her piquant face, the dangling tail wrapped around her neck for added warmth. Oh, what a fashionable sight she would provide for curious Philadelphian eyes!

Stepping inside the cabin door, Amethyst immediately snatched up the small bundle of personal belongings, and preparing to leave, sent one departing glance around the room. Strange, as foreign and hateful as it had appeared when she had awakened that first morning, it now seemed a haven of security against the unknown that was to come. Having had no recent assurances of his intentions, Amethyst could only assume Damien would follow through with the plan he had outlined the first day aboard, publicly declaring her his ward, no matter the position she privately played in his life. She assumed . . . but assumption provided little reassurance.

Turning, she walked out the cabin door, and closed it quietly behind her, her former excitement gradually replaced by anxiety as she made a slow ascent to deck.

The chill January wind nipped sharply at her face when she reached topside, and clutching her billowing cape closer against her, Amethyst was caught by several anxious stares aimed in her direction. Following Ezekiel Bellows's furtive glance as it moved from her to a spot at the head of the gangplank that had been put in place after her descent to berth deck, Amethyst saw the reason for the crew's discomfort. Her heart turning to a lump of ice in her breast, she saw Damien in passionate embrace with a slender woman whose arms were wrapped possessively around his neck. So engrossed were they in each other that they were unaware of her presence on deck. Her expression stiffening, Amethyst watched as the enthusiastic reunion continued. Suddenly aware of movement at her elbow, she turned to meet Jeremy Barnes's sympathetic smile. With a valiant attempt at lightness, the dark young man said encouragingly, "Here, let me take your bundle for you, Miss Greer. I think it will be a while before you are able to go ashore, but I'm sure Philadelphia will be to your liking."

Nodding noncomittally, Amethyst managed a small, stiff smile in his direction, her eyes moving to follow his gaze as it snapped unexpectedly toward the gangplank. Turning, she saw Damien's eyes on her, as well as the startled, somewhat mocking glance of the woman he still held in his arms. Releasing the woman, Damien advanced toward Amethyst, drawing her with him, allowing Amethyst full assessment of his companion's ample charms as they drew nearer. Struggling to disguise her reaction, Amethyst was all too aware of the woman's beauty and fashionable attire. Light chestnut hair peeked out from the hood of a magnificent maroon velvet cape, becomingly framing her lively, if somewhat haughty face as she walked with a graceful sway, possessively tucking her arm under Damien's as they drew near.

His light eyes sharp, keenly assessing her reaction of his companion's appearance, Damien spared only the briefest glance for Jeremy Barnes still standing resolutely at her side. Turning to his companion, Damien's voice was courteously formal, "Merrell, I would like you to meet my ward, Miss Amethyst Greer."

Her delicate brow raised in a manner which, Amethyst was certain, was calculated to appeal to the male instinct, Merrell coyly tilted her head to gaze provocatively into Damien's face. "Your ward? Well, I suppose that's as good a title as any you could find for her. But that's alright, darling," she continued without awaiting comment, "now that you're back, you'll have no further need for any of your . . . wards."

Amethyst's face flamed brightly, simultaneous with the small choking sound issuing from Jeremy Barnes's throat as he stood stiffly beside her in obvious embarrassment. About to turn on her heel and walk away, Amethyst was stayed by Damien's hand as it shot out to block her exit. His voice as frigid as his expression, Damien turned and addressed Merrell Bristol with a dark look.

"You have made an error in judgment, Merrell. Miss Greer is the daughter of a dear friend I transported to the islands eight years ago, and whose passing I deeply regret. I have over the years felt a great responsibility toward Amethyst's mother and her, and since her mother's death, have accepted total responsibility for Amethyst's future. You have deeply offended Miss Greer with your unwarranted assumptions, and since the situation is too delicate to be smoothed over with a few words, I will allow Mr. Barnes to escort you to the dock so you may go home and contemplate an adequate gesture of apology."

Her eyes flaring wide with indignation, Merrell gasped, "Damien! Certainly you are not asking me to apologize to this wh . . ."

"Mr. Barnes!" His own complexion becoming slightly livid, Damien interrupted Merrell with undisguised anger. "You will escort Miss Bristol to the dock!"

Refusing the courteous arm offered by a smiling Jeremy Barnes, Merrell turned in a huff and stamped toward the gangplank. Turning back only once when she reached the dock to throw a supercilious sneer in their direction, Merrell walked toward the carriage which within moments was moving with undisguised haste away from the ship.

Damien turned back to Amethyst. Surprisingly a small smile covered his lips. "You needn't worry about Merrell, Amethyst. She's a jealous bitch, but she'll come around to apologize when she realizes there's no other way back into my good graces."

Suddenly realizing that Damien fully intended to fulfill his end of their bargain, Amethyst experienced a flush of relief and inexplicably angered by her own reaction, Amethyst mumbled for his ears alone, "Insufferable, conceited boor! It would serve you right if she threw you over!"

His smile broadening, Damien replied with a slight raising of his brow, "Oh, you needn't worry about that, Amethyst. You may take my word that the possibility is extremely unlikely."

Openly amused at her heated reaction to his statement, Damien offered his arm with a gallant gesture.

"Come, my dear. I will leave Mr. Barnes to secure the ship while I introduce you to your new home."

Directing a deadly look into his grinning countenance, Amethyst accepted the arm proffered her with as much dignity as she could muster, and walked stiffly to the gangplank.

Chapter 7

PHILADELPHIA

The hired carriage moved slowly through the frozen Philadelphia streets, affording Amethyst a leisurely view of the city. Despite her mother's numerous recitations of Martin Greer's brilliant reception at the Southwark Theater when Amethyst was very young, at first sight nothing about the city was at all familiar. Her eyes wide, Amethyst missed nothing in her avid perusal of the passing streets. The city was obviously huge, many of the buildings graciously constructed of brick, the streets bustling with people despite the frigid temperatures. The further they progressed from the docks, the better dressed the pedestrians appeared to become, with many of the women wearing extremely fashionable attire. More conscious than ever of her own ridiculous appearance in the oversized man's cape and ludicrous stocking cap, Amethyst drew back further into the corner of the carriage, her concentration on the sights outside the window interrupted only briefly.

Sitting beside her, his own attention intent on the myriad of emotions passing over the face of the beautiful child/woman at his side, Damien frowned. Why had she drawn back so furtively into the corner of the carriage? Surely she was not frightened of the unfamiliar city! No . . . Amethyst had proved time and time again that very few situations proved her master. No, she would not allow a city to intimidate her. Then what . . . ? A smile dawning on his face, Damien suddenly noted the self-conscious manner in which Amethyst fingered her cap before sliding an inch further into the corner of the carriage. Realizing her peculiar attire to be the cause of her discomfort, Damien could do no more than shake his head. Leave it to a woman to surmount all kinds of difficulties, only to have an inadequate wardrobe master her confidence. Did the girl not realize that no manner of clothing could dim the radiance of her beauty . . . hide the brilliance of her dazzling smile? Even in her present admittedly horrendous costume, her lovely face stood out like a perfect rose in a field of weeds. The tense knot in his chest tightening at the silent admission of his enduring fascination with the slight woman beside him, Damien frowned. Damn!

He had handled this whole affair poorly from the beginning, and now the situation had grown completely out of hand. What had ever possessed him to say he was going to introduce Amethyst to Philadelphia society as his ward? Honesty forcing himself to finally admit it had been his own certainty that he would find himself disenchanted and anxious to conclude their arrangement by the end of the voyage, Damien gave a disgusted snort. He had been wrong again! He had not tired of Amethyst, and in fact found himself so fiercely possessive that he had come to resent more and more with each passing day the license her introduction as his ward would afford her. But he was at a complete loss for an excuse to negate his promise. On the other hand, claiming Amethyst his ward would allow him the opportunity to privately enjoy her charms while allowing him to openly indulge his fancies with other Philadelphia maidens. The only catch in the arrangement, as his recent encounter with Merrell Bristol had proved a short while previous to his utter dismay, was that the possibility provided little allure. Merrell Bristol's kiss had left him cold, her calculated sexuality too practiced and false to his taste. Having experienced Amethyst's quick mind and spontaneous personality—not to speak of her other attributes—Merrell's affected posture had dulled into insignificance in his eyes. Reluctant to admit it even to himself, he found he could not remember a woman who had appealed to him sexually since setting eyes on the matured Amethyst, damn her beauteous hide!

Engrossed in these disturbing thoughts, Damien was frowning darkly as Amethyst turned to speak for the first time since the inception of their carriage ride. They were turning off Dock Street onto Walnut and she was becoming increasingly apprehensive as to their destination.

"Is it much further to your house, Damien?"

Her anxiety was apparent, the blatant vulnerability inadvertently displayed on her face effectively bringing home to Damien the realization that she was indeed still a child of sixteen, despite the veneer of maturity forced upon her by circumstance. Managing to subdue the driving desire to pull her onto his lap and reassure her that no matter their destination, he would protect and care for her, Damien muttered gruffly, "No, we are almost there."

Accustomed to his vacillating moods, Amethyst was unaffected by his gruffness and resumed her study of the street outside the carriage.

Within moments they were pulling up before a brick house of impressive size, its gleaming oak door opening as they arrived to reveal a tall, thin, gray-haired woman in her mid-years, whose narrow, lined face was composed into a professional welcoming smile. Alighting ahead of her, Damien turned to swing Amethyst down to the ground before acknowledging the welcome of the slender woman in gray.

"It's good to see you again, Mrs. Dobbs. I'm very happy to be home." Taking Amethyst's hand, he led her lightly up the steps. "I would like you to meet my ward, Miss Amethyst Greer. She will be staying with us for an indefinite period, and I would appreciate your making her welcome."

Turning back to Amethyst, he said in a tone he hoped held a fatherly note, aware as he was of the suspicious gleam in the older woman's eye, "Come, my dear. I'll introduce you to your new home."

Suddenly acutely aware of Amethyst's trepidation as her trembling hand tightened convulsively in his upon meeting the older woman's scrutiny, Damien longed to comfort her. Did she not realize Philadelphia society had come a long way from its Quaker influence? The war had brought about a "new morality" to many of the maidens of Philadelphia, allowing them a freedom in love affairs which was curtailed only in marriage. Had he brought Amethyst into the city as his mistress, she would have been accepted by a general populace accustomed to the open flaunting of such liaisons. But it was obvious from Amethyst's reaction to the housekeeper's scrutiny that she neither knew nor cared about the "new morality," and he would not allow her to suffer at the hands of self-righteous gossip. He had no doubt in his mind that his men would be silent with regard to Amethyst's sharing of his cabin for the duration of the voyage, for each knew the price he would pay for a slip of the tongue. It now remained for him to settle to Mrs. Dobbs's satisfaction the innocence of their relationship, as much as the deceit rankled.

Acknowledging the presence of the bright young maid and rotund older woman who had just appeared in the doorway beside Mrs. Dobbs, Damien smiled.

"Hello, Harriet. It's good to see your smiling face again. This is Miss Greer who will be staying with us for a time." Turning to Amethyst he said by way of introduction, "I'm sure you will find Mary a competent lady's maid and Harriet's cooking a complete delight." Directing his next remarks to Mary, Damien continued without waiting for a response, "I would appreciate your showing Miss Greer to the guest room, Mary. She has had a tiring voyage and would probably like to refresh herself."

With a brief curtsy, the sturdy young girl smiled tentatively in Amethyst's direction. Following Damien's lead, Amethyst walked up the stairs quietly behind her.

Turning back to Mrs. Dobbs, Damien was aware of the woman's displeasure. It was, after all, the duty of the housekeeper to show the guest to her room, and she obviously resented Mary's infringement on her authority.

Leveling his gaze, Damien addressed her directly as soon as Harriet had returned to the kitchen, "Mrs. Dobbs, I have arranged for a few moments privacy with you for a very particular reason. Due to the unusual circumstances of my guardianship of Miss Greer, it will be necessary to guard her reputation with extreme care. Her mother's unexpected death did not allow me time for any immediate plans, but when such details are completed, I should like Miss Greer to leave my household with her reputation intact so as to inhibit in no way my plans for her future. I will leave it to you to make all arrangements necessary to achieve this end."

Obviously flattered by the confidence with which the new responsibility had been placed on her shoulders, Mrs. Dobbs's thin, colorless lips turned upwards in a brief smile. Her high, nasal response was determined, "You may rely on me, Mr. Straith. I will see to it that your wishes are followed to the letter."

Nodding his head, Damien replied softly, "You have my appreciation, Mrs. Dobbs. Now, if you will kindly tell Harriet to prepare some light refreshment, I will go upstairs and see how Miss Greer is faring."

"Of course, Mr. Straith."

Watching as the woman turned and headed toward the kitchen, Damien smiled to himself. Well, so far so good. "Straith, you are a devious bastard," he whispered under his breath. "Let us only hope you have not, just now, cut your own throat!"

Amethyst was startled! She had never expected that a sea captain would be able to live in such luxury! While the house did not match Sheridan Plantation's great house in size, the furnishings by far surpassed those of the great house in quality. In her nervousness, she had seen little of the foyer, but the second floor was certainly impressive. Having been ushered down a wide hallway, past two doors which she presumed were bedrooms, she was led to a third door, which, when opened, left her gasping with surprise. The room was lovely! Of moderate size, the walls were papered with a delicate blue silk paper, obviously of oriental design, the varying azure shades displayed so vividly, caught up and repeated in the lushly patterned carpet that ran to the four corners of the room. The furniture was finished in white with gold trim, the delicately curved legs greatly enhancing its graceful appeal. A huge canopied bed dominated the center of the room, its blue satin bed cover and dust ruffle adding immeasurably to its charm. A great white and brass fireplace covered the wall opposite the bed, and in the middle of the far wall French doors led out to some sort of balcony. Moving curiously in its direction, she was about to turn the knob when a deep voice behind her snapped her around to see Damien's figure in the doorway.

"Mary, please go downstairs and tell Mrs. Dobbs we will take our refreshment in the morning room."

As the short, stocky maid moved quickly through the doorway, Damien approached Amethyst, his broad, virile appearance ridiculously out of place in the extremely feminine room.

"Are you pleased with your room, Amethyst?" Damien's query was perfunctory as he gazed at the pleased surprise displayed so openly on her lovely face.

"It is a beautiful room, Damien. I was just about to go out on the balcony when you entered."

"Well, it is a bit cold to enjoy the view, but a short peek is certainly in order."

Quickly opening the door, Damien ushered her out before him, carefully watching her expression as she surveyed the small walled yard and gardens.

"It is really quite lovely here in spring when the apple blossoms are in bloom, but even more lovely in summer when the roses are in full glory."

Turning to Damien, Amethyst shot a startled look in his direction. "Somehow I never pictured you in this setting, Damien. You always seemed so much a part of the sea . . ."

Smiling at her incredulity, Damien stated with a grin, "Well, I do need a place to spend my time when my ship is in drydock. I'm happy you're pleased, Amethyst, for I expect to be in port at least until spring. Neither my men nor I fancy another bout with a winter gale so soon. We've earned a rest."

Amethyst gave no response other than to turn back toward the doorway and reenter the bedroom. When the door was closed behind them and Amethyst had still not responded, Damien continued quietly, "I have impressed upon Mrs. Dobbs the importance of maintaining your good reputation, Amethyst, because I know it means much to you, and I have given you my word. But," he continued, taking a step closer to look deeply into the lavender eyes lifted to his, "I'll have you clearly understand that as much as I dislike deceit, you may expect my company more often than not in that lovely soft bed over there."

Catching her chin as she flushed deeply and attempted to divert her gaze from his, he continued with a small smile, "And as fatherly as my actions may appear for the benefit of others, you may rest assured my feelings could not be more the reverse."

A sound at the doorway brought an abrupt end to their intimate conversation, eliciting a silent prayer of thanks from Amethyst as she attempted to overcome the trembling Damien's mere touch inspired within her. Mary had entered and was attempting to light a fire in the fireplace, and smiling at Amethyst's obvious discomfort, Damien reached out to unfasten the cape she still wore around her shoulders. Dropping it carelessly to the chair, he then turned to remove the stocking cap, which found the same destination. Turning back, a small smile formed on his lips at the sight of his huge woolen sweater hanging lankly on her petite frame.

"And certainly, the first thing on our agenda tomorrow will be to get you some decent clothing. But for now, my dear," the paternal endearment delivered with a knowing wink behind the back of the hardworking Mary, he continued heartily, "let me introduce you to the remainder of the staff."

Amethyst stood at the wardrobe door, a small smile flicking across her lips as her gaze rested momentarily on the heavy cape and stocking cap pushed into the far corner. Damien had declined their return when her own custom wardrobe had begun to be delivered by the impressive French couturiere, Madame duMaurier, but the unlikely garments had served her well, and she was strangely reluctant to consign them to the trash heap. Still, they were in stark contrast to the dazzling array of finery that now filled the ample space. At the end of her third week in Philadelphia, Amethyst found her feelings toward Damien even more complex than before. Alternating between reluctant appreciation for the unaccustomed luxuries she enjoyed as a result of his generosity, and the deep, burning anger that endured as a result of his secret, unrelenting intimate demands, she found herself in a state of complete confusion. But if there was any salvation in their present arrangement, it was the balm provided by Damien's irritation when forced to outwait the cautious Mrs. Dobbs in his almost nightly visits. Taking her responsibility very seriously, the puritanical woman seemed to feel it her duty to maintain a steady eye on Amethyst's door from the moment Amethyst retired until far past the reasonable hour for sleep. Her intense surveillance had forced Damien to skulk around his own house in the dark of the night, long after he would have preferred to retire, in an attempt to share Amethyst's bed, and forced him back to his own room far sooner than was his own inclination to leave in the morning. Still, he had kept his word and steadfastly maintained outward appearances for the sake of her reputation.

Now, nearing the end of their first month in the large house on Chestnut Street, they had been accepted as a respectable part of Philadelphia society, and were beginning to receive a steady stream of invitations to social affairs. Reluctantly, Amethyst had to admit Damien was a welcome addition to any affair, his dashing appearance and surprising charm in great demand by eager hostesses, who, she feared, merely tolerated her attendance. But still, if the Philadelphia maidens were not so keen on her addition to their ranks, certainly the male sector of society seemed to find her presence extremely stimulating. With a small chuckle, Amethyst remembered the annoyance on Damien's face at the attention she was receiving from some of the more eligible bachelors. But in truth, Amethyst found most of the young men an inadequate challenge and at times a considerable annoyance, and did not resent in the least Damien's strict screening of her ardent admirers.

Her mind wandering aimlessly on thoughts of the dinner party they were to attend that night, Amethyst's eyes moved over the gowns in her wardrobe. Now possessed of six new gowns, with several more on order, she found it most difficult to decide which she was to wear for each affair. Her brow knit in concentration, Amethyst fingered the exquisite fabrics, inwardly marveling that such a dilemma should be hers. Having come to her decision at last, Amethyst removed a pale lavender velvet from her wardrobe. Madame duMaurier had protested her selection of the color, stating lavender was a color for mourning, but she had been adamant in her choice. Too impatient to wait for Mary's assistance, Amethyst slipped the elegant garment over her head. Finally conceding she needed assistance as she struggled in vain to secure the buttons on the back of the dress, she summoned Mary impatiently.

Concentrating on her appearance as Mary worked feverishly to secure the endless line of covered buttons that stretched down her graceful back, Amethyst stared into the mirror. Having scorned the efforts of the fashionable Philadelphia hairdressers and their techniques of stiff wire forms and heavy pomades used to stretch the hair up from the face into exaggerated proportions and shapes, in many cases to be later powdered until white and stiff, Amethyst preferred to dress her hair herself. Piling the heavy, silky mass on the top of her head in a graceful pompadour, Amethyst had allowed a few curls to tumble down her back in "calculated deshabille" as her mother had so frequently termed the style. Her eyes moving to her gown, she scrutinized the garment critically. The round cut of the decolletage was complimentary, exposing only a hint of the now generous swell of her breasts, the delicate white lace lying against her flawless skin and extending down the front of her dress as far as her waist adding a touch of elegance to the simple style. The sleeves, extending as far as the elbow, ended in wide tiers of the same lace which swayed gracefully as she moved. The bodice dipped to a low point at the waist, and adjusting it uncomfortably as Mary continued securing the buttons, Amethyst frowned, finding it a trifle snug despite Madame's slight adjustment to enlarge the area only the week before. But the small sign of displeasure vanished completely as she surveyed the sweeping folds of the skirt which were caught up provocatively with deep purple bows at several points at the bottom to reveal tier upon tier of the same lace that trimmed her neckline and sleeves. On her feet, deep purple velvet slippers peeked out appealingly, completing the perfection of the ensemble. Carefully securing two small purple bows in the tumble of curls that moved lightly against the nape of her neck, Amethyst then reached for her new jewel case. Still experiencing a thrill as her eyes touched on the sparkling amethyst lavalier inside, she removed it carefully and secured it around her neck. Fastening the matching ear bobbs on her ears, she stood back to survey the total effect.

Unable to suppress the small flush of warmth that overcame her, she remembered Damien's unorthodox presentation of the beautiful gems. Having come to her room in the middle of the night the previous week, Damien had cautiously lit the lamp at bedside, and fastening the necklace around her neck with great solemnity, had declared the stones attained true beauty only when reflecting the color of her eyes. Refusing to allow her to remove the delicate jewels, he had proceeded to make love to her with a passion that still sent a rush of color to her face, whispering softly against her ear as they lay sated in each other's arms that he wanted her to recall that night vividly each time she placed the lavalier around her neck. And strangely, uncertain whether the lavalier was merely another charm to strengthen his obeah over her, Amethyst found that she did.

Shaking her head to clear her rioting thoughts, Amethyst murmured quietly, "Thank you, Mary. You may go downstairs and tell Mr. Straith that I shall be ready in a moment."

Taking a few moments longer to allow the slight trembling caused by her thoughts to abate, Amethyst dipped her fingertips into the basin of fresh water on her washstand and absentmindedly attempted to secure the small tendrils of hair that persisted in curling at her hairline. Finally admitting defeat as the stubborn curls returned within a few moments to their original position, she shrugged her slender shoulders and turned toward the door, grateful that the small distraction had allowed the return of her poise. Moving through the doorway, she walked slowly down the hallway to the staircase, cautioning herself silently. She must not allow Damien Straith to gain such control over her senses, for to do so was pure madness. She was already uncertain which disturbed her more, Damien's illicit almost nightly visits to her bed, or his occasional absences when her mind tortured her with graphic pictures of reasons for his absence. No, if she were to survive, she would have to accept the situation for what it was, a temporary possession of her will which she was now powerless to combat. Exposed to the many experienced beauties in Philadelphia who sought to win his affections, he would doubtless tire of her within a short time and release her from the spell that held her so helpless against him. Turning the corner of the hallway, she descended the staircase slowly, her mind drumming silently with each step she took, "Caution . . . caution . . . caution . . ."

Waiting impatiently in the hallway below, Damien raised his glass to his lips. "Damn the girl, where is she? We are due at the party in ten minutes, and I have no desire to be the last to arrive." Hell, no, he added silently, that would never do. Amethyst was enough of a sensation at each affair they attended. She needed no additional artifices to draw attention to her. His stomach tightening uncontrollably, he recalled the stir she had created within the ranks of Philadelphia's male contingent at the two previous affairs they had attended. Wishing fervently he was free to disperse the circle of fawning males surrounding Amethyst with a short statement declaring his own priority, he had been forced to pretend indifference, consoling himself that within a few hours he would confirm again, if only in secret, his complete possession of her. Damn! He had not expected the deception to chafe so sorely . . . had not expected he could experience such fury when another man attempted to insinuate himself into her affections. He had half a mind to call the entire farce to a complete halt by revealing the true manner of their relationship . . . but, fool that he was, he had given his word.

A small sound on the staircase drawing his mind from his disturbing thoughts, Damien glanced up, his first glimpse of the girl/woman slowly descending the stairs stealing his breath as effectively as a blow to the stomach. God, she was lovely . . . His eyes meeting and holding the glance of huge violet eyes, he felt the simultaneous tug at his heart and groin that her appearance always stimulated, and an overwhelming desire to call the charade they practiced to a complete halt by taking her into his arms then and there. But Amethyst's nervous glance toward Mrs. Dobbs as he continued his ardent, somewhat obvious appreciation of her charms stirring a jolt of conscience, he said aloud, "Amethyst, you look very well this evening, but we must hurry or we'll be late for the dinner party." Extending his hand toward her, he could not resist a small wink as their hands met, his good humor restored when Amethyst flushed uncomfortably. Hell, if he had to suffer through this ridiculous situation, he was happy to see Amethyst also suffered discomfort with the deceit. Perhaps if she became uncomfortable enough she would release him from his promise, and they could resume an open relationship. Smiling at the comforting thought, he placed her purple velvet cape around Amethyst's shoulders, his hands moving to secure the closures in a possessive manner that darkened the color on Amethyst's cheeks. Ignoring her discomfort, he said lightly, "We must step lively, my dear, or we'll most assuredly be late."

The short ride to Hiram and Millicent Strathmore's house was endless as Damien, taking advantage of their solitude, taunted her mercilessly. Sliding close to her side as the carriage started forward, he took her chin in his palm and turned her face toward his. His mouth only inches from hers, his breath was sweet against her lips.

"Don't tire yourself too much tonight, darling, for you'll surely need your strength once we've returned home and the lights go out on Chestnut Street." Slowly running the tip of his tongue across her lips, he felt a deep sense of satisfaction as a small tremor shook her slender body, and barely resisting the urge to crush her against him to conquer completely the lips so vulnerable to his touch, he slid his hand under cloak to intimately fondle the soft flesh exposed by her decolletage.

"Remember, darling," he whispered softly, "those damned fools may ogle you all they want, but you belong to me and only me ... and when we return home tonight, I'll make up for all the time wasted in this damned charade you insist upon."

Struggling to quell the weakness that assailed her at his touch, Amethyst managed a breathless retort as she attempted to stay the hand that moved caressingly on her breasts, "For all your complaints, Damien, you seem to find considerable enjoyment in the charms of Stephanie Morgan . . . and Sara Barlow . . . not to mention your forgiveness of Merrell Bristol despite the fact that she has never apologized for her insulting remarks."

His brow raised satirically, Damien responded in a soft voice, "Oh, yes, I had quite forgotten Merrell's assessment of our relationship . . ."

Her eyes sparking an anger that was apparent even in the semi-darkness of the carriage, Amethyst responded deliberately, "Are you insinuating that she was correct in calling me a whore, Damien? If that is so, it will be very easy to demonstrate the manner in which a whore truly conducts herself tonight when I'm surrounded by a group of eager admirers!"

Managing to choke down a warning against that sort of behavior, Damien responded with a control that surprised himself, "And that would be cutting off your nose to spite your face, would it not, darling?"

His small, knowing laugh at her lack of response angering her even further, Amethyst jerked herself from his restraining hands sliding as far from him as the limited confines of the carriage would allow. Startled by an abrupt movement which jerked her firmly back against Damien's chest, Amethyst gasped, only to be startled once again by the savagery in his tone as he whispered against her parted lips, "But so we may understand each other completely, I'll make myself very clear. It matters not what I do or say to *any* of the women at this party or any other we may attend. The simple fact is this. *You* belong to *me*, and the moment I feel you are forgetting this, I will end this ridiculous masquerade once and for all!"

She was trembling violently, incapable of a response and realizing they would soon arrive at their destination,

Damien released her with a sharp rebuke. "Now get hold of yourself, you little fool, or you will put an end to your own little game!"

His disposition negatively affected by the scene in the carriage, Damien entered the Strathmore residence in a surly mood barely concealed by a stiff smile. Still, he was unable to suppress a burst of pride when all heads turned on their entrance, and the almost simultaneous stab of jealousy stimulated by the instantaneous movement toward them of a small group of young men standing at the other end of the room. Acknowledging their perfunctory greetings as they approached, Damien noticed Amethyst retained her hold on his arm, her body still stiff and unrelaxed despite the profuse attentions being showered upon her.

"It's just as well," he thought, his own mood lightening as a result of Amethyst's apparent indifference to the circle of young men surrounding them, "that she realizes from the first that I will stand for none of her pretentions."

"Damien, darling!" A low, throaty greeting distracted Damien momentarily from his thoughts, turning him toward the woman who took the opportunity to move between Amethyst and himself. "Millicent was beginning to think you would disappoint her tonight and not appear, and with Hiram called away on business, she was decidedly disappointed that both her favorite men would be absent this evening. But I assured her you would never miss one of her parties. They are, after all, the most successful social affairs in Philadelphia, are they not?" Stephanie Morgan's wise brown eyes were turned up to his as he nodded with a small smile, noting Amethyst's quick glance in his direction as the group of young men around her tightened to exclude both Stephanie and himself.

"Well, since Millicent is detained in the kitchen with her small emergency, I will assume the role of hostess temporarily. Come, darling," her glance was soft and intimate, "we've been waiting for you." And then at Damien's quick glance toward Amethyst, she murmured quickly, "Leave the girl on her own for a while, Damien. You are far too protective of her. After all, if you are to marry her off, you must allow her some time with those eligible young fellows."

"Amethyst is only sixteen years old, Stephanie. I think you will agree that she is at far too tender an age to contemplate marriage in the immediate future." Striving to hide his annoyance, Damien noted out of the corner of his eye that Amethyst had turned her full attention to the most gregarious of the group and was laughing full up into his enraptured face, her discomfort of a few moments before apparently completely overcome. Damn the precocious little flirt! Well, he would not spend the evening scrutinizing her actions. He had far more interesting matters to attend to, the most appealing of which was leaning prettily on his arm. She could waste her time with those young fools if that was her wish, and he would amuse himself as well. Turning his full attention to Stephanie Morgan, he said softly, "But perhaps you're right, Stephanie. At any rate, you're far too lovely to argue with." Hardly noting her flush of pleasure at his compliment, Damien heard only the small burst of laughter from the group surrounding Amethyst. Damn her and her cleverness! She already had them eating out of her hand!

Heading resolutely toward the champagne being served at the other end of the room, Damien managed a small, intimate glance for the beaming Stephanie. "And now, I think it's time for some refreshment."

Smiling brightly into Martin Quell's animated face,

Amethyst managed to hide her anger as her mind wandered to the tall, blond figure laughing so intimately with Stephanie Morgan on the other side of the room. The man was insufferable, and he had no right to look so handsome in his formal attire. Certainly a man of such large stature should look awkward in these elegant surroundings, but he managed, as he did everywhere else, to stand out in the crowd with a subdued elegance of his own. It was not as if the other men in the room were not as well outfitted as he, but the superb tailoring of his dark blue coat was in startling contrast with his gleaming blond hair and sun-darkened skin, the light blue of his waistcoat and britches tinting his piercing gray eyes a startling blue that commanded attention. His movement was fluid and agile as he moved through the crowd. He probably dances well also, she thought with disgust at her inability to find an outstanding flaw on which to place her ridicule.

The group around her was laughing now, and taking her cue, Amethyst smiled also, realizing she had heard nothing of the humorous story Martin had spun for her amusement. Feeling a stab of guilt, Amethyst forced her attention back to the young men surrounding her. After all, it was not their fault that they paled into insignificance beside Damien's overpowering masculine aura. If it were not for them, she would probably be standing in some corner, waiting desperately for dinner to be announced so she might find a way to pass another boring hour while Damien amused himself elsewhere. Had it not been for her own unusual circumstances, she might have found Martin Quell attractive with his smiling brown eyes and glib tongue, or even Gerard Whitestone, with his appealing stammer. But moving her eyes from one to the other in the group surrounding her, Amethyst felt a sinking sensation in the pit of her stomach, for there was not one within the group that was capable of holding her interest for more than a few moments.

Thoroughly ashamed of her ungracious thoughts, Amethyst glanced away from the eyes riveted so steadily on her countenance, fearful that they might read her thoughts on her face, only to catch the glance of intense black eyes staring in her direction. Her own eyes held inexplicably by the force of his stare, Amethyst mentally noted the stranger's striking appearance. A few inches over medium height, he was extremely broad of shoulder and chest, his black coat tailored precisely to fit the unusual expanse of shoulder and narrowness of waist. His waistcoat and britches in fine white cloth fit closely against his flat stomach and powerful thighs. A masterfully tied cravat hugged closely his wide, muscular neck, emphasizing the appearance of strength and power that he exuded. But most impressive of all was the olive-skinned, devastatingly handsome face, dominated by large, black eyes which openly stared in her direction from beneath dark, heavy brows. His strong, aquiline nose added a sensual appeal, as did the firm, square chin that completed the impressive visage. His hair was a midnight black, straight and shining, tied to a queue at the back of his neck with a black ribbon, and he was, without doubt, one of the most attractive men Amethyst had ever seen.

Momentarily unable to break contact with his glance, Amethyst noted the small smile that lurked on his lips as he nodded absentmindedly to the woman speaking so vivaciously in his ear. Turning her attention back to her companions, she thought with a small stab of amusement, "Poor fellow, he's having as difficult a time concentrating on his companion's conversation as I am!"

Her amusement growing as she tossed the thought around in her mind, her smile widened, her obvious enjoyment bringing a flash of pleasure to Gerard's face, increasing his hesitant stammer. In an effort to ease the young man's embarrassment as he struggled to conclude his narrative, she reached out and placed a slender hand on his arm as she said sincerely, "Gerard, I do find you an extremely agreeable fellow," and turning quickly, hastened to add lightly, "as I do all you gentlemen."

Having obviously won their hearts with her kindness to a less fortunate of their group, Amethyst was not allowed a moment's solitude until the ringing of the bell announced the call to supper, and a deep voice sounded in her ear, "Mademoiselle Greer, Madame Strathmore has asked that I escort you to supper."

Turning, Amethyst was startled to see the dark-haired gentleman she had noticed previously standing beside her. Completely ignoring the protests of the group surrounding her, he offered his arm politely. Smiling spontaneously, Amethyst felt a rush of true warmth as her glance again met his intense dark eyes and flashing a regretful smile to the others, Amethyst placed her hand on the arm offered and turned her full attention to the gentleman escorting her toward the dining room.

"Allow me to introduce myself, *Mademoiselle*. My name is Armand Beauchamps. I am a business associate of Monsieur Strathmore. And you are the ward of Monsieur Damien Straith, the beautiful Mademoiselle Amethyst Greer."

Flushing more from the deceit that was being practiced on the unsuspecting group than she did from the man's compliment, Amethyst managed a slight nod before escaping to a more comfortable subject.

"You are new to Philadelphia, Monsieur?"

His smile broadening, the gentleman said softly, "I would be honored if you would call me Armand, *Mademoiselle*."

"And of course you must call me Amethyst, Armand." Smiling up into the darkly handsome face looking down into hers as they walked into the dining room, Amethyst did not see the anger displayed so openly in Damien's hostile expression.

The table was elaborately set with imported china, flowers, and a myriad of delicate appetizers to tempt the palate, but Amethyst saw little and sampled few of them. Armand's voice was deep and melodious, his accent unexpectedly appealing, and utterly fascinated by his vibrant good looks and sparkling conversation, she encouraged him to speak, her smile glowing with delight.

Stopping abruptly in the course of his conversation midway through the meal, Armand's glance became cautious as his brow raised quizzically. "Ah, *ma petite belle*," he whispered softly, "your beautiful face reflects far more amusement than my meager words merit, I fear. Will you be so kind as to tell me what amuses you so?"

Her own smile widening, Amethyst replied candidly, "I find you absolutely fascinating, Armand. You speak so beautifully . . . your voice is so melodious . . ."

Obviously startled by her response and uncertain if she jested, Armand replied cautiously, "*Ma cherie*, certainly you do not ridicule my poor attempt at English."

Hastening to reassure him, Amethyst moved to cover his large hand with her own as she exclaimed with obvious sincerity, "Oh, no, Armand, I am sincere. I find your speech delightful! I have not so much enjoyed listening to someone speak since the last time I heard David Douglass perform *Othello*."

His expression slightly offended, Armand responded quietly, "Do you find me theatrical in my manner of speaking, Amethyst?"

Her own expression stiffening slightly, Amethyst responded in the same soft tone as she withdrew her hand from his, "I meant it only as a compliment, sir. Captain Straith would not have me acknowledge the fact to

Philadelphia society, but my beloved father was an actor, and my mother an actress. I myself have performed on the stage and although their occupation is not generally accepted, I must say I am extremely proud of my parents' talent. My father was an artist, and although my mother and I did not quite meet the standards of his performance, I . . ."

"Cela suffit." Armand's soft command interrupted Amethyst's stiff declaration. "You need tell me no more, Amethyst, and I apologize for my ignorance."

Suddenly brightening, Amethyst said softly, "My father . . . you may have heard of him. His name was Martin Wellington Greer."

Shaking his head, Armand smiled, his voice warm as he responded softly, "No, I have not heard of him, *ma petite*, but I have not been in this country very long, and I understand theatricals have not been allowed since the revolution."

"Yes," lowering her head, Amethyst stammered softly, "that is the reason Mother and I went to Jamaica on Captain Str . . . I mean Damien's ship. Papa had died the year before, you know, and Mama could support us in no other way. But," raising her head once again, Amethyst shined the full force of lavender eyes into his, almost robbing him of breath as she whispered earnestly, "but it is an honorable profession. My father was an artist, supremely talented . . . And you, Armand, could hold audiences spellbound with your voice . . ."

Her eyes wide with earnestness, Amethyst watched as a small smile grew on Armand's face. His hand moving to cover hers, he whispered softly, *"Ma petite chou, vous êtes délicieux!"* Raising the small hand to his lips, he kissed it lightly, bringing a light flush to her cheeks as a few heads turned momentarily from their conversation with interest.

Not understanding his flagrant compliment, Amethyst

appeared momentarily at a loss, causing Armand to continue softly, "I am extremely flattered, Amethyst, but I am curious. If you have been cautioned against telling anyone of your background, why have you told me?"

Interrupting him impatiently, Amethyst said softly, "Armand, one does not have to read minds to realize that you are not the sort of person who amuses himself by breaking confidences and spreading gossip. I need no reassurance that what I have told you will go no further."

Barely resisting the urge to caress the soft cheek so close to him, Armand's dark eyes bore intently into hers. He was overwhelmed by the sincerity of the youthful beauty seated beside him, spellbound as indeed she had proclaimed audiences would be held by his voice. But his feelings were racing far ahead of the situation, and amazed that he could be so affected by a woman, especially one of such youth and innocence, he raised the small hand once again to his lips.

From his position at the far end of the table, Damien stared at the two heads bent so close together as they exchanged whispers, his anger mounting. Amethyst had not spared him a glance since she had been approached by that damned Frenchman! Perhaps she was just trying to anger him, but her expression was too intent, as if she could not take her eyes from the damned fellow's face. Barely restraining the urge to leap up and rip apart the two heads bent so close together, Damien forced his gaze back to his plate to toy mindlessly with his food until a familiar voice cooed in his ear, "Damien, darling, is something wrong?"

Glancing up, Damien looked into Merrell Bristol's amused expression. He had completely forgotten she sat beside him . . . forgotten everything but those two heads bent toward each other in shared confidences.

The insidious cooing continued. "Your little 'ward' seems to be getting on quite well with Armand Beauchamps, doesn't she? And he is such a sophisticated gentleman... I can't really believe he's sincerely interested in such a sweet, inexperienced child... But, of course, you would know her virtues far better than I..."

His head snapping up in anger, Damien hissed venomously under his breath, "Shut up, Merrell. I'll stand for no more of your malevolent innuendo."

Fluttering her lashes in mock innocence, Merrell whispered softly in response, "Why, Damien, I don't know what you mean! But it really isn't necessary for me to say more. Certainly the evidence before your eyes is far more revealing."

Turning her glance away, Merrell devoted her attention to her plate, allowing Damien the supreme torture of watching as the intimate tête-à-tête continued for the duration of the meal.

Amethyst rose from the table, smiling as Armand immediately took her arm. A small musicale was to follow, and he had already asked that she sit with him during the entertainment. Suddenly realizing she had not spared a thought for Damien in hours, Amethyst scanned the room for his tall figure, only to see it bent toward Merrell Bristol as she whispered in his ear. A flash of anger passing over her face, she thought heatedly, "I need not worry while that woman is here to entertain him," and turning, caught Armand's amused expression.

"It is obvious you are not overly pleased with your guardian's attentions to Mademoiselle Bristol."

"Oh, you're wrong, Armand," Amethyst smiled sweetly, "I'm merely not overly fond of Mademoiselle Bristol! She's a nasty bitch!"

Startled by Amethyst's unexpected declaration, Armand gave a short hoot of laughter before managing to subdue the amusement Amethyst's remark had stimulated. Taking her arm even more firmly than before, he struggled to say through his laughter, "*Ma petite chou, vous êtes une délices... une délices...*" Shaking his head at her bewildered expression, he continued in English, "I have not enjoyed myself so well in months, ma petite Amethyst, and I do not intend to have you get away from me so quickly." Darting a look toward the somber group of young men in the corner who eyed him covetously, he said softly, "Even though it was a deceit that brought us together."

Amethyst's eyes flashed wide in apprehension. Not realizing the cause of her concern, he continued hastily, "I merely mean that Madame Strathmore did not instruct me to take you in to dinner. It was my own idea, a complete prefabrication on my part, for which I apologize." Noting the relief that covered her face, he said quietly, "Then you do forgive me my small untruth, ma cherie? *Bon...* I did not wish to begin with a lie between us."

Noting the manner in which Amethyst averted her eyes from his, Armand upbraided himself mentally, Caution, fool. You frighten her with your impatience. She is still a child... you must go slowly.

Squeezing her arm gently, he urged her forward. "Come, cherie, the music room will soon be filled. If I cannot sit beside you for the duration of the entertainment, the evening will be ruined."

Bright violet eyes turned up to his once again, and shaking his head with amazement as his jaded heart leaped unreasonably in his chest, Armand was startled to realize that his statement was entirely sincere.

The first musical presentation was a cello solo of dubious merit. Seated beside Armand in one of the precisely arranged chairs in the music room, Amethyst had ample time during the performance to note that Damien sat directly behind her with Merrell Bristol on one side and Stephanie Morgan on the other. A short glance in his direction immediately ascertained his anger, and although she could not perceive its cause, she had no doubt that it was directed at her. Severely inhibited by his presence, her conversation with Armand became stiff and polite, devoid of its former spontaneity. The cello solo was nearing its end when Armand leaned toward her, a small frown creasing his brow. His hand moving to cover hers, he whispered softly, "Amethyst, ma petite, is something wrong? Have I offended you in some way?"

The lavender eyes quickly raised to his shone with obvious sincerity as she said quickly, "Oh, no, Armand. You have done nothing, nothing at all."

"Then why . . . ?"

An impatient snort from behind caused Amethyst to shoot a quick glance out the corner of her eye toward Damien. Flushing lightly at his angry glare, Amethyst dropped her eyes, her actions answering Armand's question far more clearly than words.

Relieved, Armand smiled. "You worry that your guardian does not approve of me, ma cherie? It is true that he does seem irritated, but surely we have done nothing that could cause his anger." When her eyes still remained averted from his, Armand patted her hand consolingly, "You need not worry, Amethyst. When the musicale is finished I will speak to Mr. Straith and . . ."

"Oh, no, you mustn't, Armand, please . . ."

Her agitation was obvious, and shooting Straith a quick look, Armand could see the man's irritation growing. Also obvious in that quick glance was Merrell Bristol's apparent enjoyment of the situation, and silently confirming Amethyst's assessment of the woman's personality, Armand found himself at a loss as to how to put Amethyst at ease.

The cello solo ended a few tedious minutes later. With a small sigh of forbearance, Amethyst watched as a gray-haired gentleman took his place at the piano, uncertain if she could bear another hour of Damien's dark looks and Armand's aggrieved puzzlement. A sudden burst of music from the piano startled Amethyst from her somber thoughts. The melody was lilting, the tempo gay and exciting, lifting her spirits despite herself until Amethyst smiled, turning quickly to Armand to whisper, "The melody is beautiful, is it not, Armand? What is this tune? I don't recall having heard it before."

"I cannot tell you its name, but it is a waltz, cherie."

"A waltz?"

"*Oui*. You have never danced the waltz, ma petite?"

Shaking her head in answer to his question, Amethyst returned her attention to the music. Completely overwhelmed by its beauty, Amethyst closed her eyes, swaying ever so slightly, her feet tapping the floor as the tempo increased, building to a powerful crescendo before coming to a quick, breathtaking halt. The burst of applause at the conclusion of the piece was spontaneous. Jumping to her feet, Amethyst clapped her hands with delight, her countenance sparkling with the excitement of the moment. More exhilarated by Amethyst's spontaneous enthusiasm than he was by the music he had heard a dozen times, Armand smiled into her bright young face. "I shall teach you the waltz, ma petite. It is a grand dance that lifts the heart to soaring for its duration."

The musician had taken his seat for his next piece when turning toward Armand, Amethyst whispered breathlessly, "Oh, yes, I would like to learn the waltz, Armand. I'm sure I would truly enjoy dancing to that delightful music."

In direct contrast to the gaiety of the first selection, the pianist began his second piece. Her eyes closing with a sentiment that was almost pain, Amethyst listened to the opening strains of "Greensleeves," a thoughtful expression covering her face as a kaleidoscope of memories flashed across her mind. Her eyes filled with tears, she looked to Armand's concerned expression as the haunting melody drew to a close, to answer his unspoken question.

"It is a favorite of mine, Armand. I have sung it many times..."

Seated behind, Merrell Bristol strained her ears to hear the conversation progressing between them and taking her opportunity, she snatched greedily on Amethyst's innocent remark. Her voice pitched so that it might be heard by the surrounding rows of seats, she interrupted their private conversation without hesitation.

"Did I hear you say you have sung this song many times, Amethyst?"

Embarrassed by Merrell's boorishness, Amethyst nodded lightly in response.

Directing her next remarks to Millicent Strathmore who was seated a few rows away, Merrell said loudly, "Did you hear what Amethyst said, Millicent? She has sung 'Greensleeves' many times! Perhaps we can convince her to sing for us tonight!"

Amethyst's short glance toward Armand showed her consternation, and quick to pick up her alarm, Armand replied graciously, "I do believe we are asking too much of Mademoiselle Greer tonight. Certainly you do not expect her to perform before a strange group."

"Oh, but we aren't strangers, Monsieur Beauchamps. We're friends, aren't we, Amethyst, dear?"

Damien was strangely silent during the exchange, and shooting a quick look to him for support, Amethyst saw his face darkening with anger. Whether it was directed at her or at Merrell Bristol, she was uncertain, and she was about to reply when Merrell addressed Armand again, her voice a coy innuendo.

"But perhaps Monsieur Beauchamps is afraid you will disappoint us with your offering. Oh, I assure you, Monsieur, we will be generous even though we are all certain Mademoiselle Greer's voice will match her own insouciant personality."

"And I assure you, Mademoiselle," Armand began, his face beginning to redden with annoyance at the embarrassing position she was forcing upon them both, "that I do not doubt..."

"Never mind, Armand." Rising to her feet, Amethyst began walking toward the piano. "I shall be happy to ease Miss Bristol's curiosity about my singing voice, for I fear it has suddenly assumed such monumental proportions in her mind that she will not rest until she is satisfied."

Completely ignoring Merrell's annoyed "Humph!" Amethyst moved toward the piano.

Bending down, she whispered to the stiff-faced pianist, "I apologize, sir, for this interruption in your performance, but I fear you will not be free to continue your glorious music until that bitch's curiosity is sated!"

Relieved to see a small smile crack the gentleman's facade, Amethyst smiled brightly in return and within moments the opening strains of "Greensleeves" filled the room. Allowing herself to be lifted with the beauty of the melody to a place far from the confines of the stuffy room, Amethyst began to sing. Her clear soprano filled the room, raising her on the wings of the song. Closing her eyes, she was no longer in Philadelphia, but on a faraway sunny island. She was standing on stage, looking to a box at the far side of the room where a young man stared back at her, his mahogany eyes dark and intense as she sang the words directly to him:

"Black is the color of my true love's hair,
His looks are something wondrous fair,

> The purest eyes and the strongest hands
> I love the grass on which he stands..."

Her voice rising from the verse to a gripping chorus, echoed in the room, filling it with her clarity of tone, giving those present a brief, lonely glimpse of the heartbreak of lost love. When her song was done, Amethyst found herself staring into Armand's dark eyes. There was complete silence in the room and she had just turned to express her gratitude to the pianist when a burst of applause met her ears. Turning back with a smile, she saw Armand advancing toward her. Obviously affected by her song, he enclosed her in an unhesitant embrace. Finally releasing her, he held her by the shoulders as he kissed her lightly on both cheeks.

"*Magnifique!* ... Superbe, ma petite chou. I have never heard..."

"It's time for us to leave now, Amethyst!" Damien's deep voice from behind cut abruptly into Armand's fervent exclamations, snapping him around as he protested, "Surely, Monsieur Straith, you will not leave so quickly. We have not all had the opportunity to express our appreciation..."

Directing a meaningful stare into Armand's eyes, Damien said through tight lips, "Enough 'appreciation' has already been expressed this night. It is time for Amethyst and me to leave."

Taking Amethyst securely by the arm, he ushered her firmly to the door of the room and into the foyer. With a quick nod to the servant, he summoned their outerwear before turning to Millicent Strathmore who had followed them to the door.

"I am sorry, Damien," the gracious woman offered softly. "I'm afraid Merrell does get out of hand at times, but you should be accustomed to her excesses by now, shouldn't you, dear?"

Turning to glance coolly in Merrell's direction as she moved toward them, he deliberately turned his back on her approach, saying pointedly, "Merrell? Merrell who? I'm afraid I know no one by the name of Merrell."

Her face flushing a bright red, Merrell stopped in her tracks to stare at his broad back for a few short seconds before turning abruptly and walking back toward the room in which another piano solo had begun.

Watching as Merrell disappeared through the doorway, Millicent turned to say quietly, "Well, you have put her in her place and she is properly chastised for her conduct. Don't you think you can now stay?"

His face softening only momentarily as the older woman raised a pleading look in his direction, Damien said softly, "It's I who am sorry if I disturbed your party tonight, Millicent, but if I were to stay, I'm afraid I would ruin it completely."

Turning to drape Amethyst's cape around her shoulders, he snapped tightly, "Make sure you secure the closures tightly. It is very cold outside tonight, and I don't wish to see a resumption of your ill health!"

Her own temper suddenly flaring at his manner, Amethyst clamped her teeth together for fear of the sharp response that rushed to her lips. Why was he angry with her? She had done nothing that was not forced upon her. And as painful an experience as it had been for her, her song had been a true success. Merrell's obvious plan to make her look foolish had backfired. He had no reason to be embarrassed and there was certainly no reason for the black stares he had been sending in her direction all night.

Within a few moments the carriage had arrived at the front door. Ushering her firmly outside, Damien abruptly picked her up and tossed her unceremoniously inside. Climbing inside after her, he sat at her side, his face stiff with anger.

Unable to stand his silence a moment longer, Amethyst felt her own fury rise. "How dare you embarrass me this way, Damien Straith? What right have you to treat me like an errant schoolgirl? Whatever impropriety was practiced tonight was forced by your jealous mistress, not I!"

"It is *you* who are my mistress, Amethyst, and I would have you remember that!"

Her face flushing a bright red, Amethyst exclaimed heatedly, "Yes, I am your mistress . . . one amongst many, I'm sure. But there is one difference between our relationship and your others. I did not *choose* to be your mistress, and were things as I would have them be, I would be free of your influence, of your obeah . . ."

"And in the arms of that rake, Armand Beauchamps? Hah! You are a fool, Amethyst Greer! At least I've given my word to take care of you. Armand Beauchamps is a well known womanizer who maintains at least two known mistresses in this city alone! His interest is notoriously short-lived and his mistresses rarely fare well."

"I don't believe you!"

Grabbing her roughly by the shoulders, Damien spat from between clenched teeth, "Well, it's true! He would use you just the way he uses other women, and tonight you played right into his hands!"

"I did nothing of the sort! He was a pleasant companion for the evening. What would you have me do? You were otherwise entertained for the evening, in case you have forgotten! And you're wrong, Damien Straith!" Pulling desperately at the hands securely clamped on her shoulders, Amethyst found it impossible to break from his crushing grip. Finally abandoning the attempt, she gritted her teeth against the pain his hands were inflicting and continued venomously, "You are very wrong. Once I am finally free of you, I'll allow no one to gain such complete control over my actions again.

If someone is to be used in a relationship, it will be *I* who does the using! I have learned much from you, Damien Straith, and since I'm no longer worthy of a decent man, I intend to use the indecent men just as they would use me!"

An expression of fury sweeping over his face, fathomable even in the darkness of the carriage, Amethyst felt a moment of true fear that left her momentarily weak. She had pushed him too far. She could feel his rage building, sense the wrath about to explode inside him the moment before his hand snapped free of her shoulder to slap her pitilessly back and forth across the face, time and time again, until she was almost senseless. When he finally released her, she slumped back against the seat in semi-consciousness, unaware of the fear that suddenly showed in Damien's own eyes.

His mind shrieking condemnation of his actions, Damien leaned forward, his heart thundering in his chest as he took Amethyst into his arms.

"Amethyst . . . are you alright? Amethyst, answer me!"

Her eyes still closed, Amethyst answered him shakily, "Yes, I'm alright, Damien. You haven't killed me yet."

Her soft response efficiently draining his fury, Damien whispered, his lips pressed against her temple as he held her close against him, "It's not my desire to kill you, Amethyst. Quite the reverse is the truth. You must realize that . . ."

The carriage was slowing to a halt, and realizing they had reached his residence, Damien moved back to open the door. Struggling to pull herself erect despite her dizziness, Amethyst slid herself to the doorway, but before she could attempt to alight from the carriage, Damien had scooped her into his arms, and was carrying her up the front steps.

Startled to find the master with the young mistress

almost unconscious in his arms when she answered the door, Mrs. Dobbs stepped back in alarm. Answering her unspoken question as he rushed past her up the steps, Damien tossed over his shoulder, "Miss Amethyst is ill. Send Mary up to help her disrobe. She must go right to bed."

Not bothering to respond, Mrs. Dobbs raced for the kitchen and within moments Mary and she were at the bedroom door. Moving hurriedly toward her, Damien said softly, "Quickly, help Miss Amethyst into her night rail, and call me as soon as she is in bed."

Stopping only for one backward look as Mary hastened toward Amethyst's motionless figure, Damien disappeared through the doorway. Stripping off his coat, he threw it on the chair and began pacing the hallway in front of Amethyst's door. He was impatient to return to Amethyst's side, and snorted with disgust. If it were not for the ridiculous charade Amethyst still insisted they play, he would be inside, helping ready her for bed. But then, if it were not for that same ridiculous charade, Amethyst would not be lying on that bed, barely conscious from his unconscionable blows. Whatever had possessed him to strike her? To hurt Amethyst was certainly the last thing he wanted. Why did the damned little witch insist on taunting him, inflaming his jealousy? *There* was the crux of the problem! If he were to be completely honest, he would have to admit it was his insane jealousy that had pushed him to such an extreme. Damn! Damn! Why had he given his word to declare Amethyst his ward . . . why? He wanted nothing more than to have all of Philadelphia recognize her as his own, and instead was forced to watch helplessly as other men fawned and fussed about her while he pretended to be interested in women who could not hold a candle to his Amethyst. And tonight, Armand Beauchamps had been the last straw. The damned lecher had not left her alone for one moment once he had managed to secure a place at her side. Worst of all was Amethyst's obvious fascination by the fellow . . . forgetting his own existence while the French frog was beside her!

A sound at Amethyst's door interrupted his raging thoughts, snapping Damien's head around to Mary's sober face.

"Mr. Straith, Miss Amethyst is presentable now."

Rushing past the maid without a word, Damien strode to Amethyst's bedside, mumbling over his shoulder, "You and Mrs. Dobbs may retire for the night, Mary. You'll not be needed here any longer."

A small choking sound came from the corner of the room where Mrs. Dobbs stood, her sparse brows raised in shock. Managing to find her voice, she declared stiffly, "Certainly, Mr. Straith, you do not wish to have us leave you alone in Miss Greer's bedroom!" At Damien's quick, pointed look, she stammered to continue, "I mean . . . you did insist, sir, that I do all I could to maintain propriety and Miss Greer's good reputation. If that is still the case . . ."

"That *is* still the case, Mrs. Dobbs!" Hardly able to control his impatience with the ridiculous sham, Damien could not hide the sharp edge to his voice as he interrupted the woman's faltering words, "but I cared for Miss Greer when she was close to death in Jamaica, and am certainly capable of attending her through this little spell of weakness! I would appreciate it very much now if both you and Mary would follow my orders and go to bed!"

Drawing herself up stiffly, Mrs. Dobbs signaled the quaking Mary to withdraw, and had just reached the doorway when Damien's voice met her ear. "But if you feel it will be more propitious, you may leave the door open behind you."

Turning to shoot Damien a short approving smile,

Mrs. Dobbs walked slowly through the bedroom doorway, leaving it ajar.

Keeping his attention in the direction of their exit until he could hear two distinct sets of footsteps going down the staircase, Damien shook his head in disgust. Turning back to find Amethyst's gaze once again averted from his, he reached to the night table where Mary had poured a bowl of fresh water, and reaching in, squeezed out the cloth. Firmly lifting Amethyst's chin until her eyes met his, he commenced bathing her brow, a look of inordinate sadness covering his handsome face as he noted the marks of his blows on her cheeks. Pressing the cool cloth against the angry redness, he whispered softly, "Amethyst, this farce we're living is becoming far too much of a strain on both of us. Would it not be better if we were to declare our true situation? Surely . . ."

Amethyst's response was low and instantaneous. "Better for whom, Damien?"

Anger again beginning to kindle deep inside him, Damien took a few minutes to refresh the cloth before turning back to answer her question as he continued to bathe her flaming cheeks.

"Better for both of us, Amethyst. You must see that we can't go on this way . . ."

Suddenly pushing his hand roughly aside, Amethyst turned the full force of her fury against him as she hissed in a low, controlled tone, "Do you not now have exactly what you said you wanted that first morning on the *Sally*? Complete freedom to indulge your fancies with other women while still retaining my 'services' at night? All I have gained out of this farce is a reputation that will enable me to continue with my life unhindered once you have decided to cast me aside."

"*And* the opportunity to torment me with countless flirtations conducted before my very eyes!"

"Flirtations!" Amethyst's eyes snapped wide with

shock. "Flirtations! I have never . . ."

"Then what would you call your behavior with Armand Beauchamps, my innocent Amethyst? Certainly a man of his experience and reputation would not find himself so deeply intrigued by a casual, pointless conversation, no matter how affected he was by your beauty."

"Armand Beauchamps is not 'deeply intrigued' by me! How unfair you are, Damien Straith!"

His anger rapidly abating as Amethyst's eyes filled with tears, Damien waited with a dull ache in his chest as she swallowed with difficulty and continued, "I told you, Armand Beauchamps is a fine gentleman who treated me with courtesy and respect. I enjoyed his company, and was grateful for his presence while it was obvious you were otherwise involved for the evening."

There was a short hesitation before Damien responded, his voice low and husky, "Is that why you sang your song directly to him, Amethyst?" His clear, penetrating glance held hers soberly as he continued in a voice just above a whisper, "Twice you have sung that song in my presence . . . both times to other men . . ."

Her lips trembling, Amethyst could no longer control the tears that slipped from the corners of her brimming eyes to stain the pillow beside her head. Her response was faltering. "If my eyes were on Armand Beauchamps when I sang, it was not *he* I saw, Damien. I sang my song tonight to the same man I sang it to once before, although he is far away and could not hear me . . ."

A small muscle twitching in his cheek the only sign that he had perceived the import of her words, Damien looked wordlessly into her tear-filled gaze for long silent moments. Turning, he lowered the lamp beside the bed to a dull glow. His face shrouded in semidarkness, Damien turned back to gently brush the tears from her cheeks. Taking her hand in his, he whispered softly, "Close your eyes and rest, now, Amethyst. I'll sit beside you until you fall asleep." Leaning forward, he kissed her lips lightly, lingeringly, drawing away to whisper again, "Sleep well, my darling . . ."

Emily Dobbs walked slowly up the gleaming walnut staircase, her thin, colorless lips drawn tightly together as she approached the second floor. She had been deeply disturbed by Mr. Straith's conduct of the night before, and looked forward with an actual dread to the scene that would confront her eyes when she reached the young mistress's bedroom. Taking no notice of the first two doors she passed, she kept her eyes trained on the third doorway, as she drew closer, noting that it still stood ajar. She approached hesitantly, finally taking the last two steps that would find her directly in front of the room. Slowly exhaling a relieved breath, she saw Amethyst Greer still abed and sleeping, her young face soft and innocent in the early morning light. Seated on a chair beside the bed, his head resting on the coverlet, his arm extended toward her cheek, Damien Straith also lay in exhausted slumber. A small smile moving across her face, Emily Dobbs took a deep breath and prepared to go inside. Although she was entirely satisfied nothing had gone amiss last night, it would not do to have anyone see Mr. Straith coming out of the young mistress's bedroom at so early an hour. After all, Miss Greer did have a reputation to maintain!

"Mon apologie, Mademoiselle Greer, for insisting upon another fitting today," Madame duMaurier muttered as she fussed tediously at Amethyst's waistline, "but Monsieur Straith insisted that this gown be perfect . . . made to his exact specifications, and I have no desire to incur his anger." Raising her brow expressively, Madame duMaurier did not notice the startled expression on Amethyst's face as she stared wordlessly at her reflection in the full length mirror. Having received an urgent call for a fitting that morning, she had been stunned to find that among the many other additions to her wardrobe on which the painstaking couturiere was working, Damien had contracted for a specific gown without her knowledge, which he had instructed Madame prepare for the ball to be conducted at Oeller's the following week. An establishment of much renown, Oeller's was located just across from the new Congress Hall, next to Rickett's Circus. Adopted by Talleyrand and other French emigres, it was the establishment where the German waltz which had so fascinated Amethyst was first introduced to America. But Amethyst was looking forward to the occasion with both anticipation and trepidation. Damien and she had not been out socially since the incident at the Strathmore party, and despite the fact that Damien had been the epitome of consideration and had shown her no end of devotion both publicly and in the dark hours of night in the week since, Amethyst was uncertain what another exposure to society would bring.

And now this! Shaking her head, Amethyst stared wide-eyed at the gown Madame duMaurier fitted so precisely. The dress was outrageously beautiful! A sapphire silk, its depth of color deepened the glow of her eyes to a color matched only by the true gems themselves. Her glorious mane of black curls contrasted vividly with the magnificent shade, catching its brilliance to reflect a darker, softer black than a midnight sky. Her creamy shoulders, almost bared, curved gently atop a bodice that dipped daringly to expose a tempting curve of full white breasts. Long, tight sleeves emphasized the slender length of her arms, ending at the wrist with three buttons topped with brilliants that sparkled with her graceful movements. The waistline drew to a modified point at the center in keeping with the current style; the skirt, devoid of panniers and bustles commonly used, sweeping out simply and fully to float to feet covered with matching slippers. The surface of the gown glowed subtly with sparingly dispersed brilliants, while the main concentration of the sparkling gems outlined the daring plunge of her decolletage and the generous, appealing swells rising above it. It was a gown of inordinate beauty that stirred memories of a night long before when Damien had first seen her perform . . . the night Damien had first announced his claim on her, declaring with all the assurance of his compelling masculine mystique that she was his and his alone. And although her fight had been long and arduous, she still remained as strongly under his spell as she had fallen that night . . .

Her face suddenly draining of color, Amethyst swayed weakly, raising her hand to her temple as her dark fringe of lashes fluttered against pale cheeks. Was this Damien's reason for contracting for this dress? To remind her that despite all her struggles, she would remain his until he no longer desired her?

As anxiety mounted, Amethyst swayed more noticeably, causing Madame duMaurier to gasp nervously, "Mademoiselle, are you not well? Mademoiselle . . ."

The slender couturiere's arms were too frail to support Amethyst's weight as Amethyst grew suddenly weaker, and near panic, the woman called loudly for aid. Within moments, strong arms supported Amethyst for a few seconds prior to sweeping her up to carry her to the chaise in the corner of the room.

The room had gone suddenly dim, and blinking rapidly, Amethyst struggled to identify the face bending over her, but the deep, melodious voice that spoke worriedly in her ear needed no identification.

"Mon Dieu! Are you alright, Amethyst? Cherie . . . please speak to me . . . are you alright?" Rubbing her hands briskly, Armand Beauchamps frowned darkly into

the lovely white face beneath his, a flash of relief lightening his expression as Amethyst's glance steadied and the color slowly began to return to her cheek.

Attempting to stop her as Amethyst began to draw herself to a sitting position, Armand said with alarm, "No, ma cherie, you must rest a few moments."

Embarrassed at her extreme reaction to her own flight of fancy, Amethyst resisted his restraint to pull herself up to a sitting position. Her voice still a trifle shaken, she said quickly, "Nonsense, Armand. I'm fine. I've not been sleeping well lately and I'm afraid the sleepless nights are finally beginning to take their toll."

Realizing her discomfort, Armand followed her lead, responding lightly as he kept careful watch for any telltale signs of weakness.

"Ah. I, too, have had many wakeful nights, ma petite Amethyst, but mine have been due to a vision of a lovely young woman with violet eyes which would give me no peace."

Feeling stronger by the moment, Amethyst stared at him a second before laughing lightly, "Armand, you make me fear that the rumors I have heard about you are true. I had not realized you are such an incorrigible flirt!"

His own smile widening, Armand raised his hand dramatically to his chest, his voice low and wounded, "Mademoiselle, you cut me deeply."

Her glance becoming scrutinizing, Amethyst responded warily, "Oh, I think it would be fair to say you are not a man who wounds very easily, Armand, especially when it comes to affairs of the heart."

Despite the levity of her tone, Armand frowned at her response, finally yielding to Madame duMaurier who hovered anxiously behind him.

"Are you alright now, Mademoiselle?" Madame was obviously anxious, and fearful of upsetting the woman any further, Amethyst hastened to assure her.

"Yes, I'm fine, Madame. Just a little weakness. I came out of the house this morning without breakfast, I fear."

"A cup of tea would probably help the mademoiselle immeasurably, Madame."

"Oh, but of course . . ."

Moving quickly to the back of her shop, Madame duMaurier hastened to follow Armand Beauchamps's suggestion.

"Armand, you should not have put Madame to the bother! I'm quite recovered now. It's foolish to make more of a simple bout of weakness than is necessary."

"But you do realize, ma petite, that Madame's little project now enables me a few moments to speak with you alone, which is my sole purpose in being here today."

An expression of disbelief crossing her face, Amethyst slowly rose to her feet, "You don't intend me to believe you came here today solely to see me?"

"But, of course, ma chérie. Madame and I are countrymen. I made it known to her that I would be very interested in knowing the next time you were to come in for a fitting, and she was very accommodating to my request." When Amethyst's skeptical expression remained, Armand continued with an expressive lifting of dark brows, "What other reason could I have for being in a shop of this sort?"

"From the reports I've heard, Armand, you're probably a very good customer of Madame's and quite familiar with her establishment. After all," she said slowly, widening her lavender eyes expressively, "a man who maintains *two* mistresses in this city alone . . ."

Momentarily startled at Amethyst's disclosure of her knowledge of that particular facet of his private life, Armand colored unexpectedly, and noting her amusement as a fleeting dimple crossed the velvet cheek that was now restored to its former color, he felt a flash of delight at the young woman's spontaneous wit and charm. For a woman of her youth to bring so successfully a blush to the cheek of a man of his worldliness was not a simple task, and now having brought him to this point, to turn the situation around by the simple use of her own engaging personality so that he might even enjoy his own embarrassment was indeed a wondrous feat! The girl was named well! She was a true jewel!

His handsome face breaking into a wide smile that set his dark eyes dancing, Armand laughed heartily at his own expense, taking her slender hand into his to raise it to his lips.

"Amethyst, *ma cherie, vous êtes magnifique!*"

"Oh, Armand, I do believe you're flattering me again," Amethyst responded lightly, thoroughly enjoying their light repartee.

Shaking his head in utter delight, Armand retained his grasp on her small hand, keeping her far closer to him than she would normally have dared as he smiled down into her lovely face. "Did no one ever tell you, ma cherie, that it is not polite to face a man with his indiscretions when he is trying so decidedly hard to impress you with his earnestness?"

"But I knew I had no cause for worry with you, Armand. From all reports, you are so wildly successful in your romantic endeavors, I knew you would consider this campaign a very small loss. There are, after all, countless beautiful women in Philadelphia with whom you may console yourself."

"And none of them as beautiful as you, Amethyst."

His dark eyes suddenly serious, Armand raised his free hand to her smooth cheek to continue softly, "And none of them have managed to touch the spot inside me that you warm so easily, ma petite."

A small frown covering her brow at his words, Amethyst withdrew her hand from his, grateful to

Madame's interruption as she bustled back into the room, carrying a large tray on which sat a delicate teapot and three cups.

"Some nice hot tea will refresh us all, will it not, Monsieur et Mademoiselle?"

"*Oui*, Madame." Flushing suddenly at her own French response, Amethyst laughed. "It seems this delightful company is bringing out a spark of French in a thoroughly Yankee girl!"

"Which could not please me more, ma cherie," Armand responded, his dark eyes showing a bit more warmth than Amethyst would have preferred, but certain that Armand was a thorough rake who was just passing a pleasant hour, Amethyst dismissed her worries as she gratefully accepted the cup Madame held out to her.

The tea having restored her flagging energy and the pleasant company having restored her spirits, Amethyst spent the time until Armand's departure fascinated by his engaging personality as Madame duMaurier fussed and hemmed diligently. Emerging from the boutique some time later, Amethyst adjusted the hood of her cape against the chilling cold. Lined in luxurious sable, the forest green velvet was well insulated against the winter wind that lifted its ample folds to set them dancing against the frozen street. Amethyst had just raised her hand to secure a long black curl that had whipped free of its confines when a broad figure stepped forward to tuck the windswept curl securely inside.

Surprised to find Armand waiting for her, Amethyst flashed him a startled smile. "I thought you had gone, Armand. But I'm glad you haven't because I'm now afforded the opportunity to say how much I've enjoyed our chance encounter. You are a very amusing man, Armand."

Obviously pleased, Armand's eyes moved slowly over her lovely face, allowing himself the luxury of drinking in the beauty of Amethyst's flawless ivory complexion, colored lightly on the graceful contours of her cheek with a natural pink flush. The brilliant lavender of her eyes were raised to his, the thick black lashes almost touching her slender, slanted brows as she stared expectantly into his face. Her slender lips parted into a small half smile awaiting his response, allowed a glimpse of perfect white teeth as a small dimple winked appealingly in her cheek. Lost in her beauty for a few long seconds, Armand felt the rise of a new emotion as his jaded heart began a rapid thudding against his ribs. Never had he met a female so fresh and sincere, whose glance, so free of guile, had the power to lift his heart to a plane just short of giddiness with her innocent allure. Experiencing a longing to touch the ivory cheek, to feel the delicate smoothness of her skin beneath his lips, Armand swallowed tightly, a small smile moving across his face. Amused at his own susceptibility to her unaffected manner and spontaneous charm, Armand replied softly, "And I fear I must not tell you my thoughts with regard to you, ma petite chou, or I will again be accused of libidinous desires. It will suffice to say that I should like your permission to call on you this week so I may . . ."

Her expression suddenly serious, Amethyst interrupted his declaration, putting her hand lightly on his arm as she said ardently, "No, you must not, Armand. Please . . . it would be very difficult for me . . ."

His expression slightly bewildered, Armand frowned, covering her hand with his. "Pourquoi . . . why, Amethyst? Surely you . . ."

Lowering her eyes from his searching gaze, Amethyst replied softly, "Damien . . . he doesn't approve of you, Armand. He's suspicious of your intentions." Finally raising her eyes to his, she said with an embarrassed laugh, "I think he thinks you mean to seduce me."

To Amethyst's surprise, Armand's expression grew

suddenly tight as he stiffened noticeably. His voice when he finally spoke was stiff and formal. "Then I suppose I shall have to speak to Mr. Straith myself and explain the error in his thinking."

A sudden rush of panic overwhelming her, Amethyst could feel the onset of another bout of weakness, as she exclaimed softly, "Oh, please don't, Armand. Damien is too impulsive. There will be angry words exchanged, and I wouldn't wish to see . . ."

Raising her hand to her head, Amethyst continued determinedly despite the lightheadedness assailing her, "I wouldn't want to be the cause of any problems . . ." Her eyes moving to his pleadingly, she entreated in a soft voice, "Please . . . please promise me you won't speak to Damien, Armand. Please, I ask you . . ."

Noting Amethyst's sudden pallor, Armand took her arm to steady her as he said softly, "Do not upset yourself, Amethyst. I will not speak to Mr. Straith if that is your wish . . . not yet." And then with a small smile, he added softly, "You must merely find the necessity for many more fittings, so that I will not expire from boredom without your lovely face to spark my day. *Êtes-vous d'accord?* Do you agree, my lovely?"

Nodding her head quickly to pacify his injured pride, Amethyst said softly, "I must be going now, Armand. You . . . you will remember your promise . . . you won't . . ."

"You have my word. Do not fret, ma cherie. It is not my desire to grieve you in any way."

Kissing her hand lightly, Armand handed her up into the carriage that waited at the curb. His eyes moving assessingly over her face, he noted that her color was again returning, and breathing a relieved sigh, he smiled lightly, the nervous smile Amethyst sent him in return tearing at his heartstrings. Smothering the overwhelming desire to jump into the carriage beside her, take her comfortingly into his arms, and smoothe the stress from her beautiful face, he lifted his hand, calling lightly as the carriage pulled away from the curb, "Au revoir, Amethyst. Au revoir, ma petite amour . . ."

Watching steadily until the carriage moved out of sight, Armand felt a cold fury rise inside him. The broad expanse of his chest beginning to heave rapidly with anger, his expression darkened. It was obvious Amethyst was frightened to despair of her guardian, Damien Straith. What had the wretch done to inspire such fear that the very thought of opposing him made her weak? His large hands clenching into tight fists, Armand took a deep breath in an effort to control his escalating anger. He had given Amethyst his promise, or he would go now and demand an explanation from the surly beast. But it would not do to lose Amethyst's confidence. To do so would be to lose her completely, and he was suddenly intensely aware of the horror of that thought. His darkly handsome face abruptly creasing in a small, wry smile, Armand raised his hand to his temple in a weary gesture. "Oh, Armand," he thought silently, "you are a fool. The girl is a child . . . half your age. Her world and yours are far apart, and not very likely to come together without some violent repercussions. You have led a gay life and known many women. Why did you have to pick this time . . . choose this one, this beautiful, frightened child . . . to love?"

Striding determindedly up the front steps to his Chestnut Street home, Damien Straith let himself in the front door, turning as he did to close it carefully behind him. Keeping his anger under tight rein, he carefully removed his hat and overcoat, and placed it on the chair by the door. But his hands were still trembling with the fury raging inside him and unwilling to face Amethyst until he was in complete control, he took a deep breath and again went over in his mind the conversation that had produced his agitated state.

Having just had a very favorable session with a business associate over lunch at City Tavern, Damien emerged onto Second Street extremely pleased with himself. When the *Sally* sailed again in spring, her hold would be filled with merchandise purchased at extremely favorable prices, and should he decide to go into port illegally, his profit would be just that much higher. But at the present either option was open to him, a fact that suited him perfectly. The bright afternoon sun struck his eyes, causing Damien to squint against its glare, but its golden glow was deceiving. The air was cold and a brisk wind blew, tugging at the fashionable broad-brimmed beaver resting handsomely atop his heavily sun-streaked hair. Taking a moment to adjust his hat more securely, Damien fastened the buttons on his coat against the chill. A dark blue wool, slightly fitted at the waist, the rivers in light blue buttoned back in excellent contrast to the main color, the well cut garment fell splendidly from his shoulder to black boots that rose to his knee. Two small capes encircled the neck, emphasizing his breadth of shoulder, his impressive stature drawing a few interested glances from curious female passersby as he began a brisk stride toward Chestnut Street.

It was a beautiful day, and he was anxious to return home to relate to Amethyst his successful transactions of the day. Strange, how he wished to share even this facet of his life with the disturbing little chit. But if he were to be fair, he would have to admit that the disturbance she created within him was not due to a fault in Amethyst's personality but to his own susceptibility to her charms. But her mind was quick and keen, anxious to learn any and all he wished to teach her. Her interest was unflagging, contrary to the empty-headed females to whom he had grown accustomed in polite society.

Shrugging his broad shoulders slightly as he considered the thought, he wondered absentmindedly if it were due to the life she had led, caring for her mother since before adolescence, forced to live by her wits when the sickly woman was incapacitated. But no, that explanation just would not do. A small smile twitching the corners of his mouth, he recalled the spirit in the little nine-year-old he had first seen, the intelligence so obvious in those peculiar lavender eyes when she had first fixed her angry glance on him, and the speed with which she then, at that early age, had set him back in his traces. No, Amethyst had not turned out the disarmingly lovely, spirited charmer she was today because of circumstance. No, Amethyst was merely . . . Amethyst.

The rattle of a carriage drawing alongside him at the curb breaking into his thoughts, Damien slowed his step, turning to see a vehicle that was all too familiar.

"Damien . . . Damien, darling." Motioning him toward the carriage, Merrell Bristol smiled brightly in greeting. When he hesitated in responding to her beckoning, Merrell coaxed appealingly with a pouting expression, "Surely you aren't still angry with me over that little incident two weeks ago, Damien. It isn't like you to hold a grudge."

Considering her warily, Damien approached the carriage. His response was hesitant. "Were your devious plans worked against me, Merrell, I should not have held my anger. And, for all you sought to embarrass Amethyst, your plans did backfire, didn't they? You merely succeeded that night in establishing the fact that Amethyst possesses the gift of a beautiful singing voice. Your intention, however, can't be ignored. You sought to make Amethyst a laughingstock and I can't countenance such actions."

Merrell's expression hardening, she directed a venomous glance into Damien's icy expression. "You are so considerate of your young 'ward,' Damien, and so loyal to her honor and good name. It's unfortunate that she doesn't bear the same devotion to you and your wishes, isn't it?"

His mouth tightening in anger, Damien snapped sharply, "Is this another attempt to blacken Amethyst's character, Merrell? If so, I warn you, you're wasting your time. Amethyst . . ."

"Amethyst, your sweet, innocent 'ward' is spending her spare time in clandestine meetings with one of the most notorious womanizers in Philadelphia! A devastatingly handsome and appealing man, I may add, but doubtless a rake with the experience to make full use of her rather obvious attributes."

"Damn you, Merrell," Damien swore in a low voice meant for her ears alone, "you bitch, if you start unfounded rumors about Amethyst Greer, I'll see that you suffer the consequences if I have to choke . . ."

"Save your threats, Damien." Merrell's expression held the light of victory as she rounded to deal Damien the final blow, "She has been seen by a number of our acquaintances both inside and on the street in front of Madame duMaurier's shop with Armand Beauchamps. Have you noticed that your precious ward has been spending an inordinate amount of time with fittings in the last month? Armand Beauchamps has taken to spending the duration of her fittings with her in intimate conversation. A convenient rendezvous, is it not? And so easily overlooked by a concerned . . . 'guardian.' And from what I've been told, their relationship has passed polite conversation to the point of open displays of affection."

"And by open displays of affection, you mean . . ."

"If I must be more explicit, Damien, to satisfy your burning curiosity, I will relate exactly what I've been told." Her eyes gleaming with pleasure at Damien's strained expression and rising color, she continued in an insidiously sweet voice, "They have been seen inside Madame duMaurier's boutique in extremely close proximity, heads together in whispered conversations. Armand was seen fondly caressing your ward's cheek on the street, holding her possessively by the arm, kissing her hand far more ardently than would be considered a polite gesture. As I recall, Damien, his favorite pet name for her is 'ma petite amour' . . ."

Her voice trailing off suggestively, Merrell's eyes moved slowly over Damien. Satisfied at last by the rigidity of his frame and his stiffness of expression that she had done her work well, her face relaxed into a small victorious smile. "Of course, darling, you don't have to believe me . . . but you must realize I would never have come to you if there was even the slightest possibility that what I've told you is untrue . . ."

"Of course, Merrell." His clear eyes frigid, Damien continued softly, "And I really must thank you. If I had any doubt before, you have today confirmed my assessment of you. You truly are the spiteful, jealous bitch you recently revealed yourself to be. I'm thankful to be rid of you!"

Turning on his heel, Damien ignored the quick intake of breath his words had produced and the shrill command issued to her driver seconds before Merrell Bristol's carriage pulled away from the curb.

Still seething in anger, Damien ascended the staircase. The house was oddly silent and not bothering to announce his presence, Damien turned down the hallway toward Amethyst's room. Stopping still in his tracks, Damien saw Mary outside Amethyst's door. The young woman was unaware of his presence as she stood, her stocky body pressed as close as she dared while she listened at the door. So intent was she that she maintained that posture for long moments before realizing there was another presence in the hallway. Suddenly raising her gaze, she jumped with alarm, her face flushing guiltily as Damien motioned her toward him. Coming to stand before Damien's condemning glance, Mary's eyes filled with tears, her discomfort acute.

Unable to withhold the anger from his voice, Damien demanded softly, "What were you doing outside Miss Amethyst's door, Mary?"

"Nothing . . . nothing, Mr. Straith," Mary stammered thickly. "I wasn't doing anything."

"You were eavesdropping, weren't you?" The anger in his voice escalating sharply, he added, "Are you the one I should thank for the rumors being circulated about Miss Amethyst? Have you been . . ."

Interrupting hastily, the tears brimming in her small brown eyes falling to streak her full cheeks, "Oh, no, Mr. Straith. I wouldn't do anything to hurt Miss Amethyst. She's been so wonderful kind to me . . . telling Mrs. Dobbs to allow me to take home sweets each night to my sisters and brothers. They're only babies, you know, and terrible fond of sweets . . . No, Mr. Straith, I swear, I wouldn't hurt Miss Amethyst . . ."

"Then what were you doing listening at her door, Mary, for there is no doubt in my mind that is exactly what you were doing."

A trapped expression covering her face, Mary sought to escape his assessing glance, her eyes darting away to fix on the toes of her shoes as she maintained an uneasy silence.

His voice softening slightly, Damien pressed for an answer. "You must answer me, Mary, or I'll assume you meant to do Miss Amethyst harm and you'll be dismissed."

Her eyes snapping up to his in horror, Mary gasped, "I was only worried about Miss Amethyst, that's all. She asked me not to tell anybody, not even Mrs. Dobbs, but she's been awful sick of late, and she's getting worse..."

"Sick?" A stab of fear piercing his stomach, Damien urged softly, "What do you mean 'sick,' Mary?"

Her eyes again avoiding his, Mary said softly, "She's been throwing up, Mr. Straith. Every morning she retches when she awakes until she's so weak she has to return to bed before dressing. She fainted twice, Mr. Straith, once in her room while she was trying to dress and once in this hallway, but she made me promise not to tell anyone because she said she didn't want you to worry. She says she's alright, but she's not and..."

His expression unreadable, Damien prompted stiffly, "And you were listening outside her door just now because..."

"She's sick again... I heard her choking and gasping..."

Not waiting for Mary to finish speaking, Damien interrupted softly, "You may go downstairs now, Mary. I'm sure you had Miss Amethyst's best interests at heart, and you'll not be dismissed this time, but should I ever find you listening at her door again..."

"You won't, sir." Mary's voice was relieved, her expression momentarily brightening.

"And you'll continue to keep Miss Amethyst's confidence as she requested."

"Of course, sir!"

His face expressionless, his eyes already on Amethyst's door, Damien stated dismissingly, "You may go downstairs, now."

Only vaguely hearing the soft padding of Mary's feet down the staircase behind him, Damien advanced toward Amethyst's door.

Gasping weakly, Amethyst wove a faltering path toward the washstand, stopping to grip the side tightly as she reached it in an effort to stabilize herself. Pouring some water into the washbowl with a shaking hand, she moistened the washcloth and lightly sponged her face. The coolness was refreshing, reviving her slightly, and raising her head, she took several deep breaths to steady herself. Try as she might to ignore the fear nudging relentlessly at the back of her mind, she was beginning to panic as her condition continued to worsen. She had been vomiting daily now for two weeks, the main bouts of nausea confined to awakening, but this past week found her also assailed with the same malady whenever meals were delayed beyond the usual times. And now it seemed certain foods, or even just the aroma of them, caused her to retch. She had not had her monthly flow since she left Kingston, and had at first assumed the interruption was due to her illness, but each day that passed only seemed to add more evidence to confirm her fears. She could not be pregnant! No! She did not wish to bear Damien's child! When she bore a child it would be conceived in love, not Damien Straith's lust or the strange black magic he practiced that held her powerless against him. A child would also work untold complications on her plans. Damien had only this week told her that the *Sally* would be ready to sail in March. He had not indicated what would be expected of her after he sailed, but she had been looking forward with great anticipation to the time when she would be free of his domination. She would then make good use of the few friendships she had made during this time. Above all, she wished to return to Jamaica. She sorely missed Tillie and although she dared not think of William, she longed to know how he fared. He had been so desperately ill when she had last seen him and she had never had an opportunity to explain. Once in Jamaica she would return to the theater and become self-supporting, and when the troupe decided to return to America, she would reenter the country an independent woman with a future.

But if she was pregnant, she would be entirely at Damien's mercy. Her relationship with Damien would no longer be a secret and she would be ostracized from society. And once the child was born, the complication of its presence would work untold hardships on her attempt to regain her old lifestyle.

And Armand . . . what would he think of her? Having received numerous calls for fittings in the last month, she had gone to Madame duMaurier's boutique each time to find Armand either waiting or arriving within a few minutes of her appearance. Despite his reputation, he had treated her with faultless respect and courtesy and although she chose to ignore it, she had sensed the growing warmth of his regard. Earnestly doing her best to discourage his visits to the boutique while she was present, she nonetheless enjoyed their brief encounters more than she dared acknowledge.

But just this morning she had returned from a fitting, stimulated as usual by Armand's witty conversation and ardent attentions, only to find when she arrived at the door of the Chestnut Street address the aroma of baked apples was too much for her delicate stomach to withstand. Moving with haste to her room, she had undressed and lay weakly on her bed, valiantly fighting nausea until it finally overwhelmed her. Suddenly straightening, she pushed aside her wrapper to consider her waistline in the washstand mirror. Madame duMaurier had been mumbling complaints about constant adjustments in that area, and she searched the mirror frantically for any telltale signs of widening. Abruptly gripped with another bout of weakness, Amethyst clutched the washstand tightly and dipping the washcloth into the bowl, she was running the cloth across her forehead when the bedroom door snapped open unexpectedly.

Turning her head weakly toward the door, Amethyst began quietly, "Mary, I told you I wanted to be alone . . .", her words dwindling off as she met Damien's inscrutable expression.

"Damien . . . what are you doing here this time of day? You must leave my room. Mrs. Dobbs will see you here. I'm not dressed and . . ."

"You're not well, Amethyst?" Damien's voice was cold as he deliberately advanced a few steps further into the room and closed the door behind him.

"No, I'm fine, Damien. Just a little upset, that's all. Madame duMaurier convinced me to sample some sort of pastry this morning, and I'm afraid it was too rich for my stomach." Her eyes moving slowly over Damien, she awaited his response. Something was wrong. She could sense his tension, could see it in the tightness of his lips, the cold manner in which he assessed her expression.

Slowly unbuttoning his coat, Damien took it off to throw it casually on the nearest chair, advancing as he spoke. "That is unfortunate, isn't it. But I'm sure Armand Beauchamps found the pastries delightful, accustomed as he is to the excesses of French food."

Her violet eyes springing wide with surprise, Amethyst managed to stammer ineffectually, "Yes . . . yes, Armand was in the shop this morning also. I suppose he was buying something for a ladyfriend . . ."

"And, of course, you were surprised to find him there, weren't you, Amethyst?" Damien was advancing continually closer, his chest heaving with the anger now openly apparent on his face. His eyes like gray ice as they stared piercingly into hers, chilled her, stimulating a return of the weakness she fought so desperately.

"Yes . . . of course . . ."

"You're lying, Amethyst!" Taking the last step that brought him directly in front of her, Damien gripped her shoulders roughly, his eyes no longer cold but blazing with fury. "You have been meeting Beauchamps at Madame duMaurier's shop for over a month! Have you enjoyed deceiving me, Amethyst? It is my sincere wish that Mr. Beauchamps has also enjoyed your little escapade, and will find it worth his life!"

"His life . . . !"

"You don't think I'll allow that Frenchman's little sordid plans to go unacknowledged now that I'm aware of them. He has attempted to dishonor your name, my very virtuous 'ward,' and I intend to demand satisfaction!"

"Damien, you're not serious! Just a few harmless meetings . . . that's all they were . . . certainly not worth taking a life!"

His hands biting viciously into her shoulders, Damien searched Amethyst's face for a sign of deceit. Her lavender eyes wide, she stared openly up into his face. She was extremely pale, with dark smudges under her eyes, her lips trembling lightly as she spoke. She was obviously frightened and upset, but there was no sign of deceit in her glance. His momentary weakening suddenly dissipating, he thought viciously, but then she was an actress, was she not . . . experienced in pretense . . . she had been deceiving him for over a month while she sneaked off to meet that damned Frenchman! Whatever made him think she would reveal herself now?

"Just a few harmless meetings, is that all they were, Amethyst? But he stayed for the duration of your fittings, did he not? Did Madame manage to leave you conveniently alone so you might have some privacy? Did you allow Beauchamps to kiss you, Amethyst, to hold you in his arms? Did . . ."

"Damien! Please stop this inquisition!" Amethyst's lids were beginning to flutter weakly. "Nothing improper passed between us, I swear. Armand was a gentleman at all times. He wanted to come to the house to call on me, but I told him you would object."

"Yes, I would have objected, and I *do* object! But that didn't stop you, did it, Amethyst? You managed to conduct your illicit rendezvous right under my nose!"

There was no mercy in his glance as Amethyst swayed weakly under his hands. His broad chest was heaving heavily now, his handsome face contorted with rage as he demanded, "And what other deceits have you practiced upon me, Amethyst? What else are you hiding? Tell me now . . ."

Swallowing tightly, Amethyst raised a hand limply to her brow. Her dizziness was increasing, Damien's threatening visage beginning to blur as she stammered softly, "There was no deceit . . . nothing . . . I'm hiding nothing . . ."

"Damn you!" Damien swore heatedly under his breath. "Damn you, you are lying to me again! Can you never tell me the truth? Must I shake it from you?" Giving her a vicious shake, he growled, "You've been having bouts of sickness for two weeks now, haven't you? You've been vomiting, and have fainted twice."

"How . . . how did you know?"

"Come, Amethyst," Damien offered insidiously, "you know I have powers of obeah. Did you think you could go on much longer without being found out?" Despising himself for using Amethyst's fear of his nonexistent magical powers against her, he continued, "You are pregnant with my child, aren't you?"

"No! No, I'm not, I'm not!" Amethyst protested wildly, struggling to free herself from his grip.

Realizing she was close to hysteria, Damien's voice was sharp, her struggles having no effect whatsoever on his hold. "Control yourself, Amethyst! Now answer my question! How long has it been since your last monthly flow?"

There was no response as Amethyst became suddenly still, her glance moving to a spot in the far corner of the room in an effort to avoid his eyes. His voice low, Damien demanded again, "How long has it been? Answer me, Amethyst!"

Her face still averted from his, Amethyst's voice was a small whisper in the quiet of the room. "I've not had my monthly flow since I was ill in Kingston."

Her glance refusing to meet his, Amethyst was not aware of the relief that flashed across Damien's face as he closed his eyes, a brief smile curving his lips. Three months! It had been three months since her last menses. There was no doubt!

Abruptly aware that Amethyst was beginning to sag under his hands, Damien was suddenly conscious of her extreme lack of color. Scooping her up into his arms, he carried her to her bed. Laying her down gently, he returned quickly to the washstand to take the bowl and cloth to bedside, and began bathing her brow, mumbling softly as he did, "You'll feel better in a few moments, Amethyst. That's right, just breathe deeply."

Amethyst's eyes were closed, and as Damien knelt beside her, a small tear slipped out of the corner of her eye to the pillow beside her head. Unable to suppress the tenderness welling inside him, Damien brushed the damp path from her cheek, and bent to press a light kiss against her lips, his former anger completely dissipated.

Amethyst was pregnant . . . his seed was growing within her. This small, beautiful body lying before him would soon be heavy with his child! He need worry no longer. Amethyst could not hope to escape him, and soon all Philadelphia society would be aware of their true situation! Without breaking his word, he would finally be able to establish that Amethyst belonged to him and him alone!

Slipping his arms under and around Amethyst, Damien pulled her into his arms. His face pressed tightly into the raven curls, he breathed deeply, her familiar scent shaking his body with little tremors of joy. He had sealed his possession of her. She could not go to anyone else now.

Finally loosening his hold so he might look into her face, Damien whispered softly, "Tomorrow I'll take you to see Dr. Morgan. We must make certain that everything is progressing normally with your pregnancy."

Shaking her head lightly Amethyst mumbled in a low tone, "No, Damien, I can't go. I will be mortified!" Her voice a low plea, she said softly, "Can't you just send me away, Damien, somewhere I'm not known? Would that not be better for both of us? And you won't feel pressed to acknowledge the child as your own."

His expression stiffening, Damien responded softly, "Not acknowledge the child? Why should I wish to deny paternity, Amethyst?"

Her eyes fixing somberly on his, Amethyst's voice was just above a whisper. "You have acknowledged no child before this one, Damien, and I can only surmise this child would be no different."

"And why do you assume I have fathered other children before this, Amethyst?"

"Well, a man of your experience, Damien . . . I mean, you have known many women, and the ease with which you. . . ." Amethyst's voice dwindled off significantly, prompting Damien's low response.

"I have fathered no child before this, Amethyst. Of that I'm certain. I've taken particular care in the past to avoid such a possibility."

Uncertain what he meant by his response, Amethyst stammered lightly, "If you were cautious in the past . . . then how . . . why were you not cautious this time?"

His eyes once again becoming inscrutable, he assessed

her anxious face. "Because I did not choose to be cautious."

"Did not choose... Then you did this deliberately... deliberately chose to..." Her voice trailing away in astonishment, Amethyst's wide eyes remained fastened on his face. "But why, Damien? Why?"

Yes, indeed, why? It was a question he had asked himself many times in the past three months, knowing full well his irresponsible behavior could result in the present situation. But he had continued to love Amethyst naturally, avoiding any precaution that could interfere with the glory of their lovemaking. And his reaction, his joy at the confirmation of her pregnancy was startling, even to himself! He, who had always avoided ties of any sort, had secured a bond of the very firmest kind between himself and the beautiful woman before him. Suddenly clear, the answer brought a lump to his throat as he stared wordlessly into Amethyst's beautiful face. He *wanted* to be tied to Amethyst. He *wanted* Amethyst to bear his children, to be a permanent part of his life. Lord! He loved this beautiful, infuriating child! His precious freedom so carefully guarded in the past was no longer so precious to him. Far more precious was the thought of the child she now carried, the link that would draw and hold Amethyst with him. But her eyes were accusing. It was obvious she did not share his joy. Quite the contrary. The seed growing inside her was an intrusion in the life she had perhaps been planning with Armand Beauchamps... or perhaps still dreamed of with William Sheridan. Feeling the resurgence of anger, Damien firmly dismissed his negative thoughts. Whatever the case, she would have to forget her dreams and be satisfied with reality.

His answer to her question was a soft evasion as he separated her wrapper to reveal her chemise. "I did not need a reason." Lowering his head, he pressed a gentle kiss against her slightly rounded stomach, turning back again to bewilder her with the soft glow in his silver eyes.

Amethyst was at a loss! Startled by his abrupt change of mood at the declaration of her pregnancy and his actions since, she could do no more than blink her amazement. Finally able to speak, she stammered, "But if you'll not send me away, what will I say . . . what excuse will I give when my condition becomes obvious . . . ?"

"The answer to that is very simple, my darling. We'll be married as soon as possible and no one will dare comment, no matter the premature nature of the child's birth."

There was a moment's silence as Amethyst digested his words. Her eyes suddenly growing wide with horror, she attempted to draw herself away from his embrace. "Marry? You and I? Never . . . no, never!" Her face rapidly paling, she finally succumbed to the weakness pervading her, and angry with her own inability to fight him, she turned to direct a whispered declaration into his eyes. "I'm at your mercy, now, Damien. I have neither the strength nor the means to escape this situation, but I tell you this. Say what you will . . . declare me your mistress, but I will not marry you, now or ever! I will not tie myself for life to a man who uses me at a whim and employs the threat of black magic to keep me with him! I would be free to leave when I am no longer desired. I will not be forced to stay, a martyred wife, who must endure her husband's indiscretions. Rather a brief embarrassment that will last only until you tire of me, than a lifelong humiliation as your wife!"

Damien's response was soft. "And are you so sure that you see a true picture of our life together, Amethyst?"

Her answer was swift, without hesitation. "Yes, I am sure, Damien. You do not love me and even if you did, *I do not love you!*"

His own face paling at Amethyst's adamant declaration, Damien refused to relinquish his hold. His hand lifting to slowly stroke her white cheek, he said softly, "And are you also so certain there is no love between us, Amethyst?"

Her voice bitter, Amethyst responded softly, "This child was conceived as the result of a physical attraction and a mutually physical act, but no such noble emotion as love ever played a part in our relationship, Damien."

His expression unreadable, Damien's caress moved to her hair, his fingers tangling and untangling in the glorious mass as his eyes slowly perused Amethyst's exquisite features. His glance finally coming to rest on her pink, inviting lips, he whispered, "As you wish, Amethyst. If you would bear my child without benefit of marriage it shall be as you say, for now since circumstance has put an end to this farce, I intend to punish myself no longer by this unnatural arrangement we have been living." Raising his eyes slowly, he continued, "I will no longer prowl this house in the dark hours of night to attain access to your bed. Your things will be immediately moved into the master suite which we will share. And it will give me endless pleasure to scatter once and for all that pack of drooling puppies that overwhelms you at each social occasion, with the declaration that you belong to me."

Her voice hesitant, Amethyst began slowly, "And Armand . . . you will not . . . certainly you see that nothing is to be gained by challenging him."

Allowing her to suffer his silence for a few long moments, Damien finally replied, "Yes, I suppose you are right, Amethyst. I shall enjoy his discomfort immensely when he realizes the fool he has played this past month when all the time I already possessed that which he worked so desperately to attain."

Flushing brightly, Amethyst withheld her biting

response. If she were to avoid a violent scene between Damien and Armand, she must allow Damien his moment of gloating triumph, no matter how much it rankled.

Momentarily startled from her thoughts by the sound of a knock on her bedroom door, Amethyst was too late to forestall Damien's bid to enter.

Flushing brightly as the door opened to reveal a scarlet-faced Mrs. Dobbs with Mary by her side, Amethyst quickly pulled her wrapper closed, watching as Damien slowly rose to his feet. Drawing himself to his full height, he directed a level glance into Mrs. Dobbs's outraged expression.

"I apologize for the deceit that has been practiced in this house, Mrs. Dobbs. It was necessary for a time, but I will have you know the truth now. Amethyst is my mistress, and has held that intimate position for many months. She will bear my child within six months' time. If you find this situation personally offensive, I will understand your wish to leave my employ. If not, you are welcome to stay." Giving the stiff-faced woman a few moments to digest his remarks, Damien continued quietly, "May I have your response, Mrs. Dobbs?"

Her expression strained, Mrs. Dobbs blinked rapidly as she opened her mouth to speak. Swallowing visibly, she finally regained her composure enough to respond hoarsely, "I will stay."

"Thank you, Mrs. Dobbs. You may both leave the room now."

Mrs. Dobbs's stern personage had no sooner cleared the doorway when Damien turned back to Amethyst, a surprising smile creasing his broadly handsome features.

"Well, that was the first, and by far not the most pleasurable, Amethyst!" Advancing slowly toward her, Damien began unbuttoning his shirtfront, the familiar glow in his eyes bringing a blush to Amethyst's cheek.

"But the pleasures afforded our new circumstances will far outweigh the discomfort of declaration, darling. I promise you that."

Drifting gently from an unremembered dream, Amethyst slowly opened her eyes to the light of morning streaming through the bedroom window. Warm, strong arms wrapped around her seemed to sense her awakening, pulling her closer, as if to coax her back into the quiet world from which she had just awakened. Lifting her eyes, Amethyst saw that Damien still slept, the broad planes of his face relaxed. A lock of heavy tawny hair lay on his forehead, adding to his sleeping countenance an air of youth and vulnerability which was so contrary to the aura of assured self-possession he exuded when awake. Assessing him further, Amethyst realized that even in sleep, Damien's jaw retained the stubborn, forceful look that stirred her anger, but his full, sensuous lips evoked quite a different emotion, as a memory of the wondrous delights they were capable of stirring within her returned unbidden to mind.

Beginning to stir restlessly, Damien's hand moved caressingly into her hair as he pulled her against his chest. Her cheek resting comfortably against the fine golden-brown mat of hair on the broad expanse, Amethyst felt a short moment of warm tranquillity. Damien had been a different man in the past week. Beginning and ending each day lying beside him in his arms, she had begun to see a new side of Damien Straith. Loving and tender, he withheld no sign of affection, touching and caressing her at every given opportunity, startling those unaccustomed to his open displays into open-mouthed amazement. Escorting her to Dr. Morgan's office earlier in the week, he had waited in the anteroom for the doctor's summons at the conclusion of her examination, his anxiety apparent when he met the older man's stern countenance.

His voice heavy with implied censure, the short, balding Dr. Morgan had spoken quietly. "I assume I am about to confirm a condition of which you are already aware. Amethyst is a very healthy young woman who is approximately three months pregnant. Since she has not divulged the name of the father of her child to me, I can only assume that you are he, Damien."

Obviously relieved, Damien smiled, a note of pride in his voice as he took a few short steps to Amethyst's side to lightly brush her lips with his before turning to respond, "Yes, John, it is my child Amethyst carries, and a beautiful boy he will be, too!"

A gray brow raised quizzically, Dr. Morgan said slowly, "And it does not concern you that you have taken advantage of an extremely young woman under your protection and that this child was conceived outside the bonds of holy matrimony?"

Damien's smile stiffening, he replied softly, "Will Amethyst's unwed status prohibit you from attending her, John?"

"Of course not!" Dr. Morgan's reply was slightly indignant.

"Well, in that case, I will answer your question." Damien's arm stealing warmly around Amethyst's shoulders, he pulled her gently against his side, shooting her a short look, the warmth of which brought a flush of color to her white face. "I'm extremely happy about the child, as happy as I am for the world to know that Amethyst belongs to me. As for marriage, it is a mere formality about which I have decided not to concern myself at present."

"And Amethyst, does she not . . ."

"I think I have answered enough of your questions now, John." Cutting the interview short with a smile that negated the sharpness of his words, Damien had bid him goodbye, his mood unaffected by the older man's criticism.

The following day Damien had returned from an early-morning excursion, bursting unannounced into their room to find Amethyst in her chemise as Mary attempted to aid her in dressing. Dismissing the embarrassed young woman, his eyes had moved warmly over Amethyst's petite womanly presence. Her black shining curls, yet undone, hung down her slender back, extending almost to her waist as her winsome face looked expectantly to his. The smooth line of her neck and shoulders, bared in the abbreviated garment pleased his eye as he followed it unerringly to the length of slender arms and small hands that fluttered nervously. His eyes moved to the generous swells of her breasts, exposed disturbingly in the low neckline, noting with a growing tenderness that pregnancy only enhanced her womanly appeal. Her waist was still narrow, only the slightest bulge beginning to show beneath as Damien's eyes continued downward. Edged lightly in delicate white lace, her chemise ended abruptly atop slender thighs, exposing legs that were startlingly long and willowy for a woman of her petite stature. Following their slender length to the floor, he noted the narrow-heeled shoes and dark stockings that extended upward to be secured above the knee by narrow, beribboned pink garters, and was barely able to suppress the urge to slowly roll those silk stockings down her legs, allowing his lips to follow their intimate course.

Hardly waiting for the door to close behind Mary, Damien strode to Amethyst's side to snatch her into his arms. Lowering his head, he kissed her slowly, thoroughly, his lips reawakening emotions so effectively indulged only hours before. Reluctantly drawing his mouth from hers, he noted the heat in her glance, felt the trembling of her body held so intimately against his and whispered softly as he slowly slid the straps from her shoulders, lowering the chemise to expose completely her full, perfect breasts, "Amethyst, my darling, you are my true treasure . . ."

Some time later as they lay sated in each other's arms, Damien spoke in a deceivingly casual tone.

"Madame duMaurier will come to this house for your fittings in the future, Amethyst. I talked to her this morning and she will be happy to rearrange her schedule to accommodate them."

Raising her eyes to his, Amethyst caught a fleeting hardness in his expression which stirred her uneasiness the moment before he smiled, his mouth moving to cover hers warmly, possessively, once more.

Her present tranquillity slipping away at the recollection of that fleeting moment of implacability in his expression, Amethyst stiffened. The arms holding her tightened spontaneously, and raising her eyes, Amethyst was startled to see Damien regarding her pensively.

"Damien! How long have you been awake?"

"Long enough to see you staring at me while you thought I slept. What were you thinking, Amethyst? Were you planning ways to escape me, perhaps?"

"Damien!" Disturbed by his question Amethyst drew back instinctively, only to find Damien's arms would not allow her recoil.

His voice a gentle reproof, he said lightly, "Don't waste your time with thoughts of that nature, darling."

"I wasn't planning . . ."

"Good," he mumbled softly, punctuating his remarks with light kisses which he rained on her upturned face, "because I have a ravenous hunger for you that will not be appeased, and you grow more delicious every day." His short kisses turning into teasing bites, he nibbled lightly at her ear, trailing his lips down her neck to nibble gently at the delicate curve of her shoulder. Slowly slipping the coverlet away, he exposed her nakedness, a familiar glow returning to his strange light eyes. Reaching out, he cupped her breast with his hand, lowering his head to fondle it gently with his lips.

Raising his eyes to hers, he said wonderingly, "Why is it that I can't get my fill of you?" His hands moved caressingly over her body as he spoke, delighting in the silkiness of her skin beneath his palms, his emotional plane heightening with the intoxicating intimacy. Suddenly unable to bear separation from her a moment longer, he moved to cover her small body with his, groaning softly as their flesh met. Supporting his weight on his elbows, he cupped her face with his broad palms.

"You are so tiny beneath me," he whispered wonderingly against her lips, "so fragile, and my hunger for you so compelling that I sometimes fear I will devour you in the madness you awake in me. Each indulgence of my passion only seems to lead to a desire for more of you, darling, more and more until all other thoughts are driven from my mind in my abject obsession. If you accuse me of practicing obeah on you, consider what this witchcraft has done to me. I am consumed by the very passion that enslaves us both. I can be satisfied with nothing short of complete possession, and find my dependence on this addiction growing with each passing day. And I warn you now, my darling Amethyst. I can't force you to bind yourself to me legally, but don't entertain even the vaguest dreams of escape, because there is no power on this earth that will succeed in separating you from me while I still have breath left in my body."

Her heart beating wildly in her breast, Amethyst whispered against his lips, "But why do you submit to this addiction, Damien? Would it not be better for us both if you were free again to resume your former life . . . and I, mine?"

It was long moments before Damien responded, delaying his answer to drink deeply of the sweetness of her mouth, revelling in those long moments at the wonder of its innate splendor.

"No, darling. I'm afraid I find the joy of you so complete and compelling that it overrules any negative aspects it may also entail." Lifting his eyes to exert the power of their light, transparent depths, Damien held Amethyst's glance with his. His voice a low, hypnotic whisper, he whispered, "Do you find yourself possessed by my obeah, Amethyst, helpless against its will? And so you will stay, my darling, until my own possession is relieved." His mouth covering hers again, Damien pressed apart the soft lips so pliant beneath his, his mind acknowledging solemnly even as the wild singing of passion began to race through his veins, "I will use superstition to hold her if I must, will use her fear against her if I can . . . will do any and all to keep her, for this damned willful little beauty is my life . . . my love . . . and without her is . . . nothing."

Her slender hands moving nervously against her sides, Amethyst stood beside Damien in the entrance to Oeller's Tavern, her cape still wrapped securely about her. The luxurious garment bore a wide hood that framed her exquisite face dramatically with ermine, and turning, Damien hesitated a moment to drink in her beauty before slipping it from her shoulders. Her mind racing wildly, Amethyst was unaware of Damien's appreciative glance. Their first social outing since her changed circumstances, Amethyst had anticipated the gala Winter Ball with an apprehension that had not diminished with time. Even Damien's gift of the extravagant ermine-trimmed cape did nothing to deter her mind from its path of apprehension. This night had been a long time in coming and she was certain Damien would make full use of the opportunity to fix his possession of her in the minds of those present. Not that any extra effort would have to be expended to announce his claim, for now that all pretense of guardianship had been dropped, his proprietary attitude was all too apparent. Extremely self-conscious, Amethyst was aware that Damien's possessiveness sang out in his warm glance as it rested unalteringly on her person, and his propensity to touch her with small, caressing gestures. But having had ample time to prepare herself for the evening that was now upon her, she found that anxiety had still managed to secure a hold on her emotions.

Nagging relentlessly at the back of her mind was the suspicion that Armand Beauchamps would also be present at the ball. Although she had had no communication with Armand since her last fitting at Madame duMaurier's establishment, Madame had hinted casually just the day before that Monsieur Beauchamps missed their conversations sorely and was anxious to see her again. Pretending disinterest, Amethyst had not pursued the subject, but her apprehension had heightened. She was not certain what Damien would do if Armand did attend and attempted to speak to her. His temperament was far too volatile to gauge accurately.

Walking sedately beside Damien as they approached the Assembly Room, Amethyst was thankful for one thing at least. She had not been able to wear the sapphire silk that Damien had ordered expressly for the occasion. Memories connected with the gown so similar to it which she had worn in Kingston would have been strong enough to completely subdue her confidence. She could not have been more pleased when Madame duMaurier had delivered the completed garment, only to find the waistline a bit too tight for comfort. Raising her thin brow expressively, Madame had refrained from comment while still managing to convey her thoughts. Her face coloring, Amethyst had reminded herself it was the first and probably one of the milder reactions she could expect when her condition became more apparent. Encouraged that despite the negligible widening of her waist, her condition was not yet obvious, Amethyst wore instead a fashionable white watered silk gown in the new polonaise style.

Fashioned with a round neckline, the bodice was dramatically stark, devoid of all ornamentation except a fine spray of exquisite pink silk flowers which curled gracefully at one shoulder. The sleeves, tight to the elbow, were bordered in a narrow pink satin ribbon before flaring out in wide diaphanous tiers that swayed gently with her movement. The decolletage was daring, dipping low into the bosom, the bodice continuing to a moderately pointed waistline. An overskirt of the same delicate silk was pulled back over the hips on both sides of the skirt in decorative festoons, exposing an underskirt extending as far as her slender ankles, where a narrow row of pink satin ribbon bordered the pleated hemline of the gown. Delicate pink silk roses peeked from their position tucked beneath the festooned tiers of the overskirt, in graceful complement to those on her slender shoulder.

Black and gleaming in the light of the chandeliers overhead, Amethyst's hair was swept back softly from her forehead, the remainder of the shining mass allowed to fall in a profusion of long, bouncing curls against her neck. A spray of pale pink silk rosebuds tucked into the glorious halo provided a startling contrast to the brilliant ebony of her tresses as it curved gracefully amidst the glowing ringlets.

Extremely pleased with the gown, Amethyst was unaware that the true beauty of the garment lay in its reflection of her own perfect coloring, the creamy whiteness of her skin and the becoming pink that edged her delicate cheekbones. The black of her narrow, slanted brows appeared darker still, as did the thick fringes bordering her glorious lavender eyes, while her finely drawn lips shone a truer pink than the delicate blooms themselves. Small and petite with a natural grace of bearing, she was a subtle pink-and-white confection for the eyes, appealing, tempting, utterly delicious to the sight.

Glancing down momentarily, Damien knew a moment of overpowering pride in the small, delicate apparition that walked beside him. Solemn, quietly observing, she exuded an aura of glowing innocence that pulled at his heartstrings while at the same time projecting an appealing womanliness that tantalized him heartlessly. She was completely feminine and alluring, all things to him, paling others into insignificance in his eyes.

His stomach tightening jealously, Damien noted upon entering the Assembly Room that his silent opinion was openly shared by the male contingent present as one by one, all eyes turned in her direction and an appreciative buzzing ensued.

Escaping him completely, however, was the fact that many feminine glances followed his imposing figure appreciatively, noting the superb tailoring of his maroon velvet coat as it fell from his unusual expanse of shoulder to lie casually against his narrow waist in a becoming double-breasted style. The skirt of the coat, cut away in front, sloping to two narrow coattails in back, exposed a well fitted white waistcoat and matching white britches, which hugged his body tightly to the calf, displaying to the discerning female eye a manly curve and well muscled thighs. Fine silk stockings were tucked meticulously under the leg bands of his britches, the buckles on his gleaming black leather shoes matching the smaller version securing his britches at the knee. A narrow ruffle of lace peeked from his sleeve, matching the small jabot that filled the opening of his waistcoat at the neck. The epitome of fashion, he was nonetheless one of the most blatantly masculine men in the room.

But his mind obviously far from his attire, he followed Amethyst possessively with his peculiarly translucent eyes, sober and watchful, inspiring envy in the female glances that followed him so intently. Finally taking Amethyst's arm, his manner was openly proprietary.

Hardly conscious of the man at her side, Amethyst scanned the room surreptitiously in an effort to ascertain if Armand Beauchamps was indeed present. But the room was too large . . . she had not expected such grandeur. At least sixty feet square, it had a handsome music gallery at one end, papered in an ornate gold-and-white pattern which was obviously French in design. The wall was decorated with compartments housing Pantheon figures, imitating festoons, pillars, and groups of antique drawings. To the side of the room a lavish buffet table held countless appetizing treats to tempt the palate, as well as several crystal punch bowls around which the festive crowd gathered gayly. Hampered by the confusion of the milling crowd, Amethyst was unable to see further than a few feet in each direction as she continued her anxious perusal.

At a touch on her arm, Amethyst turned to Damien's amused expression. The first chords of a reel had begun and Damien whispered above the echoing sound, "Ah, here come your faithful puppies, happy on your trail, darling. I have waited almost two months for this moment."

Her hand reaching out lightly toward his arm in a pleading gesture, Amethyst appealed softly, "Damien, you won't be unkind. They have all been extremely nice to me. I should not . . ."

"You needn't worry, Amethyst," Damien began, interrupting his response to lift his head with a small smile as Martin Quell reached Amethyst's side.

The sandy-haired fellow's face aglow with appreciation of her beauty, he said politely, "Good evening, Damien. Good evening, Amethyst. You're looking extremely lovely tonight. I can see I shall have endless competition if I hope to gain even a small portion of your time tonight."

"Good . . . good evening, Amethyst . . . Damien. I . . . it is a beautiful ev . . . evening, is it . . . not?"

Gerard Whitestone's familiar stammer turned Martin around with a frown as he declared in an annoyed voice, "There, you see, the rush has already begun!"

Before the red-faced Gerard could respond, Damien's deep voice turned the two gentlemen in his direction. "Yes, it is a lovely evening, gentlemen, but I do not think there will be any need for your good-natured squabbling tonight. Although I'm sure Amethyst is pleased to see you both, I'm afraid my betrothed will be otherwise engaged most of the evening."

"Betrothed!"

The startled expression on the two young men's faces was almost comical, and Amethyst would have been smothering a frantic urge to laugh was her heart not hammering so hard in anticipation of Damien's next words. Instead, she stood stiffly, her eyes glued on Damien's face as he stretched the moment to its fullest, prolonging the suspense while she held her breath.

Finally turning toward Amethyst with a warm glance, he slid his arm around her waist, urging her closer to his side as he continued with a smile, "Yes, I'm pleased to say Amethyst has this week consented to become my wife and I'm afraid I'm far too possessive to allow her far from my side when she is surrounded by admirers."

"Your wife!"

The words echoed on the lips of the two startled young men, their faces falling with obvious disappointment as they offered their hands in congratulations.

"Well, certainly, Damien, you are to be congratulated."

"Yes, Damien, con . . . congratulations!"

Their enthusiasm dampened by Damien's announcement, the two young men seemed to have little to say after extending good wishes and within a few moments they had faded into the crowd.

Once again alone with Damien, Amethyst turned toward him accusingly. "Betrothed! Damien, I've had my fill of deceit! I should not like to begin another elaborate prefabrication that will come to an embarrassing halt once my pregnancy becomes apparent. Better you had said nothing than to tell everyone . . ."

"But I won't have to tell everyone, darling. Just look around you. The news has already begun to spread."

Turning to survey the groups behind her, Amethyst could see a few whispered conversations concluding in pointed looks in their direction, and turning back to Damien, Amethyst whispered, "Damien, I am acutely uncomfortable."

Obviously enjoying the situation, Damien bent his head to brush a kiss against her hair as he said softly, "Come, darling, I think it's time for some refreshment. Would you like some punch?"

Not waiting for her response, Damien took her arm to lead her to the buffet table, his expression extremely pleased.

Within the hour, having been approached by endless numbers offering their congratulations, Amethyst's face was stiff from smiling and her mood depressed. The deceit, once expressed, seemed to grow with each conversation to a monstrous untruth that lay heavily upon her heart. She would never be able to face these people when her pregnancy began to show. What was

Damien thinking? Surely he realized how much they would resent being played for fools ... Did he perhaps think to embarrass her into changing her mind? Abruptly angry, Amethyst lifted her eyes to the man at her side. Involved in light conversation with two acquaintances, his arm wound possessively around her waist, he was unaware of her glance and her silent anger.

"If you hope to put me in a position where I will be forced to marry you to save my face, you waste your time, Damien," her mind screeched. "Your desire to secure me as your wife is but a transient emotion, and I don't intend to be forced to remain at your side when it dissipates into uninterest and neglect."

But Damien did not turn his head to catch her heated glance. Despite the tempest raging inside her, Amethyst began to feel a vague discomfort. Sensing the weight of someone's stare, she turned, her gaze coming to an abrupt halt when it met the dark, pensive eyes of Armand Beauchamps. Immediately certain from his expression that he was aware of Damien's announcement, Amethyst flushed hotly and averted her eyes.

"He probably considers me a coy opportunist without a shred of honesty," her mind whispered. Her spirits dropping to an even deeper low at the thought, Amethyst was startled to realize Armand's opinion mattered greatly to her. So engrossed was she in her thoughts that she failed to see Merrell Bristol approaching until she stood directly opposite them. Startlingly lovely in a gold velvet gown that brought out the highlights in her light chestnut hair, Merrell's eyes glittered with an unknown emotion as she said brightly, "Damien, darling, I understand you are deserving of congratulations! Or should I direct my congratulations to your darling ward? She has this evening, after all, managed to advance her position immeasurably, has she not?"

His eyes jerking to Merrell's bright expression, Damien frowned. His voice, when he spoke, was carefully controlled.

"You may extend your congratulations to me, if that's what you had in mind, Merrell."

"Perhaps it is, and perhaps it isn't what I had in mind, Damien." Merrell's expression tightened noticeably and Amethyst began to feel the sharp edge of apprehension as a chill moved up her spine. Merrell was obviously upset and ready to make a scene, and Amethyst was unsure what her own reaction would be. She had been so unstable these last few weeks, with spells of weakness overtaking her with startling rapidity and she was already beginning to feel a touch of lightheadedness. It would not do to faint . . . no . . .

Beginning to panic, Amethyst shot a pleading glance to Damien, but he was not looking in her direction. Intent on Merrell's flushed face, he said softly, "I will stand for none of your nonsense, Merrell."

"Will you not?" Merrell responded a trifle too brightly, her face obviously flushed. "Then I think it would be opportune for us to go somewhere where we may talk privately, Damien, for there are several things I intend to say whether other ears are listening or not!"

Taking a few moments to assess her briefly, Damien turned to Amethyst, his lips a tight line as he whispered, "If you'll excuse me, Amethyst, this bitch is determined to make a scene, and I don't intend to give her the satisfaction." Not waiting for Amethyst's response, Damien turned to take Merrell by the arm, his step rapid as he propelled her toward the doorway.

Suddenly feeling herself the center of all eyes, Amethyst turned uneasily toward the buffet table, and had only gone a few steps in its direction when she heard a familiar voice in her ear.

"It seems I must thank the graceless Mademoiselle

Bristol for the opportunity for which I have been waiting all evening, ma cherie."

Looking up into Armand's serious expression, Amethyst felt a deep sadness stir inside her. "It will not do to have Damien find us speaking together when he returns, Armand. He was furious when he found out you were meeting me at Madame's boutique."

Interrupting her with a small wave of his hand, Armand said softly, "As Mademoiselle Bristol insisted with Monsieur Straith, so I must insist with you, Amethyst. It is important that we speak. If you do not wish to be the target of inquisitive glances, we may step outside for a moment." Noting her discomfort, Armand hesitated only a moment before taking her arm and gently steering her through the crowd toward the doorway opposite the one through which Damien and Merrell had disappeared. Once outside, his dark eyes moved quickly to ascertain a spot where they might speak without interruption, and noting a secluded area behind the staircase to the second floor, he urged her forward.

His broad back completely hiding her from view of the curious as she stood with her back to the wall, Armand stared wordlessly into Amethyst's face. Almost disbelieving he could be so moved by a woman, especially one so young—barely out of childhood—Armand allowed himself a moment to gain his composure. But the pain he had experienced at Damien Straith's announcement that he and Amethyst were to marry was real, as was his overwhelming sense of loss when he looked into the lavender eyes lifted to his.

Finally speaking, Armand's voice was just above a whisper. "It is true, ma petite, what is on the tip of everyone's tongue? You are to marry Monsieur Straith?"

Her eyes moving momentarily from his, Amethyst avoided a direct answer. "Damien has announced our betrothal tonight."

Noting her furtive glance, Armand prompted softly, "And you, ma cherie, how do you feel about this match?"

"I don't know what you mean, Armand . . ."

Raising her chin lightly with the tips of his fingers, Armand forced Amethyst to meet his gaze. "Come, ma petite, you understand very well. Your expression is not that of the happy bride-to-be."

"You read something into my glance that is not there, Armand," Amethyst responded softly, almost choking on the deliberate untruth.

"And you, ma petite, do not lie very convincingly."

Unable to sustain the pretense a moment longer, Amethyst raised a pleading glance. "Armand, please, I don't wish to go into this any further. You understand my position correctly. I am . . . committed to Damien."

Raising his hand, Armand touched Amethyst's cheek lightly, his expression deeply disturbed. He was at a loss, never having felt the necessity to plead his case to a woman before, but unable to bear the thought of her passing to another, he whispered, "Was I wrong in assuming that there was a warmth between us, ma petite, something drawing us together?"

"Armand, this is senseless. We cannot retain our friendship. Damien is too jealous."

Armand's hand was caressing her cheek. "Surely you realize it is not friendship I seek, Amethyst."

"I . . . I didn't encourage your attentions, Armand . . ."

"I needed no encouragement, ma petite."

Searching his face with her eyes, Amethyst looked for a sign of deception. Surely this handsome, virile man who had loved many sophisticated women could not be serious about his feelings for her. But she could find no sign of deceit in the dark eyes of the man looking down at her.

"Oh, Armand," she whispered despairingly, "I find it

difficult to believe you are the ruthless man of the world some would have me believe. I can only believe you are sincere, and I must respond accordingly. I am indeed very fond of you, and I must admit that you stir a true warmth inside me. I find you handsome and charming, Armand. I enjoy being with you and I am sorely affected by your distress, but . . . but . . . it's too late."

"Ma petite Amethyst," Armand interrupted quietly, "I would have you for my wife . . ."

Stunned into silence, Amethyst could do no more than stare disbelievingly at the man before her. The antithesis of Damien Straith, his skin a natural olive, his dark brows, eyes, and strong features compelling, he was also Damien's antithesis in manner. Quietly considerate with a suave, understated wit and entertaining personality, he held a generous appeal, toward which Amethyst was helplessly drawn. But it was impossible . . . too late . . .

Her eyes filling with tears, Amethyst raised her hand to his cheek. Her voice was soft, wistful. "Oh, Armand, you are truly a lovely man . . ."

The obvious regret with which she spoke her soft endearment pushing him over the bounds of restraint, Armand groaned softly, "Mon Dieu . . . this is more than I can stand . . ."

Snatching Amethyst against his powerful chest, Armand covered her mouth with his for a long, searching kiss. The touch of her lips igniting the passion he had suppressed for so long, Armand strained Amethyst ever closer to him, his kiss deepening. Finally drawing away, his dark eyes bright with emotion, he said raggedly, *"Je t'aime* . . . I love you, Amethyst, *mon coeur."* Kissing her lightly again on the lips, he pleaded softly, "Come with me tonight, ma petite amour. We will leave now . . . quickly. We will drive to a spot where Monsieur Straith cannot interfere and we will be married."

"No, Armand." Struggling to free herself, Amethyst

whispered frantically, "You don't really wish to marry. You aren't a man meant to be tied to a wife."

"I did *not* wish to marry before I met you, ma cherie," Armand's melodious voice insisted, "but I am no longer the same man."

"But I am committed to Damien, I tell you. Please let me go, Armand. Damien will return soon, and I don't wish to have him find us together."

Suddenly angry, Armand said sharply, "I do not worry should he find us together. This commitment . . . it is nothing, and can be dissolved."

"It cannot . . ."

"Yes!" His dark eyes snapping angrily, Armand insisted, "Yes, it can and *will* be dissolved!"

Violet eyes slowly raising to his, Amethyst held his glance silently for long moments before responding. Her voice was a desperate whisper. "No, Armand . . . it cannot. It's too late. I carry Damien's child."

Startled into silence, Armand searched her pale face, his own expression finally registering belief as he said quietly, "When . . . when will you have this child, ma petite?"

"In six months."

Tears suddenly overflowing the great purple orbs, Amethyst whispered hoarsely, "Don't think ill of me, Armand, please. I cannot explain the circumstances that brought me to this, but I don't wish your scorn . . ."

"Not my scorn, cherie." Considering her solemnly, Armand finally whispered in return, the pain of her disclosure obvious in his darkly handsome face. "No, not my scorn . . . just my fervent wish that I were he . . ."

Gently enclosing her in his arms, Armand held her close against him for long moments, finally about to speak when a strong arm suddenly jerked them apart, flinging him roughly against the opposite wall.

Her eyes wide with fright, Amethyst saw the rage on

Damien's face the moment he turned to deliver a crashing blow against Armand's jaw. Caught unaware, Armand was unable to defend himself against the vicious blows that Damien delivered to his face time and time again, snapping his head from side to side as blood spurted from his nose and mouth. Pounding and pummelling the battered Frenchman senseless, Damien watched unaffected as Armand's powerful body doubled over, collapsing into a silent heap upon the floor.

Standing threateningly over his inert form, his chest heaving from the exertion of his attack, Damien spat venomously, "I warn you now, Beauchamps, touch Amethyst again or even attempt to contact her and you're a dead man!"

Turning back toward Amethyst, Damien grabbed her arm and jerked her forward. Dragging her down the hallway behind him, he ignored the few rushing to the Frenchman's aid as he did those who stood gawking from the doorways to the Assembly Room, and continued on to the exit door where a frightened servant stood with their outerwear in his hand. Stopping to wrap Amethyst securely in her cape, he pulled her unceremoniously through the doorway to the carriage that stood waiting. Jerking the door open, he turned and lifting Amethyst roughly, dumped her on the seat inside. Getting in beside her, he signaled the driver forward and sat stiff and silent for the duration of the ride home.

Not bothering to respond to Mary's hesitant greeting as she opened the door, Damien allowed Amethyst to precede him into the hallway. Silently sweeping her cape from her shoulders, he proceeded to remove his own overcoat and throw it on the chair near the door. His eyes burning furiously into hers, he started up the staircase, taking her arm to drag her along behind him as he did.

Her heart pounding furiously, Amethyst could not suppress her own anger as Damien pulled her into the master bedroom and slammed the door shut behind him.

Rounding to face him, her eyes sparking fire, she hissed in a low, ominous tone, "How dare you! How dare you behave so barbarically?" A picture of Armand's bloodied face flashing before her mind, she felt tears choke her throat, and struggling to speak, she continued haltingly, "You attack Armand Beauchamps brutally, without cause, and then treat me like an errant kitchen maid. You are a savage, sadistic animal, Damien Straith, and I will not stand . . ."

A sudden burst of laughter interrupted her tirade, startling her into silence while Damien regarded her with bitter amusement. Advancing slowly, he stopped to stand towering above her, his glance scathing, his overpowering size and obvious rage in blatant intimidation.

"My congratulations, Amethyst. That was an admirable try! But your ploy will not work. You will not deter me with your attack. Your noble swain, Armand Beauchamps, will not forget the lesson he learned tonight and neither will any other man present at the ball." Reaching out, Damien suddenly clamped his hands on Amethyst's shoulders, sneering as he did, "And now it's your turn, my sweet!"

"Take your hands off me!" Amethyst hissed, reaching out to push and shove against his chest in an attempt to free herself. "If you think I'll stand here and calmly allow you to abuse me, you're mistaken!"

Suddenly snatching Amethyst against him, Damien caught her wrists behind her back, holding them effortlessly with one wide hand as he used the other to force her face up to his. His voice a low growl touched with admiration, he said softly, "You're like a small, angry kitten, hissing and spitting its defiance against the inevitable." His glance hardening, he continued hoarsely, "Tell me, Amethyst, why did you allow Armand Beauchamps to take you to that secluded spot? Couldn't you resist the thought of his arms around you, the thought of his lips on yours? Did you enjoy his embrace?" His mouth descending savagely in a brutal kiss smothered her response. Finally drawing back from her bruised lips, Damien whispered softly, "Did you find his kiss more thrilling than mine . . . his touch more pleasing? Do you think Beauchamps will consider those few stolen moments worth the beating he suffered? Well, you are a fool! To Armand Beauchamps you're just another woman to add to his long list of conquests, nothing more than another feather in his cap!"

"As I am to *you*, Damien?"

His expression stiffening at Amethyst's taunting question, Damien did not deign to answer. A bitter smile curving her lips, Amethyst continued softly, her voice a whispered gasp as she winced against the pain of Damien's crushing embrace, "Well, you're wrong! Armand is sincere . . . a true gentleman . . ."

"Fool!" Suddenly realizing she struggled to catch her breath, Damien loosened his hold and freed her wrists, his hands slipping around her back to hold her more gently than before. "You merely played into his hands, Amethyst . . ."

"His intentions were honorable."

A scoffing laugh broke into her response, filling Damien's voice with ridicule, "You're a bigger fool than I thought!"

"He asked me to be his wife."

The laughter slowly leaving his face, Damien hesitated for the briefest second before responding sharply, "He was deceiving you. He would never marry you."

"I believe him. He said he loves me, Damien."

His eyes cold, Damien's response was flat, devoid of expression. "And what did you say to him?"

Lowering her head, Amethyst responded hesitantly, "I . . . I told him that it was impossible . . . that I was committed to you . . ."

"But that did not deter the Frenchman from pressing his suit."

"No, it didn't . . ."

"And?"

"I told him . . . I told him I carried your child . . ."

There was another brief hesitation on Damien's part before he said slowly, deliberately, "And what was his reaction?"

Her eyes moving to a far corner of the room, Amethyst bit her lips nervously, her barely audible whisper finally breaking the uneasy silence. "He said . . . he said he wished the child was his . . ."

Her soft response hung heavily between them, filling the silence that ensued with an air of expectancy that sent a chill of apprehension racing down her spine. Unable to bear the suspense a moment longer, Amethyst lifted her eyes to Damien's unreadable facade. A small muscle twitched in his jaw, and Amethyst braced herself for another outburst. Suddenly blinking, Damien raised a hand to Amethyst's cheek in a small, tender gesture that shook her far more than his violence of the past hour. His voice was a soft caress.

"But the child is not his, Amethyst. It is mine . . . ours . . . and nothing can change that. And you are mine, Amethyst. No one will ever take you from me . . ."

Lowering his mouth slowly, Damien covered her lips with his gently, tenderly, his arms moving to hold her against him with a sweet urgency that left her breathless. Finally drawing his mouth from hers, he moved his hands up the back of her dress, unfastening the buttons with practiced precision, punctuating his deft effort with soft kisses on her cheek and brow, small nibbles on her ear and neck, and finally another long, searing kiss that left her weak. Without her conscious realization, Amethyst's gown fell to the floor around her slender ankles. The heat of his kisses increasing, Damien slipped the delicate chemise from her body. Finally clad only in white silk stockings extending just above her knee, Amethyst stood trembling visibly before him.

Closing his eyes briefly in an effort to subdue the passion raging through him, Damien pressed a fleeting kiss on Amethyst's trembling lips before bending to loosen the ribboned garters and slip the flimsy wisps down her slender legs. Following their descent with his lips, Damien kissed the small, perfect feet as she slipped them from her shoes. Slowly retracing with his lips the path he had followed just minutes before, he continued steadily upward, his passion growing with each tender kiss until he reached her slender thighs. His blood rushing through his veins as the heat of passion assumed control, Damien looked up to Amethyst's face. Her expression bemused, she returned his stare, her body still and motionless as he lowered his head to the tender flesh between. She was trembling wildly now, as his lips circled the triangle of black, shining ringlets, finally emitting a small gasp as Damien cupped her rounded buttocks with his hands and brought her forward to press his lips tightly against the vulnerable crease.

Lost to her passion, Amethyst felt the first penetration of Damien's tongue, a jolt of ecstasy shooting through her as he pressed deeper and deeper to taste and draw from the sweetness within. No longer able to think coherently, she could feel only the joy of his erotic quest as his tongue fondled her intimately, teasing, searching, demanding a response she was no longer able to withhold. On and on he persisted, his heady penetration moving deeper and deeper until the glorious languor creeping through her veins assumed control, shaking her small perfect body with deep, heaving spasms lifting her to a euphoric plane of brilliant sensation and breathless glory, her body quivering violently as it released in gasping tribute the sweet nectar of love and total fulfillment. His mouth pressed tightly against her, Damien shared her ecstasy, accepting gratefully, lovingly, her body's homage to his passionate ministrations. Supporting her gently, he waited until the last tender spasms had passed, his lips relinquishing the tender slit begrudgingly, lingeringly. Moving quickly to his feet, he scooped Amethyst's swaying figure into his arms and carried her to bed. Laying her down gently, he quickly removed his clothing and within moments his strong, anxious body lay atop hers. Lifting her heavy lids slowly, Amethyst whispered softly against his lips, "Damien, I did not want this..."

His eyes devouring her beautiful face, Damien whispered in return, "This magic between us is too strong... too beautiful to be denied, darling." Gently sliding himself within her, Damien heard her soft gasp, a familiar glory shooting through him at the moment of complete possession. Moving inside her with increasing impetus, Damien mumbled hoarsely against Amethyst's ear, "I want to love you, darling... to keep on loving you... never to stop... never..."

With a brief, lightning gasp of rapture, Damien was brought to the culmination of his quest, Amethyst's body joining him in his final, ultimate glimpse of brilliant glory.

His body finally still, Damien moved to lay beside her, slipping his arms around her to hold her in the circle of his intimate embrace. Raising his head, Damien looked into Amethyst's face. Her eyes were closed, her expression relaxed and motionless, and he knew a moment of bittersweet joy. He had overcome her resistance once again... he had proved his mastery over her body. But he longed desperately for her spirit, her love freely given as he gave his to her. His unspoken love a heavy weight inside his chest, he bent to press a tender kiss against her lips.

"But for now," he thought silently, ". . . but for now, my darling, my dear love, for now this will be enough . . ."

Chapter 8

Insects buzzing noisily around her head, Tillie moved leisurely along the forest trail, grateful to the heavy foliage that filtered the burning rays of afternoon sun. Midway into March, the Jamaican weather had turned warmer, coupling with the humidity to preclude haste as she made her way toward Conway Plantation. Her former secrecy a thing of the past, Tillie walked slowly, appreciative of the beauty surrounding her. Giant ferns abounded on either side of the narrow path with lichens in different sizes and shapes spotting the trees in haphazard patterns, a filmy curtain of hanging moss draped across an outstretched branch completing a scene decorated with nature's matchless artistry. The fairytale quality of the secluded area did not go unnoticed by her dark, almond-shaped eyes as Tillie slowed her step in rapt appreciation.

A far different figure than she had presented only three months before, Tillie's stature was still straight and proud, her impressive height and grace of movement setting her apart from the average, but her full-breasted figure was now slender as a girl's, her brilliant mulatto beauty accented by the narrowed planes of her face where her large, heavily fringed dark eyes and full expressive lips appeared too lushly beautiful to be real. Smiling, she following the quick, darting flight of the doctor bird as it hovered momentarily before a brilliant hibiscus, finally settling to puncture the base of the flower with its long, slender, black-tipped vermillion bill, the irridescent green of its breast and black of its head, wings and long scissor-like tail fading into the vegetation as it drew the honey in pleasant obscurity. Finally satisfied, it withdrew, sounding a rather belligerent "tuss-tuss-tuss" before taking flight and darting away. Shaking her head at its sassy call, Tillie continued forward, absentmindedly humming an old song from her childhood as she walked:

"Docta bird a cunning bird—him hard fe dead,
You lick him down, him fly away,
Him hard bird fe dead . . ."

Shrugging away a sharp pang of loneliness, Tillie pressed forward again, eager to put from her mind the sadness that had fostered her heightened appreciation of the value of love. A mother who had lost her child to uncertainty, Tillie suffered the pain of Amethyst's loss each and every waking moment, but Raymond . . . her man . . . his presence had filled the aching void in her heart, making life bearable, relieving the anxieties that tortured her vivid imagination.

Her smooth forehead wrinkling into a small frown, Tillie raised her hand to her temple to smooth back a wisp of hair that had escaped her chignon, and forcing her thoughts away from the endless circle of sorrow in which all thoughts of Amethyst seemed to revolve, she concentrated on her great, handsome man. Having come to realize how extremely precious and fragile was love, which could be snatched away in a fleeting moment by the same fickle fate that had granted its inception, Tillie had decided in the three months that had passed to indulge the love between Raymond and herself, to spend as much time with him as she was able, ignoring the whisperings behind black hands as she walked the Kingston streets. Her hand tightening on the small basket she carried, a small spark of warmth moved through her as she anticipated Raymond's delight when she produced the honey cake she had baked for him this morning.

Finally reaching the small clearing used by the witchdoctor for his supplication to Pucku, Tillie turned onto the trail leading to Raymond's hut. It was still daylight, and Raymond would not return from the fields until dark, but Tillie already felt a sense of inner peace, knowing she would soon be in the simple dwelling Raymond had constructed, ". . . fraish 'n clean, jes' like Tillie want." Far better she waited there than in the lonesome house on John's Lane which held nothing more for her than memories. Yes, far better that she wait where only happy memories would fill her . . .

But what was that? Stopping still in her tracks, Tillie listened to the low mourning wail as it sounded again, her flesh crawling with fright while her ears strained to determine the location of the now familiar cry. The Mountain Witch! Tillie remembered many stories of the radiant bird whose calls were often heard while its beauty was seldom seen, and had just taken a step forward when a brilliant flash of bronze, cinnamon, and irridescent purple and black flashed before her eyes, the bird with its shaggy gray crest dipping and swooping in front of her in wild, darting dives, to flash out of sight in the space of an instant, leaving only a lonesome mourning wail behind in remembrance of its glory. Trembling wildly, Tillie clutched the handle of her basket in fear. It was a bad omen! Why had Pucku sent this brilliant bird to tease her with its beauty, giving her only a brief glimpse of its dazzling wonder, while the lonesome wail lingered on? Covering her lips with her slender, long-fingered hand, Tillie's eyes snapped wide with apprehension. What was the meaning of this omen?

Springing suddenly into motion, Tillie ran wildly along the trail, arriving at the small clearing on which

Raymond's hut stood, a low moan issuing from her throat at the sight of destruction that met her eyes. With obvious determination some malicious hand had painstakingly knocked each board from the wooden structure, trampling the straw roof into the ground until only a pile of rubble remained. And what of Raymond? Had he been inside the hut when this destruction had been practiced? Or was he perhaps safe and unaware of the maliciousness that had passed here? Tillie was trembling, her tall, imposing frame shaking wildly, one part of her refusing to accept the scene that met her eyes, while another part of her already mourned the loss she feared.

But what could she do? Where could she turn? She had no recourse, no one to turn to, a free woman of color in a slave community where she was despised for her white blood. Her breath coming in low, heaving sobs, Tillie covered her face with her hands, her strong, proud body sinking to its knees in the abject fear and misery overwhelming her. What could she do? She could do nothing . . . nothing more than sit and wait until darkness when maybe . . . maybe Raymond would return to her.

Darkness had fallen. Lantern beside her, Tillie still sat on the pallet she had rescued from the ravished hut, her face dry of the tears that had flowed so freely for the past three hours. Raymond had not come. It was long past dark . . . long past the hour of release from the fields, and he had still not returned. A heaving sickness churning in her stomach, she fought the fears inundating her mind, as she clung to the last remnants of hope left to her. Perhaps there had been an accident and Raymond was late . . .

So obsessed was she with her thoughts that she failed to hear a sound behind her the second before a small voice whispered softly, "Tillie Swann? Be dat

Tillie Swann?"

Turning swiftly toward the voice, Tillie strained to see into the darkness surrounding her, her eyes finally perceiving the figure of a small boy, black frightened eyes wide as he peered speculatively from the bushes.

Her heart pounding in her breast, Tillie turned the full strength of her gaze on the child. "This be Tillie Swann, boy. Who ask fe Tillie Swann?"

"Cudjoe bring Tillie Swann message frem Raymond," the boy hissed, his bright eyes darting back and forth as he strained to see if anyone else was within hearing distance.

Quickly moving to his side, Tillie dropped to her knees beside him as she demanded breathlessly, "Tell Tillie what happened to Raymond, Cudjoe. Tell Tillie what Raymond say."

"Massa lock Raymond up 'n knock Raymond's house t' de ground. Him tell Raymond him gowan stay locked up 'till him do what Massa say!"

"What Massa want from Raymond, Cudjoe? Raymond be best worker Massa have! Massa happy with him good blacks . . . him always say Raymond . . ."

"Massa want Raymond tek Quasheba fe him woman, but Raymond say him got woman. Quasheba young. Massa want more boys lek Cudjoe." His small face lighting with a small hint of pride, the boy continued. "Massa say Cudjoe gowan be good field hand when him growed."

"Why Massa want Raymond for this Quasheba, Cudjoe? There be plenty young bucks on this plantation that make strong children for Massa."

"But none dat Quasheba want. Quasheba want Raymond."

Her heart beating wildly, Tillie was suddenly filled with a blinding anger. "Who this Quasheba be that she tell Massa who she take for him man, Cudjoe? She be slave like other blacks here."

"Quasheba sleep with Massa, 'n now Massa tek new woman. Massa give Quasheba Raymond fe him man 'cause Quasheba choose Raymond, 'n nethin' gowan change Quasheba's mind!"

Shaking with frustrated anger, Tillie controlled the urge to scream her fury, turning to the child who stirred restlessly.

"And what did Raymond send you to tell me, Cudjoe?"

"Raymond say Tillie Swann leave dis place 'n nevah come back. Massa rygin at Raymond, 'n Massa know 'bout Tillie. If him find Tillie here, him gowan hurt Tillie, 'n sell Raymond off." His large black eyes suddenly lowering shyly, Cudjoe continued in a low voice, "Raymond, him tell Cudjoe t' tell Tillie him love Tillie Swann. Raymond say Tillie Swann him woman 'n Quasheba nethin' but black streggah. Raymond not gowan put him seed in black streggah . . . not nevah!"

Unable to do else, Tillie nodded her understanding of the message Cudjoe carried, her throat tight with unshed tears as she took the small black hand.

"Tenky, Cudjoe. Tillie Swann say tenky for bringing Raymond's message to him, and Tillie Swann ask one more thing for Cudjoe to do. Cudjoe tell Raymond that Tillie Swann love Raymond, and never stop. Raymond be Tillie's man, and Tillie do what Raymond say. You tell Raymond that, yaw?"

"Cudjoe hear Tillie Swann."

Within the space of a moment, the small black form had disappeared into the darkness, leaving Tillie alone with her boundless sorrow.

The brilliant glory of the Mountain Witch had been short and fleeting, and only the mournful wail lingered on . . .

Her eyes intent on the small garment on which she

worked, Amethyst's mind roamed far from the narrow seam. The early sun shone through the large window of the morning room, warming her as she lay propped on the chaise Damien had instructed be moved into the corner so she might reap the benefits of its southern exposure. Not of a mood to dress her hair formally, she had pulled the brilliant raven curls back simply from her face with a center part upon dressing, securing the riotous curls behind her ears with two combs. No longer impressed with the endless row of dresses in her wardrobe, she had reached in absentmindedly to pull out one of Madame's newer creations, a soft white muslin, sprigged with clusters of purple and lavender flowers. It was a comfortable gown, as were all those recently designed by Madame expressly for Amethyst's use. This particular garment was cut in a high, round neckline that circled her graceful neck with narrow white lace, the slender arms extending tightly to the elbow to puff out in a wide ruffle trimmed in the same delicate lace. A series of small purple bows moved from the center of the high neckline to the slightly raised waistline of the garment, from which the full skirt fell gracefully to feet encased in soft, purple slippers. It was an ingenious design which allowed for her ever-broadening waist and the slight rounding of stomach discernible in her fifth month of pregnancy. Small amethysts gleamed in the lobes of her ears, another gift from Damien, whose complaint that she lacked sufficient jewelry to accessorize her gowns seemed to provide him with an adequate excuse for adding sparkling additions to her jewel box with annoying consistency.

Her brow puckering into a small frown, Amethyst stifled the impatience she felt building inside as thoughts of Damien returned to mind. It was well into May, and she was still not free. Even the *Sally*'s sailing in March had allowed her no respite from Damien's domination. To her own unending amazement, Damien had seen fit to allow Jeremy Barnes to captain the ship for the spring voyage to Jamaica. Claiming pressing business matters, Damien had remained in Philadelphia at Amethyst's side, carefully supervising her activities. Not that she could complain of Damien's treatment. Endlessly considerate, he saw to all her comforts, going so far as to provide her with a carriage for her use which came equipped with a rather large, burly fellow on loan from the Strathmore household to accompany her whenever she left the house. At first terribly annoyed that she could not move without her shadow, Amethyst later came to have a certain affection for the soft-spoken Arthur Mills. A shade over average height, with a barrel chest and thick muscular tone, his features were coarse, his thin graying hair appearing decidedly out of place on the broad, jowled face. But the small brown eyes were warm, the smile shy but sincere, and she had come to accept Arthur as she had almost every other aspect of her present life.

And, strangely enough, it had been through Arthur's presence that she had come to gain her first insight into the maze of contradictions that was Damien Straith. Relating that Damien had been mysteriously abandoned at approximately ten years of age, Arthur explained that the youthful Damien had appeared at the docks, soliciting work as a cabin boy on Captain Strathmore's ship. Possessed of a quick mind and supreme determination, he had immediately won the approval of the demanding captain, who had, over the years, come to regard him as a son. Even after Hiram Strathmore had retired from the sea with a fleet of three vessels, to conduct his profitable business ashore, Damien had remained close to him and his wife, Millicent. Attaining his own captaincy at the youthful age of 24, Damien had done his mentor proud by functioning to his country's and his own benefit as a privateer during the war years, and by attaining a position of respect and importance in his home port of Philadelphia as a shrewd businessman and formidable naval opponent.

Now, guided by Hiram Strathmore's expertise, Damien was reportedly preparing to enlarge his holdings with another ship which he intended to ready for Orient trade when it opened within the year. Having known Damien as a boy when he was a wary visitor to the Strathmore household where Arthur was employed as a servant, he was truly fond of and loyal to the man he had grown to be. Excusing Damien's faults with the explanation that they were the result of a deprived and unhappy childhood, he praised the captain's dubious virtues to the heaven while shyly declaring that Amethyst was the first woman he had met that was a suitable match for Damien's outstanding qualities. Disagreeing silently with Arthur's assessment, Amethyst had merely smiled her thanks at the sincerely intended compliment, realizing the extent of her good fortune to have the loyalty of so stout a fellow as Arthur Mills.

Her daily routine considerably broadened by the use of the carriage at her disposal, Amethyst arranged to spend at least one afternoon a week at the establishment of Philadelphia's most famous bookseller, Robert Bell. Since the cessation of the war, music had begun to be widely printed and it was with great excitement that Amethyst went through the selections available. Recently passed in the Connecticut General Assembly, the *Act for the Encouragement of Literature and Genius*, securing the protection of copyright for authors, did much to encourage writing, and Amethyst was also anxious to take advantage of the literary boom that was beginning to fill the bookstore's shelves. Her eyes ever on the future, she hoped desperately to prepare for the time when she would once again be self-supporting and, hopefully, not out of touch with artistic advances.

Alienated from her native country's struggle for

liberty while living in Jamaica, Amethyst had previously had little interest in political events, but now situated in Philadelphia, at the hub of political activity, Amethyst found herself intrigued by the events progressing at the new Congress Hall at Sixth and Chestnut. Holding the same misconception as many that the painful revolution had ended with Cornwallis's surrender at Yorktown in October of 1781, she had not been aware that peace was not yet confirmed. The text of the Peace Treaty having finally arrived from Paris in March, she had been startled to learn that it had yet to be signed and ratified by Congress. Philadelphians, however, uncertain which of the interminable formalities meant certain peace, celebrated them all, and the arrival of the March text had done much to add to Damien's and her social life within the last few months.

Her avid perusal of current events in Philadelphia's newspapers had gleaned yet another bit of information that had set her heart to racing as a thrill of expectation moved down her spine. According to a small article appearing in an April newspaper, Lewis Hallam, Jr. was bringing the theater back to American shores! Amethyst remembered Lewis Hallam only vaguely as a member of the American Company of Players, as he had returned to England with John Henry when the main body of the troupe had left for Jamaica, but her mother's respect for the brilliant actor had been great, a strong recommendation indeed in Amethyst's eyes. Her hopes rising, Amethyst realized that should Lewis Hallam succeed in convincing the legislature to repeal the anti-theater laws, the remainder of the troupe would be able to return to the country, furnishing her with a means of self-support and escape from her growing dependence on Damien Straith.

But all Amethyst's afternoons were not spent in avid perusal of newspapers and political texts. Shopping meticulously for yard goods suitable to touch the tender skin of the child within her, whose life grew dearer to her each day, Amethyst carefully gathered the necessary essentials to complete a layette.

Shaking her head, a small frown drawing her slender brows together in puzzlement, Amethyst still found herself perplexed by the complete enigma that was Damien Straith. Despite Arthur Mills's generous contribution, in the long run, Amethyst was certain she would never truly understand his complex personality. Treating her with a tenderness that was almost doting since the announcement of her pregnancy, Damien obviously enjoyed her blossoming figure, his attentions so constant that he barely let a night slip by without making love to her with a passion that was unrelenting. But as complete as were his considerations of her needs, he was immune to her embarrassment when her condition became obvious, insisting that she continue to accompany him to the many social affairs to which they were invited. It was only by the strength of her own refusal that she was spared complete mortification at the mercy of the vicious tongues so anxious to do her in. So adamant had been Damien's insistence that she had begun to grow suspicious of his motives, wondering if for some deep, dark reason he wished to emphasize in the minds of society that the child was indeed his. But Amethyst had remained firm, refusing all social invitations despite Damien's vociferous protests.

A flush of color rising to her face, Amethyst recalled her chance meeting with Merrell Bristol a few weeks before on one of her shopping trips. Having stepped down from the carriage to come face to face with Merrell Bristol's haughty features, Amethyst had been startled, her surprise showing on her face as she subconsciously adjusted the folds of her cape to conceal the slight protrusion below her waist. Noting her nervous gesture, Merrell had arched her narrow brows, her eyes moving directly to the area Amethyst had attempted to conceal. Never one for mincing words, Merrell had questioned boldly, "Well, don't tell me you're expecting, Amethyst, dear!"

The hot color rushing to Amethyst's face and her lack of response speaking more adequately than words, Merrell burst into shrill laughter. "Well, it would seem that Damien's 'ward' and 'betrothed' is functioning in a far more intimate capacity than those two titles would have people believe! But, my dear," she continued, her patronizing tone irritating Amethyst far more than she revealed, "don't you think you are relying a bit too heavily on Damien's sense of commitment? After all, you've not yet exchanged vows and it would seem to me that Damien would have little inducement to do so now. Or . . ." Merrell continued without waiting for Amethyst's response, "or perhaps that was the inducement for Damien's announcement in the first place . . . and you are far more clever than I thought . . . Well, dear, he hasn't married you yet, has he? And I think it would be safe to say it's too late to save you the embarrassment of disclosure of your condition, wouldn't you? Really, darling," Merrell smiled insidiously, sharpening her claws for the final swipe, "you may have instilled in Damien a sense of responsibility for that bit of his flesh and blood you carry, but I doubt if it will do you much good in the long run. If I know Damien, when he's finished with you, he'll merely make arrangements for the child within his own household and allow you to go your merry way."

Her face paling when Merrell spoke the same fear that had been encroaching on her thoughts since Damien had begun showing such a keen interest in their unborn child, Amethyst managed to regain control enough to retort, "I suppose I should pay some heed to your words, Merrell. After all, you have considerable firsthand knowledge of Damien's short term of interest when it comes to women!"

Her own face flaming, Merrell Bristol managed to render the final barb. "Yes, my dear Amethyst. And you may believe that I look forward with great anticipation to the time in the near future—shortly after you have the child, I should judge—when you'll join our ranks."

Not bothering with a farewell, Merrell had turned on her heel and walked stiffly out of sight, leaving her words to reverberate time and time again within Amethyst's mind.

Considerably upset with the return of the memory of their brief exchange, Amethyst dropped the small shirt to her lap, her hand moving to her temple in an unconscious gesture she used when disturbed. There was no doubt in her mind that Damien would find someone sooner or later with whom he would wish to replace her. In his most violently loving moments he had never spoken of love . . . merely his desire to possess her physically. Subconsciously wincing at the picture of Merrell Bristol's face when Damien had so coolly turned his back on her, Amethyst realized that her time, too, would come. But would he be able to turn his back on his child? Somehow, she could not believe the abandoned boy inside the grown, handsome man Damien had become could reject his own child. What then? For it was with a rigid, unfaltering certainty that Amethyst realized despite the manner of its conception, she could never give up her child.

But time was passing with frightening speed, and she was still helpless against whatever plan Damien had devised for her future. Carefully allowing her all manner of luxury without the opportunity to handle money at any time, Damien had made certain she was unable to gather even the smallest sum so she might form a responsible plan to escape. And striking an even sharper blow was Amethyst's realization that even had she the resources, she would be unable to make the break. Pregnant with his child, she had nowhere to go and no one to help her in this large country of her birth where she was still a stranger. A deep trembling beginning inside her, Amethyst had also to admit to the greatest obstacle to her escape. The magic . . . Damien's obeah was as strong as ever, holding her with him more securely than iron shackles. His glance had not lost its power over her emotions, his touch still faultlessly capable of raising her past reasonable thought, his loving attentions binding her to him with the desire he stirred so unerringly within her. Oh, she was a weak fool! Unable to break from his loving prison, she would have to wait until he released her, and most chilling of all was her conviction that the time was not many months away.

In an effort to shake off her somber thoughts, Amethyst rose to her feet. It was her usual day to visit the bookseller, and she could do well with the diversion. Inactivity was beginning to make her despondent, and she would not submit to the debilitating emotion. A small wave of sadness slipping over her, she longed sorely for the comfort of Tillie's presence. Mrs. Dobbs, while courteous and efficient, managed to keep a discreet distance from the woman she so obviously considered past redemption. Harriet remained almost invisible in the household, and Mary, endlessly cheerful and attentive to her smallest wish, had not the necessary maturity to fill her need. Only in Millicent Strathmore had Amethyst sensed sympathetic understanding and a generous heart, but the woman's eyes had looked on Damien with a fondness that eliminated her unequivocally as an ally and confidant. No, she would have to go on maintaining her own good counsel. She was entirely on her own now and could lean on no one for moral support.

Within the hour, Amethyst's carriage was pulling up in front of Bell's Bookseller. Carefully gathering her light cape around her, Amethyst waited for Arthur's hand in assisting her down from the carriage. His small eyes smiling warmly into her face, he said softly, "I'll wait outside the door, Miss Amethyst, in case you should need me."

Touched by his concern, which she sensed went past the limits of duty to a sincere affection, Amethyst smiled a warm, "Thank you, Arthur," before turning to enter the store.

Nodding a short greeting to the proprietor, Amethyst moved quickly to the selection of tunebooks, her fingers moving efficiently through the stack in an effort to find any new selections available, but she was disappointed. The shop was stuffy, her cape too heavy for the warming May day, and Amethyst adjusted the closure. She still had not gained the courage to show herself completely in public in her obvious condition. Telling herself that her blossoming figure was indiscernible within the folds of her cape, she had managed to shop with a minimum of self-consciousness, but she was aware that the time was fast approaching when she would either have to sport her condition openly or spend the remainder of her pregnancy in hiding. But she would face that problem another day. For today she would bear discomfort for the sake of pride.

But for all her good intentions, Amethyst had only been in the rear of the store for a few minutes when her discomfort became so acute that she could no longer bear the weight of the cape against her shoulders. A furtive glance in the general area showed her to be hidden behind the bookshelves and quickly shedding her cape, Amethyst resumed her rapt perusal of the titles available. If she did not have any success here, she had tentatively decided to visit another Philadelphia dealer, Robert

Aitken, whom she had heard was handling the tunebooks of the singing master, Andrew Law, for his school on Chestnut Street. At any rate, she . . .

"Amethyst."

The deep, lightly accented voice of Armand Beauchamps startled Amethyst from her thoughts, bringing a flush of pleasure to her countenance as her head snapped up to his darkly handsome face.

"Armand!" Reaching out spontaneously, she continued with obvious sincerity, "Oh, I'm so happy to see you again, Armand. I so regretted the violent conclusion of our last meeting. I can only apologize for Damien's actions . . ."

"*Cela suffit*, ma cherie. That night is in the past and better forgotten. I hold no ill feelings toward Monsieur Straith for his actions, for had I been he, I fear my reaction would have been similar. You are obviously very dear to him . . ."

"Damien is very possessive, Armand, but it is his own nature that stimulates this quality rather than his particular feelings for me."

His dark eyes assessing, Armand responded thoughtfully, "I think you misjudge Monsieur Straith, but at any rate, this discussion was not the reason for my appearance here today. Rather, I came to ascertain if you are well and happy, for I knew little peace . . ."

Startled, Amethyst interrupted thoughtlessly, "But how did you know I would be here, Armand?"

"I have been away on business in New York for the past two months, cherie, but you have not been far from my thoughts during that time. I must confess to trying several desperate means of purging you from my mind, all of which were ineffective once my mind was again clear and able to function rationally. It is ironic, is it not, cherie, that while I have loved many women with my body, I have loved none of them with my heart. And now that I find the one with whom I can find total fulfillment, she belongs to another..."

"Armand..." Her eyes misting lightly, Amethyst could do no more than raise her glance wordlessly to his, inadvertently fanning the desire Armand struggled so desperately to overcome. Taking the small hand raised tentatively in his direction, Armand raised it to his lips, the smoothness of her skin sending a wave of frustrated pain through his body. Turning the palm to his lips, he kissed it tenderly, lingeringly, his gaze moving to her vulnerable mouth as he exerted a supreme effort at control.

"Ah, cherie," Armand's deep voice was husky, "you do not know what you do to me with your eyes like purple violets drawing me ever closer to you..." Still holding fast to her hand, Armand reached out to run a tentative caress along the black shining curls, his hand slipping to her narrow shoulder in a quick caress.

Suddenly conscious of her appearance, Amethyst's hand moved to her stomach in a futile effort to hide the small roundness, her eyes dropping from his with embarrassment.

Within moments Armand's hand was on her chin, raising it so she again met his eyes. "Cherie, there is no need for this discomfort between us. I do not know the circumstances which resulted in your carrying Monsieur Straith's child, and I do not wish to know. My only wish is to determine that you are safe and well treated. Now that I have seen you, I can rest, knowing that you did not suffer unduly by my foolish actions the night of the ball."

"No, Armand. Damien has been very kind."

"But he has not yet married you, cherie. Does he intend to allow..."

"Please, Armand!" Her expression distraught, Amethyst interrupted softly, "I don't wish to discuss this matter."

His expression concerned, Armand said softly, "Ma petite, if I am able to help you in any way, please tell me. If it is your desire, I will take you away from this city today and keep you safely with me."

A sudden picture of William's fevered face flashing before her eyes, Amethyst gasped abruptly, "No! I . . . I could not. Such a step would be disastrous for both of us, and I have no desire to disrupt any more lives, Armand."

His expression tightening, Armand hesitated briefly before responding. "Surely, Amethyst, ma cherie, you do not believe I fear for myself because of the manner in which our last meeting ended, for I assure you . . ."

Raising her hand spontaneously to Armand's lips, Amethyst silenced his response. "Armand, please, say no more. There is no doubt in my mind as to your bravery or integrity, and I need no reassurance."

The touch of her fingers against his lips caused Armand to flinch, and not fully understanding his reaction, Amethyst withdrew her hand. "I must go now, Armand. Arthur is waiting outside and must have seen you enter. He will tell Damien . . ."

"He did not see me enter, ma petite, because I have been here waiting for you for the past hour."

"But how did you know . . ."

"I have made it my business to be kept aware of your activities, cherie. You usually come to Monsieur Bell's establishment on Tuesdays, do you not? In any case, it was worth the chance because I could no longer suffer my doubts about your welfare." Hesitating briefly, Armand allowed his eyes to roam freely over Amethyst, his intense perusal bringing a bright flush to her face as he appeared to memorize each detail of her appearance, his eyes lingering for a few brief moments on her protruding stomach before returning to meet her eyes. His expression tight, he said softly, "I envy Monsieur Straith, Amethyst. I envy him the child you carry and his hold on you. And I curse the fate that brought you to me when it was already too late to make you mine."

Her eyes misting at the suspicious brightness in Armand's intense glance, Amethyst's voice was a husky whisper, "It is a cruel fate, is it not, Armand . . . ?"

Suddenly stepping forward, Armand took her unexpectedly into his arms, his mouth moving to cover her appealing lips. His arms tightening convulsively around her, Armand held her breathlessly tight, his searching mouth separating her lips for a brief, brilliant taste of the sweetness forbidden him. He was trembling visibly as he withdrew, his face tortured as he whispered shakily, "This will do neither of us any good, cherie, and unless you will come with me now, I must leave you before I am past control." Noting the manner in which Amethyst's eyes dropped from his glance, he whispered softly, *"Je comprends, ma cherie."*

Waiting until her eyes again met his, Armand continued, "But if you should ever need me, at any time, send word to my office. They will contact me and I will come to you." Taking her cape from the chair on which it lay, Armand slipped it over her shoulders.

"Au revoir, mon amour . . ."

His dark eyes following her as Amethyst made her way toward the front of the store, Armand whispered beneath his breath, "Au revoir, mon coeur . . . mon vie . . ."

Staring absentmindedly at the passing scenery as the carriage moved into the outskirts of Philadelphia, Amethyst dabbed lightly at her forehead with a small, lace-trimmed handkerchief. It was a ghastly hot and humid day, which Amethyst was beginning to learn was commonplace for the month of June in Philadelphia.

That reason alone was her strongest motive in finally relenting to join Hiram and Millicent Strathmore on the picnic they had arranged in a wooded spot outside the city. Extremely self-conscious of her burgeoning figure, she had all but retired from the public eye, passing her day in the confines of Damien's home. Having made good use of her time in the months previous, Amethyst had a good store of music and reading material on hand with which to fill her days, and had accumulated a fascinating array of tiny baby clothes which held a place of honor in a velvet-lined leather chest Damien had presented to her the month before.

Suddenly sensing someone's gaze upon her, Amethyst glanced to the seat beside her. His coat lying across from him in deference to the heat of the day, Damien sat casually in his shirtsleeves, the collar unbuttoned to almost mid-chest, exposing a portion of the fine mat of brown and gold hairs covering the broad expanse, and the wide column of his throat. He was studying her pensively, his strong, lightly tanned face unsmiling, his chin firm and unrelenting. A lock of heavy tawny hair had slipped to his forehead, and brushing it casually aside, he continued his perusal, a small smile lifting the corners of his generous lips to expose a trace of even, white teeth in bold contrast to sun-darkened skin. The very size of him, his broad expanse of shoulder, the strong arms and well muscled thigh lightly touching hers was overpowering within the limited space of the carriage, completely masculine and sensual. To her own disgust she realized she was still susceptible to the heat of his glance, her heart beginning to race as the cool, clear eyes moved over her face to settle for a few brief seconds on her parted lips.

Feeling a familiar dryness in her throat as Damien's head bent slowly toward her to cover her tempting lips with his own, Amethyst closed her eyes against the thrill of their touch, wishing with a futile desperation that she had the will to resist him.

His mouth finally drawing away from hers, Damien curved his hand around her cheek.

"You look beautiful today, darling. You're more beautiful every day."

Shooting a quick glance to the extended rise of her stomach, Amethyst scoffed lightly, "Impossible!"

Giving a small grunt of amusement, Damien allowed his hand to rest against the sizable protrusion, his grin growing as the child beneath stirred restlessly.

"My son does not realize the very elegant quarters he presently occupies."

A small smile her only response, Amethyst returned her attention to the passing scenery, content to allow her mind to wander for the duration of the journey.

Unwilling to withdraw his eyes from her person, Damien allowed them the luxury of moving slowly over Amethyst's appealing presence. Still slender as a reed except for the obvious rounding that preceded her, Amethyst was a ray of sunshine in her bright yellow gown, the graceful rise of her shoulders and neck, and the high delicate cheekbones displayed to greatest advantage by the upswept coiffure she had adopted for the humid summer days. An ample amount of bosom swelled atop the daring decolletage, the soft, white flesh tempting him unmercifully as it bobbed to the jolting movement of the carriage. Amused at his own reaction, Damien could not suppress the smile tugging at the corners of his mouth. This young woman need do nothing more than sit beside him to stir his desire. Who would have believed that Damien Straith would find a woman six months gone with child so fascinating that he could not tear his eyes from her? But this was not just any child . . . this was his child. And this was not just any woman . . . this was Amethyst. And soon she would be his wife. She had resisted him long and hard, refusing to relent to his demands that they marry, but when the child was born, she would no longer hold out against him. She would not allow their son to be called bastard, and by that time she would be secure in his love. For certainly he had done everything possible to demonstrate his love for her . . . everything short of saying the words. But he knew instinctively a small core of resentment remained, making him hesitant to speak the words his mind shouted over and over again . . . "I love you, Amethyst, my darling." Far better that he prove his love, a day at a time, until her resistance deteriorated and disappeared completely.

But was there ever hair more black and shining than Amethyst's, or curls that danced more gracefully even when confined in that upswept position? And were there eyes more lavender, more compelling than hers, with lashes so long that they almost touched her brow? And her skin . . . white and flawless; her nose, short and straight, the line perfect; the fleeting dimple in her cheek; and her mouth . . . Lord, the sweetness of it . . . the glory deep enough to drown within it; and the delicate grace of her body . . . the sweet comfort as it welcomed him, took him in. With delight he watched the gradual widening of her proportions, knowing she kept his child safe within her while he grew and prepared to make his entrance into the world. God, he loved her . . . had all he could do to keep from taking her into his arms here and now and proving in the way he knew best just how much she really meant to him. The mere thought causing his body to swell uncomfortably, Damien attempted to adjust his position, his squirming causing Amethyst to turn an inquiring glance in his direction. The tight fawn britches did little to disguise his momentary distress, and almost immediately discerning the reason for his movement, a deep flush covered

Amethyst's face as she gasped softly, "Damien!"

Taking her small hand to rest it intimately against the offending bulge, Damien whispered in response, "You need do nothing other than allow me to look at you to raise my desire, darling. You are indeed fortunate today that there will be others present at our picnic or you would find your day spent in a banquet of an entirely different sort, I fear."

Her hand warm against the palpitating bulge, Amethyst's expression was disbelieving. "Damien, you are insatiable! Only this morning . . ."

Her face staining an even darker color as her words dwindled off to be completed by Damien himself, ". . . only this morning I made love to you . . . held you in my arms until we were both spent and exhausted. How could I want you again so soon? The answer is simple, Amethyst. I never stop wanting you . . . I never will, darling . . . never . . ."

His glance lingering for a few moments longer on her soft lips, he shook his head firmly, removing the soft hand from his body with supreme determination. "Enough of this now. We'll be at the appointed spot in a few minutes, and I don't wish to suffer the embarrassment of arriving at full tilt!"

Laughing spontaneously, Amethyst turned her amused glance up to his. "Yes, we would be a good pair, wouldn't we, Damien? Me at full bulge and you at full tilt!"

His face suddenly serious, Damien's voice was a husky whisper as his strangely translucent eyes looked into hers, "Yes, darling, we are a good pair . . . a far better pair than you truly realize."

Arriving a few minutes later in a wooded glade, Amethyst was relieved to feel the motion of the carriage finally coming to a halt. The journey had been long for such a humid day and she desperately needed to flex her tired and cramped muscles. Preceding her out the door of the carriage, Damien turned to help her to the ground, his broad frame hiding her view of the clearing until she had descended from the carriage. Startled to see several groups of people clustered in different spots in the shade, Amethyst turned her angry expression toward Damien.

"You deliberately misled me, Damien! You told me Hiram and Millicent were arranging for a picnic. You made no mention of other guests being present!"

"And would you have come if you knew there would be other guests present?"

"Certainly not!"

"Then I'm glad I didn't tell you!"

Biting her lips, Amethyst blinked back the tears filling her huge, violet eyes as she whispered hoarsely, "Why . . . why do you wish to make a public spectacle of me, Damien?"

His face suddenly serious, Damien whispered in return, "Darling, did it never occur to you that I'm proud you carry my child?"

Suddenly interrupted by the approach of Millicent and Hiram Strathmore, Damien stepped forward to shake the hand of the tall, gray-haired gentleman who greeted him warmly. Quick to notice Amethyst's pallor, Millicent inquired quietly, "Are you well, Amethyst? Was the trip too much for you?"

"No, I'm fine." Turning to acknowledge Hiram's greeting, Amethyst was startled to find herself scooped into a brief, emphatic hug against Hiram Strathmore's tall, wiry frame. Releasing her a moment later, he bent his weather-beaten face toward hers, his tan eyes sparkling merrily. "Age grants a man certain privileges, Amethyst, and I'm the first to take advantage of them."

Turning to slip his arm around the lovely gray-haired woman who watched him with an amused smile, he said softly, "Now that these two have finally arrived, Millie, we can feed our hungry guests."

With a smile Hiram and Millicent Strathmore led them toward the waiting group in the manner of honored guests, the gesture not wasted on those who waited.

A few hours later, having eaten sparingly of the cold chicken and ham, the various assorted relishes prepared so well by the Strathmore staff and having sipped the wine chilled to perfection in the stream a few feet away, Amethyst sat quietly alone. She had been noticeably silent during the meal, her embarrassment acute. Unable to draw her into the conversation, Damien had finally given up the attempt, and allowed her to make her way to a spot removed from the group where she now sat, following her within a few minutes so she might not be alone with her thoughts.

Taking her hand, he reclined beside her, resting his back against the tree. "This place is a welcome change from the city, isn't it, Amethyst?"

Nodding silently, her glance still averted from his, Amethyst's thoughts ran riot inside her brain. It was a familiar guest list, among which were numbered Stephanie Morgan, Sarah Barlow, Martin Quell, Gerard Whitestone, and conspicuous by their absence, Merrell Bristol and Armand Beauchamps. But she was no longer comfortable in the presence of these people, despite the fact that Millicent and Hiram Strathmore were obviously putting the weight of their social prominence in favor of her acceptance. She now had no doubt that this was a scandal that would not easily be forgotten and would be quickly resumed when the time came for her to join the ranks of Damien's past loves. Her mind was racing frantically, her present embarrassing situation adding fuel to her anxiety over her poorly plotted plans for the future.

His light eyes assessing her silently, Damien felt a sinking sensation in his stomach. He had not expected this affair to have such a poor reaction on Amethyst.

Instead, he had expected that her natural vivacity would surface, allowing her to overcome the momentary embarrassment of her first appearance. Why it had been so important to him to have Amethyst appear by his side in public while in this condition was a mystery even to himself. Perhaps it was the fact that he wanted everyone to know when Amethyst and he did marry that it was not the pressure of her pregnancy that forced him to take the step. Or—damn—maybe it was just that he was so proud of her as she grew more and more lovely to him each day, the great bulge preceding her emphasizing her petite, deceptively fragile frame, giving her the appearance of a small, exceptionally lovely doll that belonged to him alone. Whatever his complicated reasoning, it all seemed pointless in the face of Amethyst's obvious suffering.

Irritated with himself, Damien rose to refill his glass, taking the few yards to Millicent's side in slow, measured steps. They would stay a little longer, and then go home. He had no wish to put Amethyst through any more discomfort than she had already suffered today.

Her light brows knit together in a frown, Millicent inquired softly, "Amethyst is not feeling well today, Damien?"

His glance direct, Damien answered the worried woman honestly. "It was a mistake to bring her here today, Millie. I had hoped . . . but no matter. Amethyst is uncomfortable."

His eyes moving to touch on the lonely figure seated a short distance away, Damien was not conscious of the loving glance he rested so openly on her person as he spoke the words racing across his mind. "I've been such a fool, Millicent. I've handled this whole thing badly from the start . . ."

"You do love her then, do you Damien?" Her voice soft, Millicent posed the question that had been uppermost in her mind.

There was no hesitation in his response. "Yes, I do. I hadn't thought myself capable of such a consuming emotion."

"And the child?"

"I'm anxious for the child, Millicent, anxious to see my son and even more anxious to have Amethyst to myself again." A small rueful laugh escaping his lips, he remarked with a shake of his head, "Selfish lout, am I not, Millicent? And the strangest part of all is that I'm aware of this shortcoming and am powerless to combat it. I intend to keep her with me at any expense..."

"Damien, dear," Millicent's tone was patient as she strove to understand the complicated man that was dear as a son to her, "if you love her, why do you not marry her... give her and your child your name?"

Finally turning to face her, Damien smiled, his expression rueful. "Am I such a marvelous catch that you could not conceive that perhaps Amethyst doesn't want to marry me?"

Her expression startled, disbelieving, Millicent said with a negative shake of her head, "But she carries your child, Damien. She lives in your house... sleeps in your bed! Why would she refuse to marry you?"

"I won't go into the rather shameful maneuvers I executed to bring Amethyst to me, Millie, nor the equally disgraceful tactics I employ to keep her. My hold is tenuous, but I had felt it grew stronger each day. But now..."

A movement from the group laughing heartily at the other end of the clearing caught Damien's eye, interrupting his flow of thought as Gerard Whitestone detached himself and began walking slowly in Amethyst's direction. Stopping abreast of her, he spoke softly, snapping Amethyst's attention to his face as he did.

"Am... Amethyst. May I b... be seated?" Gerard's familiar stammer startling her from her thoughts,

Amethyst turned in the young man's direction.

Awaiting her response, Gerard stood hesitantly, his pale blue eyes intent on her face.

"Gerard, it's extremely kind of you, but I shouldn't want to stigmatize you with my controversial company."

"St . . . stigmatize? You speak as if you are some sort of di . . . disease! Pl . . . please, Amethyst, may I sit?"

Flushing at her ungracious behavior, Amethyst replied softly, "Certainly, Gerard, I'm only too happy for your company."

His expression sincere, Gerard replied softly, "And I . . . I, yours, Amethyst. I have mi . . . missed you terribly these last few mo . . . months. These social affairs are de . . . decidedly b . . . boring without you."

Gerard's words balm to her troubled spirit, Amethyst smiled, her heart going out to the shy young man. "Gerard, you're such a pleasant fellow."

"And you have grown even more l . . . lovely since the last t . . . time I saw you, Amethyst."

"Well, you're right in one thing, anyway, Gerard. I have grown since the last time you saw me . . ." Her face flushing at her own quip, Amethyst laughed at Gerard's startled expression the moment before he too began to laugh at her outrageous remark.

Encouraged by her outspoken treatment of her condition, Gerard inquired softly, "When will you have the ch . . . child, Amethyst?"

"In September. I'm afraid I've three more months of growing yet, if that seems possible!"

His eyes dropping from hers, Gerard said softly, "Damien is a v . . . very lucky m . . . man. I en . . . envy him."

Reaching forward to place a slender hand on his arm, Amethyst said quietly, "Gerard, you're a dear man, but there are many who would disagree with you. I've already been accused of being foolish and conniving, not to speak of the many who no doubt consider me downright immoral."

His youthful, unlined face flushing with anger, Gerard spat with uncharacteristic anger, "No one w . . . would d . . . dare speak those words in m . . . my p . . . presence, Amethyst!"

Unreasonably grateful for Gerard's defense, Amethyst's eyes filled with tears, and swallowing hard, she blinked away her momentary weakness to say with a bright voice, "Well, enough discussion of this sorry business, Gerard. Tell me, what have you been doing with yourself these past months? Have you been to Rickett's Circus in recent weeks? I understand the equestrian acts are superb."

Months of reading had kept Amethyst abreast of current entertainments as well as the political climate, and anxious to speak with someone who may have actually observed the renowned equestrians who had recently performed in the tavern across from Congress Hall, she waited anxiously for Gerard's response, aware of his intense interest in such events.

His own expression brightening, Gerard replied with suppressed pleasure, "As a matter of fact, I h . . . have, Amethyst, and they were truly m . . . magnificent, the m . . . most outstanding of them all b . . . being . . ."

A familiar voice suddenly interrupted his words, snapping both heads up to Martin Quell's hesitant expression as he repeated his polite query, "May I join you, Amethyst?"

"Oh, bother!" Gerard snapped tightly. "Must we always be p . . . pestered by this t . . . tag-along?"

Startled by Gerard's outburst, Amethyst declared in a laughing tone, "Gerard! It isn't like you to be unkind!"

"Perhaps so," Gerard mumbled almost inaudibly, ". . . b . . . but I do so t . . . tire of being interrupted b . . . by this t . . . tactless fellow. And I had th . . .

thought to have y . . . you to myself for a short t . . . time, Amethyst." Turning abruptly without waiting for her response, Gerard directed his next comment to the hapless Martin Quell. "Well, do s . . . sit d . . . down, will you?"

Intensely amused by the two old opponents who had returned to battle for her attention, Amethyst's smile widened, unaware of Damien's relieved expression as he viewed the scene from across the glade.

Turning to smile into Millicent Strathmore's surprised expression, Damien said softly, "Gerard Whitestone is a rather agreeable fellow, is he not, Millie?"

"Yes, I have always thought so, Damien, but there was a time when I thought you disagreed quite violently with that opinion."

Suddenly serious, Damien responded quietly, "Neither Gerard nor Martin are threats to me, Millie, and I'm happy they have chosen to ignore the outcast status Amethyst had fostered upon herself. No, the only true threats to my claim on Amethyst are not present here today. And you may rest assured, were they present, I wouldn't be standing here making idle conversation with you right now!"

"And what are you two whispering about so confidentially, Damien, my good fellow? Has my wife finally taken the opportunity to ply you with the many questions I could see buzzing around her pretty little head?" Hiram walked toward them, smiling pleasantly.

"No, she has not. Do you suppose she has missed her chance, Hiram?"

"Not if I know my wife, she hasn't," Hiram said affectionately, slipping his arm around the still narrow waist. Then turning to face Damien squarely, Hiram said without equivocation, "You are a lucky man, Damien. Amethyst is beautiful, intelligent, vivacious and she feels damn good even in this old man's arms. She'll give you bright, handsome children, and you're a damned fool if you let her slip out of your hands. She's a true jewel. Marry the girl, damn it!"

Unable to suppress a laugh at his mentor's gruff command, Damien smiled, turning to look again at Amethyst's happily flushed expression as she supervised the friendly squabbling of the two vying for her attention. "You may rest assured, sir, that is the very first order of business on my mind. I don't intend to allow Amethyst to get away from me."

It was almost dark when Damien's carriage was again moving in the direction of Philadelphia. Her expression that of happy contentment, Amethyst was relaxed against the seat, her eyes closed, her head rolling easily with the movement of the coach. Grateful beyond words to Gerard and Martin for their attentions to Amethyst, and to Stephanie Morgan's kindness in making a point of joining the happy threesome so she might lend her support to the brave, pregnant girl, Damien made a mental note to remember to send Stephanie flowers the following day. The picnic had turned out well. Amethyst was relaxed and easy in his presence, her smile quick and spontaneous, a reflection of her state of mind, and Damien was endlessly relieved. The night had turned unexpectedly cooler, and leaning forward, Damien pressed a light kiss against Amethyst's lips before slipping his arm around her to draw her against his chest. Smiling benevolently as her sleepy eyes opened inquiringly, Damien whispered against her cheek, "Rest now, darling. I'll wake you when we arrive home."

Her heavy eyelids dropping obediently, Amethyst relaxed against his chest as Damien held her gently, possessively against him.

* * *

The torrid nightmare of Philadelphia in July with its grueling heat and humidity was taking its toll. Accustomed to the tropical climate of Jamaica, Amethyst had not expected to feel the heat so intensely, but her ponderous body in the seventh month of pregnancy seemed to hold the heat to the point of stifling her. Taking to spending long hours each day soaking in a cool bath, Amethyst found her defenses against the climate practically nil. Becoming accustomed to coming home in the middle of the day to the sight of his lovely, pregnant mistress asleep in the small, copper tub, her head resting against the high back as lavender scented water lapped gently at her full breasts, Damien was still moved to tenderness each time by her defenselessness. Time and time again he had lifted her gently from the cool water to wrap her dripping body in the light coverlet on the bed in the hope that her restful sleep would continue.

Her stomach greatly distended, Amethyst was uncomfortable in all reclining positions, and rarely slept through the night without waking. Her lagging energy was reflected in her lack of appetite and she had begun losing weight, her face and frame thinning considerably as the mighty protrusion in front her continued to grow. No longer able to restrain his fears for her health, Damien accompanied her on her visit to Dr. Morgan, only to sit in angry frustration as the doctor pronounced Amethyst healthy, and recommended she get more sleep and eat more regularly.

Thoroughly disgusted, Damien worriedly surveyed Amethyst's pale face as the carriage returned home through the stifling heat of the Philadelphia streets. Striving to present a strong facade, Amethyst smiled in his direction, the brave effort not fooling Damien for a minute as he noted her rapidly paling color and the heaviness of the black-fringed lids that drooped weakly over her glorious eyes.

Moving to the door of the carriage the moment it stopped in front of their residence, Damien turned to scoop Amethyst into his arms, ignoring her feeble protests as he lifted her from the carriage and walked quickly up the front steps. Barking gruff orders over his shoulder to Mrs. Dobbs as he moved quickly up the steps to their room, Damien kicked open the door and carried Amethyst to the bed. Laying her gently on her side, Damien began immediately to unbutton her dress.

Too weak to make a stronger protest, Amethyst said quietly, "Damien, it really isn't necessary for you to assist me. Mary will take care of my needs."

Angry and frustrated with events over which he had no control, Damien said through clenched teeth, "Kindly be quiet, Amethyst, and save your breath. I don't intend leaving for my appointment until I know you're fully recovered."

"But nothing is wrong, Damien. I was merely feeling the heat and . . ."

Turning her back to face him, Damien said in a low, controlled voice, "I do not intend leaving here, Amethyst, until your glance is again clear and you are completely comfortable."

A small smile crossing her lips, Amethyst mumbled softly, "Damien, your appointment may tire of waiting several months, I'm afraid . . ."

His stern expression softening, Damien hesitated a moment before lowering his head to touch her lips lightly with his own. "You're such a clever little chit, aren't you, darling?" he whispered, moments before turning her firmly on her side and continuing to unbutton her dress.

Within moments she was undressed to her chemise, her legs bared of the silk stockings that had seemed to encase them in warmth, her delicate limbs exposed to the pitiful breeze that moved through the bedroom window. Smiling gratefully, Amethyst was about to speak when a clunking sound at the door drew both their eyes to Mary as she struggled with the weight of two large buckets of water. Quickly pushing aside the screen in the corner of the room, Damien took the buckets from Mary's hands and emptied them into the copper tub. Without a word, Mary took the empty pails back and walked hastily through the doorway to fill them again, in a routine that had been repeated time and time again during the last month.

Her brows drawing together in a frown, Amethyst mumbled in a barely audible whisper, "I've become a terrible nuisance in this household, I fear. Poor Mary has been running herself ragged in response to my needs."

Turning, Damien said sharply, "Damn Mary! I don't give a hoot how hard she has been working! She's well paid for her services and will do well to cater to you when you're not well!"

Her face showing the first sign of color as she flushed at his remark, Amethyst replied with a trace of her old hauteur, "But I'm not ill, and I *do* care about Mary!"

The appearance of the self-same personage at the door with two more buckets of water forestalling her continued reply, Amethyst waited until the process had been repeated and Mary had again left the room before continuing, ". . . and I will not have everyone treating me like an invalid just because of a few weak spells."

Reaching the bed in a few brief strides, Damien knelt beside her, his broad hands cupping her face gently as he spoke. "Amethyst, darling, I will make this point clear to you once and for all. I care about no one but you. *You* are the uppermost thought on my mind each day, and I will not allow you to suffer one moment's discomfort that I can possibly spare you. So, darling," he whispered, a small smile softening the harshness of his words as he continued to stroke her cheek, ". . . do not speak to me of others when I can see only you . . . can think only of you . . ."

Another sound at the doorway turned Damien's head in its direction as Mary again moved toward the tub with the heavy buckets, and smiling despite himself, he said gently, "Mary, that will be adequate. I'll ring the bell should I feel the need for more water."

Nodding silently as she emptied the buckets into the tub, Mary moved back through the doorway, closing the door quietly behind her.

Quickly stripping off his shirt, Damien turned to lift the hem of Amethyst's chemise.

Moving awkwardly, Amethyst struggled to complete the task herself, mumbling under her breath, "I can do that, Damien."

Waiting only a moment as Amethyst continued her attempt to right herself on the bed without his help, Damien finally muttered under his breath, "Damn it all, Amethyst!" Gently raising her to a sitting position, he pulled the chemise over her head and threw it on the chair. Turning, he lifted her swiftly into his arms.

"Damien!" Her emphatic protest, showing the first spark of spirit within the last hour, brought a wide smile to Damien's face as he continued to hold her in his arms with a pleased expression.

"I said I could undress myself, and I won't have you treating me like a child!"

His clear eyes looking directly into hers, Damien said softly, "You are mine, Amethyst. Mine to do with as I will, and I will care for you and love you with or without your consent, darling. And right now," advancing toward the tub, his voice became more forceful as he neared the copper convenience, "and now I'm going to bathe you!"

Lowering her gently into the cool water, Damien saw the short flash of annoyance that moved across Amethyst's face as she insisted quietly, "I can bathe myself, thank you."

Startled by a short bark of laughter, Amethyst raised her eyes to Damien's amused expression as he kneeled beside the tub.

"Alright, my lady." His tone reflecting almost complete surrender, he said softly, "I'll yield. But I fully intend to stay right here so I may enjoy the result of your labors. After all, I can't allow you to spoil all my fun, darling."

Looking directly into his face for long seconds, Amethyst suddenly raised her eyes in an expression of resignation, shaking her head simultaneously as she grumbled under her breath, "Is it any wonder that I have lost all modesty?"

Pleased to see her spirit returning, Damien bent to whisper softly into her ear, "Yes, darling, but look at all you have gained . . ."

Refusing to respond, Amethyst deliberately picked up the cloth and began soaping her arm, her head firmly diverted, to Damien's deep amusement.

"Miss Amethyst . . . Miss Amethyst."

The sound of Mary's voice cut into her unscheduled nap. Blinking rapidly, Amethyst finally awakened enough to respond.

"What is it, Mary? Is something wrong?"

"No, but a number of boxes have been delivered from Madame duMaurier and I wanted to know if you wanted me to bring them in to you."

Shaking her head to clear her thoughts, Amethyst mumbled under her breath, "I don't remember ordering anything from Madame . . ." and suddenly realizing

Mary still awaited her response, she raised her voice. "Yes, Mary, please bring them in."

Laboriously pulling herself to a sitting position, Amethyst adjusted her gown, raising her eyes to stare open-mouthed as Mary brought in four large boxes and placed them on the chaise. Smiling, she turned back toward the door, her round face cheerful. "I'll get the rest of them, Miss Amethyst."

"The rest of them!"

Slipping her small feet into the slippers beside her bed, Amethyst walked slowly to the chaise, stopping to pick up a pair of scissors from the dressing table as she did. Snipping the cord efficiently, Amethyst raised the lid and lifted the tissue, her eyes widening at the magnificent pink gown lying beneath. Lifting it gingerly from the box, she ran her eyes over the sheer, delicate fabric, noticing immediately that the garment was cut to her former proportions, the waist small and fitted.

Dropping it back inside the box, Amethyst uncovered the second, the third, and then the fourth boxes, finding in each a similar airy confection in various pastels and styles, all of which were cut in her former size.

"What's all this about?" Mumbling under her breath as Mary entered carrying another batch of boxes, Amethyst shook her head, about to mutter another surprised exclamation as Damien walked through the doorway behind Mary.

"I see you've opened some of the boxes already. How do you like the frocks, Amethyst?"

"They're lovely, Damien, but you must realize that none of them will fit me."

Laughing at her confused expression, Damien bent to brush her lips with his. "Not now, of course, but after you've had the child they should fit very well. I asked Madame duMaurier to use her expertise in judging just how much of that bulge will remain, and, as you can see, she feels you'll lose most of it when the child is delivered."

"But Damien, I will have the child in September. These fabrics are really not suited to fall weather, you know." Shaking her head again, Amethyst said softly, "I really don't know what Madame must have been thinking to make up so extensive a collection of gowns in fabrics so unsuited to the fall climate."

"She probably thought you would be spending fall in Jamaica, darling, because that's what I told her when I ordered your wardrobe."

"Jamaica! Damien, I don't understand." Her heart beginning to hammer rapidly, Amethyst's face paled. Was he already intending to send her home as soon as the child was born? Were these gowns a consolation gift to a dismissed mistress? What of their child? He hadn't mentioned the child was to leave with her . . .

Raising his hand to her pale cheek, Damien said softly, "What's wrong, darling? I thought you'd be happy to sail with me on the *Sally*'s next trip. I've already arranged to remain in Kingston for a few months so you may have the child there. Dr. Martens is a capable man and I thought you'd like to have Tillie with you when the time comes."

"You're taking me home to have my child, Damien?"

Wincing inwardly at her use of the word 'home,' Damien responded softly, "You know I must captain this next voyage of the *Sally*, Amethyst, and I couldn't leave you here when you've been feeling so poorly. You're more accustomed to the climate of Kingston, and will probably fare far better there until the child is born. We'll return to Philadelphia once danger of the storm season is past." A small smile flitting across his lips, Damien mumbled gruffly, "I don't intend risking the life of my son in a hurricane at sea."

Her eyes wide, almost disbelieving, Amethyst repeated softly, "I'll see Tillie again, Damien?"

"I'm sure she'll be waiting in your house on John's Lane Amethyst. The rent was paid a year in advance, and she's certain to have remained there. She . . ."

Not waiting for him to conclude his statement, Amethyst suddenly moved forward, reaching up to throw her arms around his neck in a tight embrace as she whispered huskily against his throat, "Thank you, Damien. Thank you. I've missed Tillie so . . . and longed to have her with me when the baby comes."

Feeling the wetness of tears against the open neck of his shirt, Damien moved Amethyst to wipe them carefully from her face. "Then it's settled. We sail next week. Now I suggest you go through those boxes carefully and determine if you will have everything necessary after the child is born. If I remember, your wardrobe was not particularly extensive, and I don't want the mother of my child inadequately attired for the duration of our stay."

Swallowing tightly, Amethyst merely bobbed her head in acquiescence, her eyes brimming with happy tears.

The smile dropping from his face as he entered the hallway, Damien could no longer ignore the voice nagging insistently at the back of his brain. "Is she truly so thrilled at the thought of seeing Tillie again, or is it the expectation of seeing William Sheridan as well that has put the light back in her eyes?" Whatever the case, he had no choice. He was committed to sailing on the *Sally* at the end of the month, and he could not bring himself to leave Amethyst in Philadelphia. At any rate, it mattered very little how great was Amethyst's anticipation of seeing Sheridan again. His own hold on her grew stronger every day, and once the child was born, she would be bound to him forever. No, he had nothing to fear . . . nothing . . .

"Topmen lay aloft and loose topsails!" Damien's commands barked through the speaking trumpet echoed over the ship, sending the topmen scampering up the shrouds and out onto the footropes hanging below the topsail yards. The weather was perfect to begin the voyage. A brilliant sun blazed from a clear blue sky, the intensity of its heat cut by the stiff offshore breeze. Deciding to go out to sea under jibs and topsails, Damien was anxious to set sails, for with the wind at their back, the *Sally* would make good time that day.

Eyes squinting against the bright morning sun, Damien carefully scrutinized his men as they deftly moved across the yards, using one hand to claw at the lines holding the sails furled, while hanging on with the other.

"Man the topsail sheets and halyards!" Damien's next command sent the men on deck racing to the sheets hanging from the corners of the sails to grasp the heavy rope, while others grasped the halyards running from the center of the yards through blocks to the deck below. Eyes raised, they awaited the next command.

"Throw off the buntlines, ease the clewlines!"

Watching carefully as the men aloft slackened the lines which kept the sails furled, Damien barked, "Sheet home!" signaling the men manning the sheets to haul down on them so that the corners of the sail would touch the end of the yard below.

"Run away with the topsail halyards!" In practiced precision the men manning halyards began walking aft, lifting the topsail yards a short distance and making the sails taut.

Thrilling to the bedlam of shouted orders and

mumbled curses as the crew responded to their captain's commands, the sound of canvas cracking in the wind and the stamp of dozens of feet as they followed through the breathtaking spectacle, Amethyst watched the sails fill firm and free, her heart singing in her breast, "I'm going home . . . I'm going home!"

Feeling cool and free for the first time in many months, Amethyst stood at the rail, her eyes fixed on the distant horizon. The ocean moved swiftly beneath the ship and a warm breeze lifted the sparkling black curls hanging loose down her back to stream out behind her as the sun and wind caressed her fair skin gently. They had been at sea for two weeks, during which Amethyst's energy and appetite had returned and the child kicked happily inside her. Slowly running her hand over the surface of the now mountainous bulge, Amethyst said a silent prayer that her child would be a girl, realizing her only hope lay in the possibility that she would have a daughter, for she knew with a deep certainty that she must make a move to free herself after the child was born. She could not allow herself to submit to her strange possession any longer and sacrifice the welfare of her child. No . . . she would not allow her child to grow up under the influence of a man who practiced obeah . . . used it recklessly to his advantage each time he was firmly opposed. She could only hope that Damien would be disappointed in a girl . . . would feel a daughter would be better off with her mother when they were no longer together.

Whatever Damien's plans now, she also could not believe his infatuation with her would continue. A new face among the many women who followed him with their eyes was sure to capture his attention sooner or later, when she was no longer new to him. She must not allow herself to believe that he would remain constant, no matter the creeping reality of her own growing desire that it could be so. No . . . she must keep in mind that he had never truly said he loved her, even now, when his desire for a son to bear his name caused him to nag relentlessly at her that they be married. Perhaps he was as possessed as she . . . as confused as she . . . but of one thing she was certain. She must get away after the child was born . . . she must . . .

Chapter 9

Trembling with excitement, Amethyst watched the matchless beauty of the island of Jamaica come into view. A scene from another time flitted across her mind as Kingston spread out before her eyes, the forests lush and beautiful behind the teeming waterfront scene. The echo of her mother's sweet voice sounded softly in her ears.

"We've arrived, Amethyst! No more frigid winters to shiver through here. It is always bright and warm in Jamaica, and our troupe will be welcome. We'll begin a new and better life here, darling. I'll be well all the time, and I'll be able to take good care of you. You'll see, darling . . . you'll see."

With blind confidence she had stepped down onto the dock that first time, walking slightly behind the group as her mother dragged her along to keep up. She remembered glancing back to see the tall captain at the rail, her hatred flaring for the ruthless man who had treated her with contempt for her "stupidity." How supremely grateful she had been to leave him behind, and turning, she had left no doubt as to the manner of her final farewell. Her mother and she no longer needed Captain Straith and would never need his services again.

Swallowing the lump in her throat that the memory evoked, Amethyst recounted sadly that Jamaica had not brought the Greers the bright future they had imagined when they first touched on the beautiful island. Patient and optimistic to the end, her mama had not lost faith in the good days to come for her only daughter. Her trembling hand moving subconsciously to the rise of her stomach, Amethyst thanked a merciful God that Marian Greer could not see her daughter now.

Before noon Amethyst was stepping down onto the docks of Kingston for the second time, her heart hammering in her chest as she advanced toward the open carriage Damien had waiting. Frowning at her obvious anxiety, Damien helped her carefully inside, following behind to sit beside her. Within moments they were moving down familiar streets, finally turning onto John's Lane where Amethyst's eyes became fixed on the house midway down the street, not to budge from the unimpressive structure until the carriage pulled up before it. Oblivious to Damien's worried expression as she had been to his light conversation in the carriage, Amethyst accepted his hand to step down laboriously onto the cobbled walk. Approaching the front door with a trepidation she could not conceal, Amethyst walked slowly up the two short steps, pausing a moment in front of the door before jerking it open abruptly and stepping inside.

Complete silence met her ears as black doe-shaped eyes blinked in disbelief the moment before a familiar woman's voice, rich in depth and husky with happiness said softly, "Amethyst . . . Tillie's child . . . Amethyst be home . . ."

Her eyes moving absentmindedly around the house in which she had lived for eight difficult but loving years, Amethyst allowed old memories to roll over her, the warmth of the heady experience stirring her deeply. Damien had returned to his ship to attend to the business of settling the *Sally* comfortably in port, relinquishing her into Tillie's care. Despite the fact that the preliminary peace treaty between Great Britain and her former American colonies had been signed, he had not wanted to risk using his American registry in the British port and had used instead the false papers that had served him so well when he had last docked in Kingston. Turning his glance to Tillie, he had been sure to emphasize that he would return in time for supper, and that he and Amethyst would use the same room they had shared before leaving Kingston. Leaving the house without any further word, Damien had left Amethyst the task of clarifying his plans for residence until after the baby's birth, although he had left no doubt in Tillie's mind as to the status of their relationship or his intentions to claim his child.

Staring thoughtfully at his strong, broad back as Damien disappeared through the doorway, Tillie had said quietly, "Him be strange man, Amethyst. You be fever in him blood, and him gowan hold onto you until that fever be gone. But that man not gowan give up him child . . . no . . . never. You think on that, Amethyst Greer, because him obeah be strong, too strong to fight by yourself!"

"Please, Tillie . . ." Beginning to feel the tension again building inside her, Amethyst had raised her hand to her temple in a weary gesture. "I've been over and over this in my mind without finding a solution. I don't want to discuss it now . . . please . . ."

Conscious of Amethyst's anxiety, Tillie had nodded her head in assent.

Appreciative of Tillie's consideration, Amethyst shot her a small, grateful smile. She was too exhausted to worry now. It was well into the afternoon and the time since her arrival had been spent in deep conversation with Tillie, during which she had related the details of the previous eight months while they were separated. Tillie's own halting narrative of the manner of her estrangement from Raymond had brought Amethyst to tears, and a creeping suspicion that a dark cloud hung over them all.

Her mother, dead at a young age, her own life shattered beyond repair, and now Tillie's meager chance at happiness destroyed at the whim of a black concubine. Even Damien, in his position of command, was tethered to a situation with which he was not truly satisfied. Oh, it would be so easy to submit to the temptation to marry Damien . . . become his wife so she would no longer bear the stigma of carrying an illegitimate child, but she did not trust Damien's obsession for her. It was unnatural, as was his omnipotent hold on her senses. Tillie's words echoed loudly in her ears, reinforcing her own fears. Once the child bore his name it would be too easy for Damien to take it from her by legal means, and Amethyst would not risk losing her child.

There was no solution, at least not one she could find with her head aching wearily and her slender ankles beginning to swell. Pulling herself forward in the soft, upholstered chair, Amethyst drew herself slowly to her feet. "I think I'll lie down for a little while, Tillie. I'm far more exhausted than I realized."

Unable to suppress a smile, Tillie watched as Amethyst raised her hand to the curve of her back, her head stretching upward gracefully like a small, purring kitten. Attired in a cool green gown Madame duMaurier had designed especially for the period during which she would be *"enceinte,"* Amethyst was lovelier than ever. A floating ruffle of the magnificently light, almost transparent material followed the deep, rounded curve of the neckline, and trimmed the short tight sleeves ending just above the elbow. The raised waist of the garment cupped her generous breasts, the skirt falling softly over her protruding stomach to end in another ruffle at the hemline that touched her ankles. Small flowers delicately embroidered in variegated shades of purple were scattered sparingly within the folds of the skirt, matching to perfection the amethyst clusters decorating each dainty earlobe and lying appealingly between the swells of her breasts on a fine gold chain. Obvious to Tillie's assessing glance was the fact that Captain Straith had more than adequately provided for Amethyst's needs, and judging from the chest of clothing accumulated for the unborn child, intended to do well by his offspring. Amethyst would do well to . . .

A small noise at the doorway the second before it opened turned Amethyst's and Tillie's eyes expectantly in its direction. Her startled gasp echoing within the silent room, Amethyst's eyes remained unmoving on the man silhouetted there, feeling the weight of his glance as it moved slowly, unbelievingly over her.

Moving abruptly toward her, William reached her side and pulled her into a tight embrace, his arms crushing her swollen body against him, his voice hushed and tortured in her ear.

"Amethyst, darling, what has he done to you?"

The myriad of emotions flooding over her left Amethyst speechless with its impact. Unable to form words past the tightness in her throat, Amethyst gave a small, broken sob that pulled William back to stare for a few silent seconds into her face. His head slowly descending, William covered the warm, trembling lips with his own, a low groan sounding deep inside him as his arms tightened in a crushing embrace. Abandoning herself to the familiar security of William's arms, Amethyst allowed William's kiss to deepen, her eyes closing at the familiar warmth it inspired; did not resist as he pulled her tighter and tighter until the wild pounding of his heart was so intermingled with her own that she could not distinguish between the frantic beats. Standing passively as he withdrew his mouth from hers, neither did she resist the warm kisses William showered on her face, hearing only distantly the deep throb of his voice as he whispered hoarsely, "Darling, my darling Amethyst. I knew you would come back. You're coming home to the plantation with me, now, before Straith can return. I'll have you safe first, out of his hands, before I come back to settle with him."

Reality finally beginning to penetrate her bemused state, Amethyst began to pull back from his arms, began to struggle in his binding embrace, her voice low and faltering as she mumbled almost incoherently, "William . . . no . . . we can't. I can't go with you . . ."

His expression suddenly stiffening, William said in a low, surprisingly even voice, "Yes, you'll come back with me, Amethyst. Damien Straith took you away from me when I was unable to protect you. Tillie told me about the tactics he employed to keep you from me. How could you believe him, darling? Obeah . . . black magic . . . you had always scorned those beliefs! You knew them to be what they are, merely ignorant superstitions! How could you allow him to use such poor reasoning to take you from me? And even if it were true . . ." His voice deepening into a hoarse whisper, William continued, "don't you know I would rather have died than allow you to buy my life at the price he asked?" His voice cracking on the final words, William pulled her tight against him once again. "Darling, it's been hell not knowing where you were, seeing you in his arms every time I closed my eyes, wondering if you were safe and well . . . if I would ever see you again."

"William, I can't go with you."

There was a moment's hesitation before William drew back again to direct his glance into Amethyst's tear-stained face. "You will come back with me, Amethyst. I'll accept no other answer."

Shaking her head vehemently, Amethyst mumbled indistinctly, "No . . . no . . ." Her voice growing more adamant, she again raised her glance to his. "No, I cannot. William, look at me! Within two or three weeks I shall bear Damien Straith's child! Certainly you cannot expect me to go to your home carrying another man's child! Your parents didn't approve of me before. Now they'll merely say I've proved them right. They'll . . ."

"To hell with my parents!" His youthful face flushed, William continued heatedly, "Do you think I'll allow them to rule my life . . . my decisions? I love you, Amethyst! I want you for my wife! My life has been one long misery without you, but I knew you would come back . . . I knew . . ."

"William, Damien brought me back to have the child in Jamaica. He hasn't released me and has not yet declared his intention to do so. But even should I be free, I would make one thing clear. I could never marry you now, William. It's too late."

"Too late! Are you insane? Straith has not married you and will never marry you. He'll use you until he has had his fill and then cast you aside as he has all the other women in his life! You know his reputation, Amethyst. Certainly you don't think . . ."

"William!" Unable to bear his disturbed ramblings a moment longer, Amethyst interrupted sharply, "I cannot marry you!"

Startled by the fierceness of her response, William was momentarily silent, the dawning of fear beginning to show in his eyes as he whispered in a faltering voice, "Amethyst . . . you could . . . you don't love *him?*"

Swallowing tightly, Amethyst shook her head. "No, William, love is a tender emotion . . . it could not be applied to the feelings Damien Straith stirs within me. I don't love him, and he doesn't love me. Rather, he is obsessed with me, a temporary obsession against which he is as helpless as am I against his power of obeah."

"Obeah! Amethyst, that's nonsense!"

"No, it isn't, William! I've seen the power of his black magic! I saw you writhing in the throes of a killing fever that fled your body almost to the hour that Damien Straith released you from its spell. And I know the power he exerts over my will . . ." Flushing brightly, Amethyst paused a brief moment, swallowing tightly before continuing, "There is but one thing that allows me to bear my subservience to his will, and that is the fact that he will tire of me as he has all his other mistresses. Were it not for that thought to console me, I would not be able to live with my subjugation . . . would find escape at any expense . . ."

His expression slowly hardening, William gazed silently into Amethyst's adamant expression, his own voice firm as he responded softly, "If that is the case, Amethyst . . . that you only understand force, then I have no other recourse but to . . ."

"Don't try it, Sheridan! Touch Amethyst again and you'll be a dead man!" Damien's low, warning growl snapped Amethyst's head in the other direction. His huge hands balled into tight fists, Damien stood in the doorway, his broad shoulders silently hunched forward, his tall powerful body tensed as if for attack, overwhelmingly threatening in his obvious fury. "She doesn't want to go with you, Sheridan. She wants to stay with me. You have it from her own lips that it is I whom she wants! It is my child she carries, and I will not give her up at any cost!"

"I will not forfeit my claim . . ."

Interrupting William before he could finish his statement, Amethyst said with deliberate harshness, the words tearing at her heart as they passed her lips, "You have no claim to forfeit, William. Whatever was between us is over. You will remain forever within my heart as a friend . . . and nothing more. Now, please go . . ."

"Amethyst . . ." William's youthful face was disbelieving, his voice filled with a pain that cut deeply into her own body. Swallowing tightly, Amethyst closed her ears against the pleading tone. She could not allow him to suffer again at Damien's hands.

"Please go, William."

Standing stiff and silent, William made no immediate response. Suddenly blinking, he said in a voice just above a whisper, "Amethyst . . . if you should ever need me, I'll always love you, darling . . ."

Turning abruptly, William walked to the doorway, striding through with an unyielding step that indicated if Damien had not stepped aside to allow his passage, the confrontation would have been immediate.

Within minutes, the sound of Nero's hooves racing away broke the heavy silence of the room. Instantly moving forward as Amethyst began to sway uncertainly, Damien scooped her into his arms, his body rejoicing as he held her against his chest with fierce possessiveness. His face strained, he looked into brilliant violet eyes that attempted to avoid his glance.

"You've had a long day, Amethyst. I think it would be best if you took a nap now. I'll awake you in time for supper."

Anxious to be free of his touch, Amethyst nodded silently as he carried her into the bedroom. Laying her gently on the bed, Damien stared for long moments into her face, his expression unreadable. Slowly lowering his mouth to hers, he kissed her long and deep in a kiss devoid of tenderness but calculated to demonstrate beyond doubt his complete possession. Standing, he turned and left the room without another word, his mind going over the conversation he had overheard as he closed the bedroom door firmly behind him. "So, only the thought that I'll soon tire of her allows her to bear my possession. Otherwise she would escape me at any cost." Well, it mattered not to him if Amethyst used that blatant misconception as a crutch. Let her believe what she wished and hold that thought in the back of her mind as the years passed by. He didn't give a bloody damn how he did it, just as long as he kept her with him. His words of love would be silent, or whispered only into her sleeping ears.

If need be, she would never know how much he really loved her.

Amethyst looked fondly at the curly-haired young woman sitting across from her, smiling patiently as she went into yet another description of the fellow that had been seated in the second box to the right of the stage at last night's performance. Sally Warren would never change! Despite her vigorous search, she still had not found the man of her dreams, and contemplated with extreme interest her future success. But although a bit empty-headed and promiscuous, she was a sweet girl who had made it a point to visit Amethyst twice since her return to Kingston, carrying news of the troupe to Amethyst's anxious ears. And news there was aplenty! With rumors so rampant that the anti-theater law in America would soon be repealed, David Douglass had turned the management of the American Company over to John Henry and Lewis Hallam, Jr. It seemed that Mr. Douglass's job as councilman had become so lucrative that he could not bring himself to give it up, especially since he expected to be rewarded with a judgeship in the near future. But the company was satisfied under the leadership of Hallam and Henry, especially Sally, who found the charming and handsome John Henry irresistible, and hoped he would soon run out of Storer sisters (of which there were three) whom he seemed to be taking in turns as his mistresses—although Sally had confidentially confided she was certain she would be able to break the chain if she were to make an honest effort.

"At any rate," Sally continued with a small giggle, "John intends to sail again for America in January to petition Congress to repeal that stupid law. If he is successful, we'll return as a troupe as soon as possible. It does sound exciting, doesn't it, Amethyst?"

"Ah, but that was a stupid remark, wasn't it? I mean, whatever do you care when the troupe sails to America? You're no longer in a position where you find it necessary to work for a living."

Giving Sally's bright face an assessing glance, Amethyst realized the remark was said without malice. Sally was, after all, quite envious of her present arrangement, and made no bones about expressing her envy.

"But I am interested nonetheless, Sally, and I do appreciate your bringing me the latest news of the troupe."

Almost as if she had not heard Amethyst's last statement, Sally said dreamily, "Imagine . . . there I was describing the most handsome man I had ever seen attend one of our performances and pointing him out to you, and all the time you knew him far better than I!" Her eyes moving hopefully to the doorway for the fifth time that afternoon, Sally said in a low tone, "You are the lucky one, you are, Amethyst Greer."

"Oh, yes, Sally," Amethyst replied, patting her stomach lightly, "I have really done well for myself. You would do well to pattern yourself after my success!"

Realizing Amethyst spoke with considerable sarcasm, Sally said in a low voice, "Well, just the same, I should consider myself lucky if I were carrying the baby of that great handsome brute and sitting in luxury with beautiful clothes and . . ."

"And a brilliant future ahead of me? Oh, yes, Sally, I am truly to be envied, aren't I?" Her face suddenly serious, Amethyst continued in a low tone, "You would do far better to find yourself a nice, honest boy who will take care of you than to keep searching for your Prince Charming."

"But, Amethyst! Searching is so much fun!" Giggling wildly, Sally turned her merry glance to Amethyst's serious expression, succeeding in drawing a smile from her in return at the sheer scandalousness of her remark.

Both turning at a sound at the doorway, Amethyst shook her head with futility at the flush of pleasure that heated Sally's light complexion when Damien strode through the doorway. The girl was an incorrigible flirt!

"Well, I see you have a guest today, darling." Bending forward, Damien pressed a lingering kiss on Amethyst's lips, turning to extend a short greeting to Sally. "Hello, Sally. It's good of you to take the time to call on Amethyst. She's not in condition to go out visiting these days."

Lowering himself to the couch beside Amethyst, he slid his arm around her shoulder in a possessive manner, his hand carelessly fondling a stray black curl that lay against her slender neck.

All but sighing as her eyes moved with obvious approval over his blatantly masculine appeal, Sally said lightly, "I was just telling Amethyst that the troupe may be returning to America soon. She seemed to find the possibility interesting."

Shooting Amethyst a sharp look, Damien was instantly engrossed in Sally's conversation, his intense regard bringing yet another flush to Sally's brightly painted cheeks. "Really? And what are the troupe's plans for the future? I find I'm as intrigued by the progress of the American Company as Amethyst."

"Well, once that nasty anti-theater law is repealed, our entire company will return as a troupe to America. John Henry will be managing the company with Lewis Hallam, and John said if Amethyst were to ask to be reinstated into the troupe this very day, he would not hesitate a minute in giving her back her former place. He was always very impressed by Amethyst's voice."

"Oh, I'm sure," Damien said dryly, brightening his smile considerably at Sally's hesitant expression, his hand tightening subconsciously on the black curl he fondled until Amethyst winced with the jerking movement. His attention full on Sally, he continued drawing her out. "And what else did he say, Sally?"

"Oh, just that Amethyst has grown to be a beautiful addition to the many beauties already numbered within the troupe..." Batting her eyelashes outrageously, Sally hesitated before continuing, "And that Amethyst's father was a great actor with a fine voice, and she must have inherited her talent from him."

"Thank you, Sally." Sincerely appreciative of the compliment to her father, Amethyst smiled warmly, her eyes filling with unexpected tears. Annoyed with herself, Amethyst brushed away the tear that slid down her cheek. What was wrong with her lately? Everything seemed to move her to tears!

Noting her sudden emotional state, Damien said lightly, "I think Amethyst is getting a little weary now, Sally, and should get some rest. I do appreciate your calling." Urging her lightly to her feet, Damien escorted the startled Sally to the door, managing to raise another blush as he said in a manner meant to charm, "You are a dear girl, Sally. Do come again."

Within minutes a beaming Sally was making her way home, her mind filled with the dashing Captain Straith. Turning again toward Amethyst, Damien surveyed her silently for a few minutes, his eyes softly assessing. The soft swells of her breasts, generously exposed in the deep, square-cut neckline of her light blue organdy gown heaved in a lightly agitated manner as she regarded him intently. Black ringlets touching the graceful curve of her neck; wide, solemn eyes appearing a true, brilliant blue in reflection of her dress; she was so unbelievingly and unconsciously lovely that Damien felt a tightness in his throat just to look at her. Walking slowly to her side, he knelt beside the couch. Cupping her small face between his two palms, he kissed her gently on the mouth, his kiss slow and lingering. Lowering his head, he kissed the trembling breasts, the velvet softness of her skin sending a thrilling jolt through his veins. Lowering his head even further, he kissed the great protrusion beneath, a smile coming to his lips as his child moved actively beneath them.

Lifting his face to hers once again, Damien said softly, "Do you suppose our son will have your great violet eyes, Amethyst? Or your shining black hair?"

Seeming startled by his unexpected question, Amethyst replied softly, "You're so certain I carry your son, Damien? It may be a girl."

"You carry my son."

"At any rate, Damien," Amethyst said with a small catch in her voice, "I believe we will know soon."

His expression suddenly tense, Damien said hoarsely, "What do you mean?"

"I think the child is preparing to be born."

Suddenly whitening under his tan, Damien rose abruptly to his feet. "Tillie!" The sharpness of his tone brought the anxious mulatto from the kitchen at a run. Nodding to her unspoken question, Damien said softly, "Send for Dr. Martens immediately. Amethyst's time has come."

Moving quickly toward the front door, Tillie did not bother to answer his soft command. Leaning over, Damien scooped Amethyst into his arms in a quick movement and started toward the bedroom door.

"Damien, you needn't carry me. I've only had a few twinges. I'm quite able to walk and would probably benefit from the exercise."

His expression deadly serious, Damien responded softly, "Perhaps that's true, darling, but it gives me pleasure to hold you in my arms and I'm of a mood to indulge myself."

Without another word, he walked into the bedroom and lay her gently on the bed. Kneeling beside her he touched her cheek tenderly. Seeing she winced with another pain, Damien said encouragingly, "Dr. Martens will be here soon."

The hand that stroked her brow was shaking. Startled, Amethyst looked to Damien's face to see it a ghastly white beneath the surface tan as a small muscle jumped in his jaw. Pouring some water from the pitcher beside the bed into the small basin that sat beside it, Damien dipped the cloth into the cool water and turned to gently wipe the small beads of perspiration that had appeared on her forehead. His voice casual, he pat the refreshing coolness against her cheek, "Oh, by the way, I hope John Henry is not counting on your return to the troupe after our child is born, because he'll be disappointed, I'm afraid. You'll not go back to the theater, Amethyst. He shall have to be content with the Storer sisters, or perhaps the very willing Sally Warren, because . . ."

Angrily staying his hand, Amethyst gasped through another painful spasm, "Damien, John Henry is interested merely in my talent. He has no interest in me as . . ."

Continuing as if she was not speaking, Damien directed the conclusion of his remark into her angry eyes, ". . . because you belong to me, Amethyst, and will never belong to another while there is a breath in my body."

The following hours were vague and confused in Amethyst's mind. The brief, occasional spasms increased in frequency and duration as the day crawled endlessly by, as the night wore on, promising to tear her apart with their intensity. His austere countenance unsmiling, Dr. Martens remained at Amethyst's side during the vigil, his words short but encouraging.

Grasping for Tillie's hand as another spasm continued its grueling course, sweeping over her in relentless, inundating waves that wrenched and pulled at her body unceasingly, Amethyst uttered a low moan, tears spilling out the corners of her eyes as she struggled to catch her breath.

"Tillie . . . Tillie . . . will it be much longer? I don't . . . don't think I can stand much more . . ."

Her dark eyes moving swiftly to Dr. Martens, Tillie saw the brief nod and turning, whispered reassuringly, "Not too much longer now, child. Soon Amethyst have him baby in him arms, and everything be . . ."

Tillie's voice faded from her ears, the sound of a woman's scream taking its place as a ferocious pain stole her breath. But this time the spasm did not pass, continuing to throb and strain at her body in long, unending spirals of pain that drew her to the edge of consciousness. The cries grew louder, increasing with her own distress. Who was it who cried so breathlessly? Certainly it could not be she! She heard the wail again, this time louder as the agony inside her increased beyond bearing. The snap of the bedroom door as it opened to bang back against the wall tore Dr. Martens's attention momentarily from his frantic activity. Darting a quick look in its direction, he snapped sharply, "Get out of here, Damien. This baby is about to be born!"

Oblivious to the doctor's command, Damien's eyes went directly to Amethyst's pain-filled face, his throat choking at the agony reflected there. Brushing Tillie away as she attempted to remove him from the room, Damien moved quickly to Amethyst's side. Kneeling beside the bed, he whispered softly against her cheek. "It won't be much longer, darling. Our child will soon be born." Taking her small hands as Amethyst groaned deeply, Damien held them tightly in his, his eyes on her tortured face as she twisted and turned with the grueling spasm. Suddenly with a low, prolonged groan she was at peace, her lids dropping closed over the great tear-filled orbs, and Damien knew a moment of sheer panic.

"Amethyst!"

His low, hoarse cry was scarcely heard over Dr. Martens's short, victorious announcement as he held the child in his hand and spanked it sharply, "You have a daughter, Damien. A beautiful, perfect girl . . ."

His head snapping upward, Damien's glance came into contact with the small, blood-streaked infant who wriggled in the doctor's arms, her shrieking protest to his slap long and pronounced.

"A daughter?" Amethyst's faint query turned Damien's attention in her direction. His voice deep and husky, he whispered softly in response, "Yes, darling. We have a daughter."

Her gaze vague and disoriented, Amethyst looked directly into his eyes, her glance unseeing as she whispered softly over and over again, "Thank God, thank God it's a girl."

Her hands trembling, Amethyst lifted the child to her breast, carefully guiding the searching mouth to the enlarged nipple she sought. Gasping as the small lips closed hungrily over it, Amethyst closed her eyes briefly at the strange sensation moving through her body. Her own child, nursing at her breast . . . Opening her eyes again, Amethyst gazed down at the beautifully round, almost totally bald head, reaching out her slender fingers hesitantly to touch the golden fuzz that sparkled so brightly on the pink surface. So intent was she in her tentative exploration that she started sharply when Damien's low tone broke the silence. She had almost forgotten he sat on the bed beside her.

"She looks quite content now, doesn't she, darling?"

"Yes, she does, Damien," Amethyst responded quietly, unwilling to look up into his face. Her child had been born twelve hours before and she had yet to look Damien directly in the eye for fear of the emotion she would see reflected there. Her hand caressing the soft, rounded cheek, she ventured hesitantly, "Are . . . are you disappointed, Damien?"

"Disappointed?"

"Disappointed that I didn't give you a son?"

There was a brief hesitation before Damien spoke, cupping her cheek to turn her face toward him. Raising her eyes, Amethyst came into contact with his familiar glance, her heart beginning to race as Damien scrutinized her silently. Drawing his fingers lightly over her smooth cheek, he moved his hand to her temple to touch the black wisps curling there. "If I am to be completely truthful, darling," he began thoughtfully, "I would have to say I was slightly disappointed at first. I had hoped if the baby was a girl that she would look exactly like you, but she does not."

Startled by his answer, Amethyst stared speechlessly into his face, unable to respond, allowing Damien ample time to continue.

"If I was not to have a son, I had pictured a petite, dark-haired little girl with black lashes and brows, and blue eyes that would eventually turn a beguiling lavender. Instead, my daughter is blonde with light lashes and brows . . ."

". . . and peculiarly light gray eyes remarkably like her father's," Amethyst concluded softly. "But you are not disappointed that I did not bear you a son?"

Surveying her expression silently for a few moments, Damien replied softly, "You hoped for a girl, did you not, Amethyst?"

Steadily returning his glance, Amethyst replied softly, "Yes, Damien. I did."

"Then I'm happy you were not disappointed, darling," he returned softly. "As for me, I am content to wait. We have a beautiful daughter. Our next child will be a son."

Swallowing tightly, Amethyst jerked her glance back to the child nursing blissfully at her breast, aware of the broad hand that had slipped to her shoulder in a possessive caress. Her voice trembling lightly as she spoke, Amethyst said hesitantly, "I . . . I should like to name her after my mother, Damien. Marian Greer is a lovely name."

"I have no objection to naming her Marian, darling," Damien interrupted quietly, once again turning Amethyst's face so he might read her expression, "but her name will not be Marian Greer. It will be Marian Straith."

"In a situation such as ours, Damien, the child carries her mother's name." This time it was Amethyst that interrupted his statement, her pale face flushing.

"And her mother's name will soon be Straith." Damien's expression was stiff as he continued firmly, "As soon as you're back on your feet, I intend bringing a minister to this house and we'll be married."

Closing her eyes weakly, Amethyst said in a hushed voice, "I will not marry you, Damien." A lone tear slipped out of the corner of her eye, and brushing it away, Amethyst whispered, "The child will carry my name."

His stiff expression suddenly relenting, Damien bent to kiss her pale lips, lowering his head to kiss the pink cheek of the child that nursed at her breast before lifting his eyes again to hers. He spoke with soft conviction.

"This is my child, Amethyst, and make no mistake about it, you and she will both share my name."

"No . . . no, Damien." Shaking her head wildly, Amethyst said emphatically, "No."

Catching her cheeks between his palms, Damien effectively stopped her violent protest. She was trembling, and angry with himself for his thoughtlessness, Damien said softly, "We won't discuss it now, darling. You're exhausted, and I'm too filled with happiness to argue with the woman who has just given me a beautiful daughter. We'll name her Marian as you wish. Now just relax back against me, darling . . . that's right. You've had a difficult day . . ."

Contenting himself with the fact that the teneseness was leaving Amethyst's small body as she rested her back against his chest, Damien consoled himself with the silent thought that she would get over her foolish protest. Now was not the time to press her.

Within the half hour Tillie had removed the sleeping child from Amethyst's arm and Amethyst drowsed against the pillow. Reclining silently by her side, Damien studied her intently. Light shadows beneath drooping violet eyes and an unusual pallor, silent testimony to her ordeal, lent her an appearance of vulnerability that tore at his heart as his love for her swelled to overwhelming proportions inside him. She was so beautiful . . . so precious to him . . . the mother of his child . . . dearer than life. He longed desperately to make her his wife, to know the security that the two he loved most in the world bore his name. And it would be so, damn it! It would be so!

Leaning forward, Damien realized that Amethyst had passed into a peaceful sleep. Slipping noiselessly from the bed, Damien knelt beside her so he might look directly into her sleeping countenance. Moved to tenderness, he whispered softly against her lips, "I love you, Amethyst. I love you and I won't let you go. You are part of me, darling. There is a raging need inside me that only you can satisfy. It is past my powers of comprehension how I existed before I met you when you are as indispensable to me now as the very air I breathe." Touching the curling tendrils at her hairline, Damien felt the heat of tears beneath his own lids as he continued in a hoarse, breaking voice, "I just want you to love me, darling . . . please love me . . ."

Walking slowly along the dusty path, Raymond allowed his glance to move measuringly from side to side. Rough, one-room wooden structures with straw roofs stood one after the other in the clearing, a respectable distance from the great house of Conway Plantation, but even the fading light of dusk could not mask the ramshackle appearance of the slaves' quarters which had been his home for the last fifteen years of his life. A peculiar sense of defeat he had not known in many years permeated his senses. Tillie alone had spared him the complete futility that now filled his being, her spirit, beauty, and warmth, the promise of her presence carrying him through endless days filled with despair. But he could no longer see Tillie.

The choking smoke from the cooking fires in front of the dwellings smarted his eyes, causing him to blink rapidly against the burning sensation as he continued wearily along the path. He was a true slave now, no longer holding even the small prerogative of loving the only woman he had ever wanted. His stride slowing, he raised a broad hand to his neck and shook his head hopelessly, recognizing a familiar musky scent the second before a soft hand touched his arm possessively. Frowning,

Raymond turned to Quasheba's sultry smile. Her firm young body brushing sensuously against his, she said softly, "Raymond be back frem de fields fe hour 'n him not come t' Quasheba's hut fe him supper."

His face still unsmiling, Raymond responded tightly, "Raymond be in de stream, washing de dirt frem him body."

Her slender hand moving smoothly along the bulging sinews of his broad back, Quasheba murmured softly, "Dat be what Quasheba like 'bout Raymond. Raymond be slave, but Raymond be clean man. Proud, not like de other raw-chaw boogooyaggas on Massa's plantation."

Carefully biting back his response, Raymond eyed the wily Negress warily. She was young and pleasing to the eye, but he knew he must be cautious. Close to being sold for his disobedience to Massa's wishes, he had outwardly acceded to the command that he take Quasheba for his woman. He was a slave . . . his body belonged to his massa and his massa had given him to Quasheba for her man. Barely able to hide his contempt, Raymond sneered inwardly. Quasheba had given the massa a man child and held a place of power on the plantation even though the massa had taken another woman. Quasheba used her power well. Helpless against her, Raymond had formed a plan in his own mind. Outwardly submitting to her wishes, he slept with Quasheba and used the body that belonged to his massa to satisfy her appetites. But he did not perform well, withdrawing from her eager body every time to spill his seed. She would soon tire of him and name another to take his place. Then he would get word to Tillie and Tillie would return to him. He must be patient. Quasheba would not put up with him much longer.

"Come, Raymond." Crooking her long finger in his direction, Quasheba shot him an undereyed look.

"Quasheba ben waitin' fe Raymond."

Taking the wide, unwilling hand, Quasheba pulled Raymond behind her, drawing him further down the path until they reached the small hut they had shared for almost two months. Her dark eyes looking directly into his, she pulled him inside. Turning, she slowly removed her blouse, exposing the full dark breasts that lay provocatively against her narrow rib cage. Gradually slipping off her skirt, she ran her hands in a slow, tantalizing movement over her naked body, cupping the rounded breasts as she held his glance, moving slowly, hypnotically, to the narrow waist, along the smooth curve of her hips, descending to flutter lightly along the black triangle between her strong thighs. Stepping closer, she reached out to smooth her well tutored hands over the rippling muscles of Raymond's chest, sliding them down in a light teasing path to the closure on his britches. With a low, throaty laugh, she freed them to fall to the ground, moving down to close on his lagging member with a smooth, well practiced hand.

"Quasheba gowan mek dis man stand up 'n ask fe Quasheba, 'n when him ready, Quasheba gowan mek dis man happy."

His eyes flicking closed for a brief second, Raymond despaired at the answering swell of his body as Quasheba continued her efficient administrations, cursing inwardly as she faultlessly raised the level of his physical discomfort. Her smile knowing and satisfied, Quasheba finally withdrew her hand, urging him down beside her on the pallet, spreading her legs wide as his great body closed atop hers. Grunting as she felt him enter, Quasheba bit his neck viciously, the stinging pain causing him to pump heavily inside her, his impetus increasing savagely as her teeth dug deeply into the soft flesh of his neck. Groaning wildly as his body drove deeper and deeper into hers, Quasheba revelled in the power of his attack, moaning as he slammed heavily into her again and again. The savage violence of their joining continued as Quasheba welcomed the thrusts that assailed her eager body. Suddenly sensing the moment of climax, Quasheba wound her legs tightly around Raymond's waist, meeting and joining the pumping rhythm with the wild strength of passion raging within her, moaning in unrestrained sexual frenzy, "Gowan, Raymond, give Quasheba what him wants . . . Quasheba want it now . . . now . . . NOW!"

Feeling his powerful body quaking atop her, Quasheba smiled a wide, victorious smile, her legs locking tighter to hold him captive inside her. The swell of his throbbing manhood sending a wild jolt of exaltation through her veins, she gave a small cry of triumph the second before Raymond tore himself free of her body to bring himself to complete shuddering release. Watching mesmerized as his heaving spasms came to a complete halt, Quasheba released a cry of rage, raising her fists to beat mercilessly at the black handsome head turned from her, the fury of her blows ringing loudly within the silence of the hut as her clenched fists pounded viciously. Opening her hands, she clawed at his broad, muscular neck and heavy chest until she drew blood, hissing over and over under her breath as she did, "Quasheba gowan have Raymond . . . Quasheba gowan have him 'n have him seed!"

Her frenzy finally abating, Quasheba lay back against the pallet, her body wet with perspiration, her chest heaving with the fury of her attack. Still kneeling atop her, Raymond gradually turned his stony expression in her direction. His deep voice soft, he said slowly, "Raymond's body belong t' Massa, but Raymond's seed belong t' Raymond."

Her ebony eyes widening with heated wrath, Quasheba

whispered insidiously, "Quasheba gowan tell Massa, 'n Massa gowan sell Raymond far 'way frem here where him nevah see dat Tillie Swann again!"

The abrupt hardening of Raymond's features and the fury exposed on his face suddenly stealing her breath, Quasheba gasped in fear, reaching up to grasp his arm as Raymond made an abrupt movement as if to rise.

"No! No, Raymond! Quasheba not gowan tell Massa!" Raising herself up, Quasheba wrapped her arms around Raymond's neck, pressing her full breasts against his chest as she said softly into his ear, "No, Raymond. Quasheba not gowan tell Massa 'cause Quasheba gowan keep Raymond wid him. Quasheba gowan mek Raymond want Quasheba . . . want only Quasheba . . ."

Pulling him close against her, Quasheba finished silently, her hidden expression revealing the jealousy that twisted her face into a mask of hatred, ". . . 'n den Quasheba gowan mek Raymond feel de pain . . . gowan mek Raymond suffer . . . gowan get himself even . . . 'n den Quasheba gowan tek another man . . ."

Violet eyes alight with love, Amethyst looked down at the child suckling at her breast, her throat tight with the strength of the brilliant emotion.

"Marian Greer," she mused softly in the quiet of the room, "you bear no resemblance to your namesake, but you are a beautiful little girl, my darling baby, and nothing will ever separate us."

A small frown moving over her smooth features, Amethyst felt a nervous tingle along her spine. When Damien came home the same argument would begin again, only this time it would be stronger, more bitter than before. The bitterness had been increasing almost from the day of Marian's birth over a month before. It would soon be safe to sail for America, and Damien was determined to return to Philadelphia with Amethyst as his wife. So obsessed had he become with the thought that the tender lover had begun to slip into rage, her unrelenting refusal driving him again and again to the brink of violence, when he would storm from the small house on John's Lane to disappear for long days at a time. Returning each time without an explanation as to his absence, he would assume his loving facade until the issue of their marriage was again raised. Weary of the battle, Amethyst closed her eyes in momentary despair. What possible reason could Damien have for his demand that they marry? Surely he enjoyed all the comforts of the married state. It was not possible that he loved her. Love was unselfish . . . giving . . . generous of spirit. Damien's feelings for her were possessive, grasping, demanding, stifling and repressive. Violent feelings such as Damien felt for her were doomed to fade. But she feared more and more for the attachment forming between Damien and his child. There was no doubting the tenderness with which the tall, threatening figure reached down to take the small infant from the cradle, nor the look on his face as he whispered softly against the tiny ear, his eyes bright with an emotion she had not believed him capable of feeling. He had spoken the truth when he had said it mattered little to him that the child was a girl . . . she still was his child.

But Marian was her child, too, and she would not allow her child to grow up under the influence of a man who practiced obeah against those who opposed him, holding his evil powers as a threat over the heads of those closest to him; a man who was so insensible to human life that he would have allowed William to die had she not given herself to him. Even should his claims be sincere that he wished to keep her with him for the rest of his life, she could not fathom a future where stringent opposition to his wishes could result in disaster as a result of his powers of black magic. No... no... no matter the physical power he exerted over her, her desire to feel his touch against her body, she would not submit to the ultimate subjugation. She would not marry him.

Damien's stride was steady and sure as he walked with determination along Port Royal Street. The *Sally* would be sailing for America within a week and he had waited long enough for Amethyst to consent to marry him. He would not return to Philadelphia with a mistress and an illegitimate child. Above all things he wanted to return with Amethyst his wife and the beautiful child that had secured such a firm hold on his heart bearing his name. Torturing him even as he turned resolutely off Port Royal Street onto John's Lane were the suspicions that had begun to grow insidiously in the back of his mind since the birth of his daughter. Why was Amethyst so adamant about refusing to marry him? Did she still hope to leave him and go to William Sheridan? Or was Armand Beauchamps the man she secretly desired? Whatever the case, Damien thought heatedly, jealousy twisting his stomach into tight knots as he ascended the steps with a measured tread, her plans would be in vain. He had hesitated to use the ultimate pressure to gain her consent to their marriage, but time was growing short and he had no other choice. Since their return to Kingston Tillie's influence had only served to impress further into Amethyst's mind her belief in his powers of obeah, and once again the ridiculous conviction would serve his purpose. He would not succumb to his distaste for this method of forcing Amethyst to marry him and vowed silently that he would finally convince Amethyst of his love for her if it took the rest of his life.

Quietly opening the front door of the house, Damien

stepped into the small living room. Her expression impassive, Tillie answered his unspoken question.

"Amethyst be in the bedroom with the child."

Not bothering to acknowledge her curt statement, Damien walked silently to the bedroom door, pushing it open with quiet authority. Clad only in her chemise, Amethyst stood before the washstand, the flimsy garment lowered to her waist as she cleansed her full breasts with a cloth. Her head snapping up at the sound of his entrance, she stood framed in the light from the window behind her, the outline of her graceful shoulders and arms, delicate and fragile, her breasts full and pointed lying against the narrow ribcage, her waist narrow, gently rounded hips and long slender legs completing a picture of womanly perfection that set his heart to racing.

"Damien!" Taking a dry cloth from the stand, Amethyst attempted to cover her breasts. "What are you doing home this time of day? Marian is sleeping. I've just fed her and was cleansing..."

Her words dwindling off as Damien stared wordlessly in her direction, she watched silently as Damien approached.

"No, don't cover yourself, Amethyst." Taking the cloth from her hands, Damien bent to kiss the pointed crest of her breast, his body beginning to swell uncomfortably as his lips touched the warm flesh. Drawing his lips from her with the sheer power of will, Damien looked into lavender eyes raised questioningly to his. His throat was tight with love and desire.

"Just let me look at you a few minutes longer, darling."

Reaching out, Damien touched the raven curls that streamed past her shoulders, his hand tightening convulsively the moment before his arms closed around her to hold her close against him as he buried his face in the soft ringlets. His heart was pounding. No, he did not want to take her now as much as his body cried out for her. Having only begun to resume their lovemaking that same week, their unions were more brilliant than before Marian's birth, a particular poignancy surging inside Damien with the thought that Amethyst was the mother of his child as well as the only woman he had ever truly loved. And within a few days she would be his wife . . . his forever.

Slowly releasing her, Damien said in a whispered tone, "I've come to tell you the *Sally* will sail for America next week. All cargo has been contracted for and we will be ready to sail by midweek." Noting the small frown on her brow, he continued softly, "You may bring Tillie back with you if you desire. We shall have to arrange for a woman to help you with the child once we arrive in Philadelphia at any rate." Lowering his head, he pressed a light kiss against her lips. "I don't want all your time spent in Marian's care, you know."

Nodding slightly, Amethyst made no comment, her eyes jerking up to his as he continued in the same low tone. "We'll be married the end of this week. I'll speak to Reverend Sidley today and make the arrangements."

"Damien, please do not persist with this idea. I've told you repeatedly that I won't marry you."

"You will marry me, Amethyst. We will return to Philadelphia as man and wife."

Turning abruptly in his arms, Amethyst attempted to break free of his embrace. His grip tightening, Damien's tone dropped a notch lower. "If you value William Sheridan's life, Amethyst, you'll marry me at the end of the week as I say . . ."

The fear displayed so openly in the violet eyes that jerked back to his face gnawing at his conscience, Damien maintained his steady gaze as Amethyst began falteringly, "Damien... what do you mean? William has nothing to do with us. I've not seen him since that last time when you were present. Surely you'll not hurt William in any way."

"I'll not touch, William, Amethyst."

Her face whitening, Amethyst gasped, "You would not... you would not use obeah against him... not again..."

Holding her gaze steadily, Damien did not answer, allowing Amethyst the prerogative of judging his reply. Tears flooding her eyes, Amethyst said softly, "I don't want to marry you, Damien. Can you not content yourself with the situation as it stands now?"

Still there was no answer as Damien continued to hold her tearful gaze. Finally speaking, Damien's voice was firm and unyielding.

"Reverend Sidley will marry us on Friday. Please make sure that you are prepared."

Her body was trembling against his as Damien pulled her close, his wide hands moving smoothly over the satin skin of her back. There was a strong distaste inside him for the manner in which he was forcing her assent to this marriage, but he had determined long ago that he would do anything necessary to keep Amethyst.

Lowering his head, Damien kissed the path of the lone tear that had slipped down her cheek, his mouth moving to press light kisses along her brow and cheek, the heat inside him slowly building as he trailed his lips to hers to cover them in a deep, searching kiss. He was almost past rational thought now, conscious only of the texture of her skin beneath his palms, the sweet warmth of her body against his. His eyes holding hers possessively, he slowly unbuttoned his shirt, exposing the breadth of his chest as he pulled it free of his britches. Slowly gathering her into his arms, he pulled her against him, the touch of her naked breasts against the broad expanse sending him over the edge of desire at the ultimate sweetness of the warm intimacy.

Scooping her up into his arms, Damien carried her to the bed in a few brief strides. Gasping as their flesh met, Damien whispered softly against her lips the moment before covering them with his own, "You will be my wife this Friday, Amethyst. I will stop at nothing . . . will do anything I must, but you will belong to me."

Her ear pressed tightly against the door, Tillie listened intently, her mind filling in the picture at the silence that ensued. Shaking with frustration and fury, she searched her mind wildly for a solution. She could not allow Amethyst to tie herself for life to the obeah man. Amethyst was too strong of spirit. Eventually she would displease him and she feared for the result. Her heart twisting in her chest at the soft moan that issued from behind the closed door, Tillie turned abruptly toward the front door. She was unable to find a solution, but she would go to the only person who could help her. Moving quickly through the doorway, Tillie made her way with unerring purpose toward the market. Her eyes searching the bustling scene, Tillie's glance finally settled on the object of her search, and within minutes was seated on the wagon beside Quaco as the worried Negro urged the horse toward Sheridan Plantation with obvious haste.

His young, tired face flushed with anger, William's tone was incredulous. "Surely he doesn't intend to use the same ruse again to make Amethyst do his bidding? What was her reply, Tillie? What did she say when he threatened her with my safety?"

Her face tightening, Tillie replied in a low voice,

"Amethyst say nothin'. That obeah man know Amethyst not gowan let you die."

"Tillie!" William's voice was harsh with impatience. "Damien Straith holds no power over me or anyone! He's using Amethyst's fear against her!"

Her thin brows raising, Tillie said in quiet compromise, "It not matter what the obeah man can do, Mr. William. It matter only what Amethyst think him can do, and Amethyst believe . . . Amethyst believe . . ."

"Damn him! Damn that Damien Straith," William muttered under his breath, the truth of Tillie's statement frustrating him even further.

Turning around, William paced the small confines of the kitchen in the rear of Sheridan Plantation's great house where Tillie had called him to conference, his mind desperately seeking a solution. Suddenly coming to a complete standstill, William hesitated a brief moment, his back toward Tillie before turning back in her direction. A small smile covering his lips, William reached out a hand to grip Tillie's shoulder in a reassuring gesture. "I'll have Quaco bring you back to Kingston now, Tillie, and you may rest the night knowing that Damien Straith's plans will be thwarted tomorrow."

Her expression questioning, Tillie searched William Sheridan's face, only to have William respond quietly, "It will be better if you are unaware of my plans, Tillie. But I promise you this. Damien Straith will not use me again to gain control over Amethyst! Go home now, Tillie. I don't want Straith getting suspicious before I'm able to complete my plans."

Searching his face a moment longer, Tillie nodded briefly before her deep voice again broke the stillness of the room. "Tillie thank you, Mr. William. Tillie and Amethyst thank you."

* * *

Her face pale, Amethyst looked into Tillie's unreadable expression. She had hesitated to tell Tillie, but it was almost afternoon, and she could wait no longer. Her voice was low, almost shamed.

"Damien and I will be married on Friday, Tillie, so we may return to Philadelphia as man and wife."

Startled when Tillie showed no expression at all at her declaration, Amethyst inquired hesitantly, "Did . . . did you hear what I said, Tillie?"

"Tillie hear."

Frowning at her unexpected reaction, Amethyst said curiously, "Have you no comment to make, Tillie . . . nothing to say?"

Turning away unexpectedly, Tillie said casually over her shoulder, "Tillie say nothin' . . . nothin' at all."

Her frown deepening as Tillie walked from the room, Amethyst shook her head. What had come over Tillie? She had been so adamant against her marrying Damien and now appeared to accept the fact without a second thought. Something was amiss, but for the life of her, she could not figure out what it was.

Giving his head a hard shake, Damien again attempted to add the column he had been working at for the past fifteen minutes. He was quick with figures, and impatient with his inability to concentrate long enough to add the sums in his mind. He had gone that morning to speak to Reverend Sidley. All arrangements had been completed for Amethyst's and his wedding on Friday, but now, for the life of him, he could not understand why he had put the date off for three days. Surely tomorrow would have been ample notice for Amethyst. She need ready nothing but herself, and her wardrobe was such that she need buy nothing for the occasion. It mattered little to him what she wore anyway. She was beautiful in any garment that touched her body, and, he thought with considerable warmth, even more beautiful when she lay unclothed beneath him. Suddenly laughing at his own thoughts, Damien shook his head again, but this time in amazement. He was insatiable when it came to Amethyst.

Glancing around the small confines of his cabin, he smiled again. He and Amethyst would share this cabin on the return voyage, but he had already made arrangements for the first mate's cabin to be turned over to Tillie and Marian for the duration of the voyage home. He was almost certain Tillie would return to Philadelphia with Amethyst. She no longer had anything to hold her in Kingston now that her man, the slave on Conway Plantation, had been forced to take another woman. Amethyst tearfully confided Tillie's misfortune to him their second night in Kingston. There was true affection between Amethyst and Tillie, for which Damien was grateful. Amethyst sorely needed a woman to talk to, and it was far better it be this woman who loved her with the dedication of a mother. Tillie's presence on the return voyage would ensure them considerable privacy that might otherwise be unattainable with Amethyst subservient to the baby's needs for the duration of the voyage. Yes, he was definitely looking forward to the close quarters he and Amethyst would again be sharing . . .

Frowning at the harsh knock on the door that interrupted his pleasant flow of thoughts, Damien's response was an impatient "Come in!"

Expecting to see Barnes's stalwart figure at the door when it opened, he was startled to see an English lieutenant, with three other soldiers visible behind him.

"Damien Straith, Captain of the ship *Sally?*"

"Yes, that's right, Lieutenant." Drawing himself to his feet, Damien frowned at the young soldier, his mind racing. "Is there a problem?"

"Yes, sir. You are under arrest, Captain Straith. You and your crew will be delivered to await trial on charges of smuggling."

"Smuggling! But certainly this is a joke! We are quite legitimately in port, Lieutenant, preparing to sail next week with a cargo we have contracted in a legal manner."

His outward appearance that of startled innocence, Damien's mind worked feverishly. What could possibly have gone wrong? He had been safely in port for over two months. What evidence could they possibly have against him after all this time? Who would dare testify against him in Kingston? His "obeah" had always provided him adequate protection in the past.

"Kindly come with me, Captain Straith." The bright young officer was not to be swayed from his duty. Signaling his men forward, the young officer watched carefully as Damien reached for his coat, making certain no false moves were intended, before turning to lead them again on deck.

Blinking against the bright afternoon sun, Damien arrived on deck to see his crew under guard, their eyes moving directly to him as he appeared. His voice exuding a confidence he did not feel, he said reassuringly, "I'll have this situation straightened out in short order once I've been able to speak to someone in authority. Don't worry, we'll soon be free."

The young lieutenant's quick glance showing exactly what he thought of Straith's confident declaration, he motioned his men silently forward. Falling into place at the head of the small contingent, Damien could not help but wonder what information had inspired the lieutenant's scornful reaction. He was anxious to face his accuser.

Still puzzling at Tillie's strange behavior, Amethyst

worked quietly around the bedroom, careful not to make any sudden noises that might disturb Marian. The infant had been fretful most of the day, a reaction, she feared, from her own disturbed state of mind. But Damien had efficiently eliminated all her protests against their marriage yesterday with the threat that still hung heavily on her heart. Was this what the future would hold for her as Damien's wife? All opposition from her met with a threat on the life of someone she held dear? Who would he threaten when they were far from Jamaica? Would Tillie be the focus of his evil spells should she dare oppose him? How could she bear spending her life with the threat of black magic hanging over her? And worse yet, would Marian grow up influenced by a father who practiced the black art of obeah? A small shudder shook her slender frame. Knowing all this, how was it that she still thrilled at Damien's touch and longed for him when he absented himself from her? Perhaps she was becoming as perverse as he! Her only salvation lay in getting away from him, and now all avenues of escape were closed. William . . . dear William. She could not allow him to suffer for her again. She would not be able to live with the guilt.

The low buzz of conversation in the next room suddenly catching her ear, Amethyst walked slowly to the door. Opening it quietly, Amethyst was startled to see the subject of her thoughts talking quietly to Tillie in the living room. Her heart thudding wildly in her chest, she hastily stepped through the doorway, closing the door carefully behind her. The click of the door latch snapped both pairs of eyes in her direction.

"William, what are you doing here? You must leave! Damien may be home any minute, and if he finds you here there will be trouble."

Moving quickly to his side, Amethyst lifted pleading

eyes to his, unaware of the breathtaking picture she presented in the pale blue morning gown that lent her glowing countenance an air of delicate fragility with its fine ruffles of lace around the deeply scooped bosom and slender sleeves. Restored to her former self, she was small and lovely and infinitely appealing, and unable to restrain himself, William reached out to take her gently into his arms. Relaxing only for the briefest moment in the security of his embrace, Amethyst stirred guiltily. She could not afford to risk Damien's anger at William. He was too vulnerable to Damien's obeah . . .

"William, please, you must leave. Damien will . . ."

"Damien Straith will do nothing, Amethyst. He can do nothing to you now."

"What . . . what do you mean, William?"

"Damien Straith has been arrested, Amethyst. He and his crew are being held in the stockade to await trial for smuggling."

"Smuggling!" Startled by William's announcement, Amethyst shook her head in disbelief. "But the *Sally* has safely docked twice in Kingston. No one has dared to speak up against Damien before. Who . . . who . . . ?"

"I have named him a smuggler, Amethyst, and have declared my intention to testify against him in court. That is all the evidence needed to hold him and his men long enough to allow you to escape."

"Escape?"

"Did you really think I would allow Straith to threaten you with my safety another time, Amethyst . . . to take advantage of your ridiculous belief that he can actually hurt me with his pretended powers?"

"They're not pretended powers, William! I've seen what he can do!"

"Nonsense!"

"But it's true!"

"Darling!" Taking Amethyst's small face between his palms, William directed his glance into her eyes, abruptly stopping her protest with his unrelenting expression. "Listen to me now, please, Amethyst. I won't argue the point with you. You choose to believe Straith holds these powers of witchcraft, and I can see reasoning is powerless against your fear. But you must also see that I've taken an irreversible step against Straith. He can no longer hold my safety over your head because I'm forcing him to act against me to save himself. But you'll see, Amethyst. I'll live in perfect health to testify against him at his trial, and that will prove once and for all that any powers he claims to hold are false."

"No, William, I won't allow you to take the risk!"

"You have no choice, Amethyst. I love you, darling, and I'll have no peace until I've set you free of him."

"But William, I'm not free . . ."

"You soon will be, darling. I've arranged for you and Tillie to sail with the child on the *Whitestone* tomorrow morning. It sails to Philadelphia, and you'll be far away from here before Damien Straith even learns of your departure."

"But William, it's impossible. I have no way to pay the fare or support myself when I arrive in Philadelphia."

Reaching into his pocket, William withdrew a small pouch and placed it in her palm. "I've already paid for your tickets, Amethyst. This money will tide you over for a while until I'm able to arrange for more."

"I cannot live on your charity, William."

His glance suddenly stiff, William's voice was harsh in response. "Would you rather I demand payment for my 'charity' in the same manner in which Straith demands payment, Amethyst?"

Her face flushing brightly, Amethyst dropped her eyes.

William's voice when he spoke again was soft and apologetic. "I didn't mean to be cruel, Amethyst, but you must see this is your only means of escape."

Slowly raising lavender eyes heavy with tears, Amethyst said softly, "You're right, of course, William. How can I ever thank you?"

Hesitating only briefly, William replied in a low tone, "You may thank me by telling me the truth, Amethyst. I must know for certain before I let you go. You . . . you do not love me, do you, darling?" His clear mahogany eyes intent and serious, he whispered softly, "Please tell me now, once and for all. I must know."

Her throat tight with tears, Amethyst's response was hushed. "I don't love you in the way in which you would have me love you, William. You're so dear to me. The very sight of you lights a spot in my heart that is reserved for you alone, but it's not love as you would have it be."

Her voice choking off at the sadness reflected in William's face, Amethyst threw her arms around his neck in a tight embrace, tears streaming freely down her cheeks. "William, can you forgive me for all the heartache I've caused you? It was not my intention, really it wasn't, and I do truly love you, William!"

His arms closing tightly around her for long moments, William finally stepped back, a small smile on his lips as he whispered, "I understand, darling. I really do understand at last. Mine were always the stronger feelings. I was smitten from the first day I saw you when you were still a girl. Your feelings grew to affection while mine grew to love. I have had time to do a lot of thinking in the past months and have finally come to realize that your feelings for me never progressed past the point they reached a few years ago, while mine grew deeper with each passing year."

"Oh, William . . ." Her voice breaking into a small

sob, Amethyst clung desperately to him.

His eyes suspiciously bright, William moved her away to look into her face. "It's alright, darling, really it is. You have done the kindest thing being honest with me. And I'm satisfied at least to have freed you from this bondage you've been living with Straith. Now you must listen to me carefully."

Nodding her head, still unable to speak, Amethyst raised her eyes to his.

"You must pack all your things tonight. Tillie has agreed to go with you to Phildelphia where you and the child will be free to begin a new life. When you reach Philadelphia, you must contact my father's lawyer, Wilbur Helmswood, and give him a letter I will prepare. He will help you find accommodations and a situation."

Sensing the waning of his defenses against Amethyst's clinging helplessness, William smiled and moved her a step further from his reach. In another few moments he would ruin all his good intentions by taking her into his arms and begging her to return to Sheridan Plantation with him. He must continue to remind himself that she did not love him and could never be happy with the lopsided emotion they would share.

"Do you understand all I've said, Amethyst?" Watching as Amethyst nodded her head, he prompted again, "Do you agree with all the arrangements I've made?"

Nodding her head again, Amethyst finally managed to speak past her emotion blocked throat, "Yes, and I thank you, William . . . but . . . you will be alright, won't you? You won't allow Damien to hurt you again . . . ?"

"No, darling. Damien Straith will not hurt either one of us ever again." Allowing the impact of his words a few minutes to sink into her brain, William continued softly, "You have a lot to accomplish before tomorrow, darling.

I'll pick you up with the wagon at six in the morning and take you to the ship."

Unable to say more, Amethyst whispered hoarsely, "Thank you, William."

Staring wordlessly into her eyes for a long moment, William gave her a small smile before turning to the door. Stopping briefly at the doorway, he gave her a brief salute before closing the door quietly behind him.

Staring silently in the direction he had disappeared, Amethyst turned suddenly to Tillie's inquiring glance. Taking a deep breath, she said in a resolute voice, "We must hurry, Tillie. We have much to do before morning."

Through the long, endless day, Amethyst's eyes returned again and again to the doorway, expecting to see Damien come striding through at any second as she packed feverishly. Countless times during the long night that followed, she awoke and reached to the bed beside her, almost expecting her hand to come into contact with Damien's warm sleeping body, hating herself for the moment of disappointment the empty bed evoked. But it was true. William had given her a few days grace with which to escape Damien once and for all. There was no real evidence against Damien and his crew and he would undoubtedly be free again with a few weeks' time, but she would have arrived in Philadelphia by then, contacted Mr. Helmswood and be situated in a place where Damien would be unable to find her. Yes, she would be free, and would start her life again. Yes . . .

Smiling a small, tender smile, William waved at the petite figure at the rail of the *Whitestone*, his glance unmoving as the ship glided steadily from the dock. Watching until the ship faded into a small spot on the horizon and finally disappeared from sight, William swallowed deeply, his voice hoarse with emotion as he whispered to the image of the woman who had just sailed from his sight, "Goodbye, darling . . . my darling Amethyst. I love you, darling. I'll always love you . . ."

Pacing the dank, cramped cell restlessly, Damien stopped to swat the mosquito viciously biting his neck, uttering a small grunt of disgust as a scorpion scuttled over the damp stones of the floor at his feet. If he were to judge the passage of time by the faint ray of light penetrating a slit high on the outer wall, he had lain sweating in the blazing heat of his cell for three days, during which he was bedeviled by lice, and endless varieties of hungry insects, and the numerous "searabbits" that shared his temporary abode. He had yet to face his accuser! Frustrated to a boiling rage, Damien swore viciously under his breath, no longer bothering to raise his voice in a summons that he knew would be ignored. Uncertain where his crew was imprisoned, Damien was incensed at the manner in which his incarceration was being handled. Causing him even more unrest was the fact that this was to have been his wedding day. What was Amethyst thinking right now? Did she have any idea where he was being held? What would she . . .

The sharp, grating sound of metal against metal called his attention to the peep hole on the door. Was it again time for the revolting food that had been shoved in to him since his arrival? Brackish water, moldy biscuits and tainted meat were not his favorite fare, and he had carefully considered throwing the rancid offerings back in the face of his jailer before better judgment had assumed control of his actions. But the voice that came to him through the narrow grate was well educated and familiar.

"I just came down to check your accommodations, Straith, and find out if you're quite comfortable."

Moving to the door in quick angry strides, Damien peered out into William Sheridan's sober expression. The blood pounding to his head in a flush of rage, Damien growled heatedly, "I have waited three days to face my accuser. I should have known it would be you!"

"That's right, you should have known. I'm the only person you haven't been able to fool with that obeah nonsense and the only person who doesn't fear retribution at the hands of your black magic. In any case, what did I have to lose, Straith? You had already intended to put a 'spell' on me if Amethyst didn't marry you before you sailed, isn't that true?" His young face suddenly twisting into a vicious sneer, William continued heatedly, "Did you really expect I would allow you to use me against Amethyst again?" Stepping closer to the door, William hissed venomously, "You were to have married Amethyst today, weren't you, Straith? Well, you needn't worry. I've contacted Reverend Sidley and cancelled your arrangements. I didn't want the poor gentleman to come to an empty house and wonder what had happened to his prospective bride and groom."

"Empty house?" His hands balling into tight fists, Damien demanded in a low voice, "Where is Amethyst? What have you done with her?"

"Amethyst is quite safe, Straith. You needn't worry. She's out of your clutches once and for all. Right now she's three days into her journey back to America, and before you're released from this place, she'll have become situated where you'll be unable to find or harm her again."

His throat suddenly going dry, Damien rasped quietly, "I don't believe you, Sheridan. You'd never have let her go. She's probably at Sheridan Plantation."

"No, Straith, don't put me in the same classification as yourself. Amethyst didn't wish to marry me, or you may rest assured she would be my wife right now, and I would not force her to comply to my wishes. I love her too much to make her unhappy for my own selfish ends. But I don't expect you could understand that thinking, Straith. At any rate, she's gone! You'll never get your hands on her again, and when the authorities here finally examine your case, you may be sure I will appear to testify against you!"

"Testify!" Damien's response was an enraged shout. "What evidence do you have to give against me or my men? This is a farce!"

A smile crossing his lips for the first time, William raised his brows with a small uncertain shrug. "Perhaps you're right, Straith. Perhaps my evidence is not adequate, but by the time we find out, my purpose will have been served, will it not?"

Staring at the youthful smiling face, Damien felt a deep futility twist his vitals. "And Amethyst, what did she have to say to your plan, Sheridan?"

"Amethyst?" Hesitating briefly, William directed a cool glance into Damien's intense expression. His response was slow and deliberate. "She smiled a bright farewell to me from the rail of the ship as she sailed, Straith. She was intensely relieved to be free of you at last."

His eyes closing briefly at the pain William's words inflicted, Damien felt a sinking sensation deep inside. There was no longer any doubt in his mind that Sheridan spoke the truth. Amethyst was gone . . .

"I'll be leaving now, Straith." William's casual tone drew Damien's attention back from his dark wanderings to strike the final blow. "I've completed my mission here.

I didn't want you to live with uncertainty any longer. I wanted you to know for sure that you've really lost her."

Taking only a moment longer to stare into the light piercing eyes looking out at him from behind the rusted door, William repeated coldly, his voice clear and precise, "Amethyst is gone, Straith... she's gone. You've lost her."

Chapter 10

Struggling to clutch her cape tightly against the biting December wind, Amethyst reached up to pay the coachman. The hired carriage had been a luxury she could ill afford, but she was still unaccustomed to the penetrating Philadelphia cold after almost a full month in the city, and did not think she would be able to withstand the long walk to and from her destination from Widow Graydon's Old Slate Roof House, where she had lodgings. Shivering after only a few minutes in the piercing wind, Amethyst hurried a few steps down the street to enter the small shop near the corner.

Slightly apprehensive, Amethyst closed the door behind her, hoping her expression did not convey the trepidation inundating her spirit. But her return to Philadelphia had been frought with unexpected difficulties that had worn slowly and efficiently at her confidence until she had begun to wonder if indeed Damien had turned his obeah against her from temporary captivity in Jamaica. William had assured her that the authorities would hold Damien no longer than three weeks, allowing her at least that much time to contact Mr. Helmswood and make arrangements for a situation that would take her out of Damien's reach. But William's well thought-through plans were destined for failure. Upon arriving in Philadelphia, Amethyst had taken rooms in Oeller's Hotel, considering the expensive lodgings only temporary until Mr. Helmswood could recommend a better course of action. Having left Tillie to unpack and care for Marian, she had headed immediately to Mr. Helmswood's offices, only to find that the prominent attorney had been killed in a carriage accident only a week before. Stunned by the setback in her plans, Amethyst had returned to Oeller's in a state of desperate confusion. The responsibility for Tillie and Marian weighing heavily on her shoulders, Amethyst had spent the following weeks perusing the Philadelphia papers for situations available, only to find that her youth and beauty, coupled with the responsibility of a young child, was a severe detriment to finding suitable work. Her money fast diminishing, Amethyst had moved her small family to Widow Graydon's boarding house, which was considerably less expensive, but the drain on her funds was relentless. After a little over a month in the city, Amethyst had barely enough to pay the next week's lodgings. Desperate for funds, she had decided to sell the jewelry Damien had given her. Angry with herself that she was still indirectly dependent on Damien's support, she approached the counter and the small man behind it who eyed her appraisingly.

"You are Mr. Falworth, I presume," Amethyst began hesitantly.

"Yes, I am he. May I help you, Miss? The slender, balding man's nasal tone grated sharply on Amethyst's nerves, as did his open appraisal of her attire.

Grateful that she had had the foresight to pack her heavy winter outerwear for her intended trip back to Philadelphia from Jamaica, Amethyst knew she presented an impressive appearance in the deep gray velvet cape. With a graceful maneuver, Amethyst managed to display the heavy otter lining matching the wide band of the same fur trimming the hood of the luxurious garment, realizing the astute proprietor was mentally totaling the sum of her ensemble. She did not want him to be suspicious when she presented the costly jewelry.

"Yes, I do believe you'll be able to be of some help, Mr.

Falworth. Mr. Wilbur Helmswood's office directed me to you as a trustworthy person who would offer me an honest price for the articles I wish to sell." Retrieving a small bundle from her bag, Amethyst slowly opened a soft cloth, catching in an unguarded moment the man's obvious amazement at the jewelry inside. His eyes moving quickly over the long strand of perfectly matched pearls, the costly amethyst necklace and matching earbobs, the miscellaneous diamond and amethyst earbobs Damien had insisted on buying for her, the heavy gold chains that were to be her casual daytime jewelry, and the set of six diamond hair ornaments he had purchased to match the sapphire gown she had been fated not to wear for the previous year's Winter Ball at Oeller's; Mr. Falworth touched his index finger to his narrow lips in a thoughtful gesture. Turning, he reached for his jeweler's glass, taking each piece into his hand to examine it closely before speaking.

Apparently satisfied at last, Mr. Falworth's nasal tone sounded hesitantly, "Well, the gems do seem to be of good quality, Miss, but I'm truthfully uncertain how quickly I'll be able to move articles of this value. Frankly, I'm hesitant to purchase these items outright, but I will agree to handle them for you on consignment."

Taken aback, Amethyst was hesitant. "I'm afraid I don't understand exactly what you mean by that, Mr. Falworth."

"I mean I will take the jewels, Miss, give you a receipt for them, and offer them for sale. When and if they're sold, I'll take a percentage of the amount as commission on the sale, and give the remainder to you."

The street door of the shop opened and closed behind her, but Amethyst was too engrossed in the unexpected turn of events to pay it any mind. "But that means you will hold the jewelry for an indefinite period without my receiving any funds, sir. I'm afraid such an arrangement will not suit my situation. My needs are immediate. Isn't there any way you can help me now?"

Suddenly realizing Mr. Falworth's attention had strayed from her face to a point behind her, Amethyst began turning in the same direction as a deep, familiar voice met her ears.

"Ma cherie, I'm afraid there is much you have to learn about striking a good bargain."

Her startled glance coming into contact with warm dark eyes, Amethyst gasped. "Armand!" Uncertain whether it was happiness or embarrassment that caused the bright flush that flooded her face, Amethyst made a valiant attempt to lead the conversation away from the exchange she was certain he had overheard. "What a surprise to see you here! Are you shopping for a bauble for your latest ladyfriend, perhaps?"

"Cherie," Armand's sober expression effectively dismissed her attempt at lightness, "I came here looking for you."

"For me!" Startled, Amethyst replied unthinkingly, "That's absurd, Armand! How could you possibly know I was here?"

Touching her cheek in a light caress, Armand looked directly into the bright lavender eyes turned up to his. "The answer is quite simple, ma petite. I returned from New York this morning and was informed that you had returned to Philadelphia without Monsieur Straith." Noting the manner in which Amethyst's gaze fell from his at the mention of Damien Straith, Armand hesitated for a moment before continuing. "After numerous inquiries, I ascertained your lodgings and went directly to see you. Your maid told me you had come here."

Her brows knitting in a small frown, Amethyst muttered softly under her breath, "That Tillie! She has no sense at all!"

"Quite the contrary, cherie. She simply recognized my

deep concern and since she was also quite worried about this mission on which you had embarked, she told me..."

"... she told you why I came here." Shaking her head in futile acceptance, Amethyst finished Armand's quiet statement.

"You must not be angry with your Tillie, ma petite. It is obvious she thinks highly of you and was concerned for your welfare. But enough of this for now." Abruptly turning to Mr. Falworth, Armand said pleasantly, "I'm sorry, monsieur, but Mademoiselle Greer has changed her mind and does not wish to sell her jewels at the present time."

"Armand! What are you saying? I must..."

Laying his finger lightly against her lips, Armand effectively hushed her protest as he urged her gently toward the doorway. "First we must talk. Then you may do as you wish. Does that meet with your approval, ma cherie? If nothing else, I may be able to help you with your bargaining technique. I'm afraid it is sorely in need of improvement."

Flushing lightly at his slight reproof, Amethyst was unable to suppress the begrudging smile that tugged at her lips. "And as sorely as it chafes to admit my inadequacy, Armand, I'm afraid you're right. This past month has severely strained my self-confidence."

"Ah, then you must come with me now, ma petite Amethyst, for if there is one thing of which I am certain, it is that my unfaltering devotion will give your confidence the lift it needs."

"Oh, Armand!" Responding spontaneously to his soft-spoken charm, Amethyst's smile broadened. "You're outrageous!" Sliding her slender arm under his, she moved into step beside him as she continued, her eyes looking gratefully into his, "In any case, Armand, I will appreciate your guidance."

His eyes flicking quickly across her lovely face, Armand said quietly, "Oh, cherie, I . . ." Apparently reconsidering his statement, Armand stopped abruptly. Turning to give Mr. Falworth a brief salute, he turned back once again to smile into her eyes before drawing her with him to the door.

Carefully assisting her into the waiting carriage, Armand sat opposite her before inquiring politely, "Shall we return to your lodgings, Amethyst? Tillie will be an adequate chaperone, and I would like to speak to you in a place of privacy. Do you have any objections to my presence in your rooms, ma petite?"

"Armand!" Startled by his question, Amethyst's response was immediate. "Of course I don't! You've always been a perfect gentleman."

"Oui, cherie." Making no attempt to disguise his rueful expression, Armand shook his head with a small laugh, "But if I were to be completely honest, I would have to say it was extremely difficult at times." His smile suddenly broadening, Armand leaned forward to take her two hands into his. "But now, cherie, I want to talk about *now*. Now you are even more beautiful than when I last saw you, and I had not truly believed that possible. And the child, it is a girl, is it not? Your Tillie spoke of Marian."

"You are in for a treat, Armand," Amethyst responded brightly, her motherly pride sparkling in the lavender eyes raised to his. "She's a beautiful little girl."

"If she resembles her mother, then there is no doubt she is beautiful," Armand added, his heart warming at Amethyst's glowing response.

Her smile dimming for a brief second, Amethyst replied softly, "No, Armand, she doesn't resemble me, but . . . but she is a lovely baby, you'll see."

Oblivious to the assessing glances turned in her

direction, Amethyst quickly ascended the steps toward her room, turning to shoot Armand a small smile as he followed behind. "It was time I returned anyway, Armand. Marian will soon be wanting her feeding, and that is a task Tillie cannot perform for me, I'm afraid." Flushing slightly at her own outspokenness, Amethyst eagerly led Armand down the hall. Stopping to knock lightly at the door, she had only to wait the briefest moment before the key turned in the lock and the door opened to reveal Tillie's relieved expression. Her eyes moving quickly to the man behind her, Tillie stepped back to allow Amethyst and Armand entrance.

"I see you're not surprised to see Monsieur Beauchamps, Tillie." Directing a dark look into Tillie's face, Amethyst awaited her response as she slowly removed her cape.

"No, Tillie not be surprised." The mulatto's answer was direct. Turning her glance briefly in Armand's direction, she said quietly, "This man come here and Tillie see him worried for Amethyst Greer, just like Tillie. Tillie tell you not to go alone to see that man, but Amethyst not listen . . . Amethyst never listen to Tillie . . ."

"Alright, alright, Tillie." Waving her hand in surrender, Amethyst effectively stopped Tillie's stream of words. "You've had your way this time, and although it pains me to admit it, Armand did arrive just in time to save me from making a complete mess of the situation."

Shaking her head with a small, "Humph," Tillie muttered under her breath, "Amethyst Greer never listen to Tillie." Turning, Tillie abruptly walked away, leaving Amethyst to smile as her tall frame disappeared through the doorway into the next room.

Turning back, Amethyst met Armand's amused expression. Laughing, she said softly, "I'm afraid Tillie sometimes forgets I'm no longer nine years old, and it takes a bit of reminding now and then to make her realize I'm a grown woman now."

Laying his overcoat on the chair by the door, Armand advanced slowly toward her, his glance moving appreciatively over her slim frame. Her forest green dress was deceptively simple, the deep square neckline making the most of the smooth curve of her shoulder and the gentle rise of her breast, the narrow waistline nipping tightly to flare out in a graceful bell to her ankles; the only adornment the narrow white lace that trimmed the swaying folds that jutted out just above her elbows, and the same delicate lace that lay against her smooth breasts.

His glance warm, Armand said softly, "Ah, but I need no reminder, Amethyst. You are a delight to my eyes, ma petite." Lifting his hand, Armand smoothed back a stray curl that lay against her cheek, a small shudder shaking his broad frame as his fingertips touched her cheek ever so lightly. "Cherie," he said softly, his dark eyes looking intently into hers, "I should like very much to kiss you. You would not misconstrue?"

Touched by his sincerity, Amethyst responded softly, "No, Armand, I would not misconstrue."

His expression intently serious, Armand reached out to place his hands on her shoulders, his one hand slowly moving to the back of her neck as the other slid down to draw her close against him. Within moments his mouth covered hers, his lips moving warmly until they efficiently separated hers, his tongue finding the small separation to gently taste the sweetness of her mouth. Gradually his kiss deepened, the pressure of his mouth growing stronger, his arms straining her tighter and tighter against him until she was breathless in his embrace.

Sensing the trembling in his body as he drew away, Amethyst raised a questioning glance to his, only to see a familiar rueful smile appear on his darkly handsome face as he whispered in a shaky voice, "I am perhaps not as wise as I think myself to be, but I have missed you terribly, ma petite, and have been desperate to hold you in my arms since the moment I saw you again."

Nodding her head with a small frown, Amethyst replied softly, "Yes, perhaps that was not wise, Armand. I would not want to give you the impression that because I am no longer with Damien I am available."

"Cherie, please, say no more." His expression disturbed, Armand continued quietly, "I apologize if I have made you uncomfortable. It is not my intention to attempt to step into Monsieur Straith's shoes, no matter how appealing the fit. That is not the relationship I would have exist between us."

"What is the relationship you would wish, Armand?" Amethyst's question was soft and direct, her lavender eyes challenging his dark, pensive glance.

Realizing he had put Amethyst on the defensive, Armand shook his head in self-disgust. "Please, cherie, forget if you can what has just happened. I would not have you think I have illicit intentions when I inquire as to how I may help you."

Noting his obvious distress, Amethyst relented, a small smile returning to her lovely face. "I, too, must apologize, Armand. I'm afraid past experience has made me suspicious and distrustful. But you have never been else but truthful with me, and deserve my trust."

"*Bon!*" His expression relieved, Armand prompted quietly, "Then you must tell me all that has happened to bring you back to Philadelphia with your child and Tillie."

"Please, Armand, I don't want to go into the whole story. It's sordid and depressing, and I'd rather not . . ."

Taking both her small hands into his, Armand interrupted her soft response. "Ma cherie . . . mon coeur . . . you do believe I want to help you, don't you?"

Her eyes searched his face hesitantly for a few silent moments. His face intently serious, Armand returned her glance, his eyes a soft black, melting the last of her resistance with their warmth. "Yes, Armand. I do believe you."

"Then please tell me, ma cherie, tell me what has happened so I may assess how I may best help you out of the situation that forced you into that jeweler's shop today."

With a soft sigh, Amethyst walked to the couch and sat quietly, her glance inviting him to sit beside her. Slowly, painfully, as Armand held her hand, his quiet strength giving her the courage to go on, Amethyst related the events that had progressed in Kingston, her throat tight and aching when she came to the part where she described her departure from Jamaica. She did not tell Armand how the picture of Damien's face haunted her, how the memory of his arms around her left a deep void inside, how she wished with all her strength that his passion for her was sincere and good, and not the driven possessiveness that would have him take William's life with the evil obeah he practiced. She did not tell him that she had come to realize that she could not live her life subservient to the black magic which had become his way of life.

His keen eyes assessing her with a sensitivity that made further explanation unnecessary, Armand pulled Amethyst lightly against his chest, his arms holding her gently.

"So you find yourself in Philadelphia with only one more week of funds remaining, and only your jewels to fall back on, is that right, cherie?"

The mumbled response was barely audible. "Yes, Armand."

Moving her slowly away from him, he said softly as he looked into the wide eyes now a deep purple with unshed tears, "Then the answer is simple, cherie. You will come home with me, and I will take care of you."

Suddenly frowning, Amethyst began to rise from the couch. "That's impossible, Armand. I could not . . . I don't want . . ."

Taking her hands lightly in his, Armand restrained her from rising, his voice sincere. "Amethyst, please . . . listen to what I say, cherie. I force no arrangement of any kind on you. You will simply be my houseguest and you may . . ."

"Armand, I cannot live on your charity, no matter how generously it is given. I must find work."

"Did you not say Monsieur Henry will be coming to Philadelphia in January to petition the legislature for repeal of the anti-theater legislation?"

"Yes . . ."

"If he is successful, ma petite, the troupe will soon return to the country, and you will have your original place in the company, will you not?"

"Yes, but . . ."

"Then you will only be dependent on my 'generosity' for a few months, after which you will be self-supporting and able to pay me back if you so wish, is that not true?"

"Yes . . . but it is all so uncertain, Armand . . ."

"As is your situation now, cherie. But we can do no more than take one step at a time, can we? Come, ma petite." Raising her hands to his lips, Armand kissed them lightly, "Tell me you will come with me tonight so I may rest knowing you are safe in my care."

"Armand, you know what everyone will think . . . that I . . . that we . . ."

"Perhaps, cherie, but I for one will gladly suffer the wagging tongues for the satisfaction of knowing you are safe."

Her expression pensive for a few long moments, a small smile slowly broke through her sober facade. "And gossip no longer has the power to hurt a reputation such as mine, Armand, so I suppose I have nothing to lose..."

"C'est bien, cherie."

"Then I thank you, and will accept your hospitality until John Henry petitions the legislature. If he is successful, I will await the return of the American Company. If not, at least Marian will be less dependent on me by that time, and I will find it easier to get some work to support us. But I promise you, Armand, I will pay you back. One way or another, I will pay you back for your generosity."

A relieved expression moving across his handsome face, Armand said softly, "*Bon*, it is settled, and yes, you may pay me back if you wish, ma cherie." Leaning forward, Armand kissed her soft lips lightly, a small spark of hope beginning to grow inside his chest as his mind sang with growing optimism, "Fort bien, mon coeur, mon amour..."

His fists nervously clenching and unclenching, Damien paced his narrow cell, the grating sound of his own step mingling with the scraping pit-a-pat of other small feet as the slippery co-occupants of his dank abode scampered into a dark corner. But he barely noticed their presence, now. Rubbing his palm over the scraggly beard that covered his chin, Damien grimaced with disgust. He was filthy and uncomfortable. He had neither bathed nor shaved since he had entered this vile place over a month before. The stench of his own body was nauseating, and judging from the almost constant itching plaguing him of late, he was now a haven for the orphaned lice that had been abandoned by the last occupant of his cell. But the petty complaints of his imprisonment were not the thoughts that drove him relentlessly. Freedom and revenge... once having attained the first, he had promised himself that he would not stop until the second had been accomplished!

But his burning desire was not to avenge himself against William Sheridan. The fool had merely been a tool for Amethyst to use against him. Through the long dark days and nights, Damien had gone over in his mind again and again the words William Sheridan had spoken. "She smiled a bright farewell to me as she sailed . . ." The bitch had planned well! Wide, lavender eyes innocent and beguiling, she had confounded him, led him to trust her while she secretly planned his arrest with William Sheridan. But Sheridan had not received the reward he had expected! Hah! Amethyst had used him well, and if he knew the wily little witch at all, she had probably left Kingston with enough of the fool's money to maintain her in comfort at her destination. But where had she gone . . . what was she doing now . . . who was caring for her and his daughter? Doubtless Tillie had left with her. Kingston held only bitter memories and a dark future for the hapless mulatto. No, she would not allow Amethyst to leave alone with the child.

Damn! Damn! Pounding his clenched fist into the stone wall again and again in bitter frustration, Damien did not stop until blood oozed from the deep gashes on his knuckles, the pain succeeding in effectively eliminating for a brief moment the even stronger pain he felt deep inside. He was a fool! He had actually begun to believe Amethyst was softening toward him . . . that she was inwardly relieved that she had no other recourse but to marry him! Rubbing his aching fist absentmindedly, Damien gave a small bitter laugh. Fool that he was he had chosen to forget Amethyst was an actress by profession, skilled in the art of creating illusion. But she had not won yet, damn her! He would be free of this place soon. The authorities could not hold him much longer without granting him a hearing on the charges against him.

William Sheridan had all but admitted he had no real evidence against him or his crew. When he was free once again he would find Amethyst and his child, and make her pay for her deception. Yes, he already had a plan. All he needed now was to be free.

The sound of muffled footsteps outside his door interrupted Damien's dark thoughts, the sound of a key in the lock jerking his glance in its direction as the grating sound echoed against the wall behind him. The door opened slowly, the familiar face of the foul-smelling guard the first he saw before the squat figure was pushed aside to allow another to peer anxiously into his cell.

"Damien?" His eyes obviously not yet adjusted to the poor light, the tall wiry man's voice was uncertain. "Damien, are you in there?"

Walking slowly forward, almost unable to believe his eyes, Damien said softly, "Yes, Hiram, I'm here. But what are you doing here? You are not going to join me in my elaborate accommodations, are you, old friend?"

Shaking his head with a small snort, Hiram Strathmore said impatiently, "Enough of this foolish talk, Damien. Come out here now. You are free to leave Kingston, both you and your crew. The charges against you have been dropped."

"Dropped!" Wasting no time in following his friend's urging, Damien stepped over the threshold of the cell, expecting at any minute to have the door slammed in his face. But he walked freely into the corridor, his heart beginning to thump wildly in his chest as full realization hit him for the first time. He was free!

Turning to walk stiffly toward the wooden staircase, Hiram urged softly, "Come, Damien. This is no time for dilly-dallying. You must be out of this place quickly. Your men are in a different part of the prison, and are being released. You must make haste to get your ship out of port in the event that fool upstairs should change his mind."

Following closely behind him, Damien questioned softly, "But how did you know I was here? How did you manage this, Hiram? The charges have been dropped, you say?"

"Word of your arrest came to me in Philadelphia and I merely impressed upon the mind of that imbecile upstairs that the Peace Treaty between our two governments was scheduled to be signed this month, and a reckless act such as arresting a prominent American captain who had served his country well might be viewed by our country as an unfriendly step. That unhappy man upstairs did not want to spend any more time than necessary on this forgotten island, which was certain to be his punishment should he succeed in irritating his government. As a result, you are freed, Damien." Turning his sharp eyes in Damien's direction, Hiram hesitated only briefly before continuing. "Your men have been instructed to meet you at the ship, and I'm certain they will waste no time getting there."

Walking boldly past the guards at the entrance, Damien stepped into the open air at last, stopping to take a deep breath as he turned with a smile. "Freedom smells good, Hiram. I had not realized how truly good until now."

Looking at his friend with a raised brow, Hiram said in an almost undistinguishable voice, "Yes, it smells far better than you do right now, I'm afraid. I think the first order of business will be a bath and a change of clothes, Damien."

"Yes, my friend, I heartily agree," Damien responded with a small frown. "A bath, a change of clothes, a good meal and . . ."

"And you'll leave the island as soon as possible. I have already instructed water and provisions be delivered to your ship. The *Sally* can be loaded within a few hours, and I do not believe your men will balk at sailing so quickly. I think I can safely assume they have had enough of Jamaica for a long time to come."

"No, Hiram, the *Sally* will not sail for a few days. The men need a little time, and I must finish some very important business."

"Damien, are you insane? You must leave this place as soon as possible!"

Turning a steely-eyed glance in his direction, Damien said firmly, "No, Hiram. There is something I must do first. I will not leave Kingston until it's done. That is my final word."

His expression firm and unbending, Damien assessed the middle-aged man before him. Like the room in which he was standing, the man was obviously deteriorating with age. His thin, none-too-clean gray hair was unkempt, a heavy paunch hung over britches that had seen better days, the creased skin of his face was mottled and blotchy, silent testimony to many hours spent deep in his cups. But the rheumy eyes were alert as they openly assessed him.

"I must admit it is a handsome price you offer, Captain Straith, but I don't believe I wish to sell at any price. There are definite reasons why this one in particular is valuable to me. I do admit to being curious, however. Won't you tell me why the captain of a merchant ship has come all this way to purchase one of my field slaves?"

"My reasons are personal, Mr. Conway, but my money is good. I know you are well aware that you can easily buy two field slaves with the amount of money I'm offering you for this particular Negro."

"Yes, Captain Straith . . . and that is what is so curious . . ."

Turning at a sound at the entrance to the room, Percy Conway raised his voice in a brief command. "Come in here, Raymond. There is a gentleman here who is interested in buying you."

His eyes quickly following Conway's glance, Damien looked assessingly at the tall black man as he shuffled forward. The eyes moving momentarily to his were sharp and intelligent, the shuffling step obviously assumed for his benefit, judging from the muscular tone of the man's broad frame which indicated an excellent physical condition and immense strength. He obviously did not want to be sold from the plantation. But Damien was determined to have him.

"I don't intend answering any of your questions, Conway, and I have little time to waste in bargaining. I'll double the price I've already offered." Watching closely as the bloodshot eyes blinked with surprise, Damien said impatiently, "Alright, Conway. What's your answer?"

"I think I shall have to . . ."

"No!" A shrieking voice interrupted Conway's slow response, turning all eyes in its direction as Quasheba raged into the room, her black eyes flashing. "Massa promise Quasheba have Raymond! Raymond belong t' Quasheba, 'n Massa not gowan sell Raymond t' any backra dat come here wid him money!"

"Be quiet, Quasheba!" Conway's face flushed with anger, he looked warningly in her direction. "Be quiet this minute or . . ."

"Quasheba not be quiet! Raymond belong t' Quasheba! Dis white man not gowan . . ."

"You have said enough, Quasheba!" Raising his hand, Conway slapped the enraged Negress full across the face, knocking her backward against the chair as he moved to stand over her. "No! Don't get up or I'll knock you down again!" he hissed as she began to rise.

Turning back to Damien, Conway made a valiant attempt to control the fury that shook his obese body. "I was about to say I would not sell at any price, Captain, but my mind has been very effectively changed for me."

"No! Massa not gowan sell Raymond!" Making a quick attempt to get to her feet, Quasheba's movement was quelled by Conway's sharp command as he turned again in her direction.

"I will not warn you again, Quasheba! Stay on the floor where you are and don't say another word!"

Hesitating as the Negress slowly cringed under his intense stare, Conway then walked quickly to his desk. Rifling impatiently through the drawers, he finally pulled out the paper he sought, and dipping the quill into the ink, scribbled across its surface. Turning, he walked directly to Damien.

"As I said before, Captain, my mind has been very effectively changed for me." Holding out the paper in his hand, he continued in a controlled voice. "The transfer paper, Captain."

Slowly taking the document extended to him, Damien counted out the money in its place. "Our bargain is sealed, Mr. Conway. Good day."

Sparing only a short glance for the tall Negro standing watchfully in the center of the room, Damien said curtly, "You belong to me now, Raymond. Follow me. It's time to leave."

Falling in behind as Damien walked out of the room, Raymond shot only the briefest glance to the quivering Negress where she still sat on the floor. A small sneer crossing his lips, his heart warmed as Quasheba slipped out of his sight for the last time.

More excited than she cared to reveal, Amethyst walked briskly down the State House corridor. Her brown velvet cape streaming out behind her revealed the gold velvet of her gown. Absentmindedly pushing back the hood that covered her brilliant tresses, she revealed a lining in the same glowing color, a subtle trademark of

Madame duMaurier's artistry. Several ensembles had arrived at Armand's residence, marked for her within the past few weeks. Startled, Amethyst had questioned Armand about the extravagant purchases.

"Cherie, your wardrobe is decidedly inadequate, is it not?"

Having brought only a limited change of winter clothing with her for her return from Jamaica, Amethyst's wardrobe consisted of four day gowns, limited underwear, and one pair of sturdy shoes, in addition to the otter-lined cape that had served her well since her arrival. The extensive wardrobe Damien had purchased for her was still in his house on Chestnut Street, but she did not consider that clothing her property any longer. After all, the clothing had been bought for Damien's mistress, and since she no longer held that position, she had merely struck them from her mind. But raising her chin to a stubborn tilt, she had answered challengingly, "I believe my wardrobe will serve my needs very well, Armand. I have no need for such elaborate ensembles as have arrived today. As lovely as I must admit they are, I also must request that you send them back to Madame with my regrets."

"Ah, cherie, so you intend to punish me . . ."

"Punish you?" Momentarily startled by his response, Amethyst had slowly perused the Frenchman's hurt expression. "Punish you, Armand? I'm afraid I don't understand what you mean."

"If you will not accept these meager offerings, ma petite, and claim your needs are adequately served, then that would serve to say you do not intend to accompany me in public on our free evenings."

Hesitating briefly as Armand studied her expression, Amethyst had said uncertainly, "Armand, I truly did not think you would want . . . I mean, I didn't think it wise to be seen . . . Oh, I don't really know what I mean,

Armand, except that it would be decidedly awkward for you and me to be seen together, would it not? After all, just a few months ago I was introduced into this same society as Damien Straith's ward. A short time later, my position changed to that of Damien Straith's fiancee, and all too brief a period after that anyone but a blind man knew full well that I was his mistress."

"And now you have returned to Philadelphia, ma petite, and you are my house guest."

"Ah, I can see the eyebrows rise over that one!" Amethyst said under her breath with a small shake of her head.

"But it is true, nevertheless, cherie, and I will not have suspicious minds influence my behavior."

"But is it necessary to flaunt my position in front of the very people who only a few months ago . . ."

"Cherie, you misunderstand me. I do not intend dragging you from party to party on my arm as if displaying my latest acquisition. Nothing was further from my mind, mon amour. Surely you realize that."

"I'm afraid I'm confused, Armand. I truly don't know what . . ."

His expression softening, Armand had taken Amethyst's small face between his palms as he said softly, "These two weeks that you have spent in my house have been good, have they not, cherie?"

Nodding lightly, Amethyst had responded in a soft voice, "Yes, they have, Armand." She had not told him of the nights she had lain awake in her lonely bed, despising herself as her mind returned to Damien again and again, remembering the touch of his hands, the warmth of his strong body against hers, her longing for him so deep and acute that she felt she would expire from the endless ache inside her. Only Armand's warm presence relieved the dilemma of knowing she loved a man whose reliance on black magic had brought her to him, and possibly still held her within its grasp . . . a man she could not trust with her future and the future of their child. But, yes, the time spent with Armand had helped soothe the ache. Nodding her head she said again, "Yes, Armand, the time spent with you has been good."

"That is all I ask, cherie. I should like to attend a musicale being performed this Friday, and your presence beside me would give me much pleasure."

"Armand, do you not think one of your mistresses would better accompany you? I mean, do they not feel neglected . . . ?"

"Cherie, is it truly in your heart to punish me for my past relationships?"

"Oh, no, Armand, please believe me. I had no such intention. I merely thought . . ."

"Then think no more, ma petite. Those relationships are past. We will not speak of them again."

A small frown covering her delicate brow, Amethyst responded soberly, "My residence here is only temporary, Armand. That was our understanding from the beginning."

A light smile moving across his lips, Armand responded, "My mind understands completely, cherie, but my heart does not listen when it speaks." Bending his head to kiss her lips lightly, Armand released her face to continue in a stronger voice, "Will you accompany me to the musicale, Amethyst? I would not enjoy the music without you."

Noting his obvious sincerity, Amethyst could no longer hold out against his entreaty. "Yes, Armand, I would very much enjoy accompanying you. Perhaps I have dwelled too long on my problems."

"Bon! In that case, cherie, you must accept the gowns as suitable attire for the occasions when you will do me the honor of accompanying me . . ."

"But I cannot!"

A small sigh of exasperation passing his lips, Armand's voice began to tinge with impatience. "If you insist, cherie, I will make a proper accounting of the cost and you may pay me back sometime in the future. Does that meet with your agreement?"

Her mind working feverishly, Amethyst had considered his suggestion for a few long moments. Armand was right. And should John Henry be successful in having the anti-theater legislation reversed, she would need suitable attire when she assumed her place in the troupe. Lifting her eyes to his, Amethyst offered at last, "Yes, Armand, that does seem fine to me."

Vastly relieved, Armand had smiled broadly, his darkly handsome face lighting with pleasure. "Cherie, I can see I was very wrong about one thing at least in my estimation of you."

"And what was that, Armand?"

"Ma petite, you do indeed drive a very hard bargain."

A smile finally breaking across her own lips, Amethyst had responded with a quick, spontaneous hug that had set wings to his heart, "Oh, Armand, you truly are a dear fellow."

The clicking tempo of her heels echoing in the empty corridor as she hastened her pace, Amethyst turned to shoot an impatient glance over her shoulder as she called softly to the tall mulatto woman who maintained a steady pace behind her, "Tillie, must you lag behind so? I told Mr. Peale that I would come to view his work at eleven o'clock, and it's already a few minutes past the hour! Armand will be here to meet me at twelve and I should like to have ample time to study Mr. Peale's work."

"Tillie walking as fast as him feet will carry him, Amethyst, and Tillie not gowan push him feet any harder."

The light, cocoa-colored face was set in an adamant

expression that Amethyst knew only too well, and shaking her head with exasperation, Amethyst continued her brisk step.

Word had just reached American shores that the definitive Treaty of Peace had been signed in Paris in December. In celebration of the momentous event, the Philadelphia Executive Council planned a magnificent parade to be held one week after the treaty was ratified by Congress and commissioned Charles Wilson Peale, the same artist commissioned to do the official portrait of George Washington, to design and construct a glorious temporary structure that would serve as a brilliant commencement to the grand celebration. Having met the slight, pale artist a week previous, Amethyst had been extremely enthusiastic when he had invited her to view the work presently in progress for the display. Turning to Armand for guidance, she had been quick to sense his approval, and accepted with an eagerness that was refreshing to the dedicated painter. Having been directed to the room in the State House turned over to Peale as his painting studio, Amethyst turned another corner and approached the designated door. Taking a brief moment to regain her composure, Amethyst then raised her hand to knock lightly, her heart quickening at the prompt invitation to enter. Suddenly behind her as she opened the door, Tillie entered in her wake, her dark eyes mirroring the amazement reflected in Amethyst's as she viewed the brilliant transparencies already completed.

A pleased smile slipping over his face, Charles Peale advanced in her direction, his hand outstretched in greeting. Suddenly snatching it away again, his pale face flushed as he apologized profusely. "I'm exceedingly happy to see you have been able to come to view my work, Miss Greer, but I must apologize for my paint-smeared hands that will not allow me to greet you properly."

"It is my pleasure to come, Mr. Peale." Her sparkling

lavender eyes mirroring her enthusiasm, Amethyst smiled in return. "Armand has told me so much about your work, and I'm very anxious to view your marvelous transparencies at close range."

Obviously flattered by her interest, Charles Peale replied with equal enthusiasm, "Then you must follow me to the corner where I've made a rough model of the design on which I am now working."

Drawing her with him, Peale proudly displayed a miniature edifice consisting of three arches. "You see before you a small reproduction of the grand edifice that will stretch fifty feet across Market Street when it is completed. The structure will consist of three hollow arches, the center one being thirty-five feet high, independent of the surmounting statuary. Outside, the arches will be covered with the transparencies and mottos on which I am presently working. Inside will be positioned over 1200 lamps to illuminate the transparencies, and a network of ladders and platforms from which various mechanical devices will be manipulated by technicians. The construction of the actual framework is assigned to a group of carpenters, while my apprentice, Billy Mercer," turning, Peale indicated a young deaf mute standing nearby, "and I will endeavor to supply the artistic touches."

Much impressed by the small model, Amethyst prompted eagerly, "And how will this structure be positioned, Mr. Peale?"

"As you know, my dear," the gentleman began patiently, "the celebration is scheduled to begin at twilight on the twenty-second. A route will be published in the newspapers, and citizens will march down Market Street, carriages passing through the center arch, and pedestrians passing through the side arches. Atop a well-situated house I shall place a figure of Peace, rigged so as to suddenly appear and descend along a rope to the top of the arch. Here the Peace figure will ignite a central fuse, touching off the thousand lamps within a minute. As the arch and its paintings begin to glow colorfully, there will be a huge burst of fireworks from the top of the arch, opening the celebration!"

Gasping with delight as her mind followed the colorful description to its glorious climax, Amethyst clasped her hands together in rapt mental enjoyment of the scene. "How marvelous to have conceived such a brilliant idea, Mr. Peale!"

His face flushing lightly at her enthusiastic praise, Peale eased her slowly along the line of completed transparencies. Patiently guiding her, he pointed out the representations of the French King, of various war heroes, of the different States and of the arts and sciences, as well as a "Pyramidal Cenotaph" with the names of fallen soldiers, a tree with thirteen fruitful branches, and a picture of Indians building churches in the wilderness. Drawing her attention to the remarkable transparency rendering Washington as Cincinnatus returning to his plough, Peale explained the motto inscribed below, VICTRIX VIRTUS, as meaning "Victorious Virtue."

"The central arch," Peale continued fervently, "will be crowned with a Temple of Janus, shut to represent the close of the war, its motto echoing our new seal—NUMINE FAVENTE MAGNUS AB INTEGRO SAECULORUM NASSITUR ORDO—'By divine favor, a great and new order of the ages commences.'"

Speechless at the magnificence displayed so casually before her, Amethyst spent the following hour in rapt attention to the artist's detailed narration. Her eyes suddenly catching a glimpse of a small clock standing unobtrusively on a nearby table, Amethyst gasped audibly, "Oh, good heavens! It's fifteen minutes past the hour of twelve! I was to meet Monsieur Beauchamps outside at 12! I must leave, Mr. Peale, but not before I extend my deep appreciation for this short glimpse of the extravagant beauty you have created." Her expression obviously sincere, she continued quietly, "I do feel extremely honored to have been allowed a preview of your brilliant work."

Obviously charmed by her sincerity, completely forgetting his paint-smeared hands, Charles Peale took the delicate hand extended toward him, raising it to his lips in a gallant gesture not anticipated in the shy, slender family man, "The pleasure has indeed been mine, Miss Greer."

Taking her leave, the glow of enthusiasm still lighting her lovely countenance, Amethyst hastened down the corridor toward the front entrance to the State House. Abruptly aware as she turned a corner that Tillie was not at her side, she turned again to dart an impatient glance behind her. Maintaining the steady pace that was her norm, Tillie trailed a short distance behind, and realizing the futility of urging haste, Amethyst continued forward, her small delicate frame colliding heavily with a tall, unmoving figure that stood before her.

Embarrassed at her clumsiness, Amethyst raised apologetic eyes, only to have her glance meet and hold a familiar transparent gaze. Her heart thudding heavily in her breast, Amethyst gasped. "Damien!" Pulling free of the strong arms that steadied her, Amethyst heard a startled gasp echoing behind her as Tillie turned the corner. Turning to Tillie's incredulous expression, Amethyst followed her gaze past Damien to the man who stood behind him. Fashionably dressed, a tall Negro held Tillie's eyes with his, his stoic expression flickering only once as Tillie whispered unbelievingly, "Raymond . . . Raymond . . ."

"Raymond?" Her glance darting back to Damien's smug expression, she listened as Damien smoothly answered her unspoken question. "Yes, Raymond. It is unfortunate you left the island with such haste, Amethyst. And unfortunate for both you and Tillie that you have taken up residence with your 'friend,' Armand Beauchamps. But, of course, I would expect having planned to have me imprisoned, you would feel I was adequately out of the way for quite some time. But I have surprised you, have I not, Amethyst?"

Sensing the heat of hatred burning behind his cool facade, Amethyst trembled wildly. Fear at his obvious anger, and happiness to see him safe and well, battled vigorously inside her, fear gaining the stronger hold as Damien's fury became more apparent.

His cool facade slipping immeasurably, Damien's facial muscles became taut, his full sensuous mouth twisting into a tight line as he hissed venomously, "Did it give you pleasure to plan your escape with William Sheridan, Amethyst? I must say you played your part well, darling, the loving mistress to the end, finally succumbing with convincing poignancy to my pressures to make you my wife. I must admit I was not in the least suspicious of you, my dear. Fool that I was, I was convinced you intended to go through with the marriage . . ." His words choking off, Damien finished the statement in his mind, ". . . and fool that I was, I ached with despair at the threat necessary to make you agree to become my wife." Despising himself with the realization that even as he spewed forth his heated grievances against her, he longed to take the slight figure into his arms, to hold her tight against him until he was truly certain that she was not merely another image his tortured brain had conceived; to feel those soft, appealing lips under his again; to taste the incredible sweetness within. Clenching his fists against the almost overpowering urge, Damien continued aloud, "But I'm free, Amethyst, and I've returned to Philadelphia. I must admit I was not pleased to find you had found another protector so quickly, but I suppose Armand Beauchamps was part of your plan from the first." Jealousy twisting his stomach into knots even as he spoke, Damien continued hoarsely, "You are a consummate actress, Amethyst. I shall have to remember that when dealing with you in the future."

Her face pale, Amethyst responded with a shaky confidence, "You need not worry about dealing with me in the future, Damien. I am free of you now, and I will remain free of you."

His eyes a clear gray ice, Damien replied confidently, "You will return to me, Amethyst."

"I shall not! I shall never return to you, Damien! Marian will not grow up under the influence of your black magic, and I will not live the rest of my life in its shadow!"

His anger deepening, Damien said in a low, ominous voice, "You will do, and you will live, just exactly as I say!"

"You are very wrong, Monsieur Straith!" A deep, angry voice from behind turned all glances in his direction as Armand walked quickly to Amethyst's side. "Amethyst is with me now. She is my house guest, and under my protection. I cannot allow you to threaten her in my presence!"

"Your *house guest?* Hah! Surely you don't expect me to believe that nonsense, Beauchamps? No man with any blood in his veins could keep Amethyst Greer under his roof and still allow her to remain . . ."

"That is where you are wrong, Monsieur Straith!" Armand's heated response interrupted Damien's words. "Did it never occur to you that I might not desire to force Amethyst into my bed, only to have her run away at the first given opportunity, as she did from you? You are the fool, Straith! For what have you gained but to have the woman you desire so completely repelled by you that she would flee hundreds of miles to escape your possession?"

Armand's verbal barbs struck fertile ground, and flushing slightly, Damien responded with exaggerated sarcasm, "Truly, I am very pleased with your nobility, Beauchamps. Such an admirable quality will no doubt allow you to accept with equal grace Amethyst's decision to return to me."

"You play the fool, Straith." Armand's low tone was a direct reproof.

"We shall see who ultimately plays the fool, Beauchamps." Turning to address Amethyst, Damien mentally noted the quaking of her small frame, her growing pallor, the trembling of her delicate lips as she returned his direct gaze. "You must realize, Amethyst, you disrupt a very well rounded family group with your stubbornness. Marian belongs with her father . . . Tillie belongs with Raymond . . . and you belong with me."

"No!" Turning to look into Tillie's tortured face, Amethyst turned back to stare heatedly into Damien's sober expression. "You will not place the burden of Tillie's pain on my shoulders, Damien Straith!"

"If not on yours, Amethyst, then on whose shoulders should it rest? You have but to say the word and Tillie and Raymond will be reunited."

"No! No!" Her eyes widening in sudden rage, Amethyst charged Damien wildly, her slender arms flailing out to pummel his chest and face in frantic desperation as violent tears streamed down her pale cheeks. "No! No!" Scratching and kicking fiercely, she continued her violent attack until strong arms clamped around her in gentle restraint.

"No, cherie, this is not the answer. Come, ma petite, come." Taking her sobbing frame into his arms, Armand directed a heated glance into Damien's impassive facade before turning without a word and urging Amethyst away.

Powerless against their departure, Damien watched Amethyst's weeping form as she was drawn away in Beauchamps's sympathetic arms, the tightness in his throat growing until he could barely breathe past the swelling obstruction. Finding his voice at last, Damien allowed his voice to follow them as they made their exit, his words heavy on Amethyst's already growing guilt. "No, Amethyst. That was not the answer. You know what the only answer can be. You know . . . and you will return to me . . ."

Watching until Amethyst's forlorn figure moved out of sight, Tillie tall and proud walking behind her, Damien turned to Raymond, to see his own pain reflected in the black eyes that returned his stare. Raising his hand, Damien clamped the broad shoulder with a reassuring grip, his glance sympathetic to his pain, his voice sincere.

"I would have you know, Raymond," he began hesitantly, "that I do not enjoy using you to my advantage and deeply regret your pain. But you need not worry. This is but a small setback. We will both have our women again . . . both of us. You have my word on that."

The fine, perfectly shaped lips nursing at her breast dropped slowly open, a small stream of milk dribbling out the corner of the diminutive mouth as heavy lids closed over peculiarly light gray eyes. Her own lips turning up into a smile, a dimple skipping across her smooth cheek at the picture of absolute contentment and serenity on Marian's sleeping face, Amethyst felt a strong surge of love for the dozing infant. She was really such a good baby, and would probably sleep right through to her next feeding without a whimper, although it was a source of constant amazement that her own anxiety had not been transmitted to her blissfully sleeping child. It had been a tension-filled week since she had seen Damien in the corridor at the State House. Although she had attempted to continue with her life as if Damien had not appeared in Philadelphia, the pressure of Tillie's silent suffering weighed heavily on her conscience. If it were just for herself, she would have submitted to the personal longing plaguing her day and night, Damien's image always fresh in her mind.

She had now come to believe that she would never be free of the memory of his touch, the sound of his passion-filled voice throbbing softly against her ear, the beauty that raged between them in their more intimate moments, and his tenderness . . . his supreme tenderness . . . Inconceivable to her was the fact that she even missed the challenge of his vibrant personality, his quick mind and the sparks that resulted from the clash of their strong wills. She now convinced herself that she owed it to Tillie and Raymond—and to her own aching need—to return to Damien, were it not for Marian. But as many times as she had reviewed the situation in her mind, she could come up with only one answer. She could not allow Marian to suffer the domination of a man who practiced black magic . . . even if that man was her father. Above all, her child came first, and she could not sacrifice Marian to her own weakness.

Carefully covering her breast, Amethyst rose to her feet, quietly carrying Marian to her cradle in the corner. Armand had generously arranged that Tillie share the room next to hers with the baby so she might sleep undisturbed. At first suspicious that Armand had made those arrangements to smooth the way for the time when he would carefully insinuate himself into her bed, Amethyst was now ashamed of her suspicions. Armand had confirmed her initial respect and confidence, a fact that had allowed him to grow immeasurably in her esteem. But she feared for a confrontation to come. In the week since their meeting in the State House, Damien had appeared mysteriously each time she had left the house on an errand. Turning, she had found him behind her at the bookseller's... waiting at Madame du-Maurier's boutique when she arrived for a fitting... present at the musicale she and Armand had attended... his presence always disturbing, shaking her confidence, his sheer masculinity stirring a longing deep inside as he observed her silently, Raymond always at his side in grim reminder. But Armand was fast losing patience with Damien's haunting presence. It had only been her fervent pleas that had stopped the irate Frenchman from facing Damien down, and she feared, should the silent persecution continue, Armand's anger would not be held in check. Had she any other recourse, she would leave Armand now rather than risk his life, for she was certain it would come to that should a confrontation occur. Through her anxiety Armand became dearer to her each day, his unselfishness and obvious devotion to both Marian and herself warming an already strong affection.

Taking one last look at her sleeping infant, Amethyst moved quietly toward the door. Closing it silently behind her as she stepped into the hallway, Amethyst was caught by the low rumble of voices at the front door. Walking softly to the balustrade, she peered down into the foyer, her breath catching in her throat as her eyes touched on a familiar tawny-haired figure. Dressed impeccably in dark blue, his hat in his hand, Damien spoke insistently with the old servant as Raymond stood silently behind him.

"I've come to see my daughter, and I don't intend to leave until I have ascertained that she is well." Damien's low voice held the edge of impatience as he reasoned with the adamant woman.

"I'm sorry, Mr. Straith, Monsieur Beauchamps is not at home and he has instructed that no one be admitted to this house in his absence." Obviously flustered, the woman shook her gray head emphatically, stepping back in spontaneous reaction to the anger that flared in the cold gray eyes regarding her so intently.

"I don't give a damn what Beauchamps has instructed! It is my child he has under his roof and I . . ."

A small squeak in the floorboards as Amethyst stepped back from the railing drew Damien's attention upward, his eyes tangling with hers as she clutched tightly at the dressing gown at her throat. Suddenly springing into action, Damien pushed past the woman firmly blocking his entrance, taking the steps two at a time until he was standing in front of Amethyst. His broad chest heaving lightly from his quick ascent, his eyes slowly raked the soft outline of her body under the lavender silk of her dressing gown, the roundness of her breasts as she clutched the neckline closed with a slender trembling hand, the creamy smoothness of her flawless complexion as she turned her frightened face up to his, the quivering of the soft, warm lips he longed to crush beneath his own. But there was terror in the wide, violet eyes that regarded him intently, and suddenly sick with the realization that the woman he loved above all things should fear him so intently, he longed to take her into his arms, to whisper lovingly into her ear, reassure her that he wanted only to love her and his child . . . love them for the rest of his life. But the soft lips parted to speak, her words sending a flush of rage to his face.

"Get out of this house! You have no right here, Damien Straith! Armand would not want you up here, and . . ."

"To hell with Armand Beauchamps!" Damien growled viciously, his lips twisting into an angry snarl. "Do you think I care what Armand Beauchamps wants?"

"You are in his house!"

"And he is holding my woman and my child!"

"I am not your woman!" Amethyst declared vehemently, the fear in her eyes effectively replaced by anger as she continued heatedly, "and although you have fathered my child, she belongs to me!"

His arms snaking out, gripped her roughly by the shoulders as he hissed under his breath, "And to me. Now tell me where she is, damn you, or I'll take every room in this house apart until I find her!"

His hands were cutting into her shoulders, but determined not to wince against the pain, Amethyst said softly, "She's sleeping. I've just fed her."

"Where is she?"

"You won't disturb her?"

Giving her a hard shake, he hissed under his breath, "Tell me where she is, damn you!"

Raising her hands, she firmly dislodged his grip from her shoulders. "If you'll be quiet, I'll take you to her."

Allowing her to precede him, Damien followed behind as Amethyst walked to the door a few steps away. As he entered, Damien's gaze immediately fastened on the small cradle in the corner. Striding quickly in its direction, he looked down on the face of his sleeping child, a wave of warmth sweeping over him at the sight of her sleeping innocence. Bending down, he touched the fine blonde hair gingerly, smiling as the tiny lips turned upward in a quick, sleeping smile. His voice was husky as he spoke.

"She's beautiful, isn't she, Amethyst." Raising his eyes to hers, he said softly, "Beautiful . . . just like her mother . . ."

Disturbed by the fact that his sudden tenderness was working its usual magic on her senses, Amethyst frowned as she answered hesitantly, "No, she doesn't look like her mother."

"Yes . . . yes, she does, Amethyst," Damien insisted, taking a few steps toward her to draw her beside him as he stood looking down at the small, sleeping face. The tiny lips worked lightly in her sleep, and Damien said softly, "See . . . there . . . the small dimple in her cheek. When she grows, she will someday fascinate men with the way it flicks across her cheek as she speaks. Her hands . . . they're long-fingered and slender, like yours . . . delicate and expressive . . ." Taking her hand, Damien slowly raised it to his lips, his eyes holding hers as he kissed her fingers with tantalizing slowness.

"Amethyst . . ."

A hesitant summons from the doorway interrupted the scene as Tillie said with a tinge of anger to her tone, "Tillie be here if you need him . . ."

Her face flushing at the censure in the mulatto's eyes, Amethyst said quietly, "No, Tillie, everything is alright. Damien just wanted to see Marian. Now that he has seen her he is about to leave." Turning back to Damien, she continued in a firm voice, "Isn't that right, Damien?"

His glance hardening, Damien turned toward Tillie. "I'll be detained here a few more minutes, Tillie. In the meantime there is someone in the foyer that you might want to speak with until I'm done."

Tillie had come up the back entrance, and had not passed the foyer, but the inference was not lost on her sharp mind. Her small intake of breath the only indication that she realized Raymond was so near, Tillie said softly, "Would you like me to stay, Amethyst?"

"No, please go downstairs, Tillie. Damien and I will be through here in a minute."

Nodding her head, Tillie turned away, her steady pace not indicative of the heart that raced in her breast.

When Tillie had cleared the doorway, Amethyst said firmly, thankful for the interruption, "We're disturbing Marian's sleep, Damien. I think it would be best if we continued any further conversation outside."

Silently following behind Amethyst, Damien's eyes flicked around in the room in brief assessment.

"You don't share this room with Marian, do you, Amethyst?"

Startled, Amethyst stopped abruptly outside the door. "N . . . no, I don't. Tillie takes care of Marian through the night, waking me only for feedings. How did you know that?"

Ignoring her question, Damien suddenly demanded hotly, "Where *do* you sleep, Amethyst?" The nagging jealousy of the past months tore viciously at his insides, turning his voice into a low hiss, "Has Beauchamps convinced you to repay his 'generosity'?"

The surge of color to her face effectively destroyed the last vestige of weakening within her. Trembling with anger, Amethyst spoke slowly and deliberately, "Do not put me in the same category as yourself, Damien. If you will look back in your memory, you will recall that I was a virgin when you took me, and that was not because of any lack of pressure for me to remain so! You also do Armand a disservice in putting him in your class. He demands nothing of me. He is giving, polite, tender, everything a man should be . . ."

His expression hardening as she spoke, Damien's hands suddenly reached out to grasp her shoulders, his voice harsh as he rasped, "And does he make you quiver with wanting him, Amethyst?" His one hand slipping into her hair tightened painfully as the other slid around her waist to draw her tight against the roughness of his coat. "Does he make your heart race the way it is racing now?" His eyes holding hers hypnotically, Damien's mouth descended to cover hers with a slow possession that effectively drowned out all trace of protest as his lips pressed hers apart, his tongue slipping between to touch and fondle hers as his hand moved warmly along her back. Finally tearing his lips from hers, Damien said shakily, "Does he kiss you like that, Amethyst?" Not waiting for her response, Damien moved to spread warm kisses along her cheek, his chest heaving heavily with growing passion as his lips slid down the slender column of her throat and into the opening of her dressing gown.

In a last frantic attempt to stave the weakness swiftly overwhelming her, Amethyst whispered tightly, "No, he doesn't, Damien. Armand is a gentleman. He waits for the day when I will go to him freely. He would have me as his wife, not as his . . ."

A burning jealousy raging through him, Damien hissed softly, "He waits in vain, Amethyst, because you'll never go to him. I'll see him dead first! You belong to me . . . only me . . ."

Suddenly scooping her into his arms, Damien walked swiftly to the door beside the nursery, impatiently kicking it open as he moved inside. His voice was a low growl as he quickly surveyed the interior. "Is this your room, Amethyst?"

"Yes." Her voice trembling, Amethyst said with emphasis, "*My* room! Now put me down and get out! I don't want you in here!"

Staring knowingly into her eyes, Damien said softly, "Don't tell me what you want, Amethyst. I know what you want, and it's not that I should leave you now."

Walking swiftly to the bed, Damien deposited her on its surface, turning to quickly divest himself of his coat. When she made a scrambling movement to escape from the bed, his black look froze her in her tracks, his voice a low threat. "Stay where you are, Amethyst. I warn you. Don't make me chase after you. My patience is worn thin and I won't stand for much more."

Within seconds he was stripped down to his shirt and britches, and in a quick movement had turned to the lock in the door. Having roughly torn his stock from his neck, his shirt was open to mid-chest, the broad expanse heaving heavily with the emotion surging through him. A second later he was beside her, a low groan issuing from his throat as his mouth closed over hers and his searching hands began moving warmly beneath her dressing gown. Suddenly awaking from the lethargy that had held her immobile for long minutes, Amethyst began struggling in his embrace, clawing at the hand moving familiarly over her breasts even as her body cried out for more. But she was no match for his strength as he twisted her struggling arms over her head to grip the small wrists easily with one broad hand. The other hand, moving slowly, sensuously, stripped the dressing gown from her shoulders, and in another efficient movement, had slipped her night rail to her waist. His breath catching as her breasts were bared to his view, Damien bent to kiss the white mounds lightly, his breath warm against her skin as he said softly, "You know you don't want to fight me, Amethyst. You want me to love you . . . you want to feel me inside you, filling you, taking you to the special world where only we reside, darling." His lips moving slowly along her breasts teased the soft nipples lightly, nipped at their fullness, his tongue making a warm, erotic trail from one rise to the other until she felt she would scream with the sheer ache of her desire.

A sudden, frantic knocking on the door interrupted Damien's seeking quest, bringing his head up slowly to stare into her eyes as Tillie's voice called from the other side, "Amethyst! Why this door be locked? Let Tillie in . . ."

She was drowning in the clear gray depths of his eyes as Damien's voice whispered in her ear, "Tell her to go away, Amethyst. I could not let you go now. I've waited too long to hold you again. I will have you now at any cost . . . any cost . . ."

A sudden rekindling of fear tightened her throat, causing the voice that called out to quake. "No . . . go away, Tillie. You can't come in here now. Please . . . go away . . ."

The pounding stopped abruptly, and within a few seconds Amethyst heard Tillie's slow step move away from the door. Tillie was leaving . . . within a few seconds it would be too late . . . But her last frantic thoughts were swept from her mind as Damien's mouth covered hers once again and the rational world moved abruptly into the distance.

A world of bright, careening colors overwhelmed her, a world of warmth and raging desire as her night rail slowly slipped from her body. Damien's mouth was both gentle and seeking against her flesh, his broad palms leaving no area untouched in his aching desire to possess her completely. Her eyes closed against her tumultuous emotions, Amethyst felt the soft flutter of Damien's lips against her forehead, eyelids, temples, the smoothness of her cheek, her lips and chin. His seeking mouth moving slowly downward to her graceful throat and shoulders, paused for long moments to savor the sweetness of her breasts. His hands remaining to knead the soft white mounds hungrily, his lips trailed to her navel, and within minutes were nuzzling the dark triangle of curls below. Snapping abruptly from the hypnotic lethargy of his lovemaking, Amethyst pushed frantically at his head, tearing at his heavy gold hair in an attempt to deter his obvious intent.

"No, Damien, please. I don't want you to . . . please . . ." Amethyst's voice was a soft, broken plea. She could not allow Damien to break her down so completely, to make her give herself without reservation. She must protest this ultimate intimacy that would allow her to hold nothing back, lay her body and soul open to do with as he desired. "No, Damien, please . . . please . . ."

His eyes lifted to hers, mirrored her own passion as Damien replied huskily, "I must, darling . . . I must . . ."

His head slowly descending, parted the sensuous crease awaiting him, his tongue driving inside in quick, stabbing caresses that sent jolts of ecstasy searing through her veins. Gasping in the throes of the brilliance overwhelming her, Amethyst knew nothing but the searing heat consuming her, the exquisite jolts of erotic sensation sweeping over her in quick, overlapping waves as Damien continued his heady administrations. Pressing on to seek, consume, devour, Damien knew only the raging sweetness of his loving assault; the spasms of ecstasy moving the small, beautiful body he ached to consume with his love driving him relentlessly onward. Deeper and harder he pressed, drawing, tasting, fondling the moist inner reaches of her body with his tongue, his passionate frenzy knowing no bounds until the graceful body within his grasp began heaving in deep, jerking spasms in ultimate tribute to his impassioned lovemaking. Groaning deeply, unable to contain her body's response, Amethyst was lifted to the supreme glory of love, her passionate reward accepted humbly, gratefully, as Damien's mouth remained tightly pressed against her. Waiting until the last heaving spasm was over, Damien slowly lifted his mouth from her body, his eyes moving to cling to Amethyst's lovely face as she struggled to regain her breath.

But a deep need still ached inside him. He could not be sated until he had dispelled any doubt that she was totally his, and his alone. His lips moving down, he kissed the moist crease again, the first touch of its warmth escalating his passion beyond restraint. Again and again he brought her to brilliant climax, each shuddering response raising him on euphoric wings as he renewed his intimate claim. Slowly, insistently, his sensuous mouth worked its magic. His tongue fondling, searching, teasing Amethyst's body to the brink of yet another tumultuous descent, Damien poised to survey her impassioned face.

Slowly he slid his massive frame over her small writhing form, his throbbing hardness pressed tight against her. Passion-filled violet eyes looked directly into his, the agony of aching desire apparent in her expression. His voice hoarse with emotion, Damien rasped softly, "Tell me, Amethyst, say it now. Tell me you want me to love you ... ache to feel me inside you ... burn for the ultimate release only I can give you." But there was silence as Amethyst continued to return his stare, her soft lips working lightly as she struggled to swallow past the emotion blocking her throat.

Moving to cup her face with his palms, his elbows resting on the bed, Damien demanded hoarsely, "Tell me ... tell me, damn you, tell me! I want to hear you say it, darling." Waiting tensely for Amethyst's response, Damien's heart hammered wildly in his chest as his manhood swelled stiffly against her.

"Amethyst, I swear ..."

But she could hold out against him no longer. Her lavender eyes bright with tears, Amethyst sobbed softly, her arms moving to circle his neck in a tight embrace. "Yes ... yes, I want you, Damien. God help me, I want you so much ..."

The glory of her admission flashing a searing joy through his veins, Damien raised himself slightly to slide deep within her, her moist warmth closing around him, bringing him to a height of ecstasy without equal. Slowly, smoothly, he moved inside her, his eyes intent on her face, savoring each groaning gasp that escaped her beautiful lips as his passion quickly mounted. Her arms clinging to him, Amethyst met his thrusts with equal passion, her body lifting, meeting, crushing against his until he could suppress his response no longer. With a last surging thrust, Damien pushed deep inside her, the fury of his possession carrying her with him in a glorious, spiraling descent from the intense, dazzling ecstasy of total fulfillment.

His breathing slowly returning to normal, Damien's powerful body overwhelmed Amethyst's petite frame as he lay spent atop her. Lifting his face from the soft pillow of shining black tresses, Damien pressed light kisses against her ear as his clear, translucent gaze moved slowly to meet hers. "Darling . . . my darling . . ." he whispered softly, stopping as a noise in the hallway interrupted his ardent declaration. Reluctant to part from the warmth of her body, Damien slowly drew himself to his feet. His glance warm, he scooped her slender body into his arms, holding her tight against his chest for a few long seconds before putting her on her feet.

"You must get dressed now, darling. We'll take Marian and leave for Chestnut Street now. You need not pack. Everything is waiting for you at home." Damien's emphasis on the word "home" seemed to shake Amethyst's blank expression for the first time, her eyes blinking suddenly in reaction.

Kissing her lips lightly, Damien turned to his clothes, dressing quickly as he continued to speak, "If you wish, you may send a short note to Beauchamps explaining your departure, but I will not allow you to see him at any time, Amethyst." The fire of jealousy already beginning to kindle at the thought as he completed dressing, Damien turned back to Amethyst to see her standing in the lavender silk wrapper, her brilliant black tresses streaming down her slender shoulders in riotous disarray, violet eyes wide in a pale, expressionless face as she held in her small, delicate hand a pistol pointed directly at his stomach.

Almost disbelieving his own eyes, Damien frowned darkly, waiting as Amethyst swallowed tightly. Finally able to speak, she whispered haltingly, "T . . . take your coat, Damien, and walk slowly toward the door.

Now . . . you are leaving, and you will never come back here . . . do you hear what I say? Never . . . *never* come back."

Damien's response was low and confused. "Amethyst, you don't mean what you say." Taking a step forward, he continued ardently, "You're coming home with me now, you and Marian."

"Stop!" Amethyst's harsh command halted Damien's advance as she continued in an almost pleading voice, "I don't want to shoot you, Damien, but I swear on the life of my child, if you take one more step toward me or attempt to take Marian from this house, I'll pull this trigger. At this close range, it won't matter how good a shot I am. I won't miss."

The small hand that held the pistol was shaking badly, and steadying it with the other hand, Amethyst repeated her soft command. "Now, quickly, move to the door and unlock it."

His eyes quickly assessing her strained expression, Damien had no doubt she meant what she said, and picking up his coat, Damien turned wordlessly toward the door. Unlocking it, he swung it wide and walked into the hallway. Waiting until Amethyst stood a few steps behind him, he directed his glance into the foyer where Tillie and Raymond sat together, engrossed in quiet conversation. Their glances springing to him as he appeared at the rail, their eyes widened incredulously as Amethyst appeared behind, holding the pistol.

Turning to give her one last glance, Damien said softly into her eyes, "You're not thinking clearly now, Amethyst. I've pressed you too hard . . . confused you, and for that I'm sorry, darling. But there are some truths that we cannot deny. We are meant to spend our lives in each other's arms, you and I, just as those two down there are meant to be together. A word from you is all that is needed to bring us all together."

Her hand was beginning to shake violently on the pistol as Amethyst mumbled softly to herself before suddenly saying aloud, "Go, Damien! Go now, without another word! Now, damn you . . . Now!"

Taking only a moment more to allow his eyes a full sweep of her presence, Damien walked slowly down the staircase. Signaling Raymond to fall behind, he walked silently through the front doorway and down the steps. It was only when the door was firmly locked behind him that Amethyst allowed the hand holding the pistol to drop to her side. Racing quickly up the steps, Tillie was just in time to steady the small figure as she swayed weakly. Supporting her against her sturdy frame, Tillie held her silently as deep sobs began to shake Amethyst, her words coming out in small, jerking sentences.

"Tillie . . . you don't . . . don't hate me, do you? I'm . . . I'm sorry. I don't want to keep you and Raymond apart. I wish . . . I wish I could help, but I can't go back to him . . . I can't, Tillie! I'm frightened of his power over me . . . of what he can do to our lives . . . to Marian's life. Please . . . please don't hate me, Tillie . . ."

Taking Amethyst soothingly into her arms, Tillie rocked her gently, her smooth cocoa-colored cheek resting lightly against Amethyst's silky tresses as she cooed softly, "You not to worry, Amethyst Greer. Tillie not hate you. Tillie love you like him own child. Tillie and Raymond be together some day. You not to worry, child. You not to worry."

Gulping softly, Amethyst nodded her head, her eyes thankful as Tillie led her gently into her room.

A few hours later Armand returned to a well functioning household that showed no signs of the disruption of earlier in the morning. Moving quickly up the steps, he knocked lightly on Amethyst's door, his darkly handsome face creasing into a smile as Amethyst opened the door. Dressed in a light blue velvet gown, the high neckline bringing the bright color up to her face to reflect brilliantly in lavender eyes appearing a startling blue in reflection, Amethyst was fresh and lovely to his eyes. Taking her hand, he kissed it lightly.

"You are lovely today, mon coeur. Have you had a good day?"

Her eyes flicking away from his for only the briefest second, Amethyst's voice was a trifle husky as she responded, "Yes, a lovely day, Armand." Sliding her hand tightly into his, she led him quietly to Marian's door. "Come, Marian is up now. I can hear her cooing. She'll be happy to see you." Raising her clear eyes to his for a short moment, she said quietly and sincerely, "We are both very fond of you, Armand . . . so very fond . . ."

Shaking her head lightly in answer to the thoughts running riot inside, Tillie dropped the small articles of clothing into the tub of warm water. Absentmindedly taking the soap into her hand, she began scrubbing the dainty apparel, her mind far from the task before her. It had been two days since Captain Straith's and Raymond's visit, and she was still confused and perplexed. Certain she knew what had transpired behind the locked door of Amethyst's room, her heart bled for Amethyst's agony, realizing her soul-child was completely possessed by the same black magic she feared. But frightening her even more was Amethyst's reaction to the assault she had suffered. Obviously frightened beyond rational thought, she had turned fully and completely to Armand Beauchamps, her dependence on him for the stability she sought growing greater each day. Her eyes turning to him glowingly when he spoke, her obvious preference for his company, the brilliance of her smile when Armand held her small daughter so tenderly in his arms, did not go unnoticed by the handsome Frenchman. Obviously growing more secure in her apparently blossoming affection, Armand became less cautious, the true magnitude of his feelings often openly displayed. To Tillie's knowing eyes, it was obvious there was soon to be a breaking point in Armand Beauchamps's strictly controlled passion . . . and she feared for the result.

Suffering her own torment, Tillie fought to strike from her mind the longing in Raymond's dark eyes as they had stood so close, realizing his suffering mirrored her own. But she could not set herself free from the memory. Nor could she forget the trembling of Raymond's massive body as he took her into his arms, or the passion in the deep whisper that still echoed in her brain, "Tillie . . . Tillie Swann . . . Raymond hold him woman again. Soon Raymond 'n Tillie be together always . . ."

But their ecstatic reunion had almost ended in a violent dispute as Raymond had insisted adamantly, "Cap'n Straith be good man. Him say Tillie and Raymond gowan be together when him 'n him woman be together again. Him say . . ."

"Him be obeah-man, Raymond! Him use him magic on Tillie's soul-child, make him soul-child suffer!" Tillie had countered heatedly, aghast at Raymond's traitorous words.

"Cap'n Straith not be obeah-man, Tillie." Raymond's voice had been softly persistent. "Him love him woman, 'n him gowan get him woman back . . . 'n Raymond 'n Tillie be together."

"No! Tillie Swann not gowan let that man take him child forever! No! Amethyst Greer gowan marry good man and him child gowan grow up happy and safe . . ."

". . . 'n Cap'n Straith gowan be dat man, Tillie . . . Cap'n Straith gowan be dat man . . ."

Gently squeezing out the small garments, Tillie hung them near the fire, a quick step behind her interrupting her thoughts as she hung the last piece up to dry.

Turning, she saw Amethyst behind her, a hesitant smile on her beautiful face.

"How do I look, Tillie? It's to be a grand celebration tonight, and many of Armand's friends will be present. I should not like to be the cause of any unfavorable comments."

Her glance assessing, Tillie's dark eyes moved swiftly over the brick-colored velvet gown Amethyst wore, noting the superb fit from the gently scooped neckline, the sleeves that moved snugly from shoulder to elbow to flare out in frothy white ruffles that hung almost to her wrist, to the minuscule waist emphasized by the billowing flare of the full skirt that hung gracefully to her narrow ankles. Taking the matching cape she carried from her hands, Tillie adjusted it on Amethyst's shoulders with maternal pride. Lined in sable, it was a luxurious garment, further enhanced by the overwhelming beauty of the small woman who wore it.

"Amethyst Greer gowan be the most beautiful woman at that parade tonight, and Monsieur Beauchamps gowan be so proud him gowan beam like Mr. Peale's lamps!"

Laughing at Tillie's response, Amethyst hesitated briefly. "Are you certain you don't want to come to the parade, Tillie? Having seen the work Mr. Peale did in the State House, don't you feel even the slightest curiosity to see the finished product? It will be a spectacular event."

Shaking her head, Tillie smiled at Amethyst's persuasive argument. "No, Tillie gowan stay home with Marian. Monsieur Beauchamps not gowan want Tillie in him carriage tonight . . ."

"But we're not taking the carriage, Tillie. We've decided to walk to Market Street so we may pass through the arches at our leisure and situate ourselves so we might take full advantage of the display when the fireworks are lit." Eyeing Tillie closely, Amethyst said quietly, "Are you certain you won't change your mind?"

"Tillie sure." A smile curving her generous lips, Tillie's eyes moved behind Amethyst, her heart warming at Armand Beauchamps's loving glance as he observed from the doorway. "Monsieur Beauchamps be waiting."

Turning, Amethyst shot Armand a quick smile before returning her glance briefly to Tillie. "Alright, Tillie. I'll tell you all about it when we return."

In a quick, graceful movement, Amethyst turned to walk toward Armand, taking his outstretched hand as he whispered softly, "Ma petite, vous êtes magnifique!"

Bobbing her head with a light flush, Amethyst said lightly, "*Je vous dis un grand merci*, Armand."

Obviously pleased by her well executed response, Armand's smile widened. Taking her small hand, he tucked it proudly under his arm. "Come, cherie, I have the privilege of taking the most beautiful woman in Philadelphia to the parade tonight, and I am anxious to show her off."

Her hand clutching his arm a bit more tightly than necessary, Amethyst walked beside him to the front door, and within minutes they were walking briskly toward Market Street.

Rubbing his chin in an anxious gesture, Damien was oblivious to the January cold in which he had been standing for the past hour. Partially concealed in a doorway, his unusually light eyes glowing in his still sun-darkened, sober face, he carefully perused the growing crowd. Without taking his glance from the groups beginning to gather along the walks, he mumbled to the tall Negro beside him, "She should be here soon, Raymond. I'm certain she'll not miss the parade."

It became obvious when he had not been called out by Beauchamps after his visit to the Frenchman's household that Amethyst had managed to conceal his visit and the events which had progressed. She would have no plausible excuse to miss the parade or display in which she had shown so much previous interest without raising Armand's suspicions. He was certain he would see Amethyst tonight. She had not left the Beauchamps household for three days; three days during which Damien had searched his mind for an argument that would convince Amethyst to return to him once and for all. Time was growing short. His violent jealousy of Armand Beauchamps was growing out of hand, and he was uncertain how much longer he would be able to withstand the growing urge to physically remove Amethyst and his child from the household in which they hid from him.

Sparing not the slightest glance for Charles Peale's masterpiece, its three towering arches stretching across Market Street almost directly in front of him, Damien continued his perusal of the rapidly thickening crowd, his heart jumping in his chest as a familiar figure turned the corner. Burning with jealousy, Damien noted Beauchamps's proprietary air as Amethyst walked briskly beside him, her arm tucked securely under his. Her face turned up to Beauchamps, she smiled glowingly, causing the knot in Damien's stomach to tighten painfully. He had to get her away from Beauchamps soon. As they moved steadily closer, Damien's eyes moved lovingly over Amethyst's face. God, she was beautiful! His love an aching need inside him, Damien stepped back further into the doorway as they drew nearer, motioning Raymond to follow. He would not allow them to see him until the right moment. He ached to hold her, burned to have Amethyst look at him the way she was presently looking at Beauchamps, and in that fleeting instant a firm decision was formed in his mind. He would have her tonight. One way or another, he would not spend another night without her.

* * *

Stopping almost abreast of the doorway in which Damien and Raymond were secreted, Amethyst and Armand paused to observe the monumental arches. It was twilight, and the proceedings were scheduled to begin, but a frantic scrambling on the network of ladders and platforms from which the technicians were to manipulate the mechanical devices was causing some delay. Answering a call for assistance from a platform high above the street, Armand moved from Amethyst's side to untangle a series of ropes that had become tangled in the wind. Within moments his broad figure was swallowed by the crowd as Amethyst waited patiently for him to return to her side.

Taking his opportunity, Damien moved quickly to her side. Touching her arm lightly, Damien whispered in a husky voice, "Hello, Amethyst."

Jerking around at the sound of his voice, Amethyst made an attempt to snatch her arm from his grip, succeeding only in causing Damien to tighten his hold as he spoke softly, "Are you still angry with me, darling? I hope you're not carrying a pistol hidden somewhere within that voluminous cloak." His chiding tone falling flat in the face of Amethyst's obvious anxiety to be free of his tenacious grip, he continued in a sober tone, "How much longer are we going to go on with this farce, Amethyst? You're not only putting us both through unnecessary torment, as well as Tillie and Raymond, but you're being unfair to Beauchamps as well. You encourage his hopeless attachment to you when you know in your heart you love me."

"No! No, I don't love you! It's not true!" Amethyst hissed, her eyes wide with denial.

The surging crowd aiding his cause, Damien pulled her closer against him as he said softly, "Do you deny the emotion between us, Amethyst? Do you deny the way your body trembles at my touch, the longing I can see in your eyes even now when you refute our love?"

"There is no love between us, Damien. You don't *love* me. You lust for me and have succeeded in stimulating a similar need inside me. But I will submit to my own weakness no longer, no matter the manner of threat you hold over my head."

A tenseness growing inside his tall frame, Damien responded tightly, "You will allow your selfishness to keep Tillie and Raymond apart . . . to keep Marian from her father . . ."

"Yes! Especially to keep Marian from her father's influence! Do you think I will allow you to dominate Marian as fully as you attempt to dominate me?"

"Damn you, Amethyst!" Damien exclaimed in a low voice. "It is not I that is domineering! Instead, it is yourself that is obstinate, automatically challenging my every word, balking at my every suggestion!"

"And when did you ever make a *suggestion* to me, Damien Straith?" Amethyst hissed vehemently under her breath. "You do not know how to *suggest*. You merely *command!*"

Clenching his teeth tightly together against the heated response that rose to his lips, Damien hesitated before answering. "You are behaving like a child resisting authority, Amethyst."

"You have no authority over me, Damien Straith! You merely wish it to be so, but I will never allow that to happen!"

Grabbing her roughly by the shoulders, despite sharp glances from the passing crowd, Damien demanded softly, "Damn you, Amethyst Greer! Why do you resist me so? You know you want me as much as I want you . . ."

Tears filling her eyes at the truth of his whispered statement, Amethyst whispered softly in return, "Whether that be the case or not, Damien, I cannot allow my child to live her life under the influence of black magic..."

Anger flooding his face at the mention of the obeah that had haunted their relationship from its inception, Damien responded heatedly, "Since you are so insistent on crediting me with powers of obeah, Amethyst, then I would think it would not be too wise to defy me so blatantly by remaining with Armand Beauchamps. It might not be safe for him..."

"...might not be safe for him..." Her eyes widening, Amethyst demanded, a sudden harshness to her tone, "Let me go... let me go, I say! I will not listen to your threats! I will not listen, do you hear me?" Her voice becoming shrill caused several anxious glances to be sent in her direction by passersby, and realizing she was close to hysteria, Damien slowly loosened his grip, his voice low as he spoke directly into the wide, fear-filled eyes holding his gaze, "Alright, Amethyst, I'll let you go. I've said everything I have to say. The rest is up to you..."

Taking only a moment to digest the portent of his words, Amethyst shook her head, mumbling softly under her breath as she did, "No... no, I will never come back to you... never..."

Turning quickly, Amethyst moved into the crowd that now surged toward the magnificent arches, allowing it to carry her to the spot where Armand still stood as the ropes began moving faultlessly through the complicated mechanisms that worked the display. Grasping his arm, she said breathlessly, "Armand, I thought you had been swallowed by the crowd."

His dark eyes moving to her face showed deep regret at the anxiety present in her expression. "Cherie, forgive me for my thoughtlessness. I thought only to be involved here for a short moment, but the problem has been corrected and we may now join the onlookers." Pointing to the top of the center arch, he smiled. "See, up there, Amethyst. Your friend, Charles Peale, is atop to give the signal for the Peace figure to descend to light the central fuse."

Appearing to follow the direction Armand indicated, Amethyst shot a furtive glance out of the corner of her eye to see that Damien had moved to a storefront where he stood with Raymond by his side, his glance intent on her person. A sudden shiver of fear moving down her spine, Amethyst slid her arm through Armand's, returning her glance to the top of the arch just as the Peace figure started to descend.

Watching as it moved at a calculated speed to the top of the arch, the crowd held its breath in anticipation of the brilliant display as the Peace figure struck the main fuse. Unexpectedly, a sudden deafening explosion rocked Market Street, raining a shower of flames and rockets into the eager crowd. Screams and shouts filled the air as spectators scattered wildly in an attempt to elude the rockets careening into the frantic crowd as the towering arches suddenly burst into flames! Too startled to move, Amethyst felt a strong tug on her arm as Armand jerked her forward. A man ran wildly past them, his clothing afire, his mindless fear fanning the flames already consuming his overcoat. His screams echoed in her ears and Amethyst turned toward him just as another spectator threw him forcefully to the street to beat the flames from his clothing.

Armand's voice was hardly distinguishable as he shouted above the growing melee of hissing rockets, terrified screams, and the growing crackle of flames. "Quickly, Amethyst . . . this way! I must get you to a point of safety before . . ."

But he could say no more as a burst of fire suddenly seared past. Moving to shield her with his body, Armand took the full force of the strike in his shoulder, his overcoat igniting in the space of a second as he fell backward against her, knocking them both to the ground. Stunned as her head hit the ground, Amethyst suddenly felt a searing heat at her ankles. Looking down, she saw flames engulfing her cape at the same second she heard Armand's anguished cry. Before her eyes Armand's entire coat became engulfed in wild, leaping flames as he attempted ineffectively to beat them out. Unable to clear her head enough to move, Amethyst felt the first lick of flames sear the flesh of her leg when a tall figure was suddenly bent over her, his strong hands ripping the cloak from her body in one fell swoop. Taking another second to stamp out the flames, he then crouched by her side.

"Darling, are you alright? Amethyst, please answer me, are you alright?"

She was strangely unable to respond to his frantic query, and suddenly standing up, Damien stripped his overcoat from his back and pulled her to her feet. Supporting her wavering form, he slid her slender arms into the massive garment. Closing the collar under her chin, his expression was tortured. "Darling, I was so afraid I had lost you . . ."

Suddenly coming to her senses, Amethyst pushed herself free of his hands, the first sound out of her throat a harsh, croaking scream.

"Armand!"

Pushing Damien aside, Amethyst moved a few steps forward where Armand lay on the ground unconscious. Raymond's tall broad form was bent over his as he beat out the last of the flames that had seared through Armand's clothing to the skin of his torso. The smell of burning flesh filled her nostrils as Amethyst bent over Armand's inert form. Her eyes wide, she mumbled over and over again, her low tone hardly audible over the melee that ensued around them, "Armand . . . Armand, please don't die. Armand . . . please don't die . . ."

Spotting a carriage picking its way cautiously through the smoke-filled street, Damien rushed to its side and jerked open the door to shout into the frighened faces of the occupants, "We have a badly injured man here. He lives close by."

"By all means put him inside, sir," the elderly gentleman responded, pulling the woman at his side to the far edge of the seat.

Nodding a brief thanks, Damien returned to Amethyst's side.

"I've secured a carriage, Amethyst. Quickly, move out of the way so Raymond and I may lift him."

Cringing as his hand touched her shoulder, Amethyst turned to hiss into his face, "Don't touch me! You did this! You did this to Armand! You warned me, but I wouldn't listen, and now Armand is . . ."

Turning her gaze back to Armand's unconscious face, Amethyst stared speechlessly, unable to force the words past her throat. Moving her abruptly aside, Damien said harshly, "Raymond, take his feet gently. I'll take his shoulders."

Suddenly screaming wildly, Amethyst charged Damien's towering frame, her small fists beating at his chest and face as she shouted hoarsely again and again, "Don't touch him! You did this to him! Don't touch him!"

Stepping back a step, Damien caught Amethyst's flying wrists in his hands, twisting them behind her to shout harshly into her wild-eyed expression. "Amethyst, stop this! Beauchamps cannot lie in this street much longer if he is to survive. Now get out of my way so Raymond and I may carry him to that carriage and take him home!"

Suddenly blinking, Amethyst nodded briefly, allowing Damien to release her wrists. Moving quickly to

Armand's side, Damien nodded to Raymond. Lifting him slowly, they moved Armand's inert body to the carriage. Signaling Raymond to slowly lower his feet to the ground, Damien supported Armand's weight as Raymond climbed into the carriage to pull him inside gently and lay him on the seat opposite the old couple who cringed visibly at the sight of his burns. Quickly lifting Amethyst inside, Damien followed, signaling Raymond to sit atop beside the driver.

The moments during which the carriage picked its way slowly through the debris littered street dragged on interminably. Finally arriving at Armand's residence, Amethyst was the first out of the carriage, as she ran up the front steps to ring the bell. Carefully handing Armand's unconscious body down to Raymond, Damien alighted from the carriage to share the burden of Armand's unconscious form as they carried him through the open front doorway and up the steps as directed and into his room.

Dispatching a servant for the doctor, Amethyst turned to Damien, her violet eyes dark with fury.

"Now, get out of here! Get out of here, Damien Straith! You did this to Armand and I will not allow you to stay to enjoy the fruits of your obeah! Get out!"

His face blanching white at the vehemence of her accusation, Damien said softly, "You're upset, Amethyst. You don't know what you're saying . . ."

"I know what I'm saying, Damien! You warned me, didn't you? But I wouldn't listen, so you have attempted to destroy Armand just like you attempted to put an end to William's life! But I won't submit to your demands this time, for after this time there would only be another and another and another, with endless lives affected by your obeah! You've done your black deed now, and I'll do my best to nurse Armand back to health. And I tell you now, Damien Straith. I will never, *never* come back to you! *Never!* Do you hear what I say? NEVER!"

Turning abruptly toward the bed, Amethyst joined Tillie who worked laboriously over Armand, completely ignoring Damien's existence. Watching for long minutes as Amethyst gently bathed Armand's face with cool water, whispering softly into his ear as she did, Damien finally turned around and walked slowly into the hallway. Closing the door behind him, he met Raymond's dark, observant gaze.

His voice hushed, Damien said hoarsely, "Stay here, Raymond. They'll need your strength to take care of Beauchamps. I think it's best if I leave here now. My presence will only serve to disrupt, but you'll be welcome. I'll come back tomorrow. Maybe by then, Amethyst . . ."

His words suddenly choking in his throat, Damien turned abruptly and moved quickly down the staircase and through the front doorway, unable to say the words that flashed through his mind, ". . . maybe by then, Amethyst will believe me . . ."

The full result of the disaster on Market Street had left one man dead, and many others injured. Charles Peale himself had fallen twenty feet from the flaming arch, his clothes afire, to break several ribs and suffer severe burns. For several days during which Amethyst never left his side, Armand Beauchamps continued to waver between life and death. Her life revolving between her child and the man lying mortally wounded, Amethyst spared little thought for anything else. Each request to speak with her sent into the sickroom by Damien Straith was met with the same negative response.

"I do not wish to see him."

Raymond remained her only contact with Amethyst. Plying him with endless questions, Damien listened anxiously as Raymond responded carefully.

"Miss Amethyst nevah leave Mr. Beauchamps. Him stay there day 'n night, 'til Tillie make him leave him room t' rest. Miss Amethyst say him nevah gowan see de cap'n 'gain, dat it be de cap'n dat bring dis trouble down on Mr. Beauchamps's head, 'n Miss Amethyst nevah gowan forgive him."

Staring steadfastly into the black eyes level with his own, Damien said softly, "You know that's untrue, don't you, Raymond? I never possessed any powers of obeah . . . never conjured any black magic . . ." Somehow it was important that Raymond believe him innocent of the crime for which the entire household seemed to hold him guilty.

Returning his glance, Raymond hesitated only a moment before responding. "Raymond hear de stories of de white obeah-man when him on Massa Conway's plantation, 'n him believe den. But Raymond know de cap'n now, 'n him know de truth now. Him believe de cap'n."

Grateful for Raymond's confidence, Damien smiled briefly. "If only I could convince Amethyst of my innocence, perhaps then she would . . ." Not bothering to finish his statement, Damien shook his head in a small gesture of defeat. With each day that passed he was beginning to believe more strongly that he had lost her.

A month passed slowly, during which the reports from the sick room grew increasingly better. Armand Beauchamps would indeed live, but his recuperation would be long and slow. No longer able to withstand the deadly ache inside him, Damien arranged to wait at the back door of the Beauchamps household at the time when Amethyst regularly went to the kitchen to prepare Armand's tea. It had become a daily ritual, on which he was certain he could depend in order to finally speak with her. The skin on the back of his neck prickling with anticipation, Damien waited silently outside the rear door, his eyes catching a short glimpse of Amethyst as she moved past the window toward the fireplace. Slipping quickly through the door which had been left conveniently open, Damien ignored the gasps of the startled servants, his eyes transfixed on Amethyst's figure as it turned toward him.

"Damien! What are you doing here?"

Her eyes wide with shock, Amethyst stared into his face. His heart twisting in his chest, Damien noted she was painfully thin, the stress of the past month showing in the vague circles under her eyes and her unusual pallor. But she was even more beautiful to him in her fragile state, her vulnerability drawing a fierce protective instinct to the surface. Longing desperately to take her slimness into his arms to shield her from all she had suffered, Damien said softly, indicating the two servants who stood hesitantly, uncertain how to react, "Please tell them to leave, Amethyst. I would like to speak with you alone for a few minutes."

"We have nothing to discuss, Damien."

"There are some things we must settle, Amethyst. Please tell them to leave."

Hesitating a moment, Amethyst finally nodded her head to the two uncertain women who scurried from the room with relieved haste. Taking a few steps further into the room, Damien attempted to close the gap between them when Amethyst's sharp command stopped him in his tracks.

"Stay where you are, Damien! We may speak very well with this distance between us." Amethyst's breast was beginning to heave with agitation as she struggled to resist the magic his presence always worked on her senses. Unable to stop her eyes from moving over him, she noted the tenseness in his expression, the supreme control he exerted as he stopped his advance, the manner in which his broad hands clenched nervously as if longing to reach out and pull her into the haven of his arms. And how she longed to be in his arms . . . to hear his heart hammering against her ear, to feel the touch of his hands in her hair and his mouth upon hers as he crushed her against him. But she could not submit to her weakness. He would only use it against her as he had done in the past. Armand needed her desperately. Damien was strong. His lust could be sated by any number of willing bodies that had served him in the past. She must keep in front of her mind his selfish use of her and anyone who would serve his purpose. And his black magic . . . Please, God, help her to remember the misery and near death he had caused in the past in order to achieve his selfish ends.

"Amethyst," Damien's voice was hoarse, filled with emotion, "I would have you know . . . impress upon your mind once and for all that I was not to blame for the events that took place on Market Street."

"Don't bother to deny what you have done, Damien."

"Surely you don't truly believe I was to blame? You could not possibly believe I could have caused that tragedy with the mere power of wishing, or wave of my hand . . ."

"I have no idea how you conduct your magic spells, nor do I care to learn, Damien. I only wish to be free of you."

Covering the distance between them in three quick strides, Damien reached out to grasp her shoulder in obvious desperation. "Have you not been listening to what I have said, Amethyst? How can I convince you that I never held powers of obeah, never conducted spells of black magic?"

Standing stiffly in his grasp, Amethyst responded disbelievingly, "You wish to convince me now that you are innocent, when you openly admitted to binding me to you by the power of possession you exerted over my will."

"God, help me, it's true, Amethyst. I used your fears against you so I might keep you with me. I love you, darling. I have loved you from the day I returned to Jamaica and first saw you as a mature woman, although I suspect my deep feelings for you went back even further than that. I know only one thing for sure, darling, that I have been unable to wipe your memory from my mind since you were a child, and my need for you is so great that it consumes me." Drawing her into his arms, he whispered softly against her ear, "Let me prove how much I love you, Amethyst. Don't shut me out. I'll agree to any arrangements you wish to make if only you'll give me a chance to prove my love."

Mesmerized by his ardent plea, Amethyst stood helpless as Damien slowly moved his mouth to cover hers, the first touch of his lips sending the fire leaping in her veins as his arms closed roughly around her to crush her against his chest. The magic of his kiss was working again, lifting her on brilliant wings to a familiar euphoria. Her arms ached to go around his neck, to tangle in the heavy gold of his hair as he crushed her endlessly against him. She was slipping away, slowly, steadily . . .

The clear tones of a bell from upstairs suddenly entered her love-drugged mind, snapping Amethyst to the present. Abruptly ashamed that Damien had so easily overcome her resistance, she shoved violently at his chest, her face twisting into a sneer of self-contempt, "I'm still the same old fool, aren't I, Damien? But you won't lull me into tranquillity now only to later use the same threats against me when I oppose you. I will no longer be taken in by you."

The bell rang clearly again, snapping Amethyst's head in the direction of its sound. "That's Armand. He's wondering what is keeping me so long. I'm going to him now and will send Elizabeth back to prepare the tea. Leave now, Damien, and don't return. I hope you will believe me when I tell you once and for all I never want to see you again."

Turning abruptly, Amethyst strode through the kitchen doorway, her purposeful stride belying the heavy weight in her heart.

Sitting motionless at his desk, Damien slowly lifted a broad hand to his forehead, closing his eyes wearily for long moments as he struggled to put in order the words whirling around his troubled mind. It was over at last. He had lost her . . . his Amethyst. Mishandling the whole affair from the beginning, he had finally succeeded in driving the only woman he had ever loved into another man's arms. Like a fool he had allowed her to believe in his mystical powers because it suited his purpose and he was now trapped by his own deviousness. Had he not been so frantic to have her from the first; had he allowed their love time; been adamant when she had returned to him from Sheridan Plantation and denied his part in William Sheridan's illness . . . But no, he had not been strong enough to fight his desire for her, and having taken her once, could not risk losing her.

"Fool! Fool!" his mind harangued, "you have only yourself to blame. How can she trust you now when you have deliberately led her to believe an untruth on which you have based your relationship? A belief that inspired only one emotion . . . Fear."

Picking up his pen, he dipped it into the ink and began again the letter he had been attempting to compose for the last two hours.

"My darling Amethyst,
    I have tried many times to begin this letter,

thinking of endless excuses for my gross mishandling of our lives, but there is no true excuse for my actions. You are so desperate to be free of me, to make a new life for yourself and Marian, and I know of no other way to prove my love for you except to make your most ardent wish possible.

I have today deposited in the Bank of Philadelphia a draft in Marian's name, designating you as trustee of the sum. I am hoping you will use that money in any manner you see fit so you will no longer be dependent on others for survival. Should you desire to stay with Beauchamps, I can only wish you happiness.

I will always love you, darling, and I hope you will someday be able to forgive me for all you have suffered at my hands. My thoughts will always be with you and Marian.

Damien"

Dropping the pen hopelessly, Damien muttered under his breath, "It's done." The letter was inadequate, but it would have to do. Rising slowly to his feet, Damien walked to the door of the library, dreading the moment he would ascend the steps to the master bedroom on the second floor. The house was haunted with Amethyst's presence. In the morning room he saw her reclining on the chaise in the sun, her body swollen with his child; in the hallway descending the staircase, completely selfless and unconscious of the innate grace and beauty in which she walked; and across from him at the dinner table, her sharp mind and quick wit sharing his burdens, lightening his cares. But it was in the privacy of his room at night where countless memories assailed his mind, giving him no peace through the long hours of the night. He longed to hold her again in his arms, to feel her warmth against him as she slept, breathe in her fragrance, feel the silky texture of her skin against his palms as she lay warm and tight against him. He ached to love her . . .

Awakening early, Damien immediately dressed, unwilling to spend any more time than necessary in the room that harbored so many strong memories. Walking to the staircase to the first floor, he descended it slowly, with the same lack of enthusiasm with which he had begun each day during the past month. His eye catching on a tall, dark figure standing hesitantly in the foyer, he hastened his step.

"Raymond, you need not have come so early in answer to my summons. I did not expect you for at least another hour." Damien's smile touched the silent Negro with true respect and affection. His impressive frame straight and proud, Raymond maintained a sense of dignity that a life of slavery had left undaunted. True intelligence gleamed in the black eyes regarding him intently, as well as apprehension at the reason for Damien's urgent summons.

Signaling Raymond to follow as he walked toward the library, Damien began hesitantly, "We have some things to discuss, Raymond. Please come in and close the door behind you."

Walking directly to the desk, Damien picked up the letter over which he had labored so arduously the night before, wincing slightly as his fingers touched its smooth surface.

Turning back to Raymond he said soberly, "I would have you deliver this letter to Amethyst personally, at your first opportunity of privacy. I wish only to be certain she reads it, for there is something of importance contained inside of which she must become aware."

Nodding silently, Raymond accepted the letter, and

putting it in his pocket, waited for Damien to continue.

Beginning hesitantly, Damien said in a softer tone, "Secondly, I would know if you are happy in the Beauchamps household, Raymond."

His stoic features revealing little of the surprise he felt at the question, Raymond's answer was equally hesitant, "Raymond be content deh, Cap'n."

"And Tillie . . . is all well between you and her?"

A small smile curving Raymond's lips for the first time, Raymond replied softly, "Tillie Swann 'n Raymond be happy t' be together 'gain."

Smiling at the twinge of envy deep in his own heart, Damien responded softly, "Well, at least one good thing has come of this fiasco." Walking back to the desk, Damien picked up a paper lying on its surface, and returning to Raymond, placed it in his hand. "I had this certified yesterday, Raymond. This paper says you are a free man now . . . as free as Tillie Swann. When you return to Beauchamps's household today, you need never report back to me again. You will be needed there for a long time to come, but should you find yourself in need of employment in the future, you may return here at any time. But as a free man, Raymond, not as a slave."

Appearing unable to comprehend the full portent of Damien's statement, Raymond blinked into Damien's clear, penetrating eyes, his broad features drawing into a deep frown. When he finally spoke, his deep voice was low and hesitant.

"Cap'n say Raymond be free man now? Free as Tillie Swann?"

Nodding his head, Damien continued softly, "And I offer you my sincere apology for using you so heartlessly. I was thoughtlessly cruel in flaunting your presence so I might convince Amethyst to return to me.

I caused both you and Tillie unnecessary pain . . ."

Refuting Damien's statement with a shake of his head, Raymond responded softly, "Raymond know how it feel t' need him woman 'n not have him. Raymond understand what de Cap'n do." Hesitating another moment, Raymond continued in a lower tone as he tightly clenched the paper Damien had put into his hand, ". . . 'n Raymond say tenky, Cap'n, tenky for making Raymond free man."

Smiling, Damien offered softly, "Raymond never truly belonged to me, anyway. The only person Raymond ever belonged to was Tillie Swann."

A broad smile slowly moving across his lips, Raymond laughed, the low heavy rumble pleasant on Damien's ears. "Dat be true, Cap'n, dat be true."

Extending his hand, Damien said sincerely, "Goodbye, Raymond. Let me hear from you again."

Nodding his head, Raymond accepted the hand held out to him, and turned to the door. Watching as Raymond's tall proud frame moved with a rapid stride through the foyer and out the front door, the smile slowly dropped from Damien's face. Turning, he walked slowly toward the morning room. Another long, endless day had begun.

Bright violet eyes looked clearly into his as soft lips parted in anticipation of his kiss. Her fragrance was strong in his nostrils, her body soft as she pressed against him. "Amethyst . . . Amethyst, my darling," he whispered softly as his lips moved slowly to cover hers, "I've waited so long . . . so very long . . ."

But she was fading from his sight, slowly slipping away, her image paling until only the aura remained, and suddenly, with a start, he awakened. He was trembling uncontrollably, his body covered with a veil of perspiration that pasted the coverlet to his body like a damp shroud. Disgusted with himself, Damien struggled to his feet, moving quickly to the washstand to pour the pitcher of water over his head in an effort to release himself from his semi-conscious state. It had just been another dream! One he had been subservient to for the past month, during which he had waited in vain for some word from Amethyst. Raymond had brought her his letter a full month before, returning the next day to tell him Amethyst had read it in his presence and turned away without a word. Clinging desperately to the last thread of hope, Damien had found all manner of reason to remain in Philadelphia in the hope of seeing Amethyst again, even though he knew full well she did not stray from the Beauchamps' household where she continued steady nursing chores for the recuperating Armand Beauchamps.

But the dreams had been recurring more often of late as hope began to fade, his subconscious mind endeavoring to compensate for his waning hope. But he could go on like this no longer. It was time he faced the truth of the hopelessness of his love and went on with his life, no matter the pain of final acceptance.

With a new sense of resolution, Damien brushed his damp hair into place and slipped into his fawn britches and white shirt, making haste to leave the room before his determination failed. It was March, and the *Sally* would be sailing again within a few weeks. He would take her out this time and damn the memories that haunted him! Walking purposefully down the staircase to the first floor, he was in time to see Mrs. Dobbs open the front door. Blinking his eyes in disbelief, Damien saw a small, slender figure in the doorway and heard a soft, familiar voice saying quietly, "It's good to see you again, Mrs. Dobbs." Turning to the tall mulatto behind her, the apparition said softly, "You may take Marian upstairs first, Tillie. Our early rising has interrupted her sleep and she will benefit from a few more quiet hours."

Nodding her assent to Amethyst's instructions, Tillie began moving quickly in the direction of the staircase, stopping only briefly when she saw Damien paused on the stairs. Within moments she had brushed past him without a word and was continuing up the staircase.

But Damien's eyes had not strayed from the slim figure that now stood in the foyer, removing her cape. Turning as Raymond came through the doorway, his arms loaded with assorted boxes and cases, Amethyst directed softly, "Please put them in the upstairs bedroom, Raymond. I'm sure Mrs. Dobbs will be happy to indicate which rooms to use."

Taking her cue from Amethyst, Mrs. Dobbs quickly preceded Raymond up the stairs, obviously grateful to escape the tension-filled scene.

His eyes unmoving from Amethyst's countenance, Damien slowly descended the staircase. His heart pounding in his chest, he advanced toward her, reaching out as he did to lightly touch her cheek. Closing his eyes for a brief second, Damien slowly released his breath. She was real, not just a figment of his imagination or another dream. His eyes slowly moved over her face, drinking in the sight of her, his throat too choked with emotion to speak.

Bright violet eyes held his for long silent moments before Amethyst swallowed tightly, the slight trembling of her soft lips betraying her emotion as she whispered huskily, "We've come home, Damien. Marian and I have come home."

Waiting, holding her breath in the long moments of silence that followed, Amethyst watched as Damien's gray, translucent eyes moved slowly over her face, his broad chest heaving with the intensity of emotion clearly coursing through his body. His fingers still rested against her cheek as if he dared not move and break the spell of the moment. A small smile slowly broke the stiffness of his expression, turning up the corners of his mouth, the stillness between them shattered abruptly as his strong arms snaked out to crush her against him and he groaned in a deep, hungry voice, "Amethyst, oh, God, Amethyst, you've finally returned to me." Savoring the ecstasy of holding her again in his arms, Damien clutched her against him for long moments, his hands luxuriating in the black, silky curls that streamed down her back, revelling in the wild beating of her heart as it raced frantically against his own; the intimate sweetness of her body, warm against his as his mouth slowly descended to cover her soft lips. And it was there . . . the rapture singing through his veins as his mouth touched and tasted the innate beauty it had been denied for so long.

Releasing her momentarily, Damien bent and scooped Amethyst into his arms, holding her tight against his chest as he turned to scale the staircase two steps at a time in his anxiety for the privacy of their room. Unconscious of Raymond's and Tillie's smiling glances as he moved through the doorway of the master bedroom, Damien kicked the door shut behind him, carrying Amethyst to the bed where he lay her gently on the rumpled linens. His hands cupping her face, he stared for long moments into the purple jewels of her eyes, still hardly daring to believe she was once again in his arms. His voice hoarse from the emotions still shaking his strong frame, Damien said softly, "Darling, I want to say this first, so you may know unequivocally, never to doubt again, that I love you, Amethyst. I love you more than I thought it possible to love. The past months have taught me in the most brutally painful way that life without you is flat and empty, darling. Yet, within the space of one moment you have returned the spark to my life . . . the brightness to my soul, and now that you have returned, I will never allow you to leave me again. You will marry me . . . you will be my wife, the mother of our children . . .''

Suddenly realizing Amethyst remained silent, Damien felt a moment of soul-shaking doubt, his body stiffening as he said softly, "You will marry me, Amethyst . . . you will not insist on the same situation as before . . ."

A lone tear slipping out of one corner of the brimming violet eyes returning his gaze, Amethyst whispered huskily, "Oh, yes, Damien, I will marry you. I will be your wife. I, too, have learned something over the past months. Affection and sympathy cannot be transformed into love, no matter how deep their proportions, especially when the heart is already filled with love for another. I love you, Damien, and have finally come to realize that the possession I so feared and which held me bound to you was merely the power of that love, drawing me ever closer to you as I struggled to pull away. Once you had turned me free, with no thought for the pain I knew you suffered, for I suffered it also, I came to realize the true depth of your love, and the depth of my own as well." Hesitating a moment longer as Damien stared soberly into the exquisite face filled with love, Amethyst finally whispered in a hoarse, breaking voice, "No, Damien, I will not leave you . . . ever again." A small smile turning up her lips as a fleeting dimple danced across her velvet cheek, she said softly, "This obstinate, impulsive, foolish woman is yours for the rest of your life, darling . . ."

"And this domineering, overbearing, unreasonably jealous man is yours, Amethyst," Damien responded softly against her lips, pausing momentarily to add in a low tone that held a lingering trace of the Damien of old, "but you may believe me now when I say that this time, Amethyst, I'll never let you go . . . not ever . . . ever again . . ."

Amethyst's wordless reply was the lifting of her mouth to his and the ultimate, sweet surrender that spoke more clearly than words.

Epilogue

Philadelphia—March, 1789

The Southwark Theater was filled to capacity, demonstrating the city's support of the repeal of Philadelphia's anti-theater law and the American Company's production of *By Authority*. The first act had gone well, the combined talent of the troupe, especially the handsome John Henry, standing them in good stead, but intermission brought the usual restless stirring in the body of the audience. The first notes of the haunting melody went unnoticed as the strains of "Greensleeves" began amidst the growing din. The slender guest artist whose efforts had contributed so significantly to the repeal of the city's anti-theater law, came on stage, the startled gasps of a few drawing the attention of the remainder of the audience to the startling beauty of the woman who moved slowly across its expanse, the turquoise silk of her gown shimmering in the footlights, the light of the candles reflected a hundred times in the brilliants dispersed sparingly over the splendid garment and around the deep decolletage which glowed with the greatest concentration of the sparkling gems. Black silky curls tumbled gracefully from the curving sweep of her coiffure to bounce against slender shoulders, drawing the eye to the delicacy of her petite frame. But most arresting of all was the supreme beauty of the exquisitely sculptured face dominated by huge, luminous eyes that sparkled with a beauty more magnificent than the gems she wore.

Her true, soft soprano, the tone light and sweet to the ear, caught the hearts of the audience as she moved slowly across stage, the rhythmic sway of her delicate form further mesmerizing an audience already helplessly enraptured. Her voice rose in gentle supplication, her hands clasping in a graceful gesture as the melody moved on, drawing the hearts and minds of the spectators to well remembered echoes of futile love.

From the audience, clear, translucent gray eyes followed the graceful figure with a hint of a deeper passion than that stimulated by the haunting melody. His handsome face sober, he sat motionless in the box nearest the stage, his glance unmoving from the lovely figure that so entranced him . . . the woman who was his wife. From a spot offstage a tall mulatto woman observed, grasping the hand of a tall, handsome Negro who stood at her side, the velvet softness of her black, almond-shaped eyes moving to hold his glance with a warmth indicative of the strong emotion that bound them together, drawing them ever closer as the years pressed on.

The clear bell-like tone raised in a soulful cry, extolling the virtues of love fully accepted and returned, the brilliant violet eyes of the artist moving to meet the steady gaze of the broad, tawny-haired man whose eyes never left her face. Her glance holding his, she sang softly, convincingly, the truth of her gentle acclaim:

"I love my love and well he knows
I love the grass on where he goes
If he on earth no more could stay
My life would quickly pass away . . ."

The audience slowly faded away as the two remined locked in a special world of their own creation, the splendor of their love carrying them on the wings of the song to memories of ecstatic glory and the brilliant promise of rapture yet to come. His heart beating rapidly in his chest, Damien acknowledged the truth of Amethyst's love, at last accepting it to be as strong and true as his own, a love that would truly last . . . and even grow.

HISTORICAL ROMANCE IN THE MAKING!

SAVAGE ECSTASY (824, $3.50)
by Janelle Taylor
It was like lightning striking, the first time the Indian brave Gray Eagle looked into the eyes of the beautiful young settler Alisha. And from the moment he saw her, he knew that he must possess her—and make her his slave!

DEFIANT ECSTASY (931, $3.50)
by Janelle Taylor
When Gray Eagle returned to Fort Pierre's gates with his hundred warriors behind him, Alisha's heart skipped a beat: would Gray Eagle destroy her—or make his destiny her own?

FORBIDDEN ECSTASY (1014, $3.50)
by Janelle Taylor
Gray Eagle had promised Alisha his heart forever—nothing could keep him from her. But when Alisha woke to find her red-skinned lover gone, she felt abandoned and alone. Lost between two worlds, desperate and fearful of betrayal, Alisha hungered for the return of her FORBIDDEN ECSTASY.

RAPTURE'S BOUNTY (1002, $3.50)
by Wanda Owen
It was a rapturous dream come true: two lovers sailing alone in the endless sea. But the peaks of passion sink to the depths of despair when Elise is kidnapped by a ruthless pirate who forces her to succumb—to his every need!

PORTRAIT OF DESIRE (1003, $3.50)
by Cassie Edwards
As Nicholas's brush stroked the lines of Jennifer's full, sensuous mouth and the curves of her soft, feminine shape, he came to feel that he was touching every part of her that he painted. Soon, lips sought lips, heart sought heart, and they came together in a wild storm of passion. . . .

Available wherever paperbacks are sold, or order direct from the Publisher. Send cover price plus 50¢ per copy for mailing and handling to Zebra Books, 475 Park Avenue South, New York, N.Y. 10016. DO NOT SEND CASH.

THE BEST IN HISTORICAL ROMANCE
by Sylvie F. Sommerfield

SAVAGE RAPTURE (1085, $3.50)
Beautiful Snow Blossom waited years for the return of Cade, the handsome halfbreed who had made her a prisoner of his passion. And when Cade finally rides back into the Cheyenne camp, she vows to make him a captive of her heart!

REBEL PRIDE (1084, $3.25)
The Jemmisons and the Forresters were happy to wed their children—and by doing so, unite their plantations. But Holly Jemmison's heart cries out for the roguish Adam Gilcrest. She dare not defy her family; does she dare defy her heart?

TAMARA'S ECSTASY (998, $3.50)
Tamara knew it was foolish to give her heart to a sailor. But she was a victim of her own desire. Lost in a sea of passion, she ached for his magic touch—and would do anything for it!

DEANNA'S DESIRE (906, $3.50)
Amidst the storm of the American Revolution, Matt and Deanna meet—and fall in love. And bound by passion, they risk everything to keep that love alive!

ERIN'S ECSTASY (861, $2.50)
Englishman Gregg Cannon rescues Erin from lecherous Charles Duggan—and at once realizes he must wed and protect this beautiful child-woman. But when a dangerous voyage calls Gregg away, their love must be put to the test . . .

TAZIA'S TORMENT (750, $2.75)
When tempestuous Fantasia de Montega danced, men were hypnotized. And this was part of her secret revenge—until cruel fate tricked her into loving the man she'd vowed to kill!

RAPTURE'S ANGEL (750, $2.75)
When Angelique boarded the *Wayfarer*, she felt like a frightened child. Then Devon—with his captivating touch—reminded her that she was a woman, with a heart that longed to be won!

Available wherever paperbacks are sold, or order direct from the Publisher. Send cover price plus 50¢ per copy for mailing and handling to Zebra Books, 475 Park Avenue South, New York, N.Y. 10016. DO NOT SEND CASH.